P...
New Yo... ...r
Gena Showalter

"Showalter's signature blend of sizzling attraction,
breathtaking worlds, and lethal stakes
rocks me every time!"
—Sylvia Day, #1 *New York Times* bestselling author

"With compelling stories and memorable characters,
Gena Showalter never fails to dazzle."
—Jeaniene Frost, *New York Times* bestselling author

"The Lords of the Underworld series…keeps getting more
satisfying. The chemistry has never been hotter and both
the characters and the world they live in
are beautifully detailed."
—*RT Book Reviews* on *The Darkest Craving*

"One of Showalter's biggest strengths is her ability to
create wounded characters who are riveting and intense,
but who also hold out the hope of redemption."
—*RT Book Reviews* on *Beauty Awakened*

"Showalter does her magic with an intricately developed
world, complex and intensive character arcs and dark,
compelling paranormal themes. She releases that literary
punch to the gut with excruciatingly detailed scenes that
haunt the senses long after reading the pages."
—*USA TODAY* on *Wicked Nights*

"Gena Showalter knows how to keep readers
glued to the pages and smiling the whole time."
—Lara Adrian, *New York Times* bestselling author

"Another sizzling page-turner….
an utterly spell-binding story!"
—Kresley Cole, #1 *New York Times* bestselling author,
on *Playing with Fire*

GENA SHOWALTER

Burning Dawn

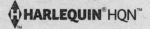
HARLEQUIN® HQN™

Recycling programs
for this product may
not exist in your area.

ISBN-13: 978-0-373-77844-7

BURNING DAWN

Copyright © 2014 by Gena Showalter

All rights reserved. Except for use in any review, the reproduction or utilization of this work in whole or in part in any form by any electronic, mechanical or other means, now known or hereafter invented, including xerography, photocopying and recording, or in any information storage or retrieval system, is forbidden without the written permission of the publisher, Harlequin HQN, 225 Duncan Mill Road, Don Mills, Ontario M3B 3K9, Canada.

This is a work of fiction. Names, characters, places and incidents are either the product of the author's imagination or are used fictitiously, and any resemblance to actual persons, living or dead, business establishments, events or locales is entirely coincidental.

This edition published by arrangement with Harlequin Books S.A.

For questions and comments about the quality of this book, please contact us at CustomerService@Harlequin.com.

® and TM are trademarks of Harlequin Enterprises Limited or its corporate affiliates. Trademarks indicated with ® are registered in the United States Patent and Trademark Office, the Canadian Trade Marks Office and in other countries.

Printed in U.S.A.

HARLEQUIN®
www.Harlequin.com

To Jill Monroe. You're pretty freaking amazing. You deserve only the best—which is why I hang around you so much. (Yes, I somehow managed to make your awesomeness all about me. I'm THAT good.)

To Emily Ohanjanians. You always go above and beyond the call of duty, and I'll be forever grateful.

To Kathleen Oudit, Tara Scarcello, Glenn Mackay, and Alan Davey. You guys gave me the cover of my dreams—my sweet, sexy dreams. Thank you!

To Craig Swinwood, Loriana Sacilotto, Brent Lewis, Christina Clifford, Stacy Widdrington, Diana Wong, Ana Luxton, Amy Jones, Melissa Anthony, Erin Craig, Michelle Renaud, Margaret Marbury, Susan Swinwood, Natashya Wilson, Emily Martin, Don Lucey, Lisa Wray, Aideen O'Leary-Chung, Larissa Walker, Arista Guptar, Reka Rubin, Jayne Hoogenberk, Kate Studer and Chris Makimoto (and Emily O, of course—you get it twice!). You guys are an awesome team, and I'm blessed to have you in my corner!

To Deidre Knight and Jia Gayles. I think Hard Work and Dedication are your middle names. Thank you!

Burning Dawn

CHAPTER ONE

HE LIVED SEX. Breathed sex. Ate sex.

He *was* sex.

Maybe that was his name.

No. That wasn't what *she* called him. She—his heart. His reason for being.

She would straddle his waist, feed his aching length into her hungry body, and say, "My slave needs me more than air to breathe, doesn't he?"

My Slave. Yes. That was his name.

My Slave wanted his woman. Craved her like water to drink.

Must have her.

Only she would do. He couldn't live without her smoke-and-dreams scent…mmm, or her too-close-to-the-sun heat…or her fiery claws. How deeply those little daggers cut into his bare chest. And her peekaboo fangs…how deliciously they nipped at the vein in his neck.

She was perfect, and only when she was with him, her strong body taking and receiving pleasure, was the gnawing hunger within him finally satisfied.

Must. Have. Her. NOW.

But…he looked around. She wasn't with him. He tried to rise from the bed. Something bound his wrists and ankles again. Not rope. Not this time. Too cold, too hard. Steel? He didn't care enough to look.

Problem. Solution. My Slave gritted his teeth and jerked with all his considerable might. Skin tore, muscle ripped, and bone snapped. Pain. Freedom. He grinned. His woman was out there. Soon he would find her. He would thrust inside her and slake his need for her. Again and again and again…

Nothing and no one would stop him.

"HE'S LOOSE AGAIN," someone grumbled.

At the pond washing clothes and dreaming of salted caramel cupcakes…and frosted brownies…and, oh, oh, oh, peanut butter cookies, Elin Vale lumbered from the over-warm water. Brittle grass covered the small bank provided by the gorgeous desert oasis of Sahel, abrading her bare feet. As the sun glared from the clear morning sky, golden sand dunes undulated on every side; she sought shade under one of the handful of trees. A gentle breeze carried more grit than she was ever able to wash away.

At least there was a silver lining. A free daily body scrub meant her sunburned, freckled skin always glowed. *Yay me.*

Now, if only she could accomplish her life goals so easily. 1) Escape the Phoenix warriors holding her captive, 2) make big bank, and 3) open a bakery. She would sell desserts good enough to induce orgasm… except peanut butter cookies because she would single-handedly consume the entire stock.

Life would be over-the-moon crazmazing. She would be doing what she loved and eating what she craved. Except, for one wee problem—she hadn't yet managed to cross number one off her list. Phoenix were immortals with the ability to flame to ash and rise from the dead, stronger than ever before. They were vicious. And, ironically enough, they were cold-blooded. They enjoyed pillaging and plundering, and killed for grins and giggs.

Elin had seen the worst of their handiwork up close and all too personal, and even now, a year later, the memories were formidable enough to break her down. Memories she couldn't stop...*please, please stop*...but there they were, flashing through her mind. Her father's head rolling across the floor—without his body. Bay's pain-filled moan echoing in her ears as he sagged to the floor, a sword sticking out of his chest. Silence descending. Such dreaded silence.

Even now her heart rate went full throttle, with enough horsepower to break records. *Going to vomit.*

"Catch him!"

The frantic shout was a welcome and wonderful distraction, the only life raft in a sea of horror, halting the oncoming breakdown.

Her gaze scanned—there.

Oh, blimey. *He's magnificent.*

Because of Elin's supposedly disrespectful mouth—some people couldn't tolerate the truth—she had spent the past two weeks stuffed inside a small, dank hole, unable to see the new prisoner "worth toppling an entire empire to possess."

The quote had come from every female in the village.

For the first time, Elin had to agree with her captors. The princess's immortal slave was a god among men.

He stomped through the sand, flinging expert soldiers out of his way as if they were stuffed animals.

He did this *despite* the fact that his wrists and ankles looked like raw hamburger meat.

His scowl was dark, frightening, and despite her fascination, she instinctively lowered her gaze.

Oh, wowzer. Hello, massive erection. The beast was in no way concealed by the leather loincloth the slave wore.

The ability to breathe abandoned her. Who knew penises did actually come in size magnum, as romance novels proclaimed? And, sweet fancy, as the scrap of material rose…and rose…and eventually fell to the side, she saw a glint of silver. Was the head of his shaft— It was! It was actually pierced with a long, silver barbell.

Her knees went a bit weak.

Eye-raping the princess's slave, Vale? Really? Stop!

First, entertaining lustful thoughts for another woman's man was a crime punishable by death. Second, it was 100 percent skeevy.

That was why she would look away…in a second. A peek at the rest of him, that was all she needed. He was at least six and a half feet of primal male aggression, with the defy-me-at-your-own-peril muscle mass of a dedicated, centuries-old warrior. But what truly snagged her attention—besides the jumbotron, of course—were feathered wings of the most luminous pearl and gold arcing behind wide, bronzed shoulders. Actual, honest-to-goodness wings, fit for the most cherished of angels.

But if the whispers and giggles she'd heard about the male were to be believed, he wasn't actually an angel, and calling him one would have been an insult, since angels were lower on the totem. He was a Sent One. An adopted son of the Most High, the ruler of the highest realm of the heavens.

Sent Ones were expert trackers and merciless demon slayers. Defenders of the weak and helpless. They were honest to the point of seeming brutality. And, okay, wow, that was like a checklist of awesome. But the things that were supposedly specific to this male's character: cold, calculated and demented. *Not* awesome.

Apparently, he laughed when he killed his enemies... and laughed when he killed his friends.

But...that couldn't be true. Could it? He was too pretty to be so cruel.

Shallow much?

What? She was starved. A mind was mush when a body was hungry.

According to gossip, he was part of the Army of Disgrace, one of the Most High's seven heavenly defensive forces. Six of those forces were well respected and admired. The AoD, not so much. They were a group of wild, untamable mercenaries in danger of losing their homes, wings and immortality; in other words, permanent time off for wicked behavior.

The twenty or so men and women were on a year-long probation, their every action scrutinized. One more screwup, and they would be adiosed forever.

The grapevine hadn't stopped there. The male directly below the Most High was named Germanus, and he was the Sent Ones' boss. Or rather, had been. Germanus was killed recently by demons. But before his death—obviously—he controlled the Elite Seven, the seven men and women who were the fiercest of the fierce, and the leaders of those seven defensive forces. After his death, the Most High appointed a new second-in-command, Clerici, and this Clerici guy had tweaked some long-standing rules.

Before: do not harm anyone or thing but demons.

After: unless a fellow Sent One is being held against his will.

Then, and only then, the entire race could play a Kill Everyone Card.

Elin's takeaway: once Sex On Legs' army buddies found out what had happened to him, everyone in the village would bathe in blood. And—if the expert-tracker thing proved true—bath time would come soon.

Have to be long gone by then.

"Woman!" he bellowed, his voice more smoke than substance. And yet, that one word dripped with command, expectation and raw animal carnality.

She shivered with vibrant anticipation.

Reacting to him, too? Why don't you just chop off your own head and call it good?

He belonged to Kendra the Merry Widow, Princess of Clan Firebird; she'd addicted him to the poison her body produced, a nonlethal substance worse than any drug, making him desperate for her touch. *Then* she'd cinched the deal by tricking him into killing her.

With Kendra, everything began and ended with death.

Shortly after drawing her final breath, she flamed to ash, reformed and rose again, the bond between mistress and slave firmly in place.

Apparently, she'd done the same to six of her husbands—and was currently doing it to her seventh, who was away from camp at the moment, the lucky jerk. Because, when she tired of her men, she cut out…and ate…their hearts, ensuring they stayed dead.

A shudder crawled the length of Elin's spine.

As punishment, the late King Krull, Kendra's father, had bound her with slave-chains to negate her abilities and sold her on the black market.

Where and when the Sent One had come into play, Elin wasn't sure. She only knew he'd returned Kendra to camp decades later, dropping her from the sky and flying away. Krull, thinking the time apart had mellowed her, had removed the chains and given her to his third-in-command, Ricker the War Ender.

But with her abilities fully restored, she'd been able to addict Ricker to her poison, and gain his permission to leave the camp to hunt the Sent One.

The princess was sweet like that.

"Woman! Now!"

Elin swallowed a dreamy sigh. Even laced with anger and annoyance, the Sent One's voice elicited images of strawberries dipped in warm, rich chocolate. *Mmm. Chocolate.*

Maybe I should help him.

The thought struck her, surprising her. She wasn't exactly on speaking terms with courage, and to be effective, she'd have to endanger her own life. But if she could free the male from the princess's bond, she could use him to escape.

Elin pored through every bit of information she'd gleaned during her enslavement but came up with only a few ways to free him. None that were particularly helpful. She could kill him, but that kinda threw a wrench in her plan, because he wouldn't come back to life. She could kill Kendra (again), but the princess would come back to life, and Elin would have a very determined enemy for the rest of her (probably) short, (definitely) miserable life. Like the Sent One, death was the end for her.

Elin was half Phoenix, half "weak, lowly human," with zero abilities to show for her dual parentage. And it sucked, because here—or in any immortal colony, really—halflings were an abomination. A stain against the race. A threat to the vigor of the bloodline.

She'd known she was half-immortal, but she'd had no idea she was so despised, living in happy ignorance until a group of Phoenix ambushed her mother, Renlay, a little over a year ago. All because her mother—a full-blooded soldier—had fallen in love with Elin's father— a human—and had deserted her clan to be with him. As punishment, the group murdered Elin's father, as well as sweet, innocent Bay.

So much loss... She tried to ignore the knot growing in her throat.

She and Renlay were taken prisoner. Then, four months ago, Renlay experienced the ultimate death. It happened to all Phoenix eventually—even if their hearts weren't eaten—leaving Elin alone, *so alone,* suffering in the cruelest of ways, battling loneliness, grief, sorrow. Heartbreak.

Oh, the heartbreak. It was a constant companion. Cruel and merciless, darkening her days and soaking her nights with tears.

To be honest, the beatings and degradation did not compare to the torture of her emotions. Not even when she was treated like a dog, told to eat her meals on her hands and knees, without the use of her hands. Not even when she was made to take care of her bladder's needs in front of a laughing audience.

Elin blinked away tears.

In a sick, twisted way, she kind of…welcomed the abuse, she supposed. After all, she deserved it. Her parents and Bay had been strong and brave. She was a weak coward.

Why had she lived and not them?

Why did she continue to live?

As if you don't know.

Her mother's final words echoed in her mind. *Whatever proves necessary, my darling, do it. Survive. Do not allow my sacrifice to be in vain.*

"Woman! Need. Now." The Sent One once again ripped her from the past. He neared the river…neared her.…

Soon, he would pass by, and the opportunity would be lost.…

Her hand twitched as she debated whether or not to palm the glass shard another prisoner—now gone—had given her. A shard she'd hidden in the fabric of her leather dress, just in case one of the males decided to stop looking at her and start taking. She would have to do something drastic to break through the Sent One's obsession long enough to capture his attention. Maybe cutting him would do the trick. Maybe not. Maybe it would enrage him, and he would snap her neck with a single flick of his wrist.

Should she risk punishment? Death?

Decision time.

Pro: there was no better time for an escape. Many in the camp were distracted, as King Ardeo—who'd replaced the late Krull—had taken his most trusted men to who-knows-where to hunt Petra, Kendra's aunt, the Phoenix who had murdered Malta, Krull's widow and

Kendra's mother and, for a short time, Ardeo's most beloved concubine.

Ugh! What a mind-maze of names.

Ardeo had waited centuries to claim Malta, only to lose her two days later when a jealous Petra stabbed her in her sleep—and, taking a page from Kendra's *How To Be A Psycho* book, ate her heart.

Con: Elin wasn't in possession of Frost, a new "medication" for immortals, and the only thing capable of diluting Kendra's poison.

Pro: she might be able to get some.

Krull had purchased a handful of cubes right after Kendra's marriage to Ricker. Kendra now kept them inside a locket she wore at all times.

If Elin could steal that locket...

Another pro: never again having to worry about Orson.

He was away with Ardeo, but when he returned...

She shuddered as she recalled his parting words to her. "I *will* have you, halfling, and the way I'll take you, there'll be no chance of a babe."

Hellmongrel!

Con: she could die horribly.

The Sent One was almost in front of her. Any second now...

If her mother were alive, she would tell Elin to go for it, despite the risk.

Well, then. *Decision made.*

Moving as fast as her reflexes would allow, Elin palmed the shard and swiped the jagged edge across the Sent One's arm.

As crimson droplets trickled down his skin, she

gagged. Dizziness struck her, and a burning tightness bloomed in her chest.

Panic…threatening to consume her…already restricting her airways…

No! Not this time. She focused on her life goals—freedom, money, bakery—breathed in and out with purpose, and the storm passed.

The Sent One ground to a halt.

He's a slave, like me, and I'm his only hope. Heck, he's my only hope. I can do this. For my family.

He turned his head, looking at her over the arch of his wing, and she shivered. Curly blond hair innocently framed the face of a born seducer…exquisite, flawless. In contrast, his bedroom eyes were at half-mast, beseeching a female to naughtiness.

Anything for you…

Too bad those eyes were so poison-fogged she couldn't guess their color. Long, spiky lashes of the deepest jet rimmed his lids, and his soft, full lips practically begged for reckless kisses.

A ring of angry scars circled his neck, and she frowned. Evidence of an injury, no matter how great or small, did not usually remain on an immortal's flesh. Had someone tried to kill him before he'd been old enough to regenerate?

Even with the imperfection, he was beautiful. A visual feast. A rare eye candy. A delicacy to be savored. *And now I'm struggling to breathe again, drowning, seriously drowning in his utter masculinity, and now in guilt…grief… I haven't lusted for a man since Bay, my sweet, darling Bay, my husband of only three months, dead now, and I should be ashamed…*

"Female."

The smoky voice caught her off guard. *What the flip am I doing? Concentrate!*

"What's your name?" she asked, the words scraping against her throat.

Scowling, the warrior faced her fully.

Note to self: *gaining his attention is a mistake.*

His expression was all kinds of scary: hot and dark, radiating the evilest of intents. She gulped, expecting to be batted aside like everyone else foolish enough to engage him. But maybe she'd be gutted first.

Instead, he reached out to pinch a lock of her hair, the dark color an intriguing contrast against the bronze of his skin. His scowl softened. "Pretty."

Her rebellious heart hitched into her still-throbbing throat. Another living creature, touching her with no intent to harm…making her tingle…*so danged good.*

How starved she had been for some kind of affection, she realized.

A distant shout jolted him, and he dropped his arm to his side. She swallowed a humiliating whimper. Like an addict, she already wanted more from him. Nothing sexual. Never that. Bay would be her first and last lover. There would be no second chances for her. But she couldn't help wanting the Sent One's big, strong hands on her…rubbing her nape, maybe…or massaging her aching shoulders…no, her feet…as a friend! Just a friend.

A friend with a magnificent body surely chiseled from solid gold.

Whatever!

He turned away to resume his stomping, Elin already forgotten. No! She tried to wrap her fingers around his biceps, but couldn't. He was so large, his muscles so knotted with purpose. But, oh, his skin was deliciously warm and smooth.

"Please. What's your name?" she whispered. "Think."

Again he paused. His head tilted to the side, as if he gave serious consideration to the question. "I am My Slave."

"Wrong. What's your real name?" The more he reflected on the answer, the faster he would fight his way through the fog. *Without* the aid of the medication she may or may not be able to steal.

"My Slave," he repeated, angry now.

O-kay. Message received. Conversation over.

He moved away as a group of Phoenix soldiers inched closer to him, their determination to subdue him by any means necessary evident with every step.

He threw them aside as easily as he'd thrown the others.

Hunting his prey, he tore several tents apart.

In the fifth, the infamous Kendra sat in front of a vanity mirror, brushing her gold-and-scarlet hair. She rolled her eyes as the Sent One approached.

"You didn't have permission to leave your bed," she said, standing and glaring at him. "Therefore, you must be disciplined." She drummed her fingertips against her chin. "I know. You will spend an entire night away from me."

Oh, no. Not that. Anything but that, Elin thought drily.

Low growls erupted from him as he snatched Kendra by the waist, turned and tossed her on the mattress. The muscles in his back and thighs rippled with strength. "My Slave wants his woman."

"Thane!" Kendra scrambled to her knees, excitement

now glowing in her eyes. "You didn't have permission to touch me, either. If you do it again, I'll have to deny you the luxury of my body for a week."

Thane. His name was Thane. Seductive, like the man himself.

He moved in front of his mistress, breathing hard and fast, his hands clenched into fists. Elin could guess his dilemma. He wanted to do the princess's bidding, but he also wanted—needed—what only she could give him.

"Nothing more to say? Oh, how the mighty has fallen," Kendra cooed, tracing a fingertip down the center of his chest. She must have forgotten about her audience—or she just didn't care. "I wish the male you were could meet the male you've become. You'd realize just how desperately you crave the woman you once abandoned." She thought for a moment, brightened. "You're in luck. I *can* arrange a meeting." She unsealed the locket hanging from her neck and scraped a few flakes of Frost onto her fingertip.

"Open," she commanded, and he obeyed.

He groaned with pleasure as she rubbed the flakes against his tongue.

With such a small amount, he would be aware of his predicament, for a little while at least, but unable to deny his body's needs. Far more would be required to break the bond between master and slave.

Tense, Elin watched him. What would happen when reality hit?

A minute passed. Then another. Then he threw back his head and roared with unfettered rage.

The Frost had worked. Part of him had just realized what had become of him.

Elin covered her mouth to stop a cry of dismay.

"That's right. You worship a woman you despise." Grinning, Kendra stretched out on the bed. "I've changed my mind. You will take me, my slave. You will take me now, while your mind curses me."

"No," he snarled, even as he stroked his erection.

"Oh, yes. Do it." Her tone hardened. "Now."

Gritting his teeth, as if he fought a war within himself, he tore at her tank and shorts.

How did he treat a woman when he wasn't enthralled? Gently? Would he care that others watched him have sex? Or that his lover actually belonged to another man?

"Isn't this fun?" Kendra purred. Never had a person so emanated evil.

What had caused her to become…this?

Didn't really matter now. She was what she was.

They all were.

Survival instinct 101. Put your head down. See nothing. Say nothing.

"Hate you," Thane spat.

Kendra laughed. "Do you really? When you love me so thoroughly?"

Crack. Elin's gaze jerked up. The warrior had just punched a hole in the headboard.

"Now, now. None of that," Kendra cooed. "You've been given an order. See to it."

Thane flipped her over and pushed her face into a pillow. Not wanting to look at her, even though he was still desperate for her? He nudged her legs apart with his knee, and Kendra gave another laugh.

"Just the way I like it," she taunted, glancing back at him to smirk.

He turned his head to the side, and Elin could see the humiliation and disgust contorting his features.

A conflicting blast of emotions raced through her. Pity that he was being driven to this. Anger that he was being treated this way. And raw determination. He was a slave, like her, and needed a savior.

Screw survival instinct.

Elin raced inside the tent. "Stop. Please, Thane. Stop."

He grabbed the base of his shaft and positioned himself for entrance.

"Thane!" she shouted, trying again. *Fight Kendra's allure. Don't give her what she wants.*

He halted just before the damage was done, his entire body vibrating as he resisted the urges thundering inside him.

"Please," she repeated, and cupped his shoulder. "You don't have to do this."

His nostrils flared as he drew in a sharp breath. Then he licked his lips, as if he'd just scented a tastier meal.

Me? she almost squeaked.

"How dare you speak to my slave, human." Kendra swiped out a claw, intending to rake Elin's thigh. Only, Thane grabbed the princess by the wrist, saving Elin from a severed artery. "Ow! Let go."

"No...hurt," he gritted.

The Phoenix guards snapped to attention, realizing they needed to protect their princess, and attacked Thane in unison, wrenching Elin from his side.

Stomach rolling from the sight of the attack, dizziness swimming in her head, she scrambled from the battle and waded shakily into the pond. She ducked under the surface, submerging herself, and vowed to stay under water as long as her lungs would allow.

Coward!

Yes. Yes, she was. But there was nothing she could do about it. Violence was her kryptonite, and if she didn't hide, if she saw it happening, she would splinter apart.

Aren't you already?

At least Thane's life would be spared. Upon his arrival at camp, he had been clear enough to realize he was in the middle of a crap storm, and had killed Krull, who would not be coming back. Ever.

Kendra had been due a punishment for what she'd done to Ricker, and, to avoid it, she'd reverted to her old ways and eaten the old king's heart. Ardeo had then taken the throne and as thanks for Thane's part in the whole deal, granted him life eternal among the Phoenix. As a slave, yes, but life was life.

Lungs…burning…

Elin came up for air, gasping, relieved to see Thane and the warriors were gone. She wiped the water droplets from her lashes and trudged to the shore.

"Human!" Kendra screamed. "We have business."

Uh-oh. *Time for my newest beating.*

Her mind whirled with a new plan. *Bear whatever happens next, recover and steal the cubes out of the locket. Kendra has to sleep* sometime.

Thane would come to his senses and fight his way out. Grateful for her service, he would take Elin with him. Finally, she could start her new life.

CHAPTER TWO

New bonds. Same problem.

Same solution.

My Slave yanked his way to freedom, ignoring the pain sweeping through his body. He stomped toward the exit of the tent. He wanted his woman with a desperation that—

He stumbled back a few steps, momentarily distracted. He frowned. Something small, square and cold had just been shoved into his mouth; it was sweet. He liked it. Also, there was a strange weight pulling at his shoulders. Why?

He took stock. A female had her arms locked around him, her small body pressed against him, her legs dangling above the ground.

New problem.

New solution. He grabbed her by the waist with every intention of pitching her over his shoulder. But the sweetness of her curves registered, and he quickly changed his mind. She was delicate, like an exquisite piece of china in need of protection.

He didn't think he'd ever held anything so fine.

Careful, so careful, he wrapped his arms around her and held her against him, using his body as a shield against the world. *He* would protect.

She sucked in a breath, as if the embrace surprised her. "Your name is Thane. Remember. Please."

Her voice—he recognized it. It was unnaturally raspy, as if she'd just had the most intense orgasm of her life and would die without another. And it was an intonation that had invaded his dreams for the past six nights, sparking something inside him to life…something almost tender…driving him, arousing him.

An arousal he didn't understand. She wasn't his woman.

"Thane," she said on a trembling breath. "Your name is Thane. Kendra tripled your dose of poison, so I need you to concentrate on the cold now spilling through you. Do you feel it? Do you feel the cold?"

The cold—yes. A thin layer of ice coated his insides. "Yes."

"Good. Now concentrate on me," she said, and he was helpless to do otherwise. "Hear what I say. You are a Sent One. You aren't here of your own volition. You were drugged. You're still drugged. The woman you desire has made you a prisoner of the Phoenix. Clan Firebird."

In some forgotten corner of his mind, the words held his interest. Sent One. Drugged. Prisoner. Phoenix.

The words were accompanied by emotions.

Sent One—longing.

Drugged—confusion.

Prisoner—rage.

Phoenix—hatred.

"—still listening? You can free yourself, Thane. There is a way."

The cold intensified, until a winter storm raged through every inch of him. All the while the female continued to speak—that voice, so carnally perfect—and he began to feel as if he were floating higher and higher, his head finally peeking above a sheet of dark clouds.

His name *was* Thane. He *was* a Sent One.

He was here for a woman. No, he thought a second later. He was here *because* of one.

Kendra. Yes. That was her name.

He despised Kendra. Didn't he?

No. He wanted her. Only her.

But…if that were true, why was he clinging to the female in his arms?

The, oh, so tempting *female in my arms.* He ran his nose along the line of her neck, inhaling deeply.

"Wh-what are you doing?" she asked on a wispy catch of breath. "Smelling me? I've bathed. I swear I have."

No hint of smoke or flowers, only soap and cherries. She didn't smell like Kendra, and he was glad.

He rubbed his stubble-covered cheek against her skin. Soft, mildly warm rather than searing hot. She didn't feel like Kendra. But…better?

Yes, oh, yes.

He flicked his tongue across her fluttering pulse. Melted honey, summer fruit. She didn't taste like Kendra. *So much better.*

"Stop." She moaned, and he liked that, too. Wanted to hear it again…and again. "That's not going to happen between us, warrior. We're going to save each other, nothing else."

What he heard: *going to happen between us.*

He agreed.

He carried her to the bed and eased her onto the mattress. "Have you," he said.

"No, Thane," she replied, wary—and even more breathless.

Floating higher and higher...

Peering down at her, he felt as if he were seeing her for the first time. Maybe he was. Or, maybe his focus was sharper with every second that passed, new portions of his mind clearing, cobwebs falling away.

His friends would have called her "plain," he thought, but to Thane she was utterly breathtaking.

Long, dark hair spread around her like a midnight curtain. She was human. Petite. Delicately honed, like a cameo. Her pale skin had been burned by the harsh rays of the desert sun and had freckled. He could trace those freckles with his tongue. She was young, perhaps twenty, with big gray eyes that reminded him of smoked-glass mirrors. He could see himself in those eyes...all the way to his battered soul.

Something in her called to something in him—like to like—and a part of him he'd never known, a part once hidden even from that forgotten corner, responded. It was strong, this something. It was alive. Demanding. And it was saying, *This one. Take her.*

He watched as her gaze dropped to his erection... and quickly shot back up. A blush stained her cheeks. The sight aroused him, lighting a new fire in his veins.

"Uh, if you want to be free of Kendra, you can't make love to her. Not that that's what you've been doing to her. Barf! I'm just saying you have to kill her."

He would have to proceed with caution. He could easily hurt so fragile a female.

Her words registered, and he paused. Kill...Kendra?

"There's no better time. She's sleeping. That's how I managed to steal the Frost."

Higher...

Kendra... His friend Bjorn had found her in the slave market. She'd been bound by gossamer chains—somehow unbreakable—when the warrior presented her to Thane as a gift.

Higher still... Bjorn. A sharp, stinging pang razed Thane's chest. Bjorn and Xerxes. His boys. His only friends. They had fought demons together, bled together. They had shared lovers and guarded each other's backs. The boys were as close as brothers. He trusted them with his life. Loved them with all that he was. Needed them more than his heart or lungs.

They felt the same way about him. Bjorn probably blamed himself for what had happened with the princess.

He shouldn't. Thane had welcomed Kendra into his bed because she hadn't minded his peculiar sexual tastes...his enjoyment for things that had horrified so many others. In fact, she had begged for the terrible things he'd done to her. For more. But she had also grown possessive and clingy, and he'd decided to let her go.

To punish him for his defection, Kendra had tried to torch his club, the Downfall. He'd stopped her before any permanent damage was done and hauled her back to her people, happy to be rid of her.

Only, her father had freed her from her chains, and she had returned for Thane. With full use of her powers.

Some Phoenix could change their appearance with only a thought, and Kendra was one of them. Again and again she'd come to Thane, never appearing to be the same woman, and each time he'd taken her. All too soon, he'd become dependent on the fiery poison her body produced.

That was when she'd revealed her deception.

Enraged, he'd killed her and, in turn, sealed some kind of bond between them, giving her what she'd wanted most. His slavish devotion.

Sparks of remembered rage scalded him.

She. Had. Enslaved. Him. Had bound his mind as surely as she'd bound his body. Only, the chains on his thoughts had been invisible.

She was the enemy.

She had to die.

It's working. He's beginning to understand.

Elin's joy was sweeter than the banana cream pie Bay used to make her.

"If I kill the princess," Thane gritted, "she'll become even stronger."

Elin debated whether or not to risk sitting up. Lying in bed while a superstrong warrior with a massive hard-on loomed over smacked of stupid. She was vulnerable. And shaky. And achy. But one wrong move could send this particular warrior into a tailspin that led straight back to the grunting, psychotic caveman.

Stupid or not, she remained in place.

"Kendra will strengthen, yes, but her tie to you will not. That will be broken with her second death, and won't reform with her next regeneration. You'll be free—and then, if you want to, I don't know, escort me, your new best friend, back to civilization, I would be forever grateful."

He thought for a moment, more and more fury rolling off him. "You are sure my tie to her will be broken?"

"Yes. But if you feel yourself falling back under her spell, take one of these." She opened her hand, revealing the remaining two cubes of Frost.

Removing the medicine from Kendra's locket had been easier than she'd anticipated. The Phoenix had drunk herself into a stupor and hadn't noticed when Elin tiptoed to the side of the bed and fiddled with the locket.

Thane snatched the cubes and tossed them in his mouth, swallowing.

Or eat them now. Whatevs.

The tent flap lifted, and in stepped a guard on patrol.

Great! Premature rejoiceulation. Thane wasn't ready for a full-on rebellion.

Sand flung from the guard's boots as he stomped toward her. "Hey," he barked. "You're not supposed to be in here."

Fear drove her to the other side of the bed. *Head down. See nothing. Say nothing.* The guard followed her, unconcerned by Thane, assuming he was on another lust-induced rampage to reach Kendra.

"Looks like someone's due another reminder about her place." Strong hands wrapped around Elin's upper arm, surely bruising her. A whimper escaped her. She was jerked to her feet. "I'll be happy to— Hmph."

Thane grabbed the guard by the neck and snapped his spine.

The hold on Elin's arm broke, and the male fell to the ground.

There was no crimson pool to stir her panic, and she released a sigh of relief.

Maybe Thane was ready for a full-on rebellion after all.

"Thank you," she panted.

He was breathing too heavily to respond, his attention focused solely on the bed. Elin backed away. Just in time. Perhaps he was remembering all the horrible things Kendra had made him do there, perhaps not, but the tether to his control shattered. With a roar, he punched and clawed at the iron railings, until only shards of metal remained. He ripped the mattress into eight different pieces before turning his attention to the walls, tearing through the fabric, shredding the entire structure.

Without the barrier, bright sunlight glared overhead, spotlighting him. Dust motes performed a wild ballet around him, as if to celebrate the birth of vengeance.

I've partnered up with a crazypants.

Uh-oh. She must have said the words aloud. He focused on her, the fog gone from his eyes...eyes a bright electric blue, beautiful beyond compare and so charged and turbulent she could feel the crackle of them all the way to the bone.

"Stay here, and you'll stay safe," he said through clenched teeth. "Do not run. I'll catch you, and I don't think you'll like the results."

Oh, no. What had she gotten herself into? "D-don't threaten me."

"Don't run," he reiterated.

Shouts sounded, drawing his attention. He marched into the heart of the camp. Elin watched, wide-eyed, heart thumping, as he worked his way through the masses, breaking the neck of anyone foolish enough to step into his path.

Was this really happening?

When he reached Kendra's tent, he removed the blockade with a single brutal yank.

Yes. This was happening.

The princess had awakened. She stood in front of a full-length mirror, admiring her reflection, unaware her locket was empty. Seeing Thane, she smirked. "Someone enjoys his punishments a little too much, doesn't he?"

He wrapped a hand around her neck, lifting her, causing her legs to dangle in the air. He squeezed so tightly her eyes bugged out, and her skin quickly turned blue.

She tugged at his wrist—he held firm.

She clawed at his face—he held firm.

"You're going to die, and you're going to come back, and then we're going to have some fun." There was absolute, utter command in his voice. "Do you hear me? Don't you dare try to deny me my retribution by staying dead. You do, and I'll track your spirit into hell and drag you back."

Blood leaked from her eyes and nose and then...then her head flopped to the side. Her motions ceased, and Thane dropped her.

Elin fought a hot rise of panic. Blood...blood...not much, but enough. *Stay calm. Find a happy place. Somewhere. Anywhere but here.*

Thane threw his head back and released a war-hungry roar.

Anyone unaware of what was going on suddenly understood. Warriors noticed their fallen comrades on the ground and charged toward Thane. His back was to them. He didn't know he was about to be tackled.

Elin cried out, distressed. Then Thane squared his

shoulders, flared his wings—so long, so glorious, art in motion—and spun, a sword of fire appearing in one hand, a short sword in the other.

The Phoenix moved too quickly to backpedal and avoid impact.

He was calculated, methodical and lethal as he sliced through their ranks. Appendages fell. Bodies followed. Blood splattered and gushed.

Dizziness. Nausea. More heat.

Don't scream. Please, don't scream.

She'd witnessed this much devastation before, the day her father and husband were killed by the very men being dismembered. The only reason Elin had been spared was her mother. The beautiful Renlay had agreed to return to camp as a breeder, sleeping with whomever the king desired, so that she would give birth to full-blooded warriors for the rest of her miserable life.

Elin had been her insurance policy.

Renlay had become pregnant right away. But then, four months ago, both she and the child died. Neither regenerated.

The agony of Elin's loss was still so terribly fresh. A wound that had yet to heal.

A wound that might not ever heal.

Finally, a reckoning had come. She should enjoy it.

Tears tracked down her cheeks, a scorching deluge.

An arm went flying through the air—without a body attached. A foot soon joined it. What little calm she'd managed to retain left her in a puff of smoke, and she hunched over to vomit.

In a desperate bid to end Thane, the final soldier threw a ball of fire at him. A very foolish move. Creating the ball zapped the rest of the male's strength.

Thane easily dodged, his wings snapping together. Then he stepped forward—only to disappear from view. He must have entered the spirit realm, becoming unseen to the ungifted eye. A few seconds later, as if he'd flown the distance, he reappeared directly in front of the culprit.

Head—severed. Blood jetted from the open artery.

Elin vomited again, saying goodbye to the rest of her measly breakfast...and maybe even parts of her stomach. At least the battle was over. Violently. Brutally. But over and done.

Across the way, a tent erupted with flames. Crap. The fireball had not extinguished. Smoke curled through the air, thick and dark, drifting toward her, stinging her eyes and nose. Still, she remained where she was, just as she'd been told. Thane's rage and bloodlust would soon fade—*please, fade*—and he would remember her. He—

Pivoted on his heel to look back at her, his expression dark with manic satisfaction. Icy fingers of dread crept through her. *This is the man I'm going to trust to escort me back to civilization?*

She stepped backward, the decimated remains of the bed stopping her.

"Female. Come here."

Before she could take a step forward—was she really going to move *closer?*—two other Sent Ones appeared in the camp, claiming Thane's attention.

Expert trackers...cold-blooded killers. The males were just as tall as Thane, just as muscled...just as intimidating. Maybe more so. They looked to be worked into frothing tempers.

They reminded her of rabid wolves.

She had a choice to make: fight or flight?

Did she really need to think about it? Flight! Surviving the desert and surrounding safari on her own would be difficult, but difficult beat insane any day.

As quietly as possible, she inched to the side, away from the males. If she drew their notice...

Careful...

Another inch...

She froze when Thane squeezed the shoulder of the guy on his left. The one with bronzed skin veined in gold and multicolored eyes glistening with violent determination.

The one on the right nodded, as if answering an unspoken question. His white hair was slicked back from his face, revealing the palest skin she'd ever seen, with tiny scars etched over every inch. Not exactly model-attractive...unless he was doing a spread for *Hell on Earth Magazine.* His freaky, neon-red eyes were straight out of a nightmare.

She gathered what little courage she possessed...and gained another inch.

The three warriors angled toward each other, forming a private circle smoldering with emotion—a sweet emotion that astonished her. Joy. Relief. Sorrow. Love. So much love. Despite everything that had happened, the worst of her fears were assuaged.

Without a word, the three males branched apart and vanished.

Elin spun, searching for any sign of the trio's presence, finding none. Perfect. She swept through the surrounding area, gathering the things she needed: a canteen of water, a blanket and a bag to carry food.

Neon returned, seeming to step through thin air, and she jolted, a scream brewing in the back of her throat.

He lifted two motionless bodies from the ground, unaware or unconcerned by Elin's presence, and threw
them in her direction. They landed at her feet, blood
leaking from the bodies, pooling, winding around her.
She began to tremble.

Rainbow came back next, then Thane, and the three
continued to add bodies to the pile. The death...the destruction.

Do not vomit. Do you hear me? Do. Not. Vomit.

She must have made a noise. Neon's gaze hit her
with laserlike intensity. Gasping, she dropped her bundle and backed away. He stomped toward her, moving
around the wall of death. The scream finally fought
its way free...and just...never...stopped. Sharp pains
ravaged her throat as her already damaged larynx protested further abuse.

Strong hands cupped her cheeks. "Female."

Thane's midnight-fantasies voice penetrated the haze
of panic.

She blinked into focus. Piercing blue eyes watched
her, diamond hard and determined. He was all that she
saw. All that she wanted to see.

"You're safe from my wrath. I told you this."

Safe.

Yes. Deep breath in...out... Yes, she was safe. He'd
said so, and Sent Ones couldn't lie.

"Th-thank you," she managed.

He traced his thumbs over the rise of her cheekbones—*more contact, even better than before*—every
cell in her body coming to unexpected, dreaded life,
snagged by the magnetic pull of him...reaching for him,
desperate, hungry....

Vulnerable already, she was no match for his dark,

wicked allure… It was as unattainable as a whisper, as heady as a caress. Undeniable. Inexorable. So powerful it nearly dropped her to her knees.

I'm so sorry, Bay. I promised you forever, and now I'm reacting to another male. I'm slime. No, I'm worse than slime. Though all she wanted to do was burrow closer, she forced herself to tug from Thane's hold.

"You have two choices, female," he said with a frown. "Return to the humans and chance being hunted and tortured by the Phoenix. Or come with me to the third level of the skies and work at my club, where you will be guarded."

Work for him? Stay with him?

Determination pushed her shock to the curb.

"You'll pay me?" Life goal one: escape. Life goal two: make bank. He could be offering both.

"Yes."

"How much?" She may be tempting fate, but in the past few seconds, a mini-war had waged in her brain, and shrewdness had won.

His frown deepened. "We'll figure it out."

A nonanswer. "I…I…" Didn't know what to do.

His gaze sharpened. "Never mind. I've decided for you. You're coming with me, and that's final."

What! "Now hold on a second, angel boy."

"I'm not an angel." He clasped her by the waist— holding on—and passed her on to Neon. "See that she gets there." Then he vanished, ending the conversation.

Well, well. Next stop: the skies.

CHAPTER THREE

ENDLESS RIVERS OF EMOTION cut different paths through Thane, though they each intersected with his heart, one bleeding into another, until he could no longer tell them apart.

Last night, thirty-eight Phoenix prisoners regenerated, the oldest and strongest first. Two had yet to reform, and might have reached their final death.

Kendra had been the fourth to reform.

One by one, Thane had hauled every single warrior to the courtyard in front of his club—and staked them to the ground. Hands, shoulders, pelvis, knees and ankles. He'd ensured every head was propped up with a rock…so that every warrior could witness the suffering of his friends.

Kendra was at the head of the line.

The Phoenix wouldn't die quickly. As children of the Greeks, they were immortal. For weeks, perhaps months, they would starve, the sun blistering their exposed flesh, crows constantly pecking at their eyes and, later, their organs. And when the warriors finally succumbed to the sweet oblivion of death, they would regenerate, and Thane would be right there to repeat the entire process.

Merciless, yes. He didn't care. Now enemies would think twice before challenging him.

The problem was, this would upset Zacharel, the leader of the Army of Disgrace. *Thane's* leader. This would anger Clerici, the new king of the Sent Ones, Zacharel's boss, for Thane was abusing the spirit of the amended law—do not kill, unless captured—not acting in an effort to protect others from the same fate, but to exact revenge. This would also disappoint the Most High, the commander of them all.

This would jeopardize Thane's future.

He already stood at the corner of Last Chance and Doomed, and with one wrong move, he could lose the only thing he loved.

His boys.

Can't be parted from them.

But he couldn't let the Phoenix go, either. Not until their suffering blotted out the hated memories they'd given him.

Thane sat at the back end of his tub, boiling water pouring from the overhead spout, raining over his naked body. His hands clenched the edge of the porcelain so tightly it was already cracked. His legs were bent to his chest, his forehead resting against his knees. It was a position of shame. One he knew well.

He should have already rebounded. He was no stranger to sex and bondage. For almost a century, he'd found a delicious sort of comfort in the way pale, feminine flesh reddened under his ministrations. He'd adored watching wrists and ankles strain against bonds. Delighted in seeing the first gleam of fear in his lover's eyes...knowing tears would soon follow.

Messed up? Yes. But then, he'd also enjoyed being on the receiving end of such treatment.

He was probably worse than messed up, and it didn't

take a lot of digging to figure out why. The months he'd spent inside a demon prison— *Stop. No.* Every muscle in his body tensed as his mind fought the abhorrent direction it was traveling, but he forced himself to continue on. Remembering kept his darker emotions at a razor's edge, each ready to cut him, make him bleed.

He liked to bleed.

He remembered the way clawed hands clutched at him as they dragged him into a dank cell, stripped him, and strapped him to an altar. He remembered Bjorn, a stranger then, being strung up above him—and skinned. He remembered the copper scent of fresh blood, the warmth of it as it dripped onto Thane's face, chest and legs. He remembered Xerxes, also a stranger, being chained to the wall across from him and raped repeatedly.

A roar of denial clogged his throat. Thane punched the side of the tub, leaving a gaping hole in the porcelain. What do you know. There was a limit to what even he could bear.

The pain of his friends.

As the days passed inside that terrible prison, Thane was never touched. He hurtled threats and insults, but the demons laughed rather than feared. He begged, desperate to remove focus from the other men, but the demons ignored him.

His frustration…

His hatred…

His rage…

Each had slunk to the back of his mind, and just never left him. Eventually, after his escape, his sexual gratification became tied irrevocably to the very things he'd been denied, creating a hell of a lot of crazy.

"I put your human with the barmaids."

Xerxes's gentle voice came from inside the bathroom, a comfort to him.

"Thank you." Thane had questions for his lovely, unlikely savior. How had she, a human, come to live with the Phoenix? What was her name? How old was she? Did she smell as clean and sweet as he remembered?

Did she belong to one of the warriors staked outside, or perhaps to one of the soldiers out hunting with the new king?

How had she helped Thane? His memories were clouded. *Why* had she helped him?

The moment the urge to touch her faded, Thane would approach her and ask.

Right now, he was too aware of her. Too…absorbed in her. She made him feel soft, protective and tender, something he didn't just not like; something he despised. And yet, his sexual desires had never been so intense. The urge to throw her down and ravage her was almost blinding.

Why the unlikely juxtaposition?

She wasn't the type of woman he usually pursued. Line up his last hundred conquests, and each would be tall, leanly muscled and stalwart. This girl was delicate in every way.

It made no sense.

A growl rose from deep in his chest. Instinct demanded he destroy whatever he didn't understand. What he didn't understand, he couldn't control.

Control was more important to him than water.

But he wouldn't destroy the girl—he didn't *want* to destroy her. Not after everything she'd done for him.

He could send her away, he supposed. But she would have zero protection.

Pass.

He could frighten her and—

No. Pass. She would scream.

Once, a screaming female would have aroused him. Now? When the slave girl did it? He experienced only rage.

At least he understood why her voice was so raspy. At some point in her life, she had screamed to such a degree, she had permanently damaged her vocal cords.

"I've placed guards around the courtyard." Bjorn's statement drew him from his thoughts. The warrior entered the bathroom behind Xerxes. "They will alert us when someone dies."

Always these men supported him, loved him. Never did they judge him or push him for details he wasn't yet ready to share. No man had ever had better friends.

Little wonder Thane was willing to die for them.

"Thank you for coming for me," he said quietly.

"We will always come for you." Xerxes walked over and shut off the water. "We heard about a Sent One who wreaked havoc in a Phoenix camp weeks before, and so we were in the area, looking for you. But they hid you well. If you hadn't told us where you were…"

All Sent Ones could direct their thoughts into the minds of their brethren, so, the moment Thane had come to his senses and realized his location, he'd used the mental connection to shout for aid.

"Time to dry off," Bjorn said. "You're already waterlogged."

As Thane stood, Xerxes offered him a towel.

He draped the cloth around his waist, a lance of anger

cutting through him. Kendra had dressed him in a loin-cloth and forced him to parade around her people, a target for any wayward caress.

And her people had caressed him.

"Have Kendra's robe removed," he demanded. "Put her in a bra and panties." Tit for tat. No mercy.

Xerxes nodded. "As soon as I leave you, I'll see that it's done."

To distract himself from his black mood, Thane studied the opulent en suite adjoined to his bedroom. Steam coated the air, curling to the domed ceiling, with its elaborate chandelier hanging in the center, glistening with a unicorn's petrified teardrops. The walls and floors were made of the same gold-veined marble. Towering archways framed large, alabaster lions and led into a closet—the one storing his...toys. A gilded mirror hung over a sink carved from a melding of rubies, sapphires and emeralds.

He'd designed the space for the women he bedded. And yet, he had never allowed a single woman inside it. Not even Kendra.

What would the human think of the decor—

He cut off that line of thought before it could tempt him. Her opinion didn't matter.

In the living room, he eased onto the couch and, after collecting a tray of cookies and breads, Bjorn settled at his left. Xerxes poured him a glass of whiskey laced with ambrosia before claiming the spot at his right.

Thane accepted an offering from both men with a nod of thanks. He devoured the shortbread and drained the contents of the glass in a lone gulp.

"You have questions, I'm sure," Xerxes said, settling back with a cookie of his own.

Grown men with a dessert fetish, he thought with the first stirring of amusement in his chest. Domesticated manimals in their natural habitat. Nice.

"Many questions," he said, but he would start with the one that tortured him most. "How are you here, Bjorn?" Thane wasn't the only one to suffer tragedy lately. "Before I ended up in the Phoenix camp, I watched you disappear in a dirty alley."

A fateful night. Just before Kendra had died and risen from her ashes, effectively enslaving Thane, he and his friends had fought a new breed of demon. Shadows that slunk along stained, cracked concrete, hungry for more than human suffering...hungry for flesh.

Bjorn had been injured, the wound oozing some kind of black goo. Then he'd vanished.

Thane and Xerxes had been frantic, but before they could search for the warrior—the other piece of their hearts—Kendra had opened her eyes and commanded Thane to journey to the Phoenix camp.

He'd obeyed unquestioningly.

Oh, Kendra. The things I'm going to do to you...

With a new slave band hooked around her waist, negating her powers, she was as helpless as he had been.

"I can't tell you what happened, or explain what will happen to me in the coming months," Bjorn finally said, and Thane heard the torment in his voice. "I'm avowed to secrecy."

He swallowed a curse. Sent Ones never broke their vows. Physically, they couldn't. Not even degenerates like them. Thane knew Bjorn, and knew his friend never would have offered one unless those he loved were being threatened.

This was another crime to place at Kendra's door.

Had Thane been around, he might have found a way to save his friend from his current fate. "If ever I can help you…"

"I know," Bjorn said, sad now. "I always know."

I must do something. Anything that affected his friend's happiness affected his.

"Have the demons responsible for Germanus's death been found?" he asked, voicing the second most pressing subject. Before Kendra, hunting the six fiends who'd ambushed and decapitated the former king of the Sent Ones had been his only duty and his greatest privilege.

"Unfortunately, no," Xerxes replied.

So much to do. Seek answers for Bjorn. Find the demons. Punish the Phoenix. Talk to the slave girl.

He looked forward to the latter most of all, and that irritated him. Looking forward to an interaction with a specific female was the same as looking forward to a specific meal. He'd eat, and it would taste good, but then he would be done.

He did not need a clinger situation.

Maybe it'd be best to avoid her now and always, his questions forever unanswered.

A sharp lance of…something…shot through him—it wasn't regret, couldn't possibly be regret—but he forced himself to nod. He would avoid her. And it would be easy. Within the hour, he would have forgotten she was even here.

Motions clipped, he leaned over and grabbed another cookie. To lighten the mood, he said, "I don't have to ask what you were doing during my absence, Xerxes. Clearly, you were lost without me."

"Clearly," Xerxes said, his lips quirking at the corners. "Oh, but before you adjourn to your room, I'll need a few minutes to move my things. I used the opportunity—I mean tragedy—of your absence to my advantage."

Ha! "Did you turn it into the knitting room of your dreams?"

Bjorn wiped his lips with the back of his hand. "If you're into knitting now, I want a sweater for Christmas."

"Well, too bad," Xerxes said. "You're getting a muzzle."

"A sweater muzzle? That's effective," Thane quipped. "I want socks."

"To hide your hooves?" Bjorn asked casually.

Funny man. "I'll have you know I have beautiful feet."

"If you wax poetic about the great beauty of your toes, I'll heave." Xerxes clutched his stomach in mock disgust.

"Oh, little piggies," Thane said, his voice soft yet dramatic. "Such sweet treats. How you send so many women…into heat."

Bjorn burst into laughter.

Xerxes shook his head, clearly fighting a grin. "How did we get on this subject, anyway? The day I learn to knit is the day I want you both to put a dagger through my heart."

This. This was why Thane loved these boys. The easy camaraderie. The teasing. The acceptance. "Deal," he said with a full-blown smile. "But what should we do if you take up basket weaving?"

"Can you believe…? It's just so… Wow… I've never seen anything quite so magnificent. Do I have tears in my eyes? I think I have tears."

Elin studied the four women pressed against the only window in the spacious and weirdly decorated bedroom they were to share. Octavia the vampire, Chanel the Fae, Bellorie the Harpy, and Savanna Rose—Savy—the Siren.

As a child, Elin's mother had taught her the Who's Who of the Different Immortal Races.

Phoenix and Fae were natural-born enemies, because Fae were descendants of the Titans—current rulers of the lowest level of the skies, *this* level—and Phoenix were descendants of the Greeks—former rulers of the lowest level of the skies.

Harpies were country cousins to the vampires, with a splash of demon ancestry, and lived for bloodshed rather than blood taps. However, they *did* need to drink blood to heal from mortal wounds.

Vampires were a blend of both Greek and Titan DNA, and despite human opinion, they didn't burst into flames—or glitter—when out in the sun. And unlike other races, they didn't choose to live in secrecy. They were the glory hounds of Mythtopia.

Mythtopia: Elin's second choice name for the world of immortals. Her first? Suckville.

Sirens were secretive, usually only emerging from their oceanfront caves once a year to seduce and kill unsuspecting humans.

From the moment Neon—aka Xerxes—had pushed Elin into the room, saying, "She's human, and will help you around the bar—do not harm her," all four beauties had been nice to her, telling her all about their lives.

It shocked the crap out of her, the uncomplicated reception, and she was still reeling.

"Elin, come take a looksie," Chanel said, motioning

her over. "Prepare to be blown the eff away." She smiled sheepishly. "And please forgive my lack of potty mouth. Savy has put me in a curse-word recovery program— even though only losers go to rehab."

The girls snickered.

Bjorn, aka Rainbow, had found the pale-haired, blue-eyed Fae as a child, after her parents had kicked her out of her realm, Séduire, for reasons Chanel refused to state.

Steps hesitant—was this a trick?—Elin closed the distance. The girls made room for her, and suddenly she was peering out at the most gorgeous setting sun. Pink and purple spilled across an endless expanse of gold and blue. Clouds were in the process of thinning and breaking apart, wisps of white forming an intricate game of connect the dots.

"Beyond lovely." She'd never seen the sky so up close and personal.

"I don't think we're looking at the same thing," Octavia said. Thane had rescued the brunette bomb-shell from humans determined to hammer a giant nail through her beating heart. "As a plasmaterian, I think it's lovely. And magically delicious. But I doubt we share the same tastes. Glance down, petal."

Petal? It was better than "Servant Girl." She glanced down—and screamed. Phoenix after Phoenix lined the courtyard in front of the club, each body held in place by multiple stakes. Blood dripped from each of the vic-tims, creating infinite pools of red.

Elin pressed a fist into her mouth to stop another scream from escaping. As her stomach churned with sickness, she backed away from the window.

Most of the immortal races are vicious, her mother once told her. *They are predators whose instincts have*

been honed by a single blade—survival of the fittest.
Remember that. And if ever I'm not around to protect
you, trust no one and use everyone. Do you under-
stand? It's the only way you'll survive.

Elin's chin trembled. Thoughts of her mother's life
always came with thoughts of her death. Annnd, there
they were. Renlay's image flashed. She was sprawled
across the floor of her tent, drenched in sweat and
blood, clutching her dead baby in her arms, crying as
her life drained away.

Heart...breaking all over again...

"One thing is clear, girls," Bellorie said, tugging Elin
away from the dark place she'd been racing toward. "We
need to wear rain boots the next time we leave the club."

That was what was clear?

"Baking soda and vinegar might work on blood-
stains," the girl continued blithely, "but they do *not*
work on blood soaks."

Xerxes had purchased the redheaded stunner from
the slave market and set her free. But like Elin, her
family was dead and she was alone; she'd chosen to
come here.

"Do you think Thane will greet all fire whores with
a stake from now on?" Savy was the youngest of the
group, and the most exquisite, with her blue-black hair,
golden eyes, and toffee-colored skin. She'd once aided
Thane, "the darling man," during a mission, and he'd
rewarded her with a home and a job.

The darling man? It was hard for Elin to reconcile
the magnanimous Thane these girls had described with
the cold, withdrawn Thane who had shoved her at his
friend, disappeared, forgotten about her, and then, oh,
yeah, decorated his walkway with living beings.

Who was the real Thane?

Actions mattered more than words. So. This one, she thought, was the truest reflection of him. No question. She shuddered, horrified. Thane might do this to her, if ever she crossed him.

Might? Ha! He was just like lightning. Pretty to look at, but dangerous and deadly. At the first sign of a storm, he would strike at her.

"Yeah. Probably," Bellorie finally said. "Revenge goggles will paint targets on all their backs."

Well, that settled it: Thane could not know of Elin's mixed heritage.

Thane must not *ever* know.

Use the girls for information.

"Has, uh, he ever done anything like this before?"

One by one, they turned to face her. Their expressions ranged from pity to resignation.

"He's always been brutal when it comes to his enemies. I mean, we've heard the results of some of his torture sessions with demons," Savy replied. "Trust me, that Sent One knows how to work a blade."

"And a hammer."

"And a hacksaw."

"And a bow and arrow."

"But he's never done anything this violent to so many at once," Savy finished. "At least, not to my knowledge."

"Don't worry, petal," Octavia added. "He's very good to his employees. As long as you don't steal from him, you'll be fine."

"Or lie to him."

"Or betray him."

"Or insult one of his friends."

"Or try to physically harm him," Octavia said with a shrug.

Elin gulped a mouthful of acid. *I once cut him with glass.*

Would he remember and retaliate?

She decided then and there to be such a good employee, he would never have any reason to punish her… or talk to her…or notice her in any way.

If ever I decide to write my biography, I'm calling it Head Plus Sand Equals Buried. *Like the rest of me might be, if I'm not careful.*

"Oh, a word of advice." Wagging a finger in her face, Bellorie said, "Don't try to lure Thane into your bed."

"Or a closet."

"Or onto a kitchen table."

"Or the floor."

Bellorie nodded in wholehearted agreement.

"Uh, don't worry," Elin said. Bay's life hadn't just been cut short. Bay's life had been cut short *because of her.* Her! Because she'd surrendered to her feelings for him, dragging him into the crosshairs of the Phoenix.

If he couldn't live to the fullest, she wouldn't live to the fullest, either. Fair was fair.

And, yes, it was a self-inflicted punishment; a therapist could probably excavate a gold mine of neuroses out of her. But she'd made up her mind, and she was sticking to it.

So, that wasn't you panting after Thane and his massive hard-on?

Whatever. A woman would have to be comatose to miss Thane and his hard-on.

"Anyway, Thane doesn't sleep with his staff," Bellorie continued. "Don't get me wrong. I could totally seduce him if I wanted. I'm *that* good. But I choose to dial down my sexual appeal while I'm here. FYI, that's why you haven't jumped me, Elin. You're welcome."

Savy rolled her eyes. "You are beyond mistaken, Rocket."

Interesting nickname. "How dare you!" Bellorie stomped her foot. "Elin would totally jump me if I unleashed my full prowess!"

The siren pinched the bridge of her nose. "Why do I even bother? I wasn't talking about your sexual prowess, moron."

Instantly appeased, Bellorie waved her hand through the air. "Then you may continue."

"He *does* sleep with his staff," Chanel tossed Elin's way, "but only very rarely. And once the deed is done, the girl is gone. She never works here again. Never even comes back for an effing drink—because she's forever barred from the effing premises."

Got it. Thane was a serial bang and bailer.

According to her friends at college, it took a pretty hard-core personality to be a repeat offender. The shame of the broken hearts left behind and all that.

After a while, Elin had developed an unhealthy dread of being used. Not because she didn't think she could handle the emotional baggage, but because her mother would have found out—Renlay always found out—and would have gone hunting for vengeance.

Renlay wouldn't have been able to beat a second assault and battery charge.

Yeah. Try being *that* girl. The one whose mother broke a girl's nose for giving her precious daughter a case of the sniffles.

Renlay might have lived among the humans, but she'd never been fully tamed.

A vise squeezed at Elin's heart. Her eyes misted over.

When Elin had realized things with Baylor Vale were serious, she'd suggested marriage, despite how young they were. He loved her more than anything, he'd said, and happily whisked her off to Vegas. Three months later, he was dead and she was enslaved.

Had she known what was coming, she would have avoided him.

Oh, Bay. You'll never know how sorry I am.

"I don't want Thane in that way," Elin reiterated. *Really.* "And I won't. Not ever." Determination could defeat tsunami-like lust, right?

Savy and Bellorie smiled at her, all sure-sure. Chanel shook her head and sighed, her disbelief obvious.

Octavia gently chucked her under the chin. "Everyone in this room is nursing a serious lady boner for him."

Nice.

The girl continued, "Night after night you'll watch him enter the club, select his female for the evening, and charm her into his special bedroom. You'll be charmed, too, petal, I guarantee it. You won't care what he likes to do in there. Hint: chains are involved. You'll start to crave an invitation you know you'll never get."

Wait. "What does he do with chains?"

Smiling, Chanel wagged her finger at her. "Gossiping is another thing Thane abhors. So, you'll just have to find out for yourself. And you will. Some mornings, you'll have to go in there to clean the room *and* the effing woman."

No way. Just no way. Love nest mop-up wasn't what

Elin had signed up for. It wouldn't even look good on her résumé.

"Okay, enough chitchat." Bellorie anchored her hair into a bun at the crown of her head. "Let's get our girl into a uniform. The club opens in a few hours, and I have a feeling she's not even close to being prepared. No offense," she said with a grin. "But you look about as ferocious as a newborn bunny."

"None taken." Elin *wasn't* prepared, and she couldn't deny she was unaggressive and ready for a cuddle.

"Questions? Comments?" Savy asked. "No? Good."

"Yes!" she rushed out. "I have questions." But she would throw only the first thousand at them. The next thousand could wait.

"No?" Savy said again. "Good. Tonight you'll simply shadow us, learning how to take orders and how to deal with unruly customers. Of course, that means we get to keep all your tips. The money, the gold." She sighed with dreamy pleasure. "And the jewels."

Gold? Jewels? Forget the questions. "Tell me more."

Bellorie pulled down the collar of her shirt, revealing a sapphire skull-and-crossbones pendant. "Last night, a bear-shifter gave me this little beauty just for adding honey to his beer."

Sweet juicy sparkles! How much would a handful of baubles like that go for? Enough to finance Elin's bakery?

"Oh, before we forget," Bellorie said, clapping her hands. "At the end of your shift, you may bed the male of your choice, but you can't bring him to this room. Patrons aren't allowed back here and are killed on sight. You can leave with him, and go anywhere you wish. Just make sure you know how to get back. Since you aren't immortal, we don't want you to accidentally walk over the edge of a cloud."

Note to self: stay inside the building forever.

"I'm not looking for a relationship," she assured them, "so I won't be leaving with anyone."

Octavia arched a brow. "Backtrack, petal. No one said anything about a relationship."

Good point.

Chanel put her hands on her hips and studied Elin more intently. "If I know men, and I do, like, seriously effing well—good?—you'll appeal to the protector types. You're not a great beauty, but there's something about you…a vulnerability, maybe. They're going to want to save you."

She wasn't offended by the "not a great beauty" comment. She'd come to grips with her plain-Jane status a long time ago and made up for it with one heck of a personality. Or so she liked to think. "I don't need saving."

All four girls burst into laughter.

"What?" she demanded, a little peeved. "I don't." Not anymore. Thane had already checked that off her Life Goals list.

Savy shrugged her delicate shoulders. "If you have any problems, go to Adrian, the head of security. If you can't reach him, go to Bjorn. He's in charge of the club's employees. If you can't reach him, either, go to Xerxes. Whatever you do, don't go to Thane. Especially now." She glanced out the window and smiled proudly. "I have a feeling this isn't the last dispute he's going to end with major bloodshed."

Great! Now Elin was thinking about being staked again.

Did I make a terrible mistake coming here? Should

I have taken my chances out in the wild, a target for Ardeo and his men?

Octavia's flawless emerald eyes twinkled as she came to stand at Elin's side. Smacking her on the butt, she said, "Come on, human. Let's get you a uniform. And while you're being fitted, we can tell you the best part about your new life. As of now, you're a member of our dodge-boulder team, the Multiple Scorgasms!"

CHAPTER FOUR

A BELLOW WOKE HIM. It was ragged. It was raw.

It came from him.

Thane jolted to awareness. He was in his room, in his bed, and it was dark. He was drenched in sweat, his lungs desperate for air. His muscles sore…from thrashing.

Bjorn and Xerxes were beside him, pinning him to the mattress.

He'd had another nightmare, harkening back to his time inside the demon dungeon. To captivity. Humiliation. Frustration. Pity. Sorrow. Rage. Helplessness. His eyes adjusted, and he glanced down, saw the bloody marks on his chest. As usual, he'd attempted to rip out his own heart.

Anything to end the torment he was so good at hiding, even from himself. Until his guard lowered…

Well, enough. He would take a lover today, he decided. He hadn't done so since returning from the Phoenix camp, and he was feeling the effects of abstinence. He would exhaust himself so thoroughly, he wouldn't have the strength to move when the next nightmare came.

And it would. They always did.

Bjorn and Xerxes sensed his change of mood and released him; he sagged, boneless, atop the bed.

"Thank you," he managed.

"Defeating nightmares happens to be one of my many specialties." Xerxes switched on the side lamp, a soft golden glow chasing away the shadows.

"What about the times *you* are the nightmare?" Bjorn quipped.

"I'm never the nightmare. I'm always the fantasy."

Bjorn snorted.

A second later, the pair piled onto the bed, unwilling to leave. Thane knew why. They were willing to forgo much-needed rest in the hope of distracting him.

A man could not ask for better friends.

"Anyone else feel like girls at a slumber party?" Xerxes asked drily.

Thane's heart calmed. Grinning, he sat up and leaned against the headboard. "If you start talking about cute boys and prom dresses, I might shoot you both in the face."

"Wait. We're having a prom?" Bjorn asked. He gave a fist pump. "Finally, a chance to be king."

"If anyone's going to be prom king," Thane said, voice stern, "it's me. Look at this face. It's a money-maker."

Propping his hands behind his head, Bjorn said, "Hate to break it to you, *angel boy,* but even circus sideshows have moneymaking mugs."

Thane kicked him off the side of the bed. *Thud.* Xerxes laughed as Bjorn came up sputtering.

Bjorn crossed his arms over his chest, and narrowed his eyes on Thane. "About that prom…shall we guess who you'll crown as your queen?"

Thane stiffened. "Well played, my friend. Well played."

Bjorn grinned. "That's the only way I play."

Life as a barmaid both rocked and sucked.

The plus: tips. Not that Elin had earned any of her own yet. Having shadowed the girls for the past four nights, she had seen the potential of her paydays, and was practically foaming at the mouth.

The minus: the uniform. A bra was trying to pass itself off as a shirt, and a piece of tulle was trying to pass itself off as a skirt. Elin was pretty sure she would cover more skin at a nude beach.

But, okay. Fine. Whatever. When in Rome…or, in her case, the clouds.

The clouds. Ugh. Even though Elin now resented the word *splat,* and *fall* was practically a curse word, she'd convinced herself to explore the backyard. There, she'd found a garden in need of major TLC and had spent hours pulling weeds, a chore she used to do with her mother in Harrogate, before her family had moved to Arizona.

It had been nice, but… How long should she stay here? A few months? A year?

No. A few weeks at most. The longer she stayed, the more likely Thane was to learn of her origins.

I would rather die than face his wrath.

But, there was a plus to waiting. If she were on her own, the Phoenix king would surely hunt her, then torture her for information, willing to do anything to learn what Thane had done with his people.

She sighed, hating the thought of living in limbo, her goals once again on hold. But at least she was safe for the moment. She wasn't beaten for speaking the truth…or at all…and she wasn't locked in a cage for some imagined crime, or buried in the sand, fire ants allowed to bite the only exposed part of her body, which always happened to be her face. She wasn't treated like an animal because of her human blood.

She was fed regularly, had access to a television, a game station, and a computer—with surprisingly good internet connection, considering her distant locale—and she was getting to spend time with four of the most endearing women in the skies, each reminding her of her beloved mother in some way.

Elin smiled as she replayed a conversation the girls had last night.

Bellorie: *So, get this. A gorgeous were-shifter stumbled into the bar. He was already drunk, and paused to stare at me like he'd never seen anything more beautiful. Because, of course, he hadn't.*

Savy: *Until I walked in.*

Octavia: *I must have had the day off.*

Chanel: *I'm pretty effing sure I was hanging out with Octavia.*

Bellorie: *Wow. Could you guys be any more narcissistic?*

Chanel: *I'm not narcissistic. I'm perfect.*

Bellorie: *Anyway. He kissed me, only to pull back and mutter an apology. He said he thought I was his wife, 'cause I look just like her. I kneed him in the balls, and called him a lying, cheating son of a troll. He then said I sounded just like his wife.*

Octavia: *I bet you told him to bring the female with him the next time he visited the club, because she had to be the wittiest, smartest person ever.*

Bellorie, blinking innocently: *So you* were *there?*

Immortal divas were fun.

But the girls were more than beautiful—and more than aware of that beauty. They were kind, uninhibited danger junkies, and quite competitive. They were serious about their dodge-boulder league, which was exactly what it sounded like. Dodgeball with boulders.

If only they were members of a jazz club instead.

They practiced every day. Hard-core practicing, at that. Running for endurance. Throwing their bodies against slabs of concrete to increase pain threshold. Navigating complicated obstacle courses while dodging the weapons the other girls pitched at them. Things like knives, metal stars and hammers.

They were determined to become national champs.

Elin barely survived the practices—even though, for the time being, she was only allowed to watch.

A clatter of dishes snapped her out of her musings.

Mind in the game. Right. Tonight, a live band would be playing. The group of five Sent Ones—Shame Spiral—were in the process of setting up. Elin found her gaze constantly returning to the lead singer.

Sexy did not even begin to describe. He had a slow, sensual smile loaded with all kinds of naughty suggestions.

Mind in the work *game, Vale.*

She would soon be toiling at the tables, on her own for the first time. And she could do it. She knew she could. She'd learned a lot. The most important lesson? Find a niche and stick to it. Each of the girls had one.

Bellorie flirted outrageously.

Savy was a stern taskmaster.

Octavia acted shy.

Chanel pretended to be an airhead.

Elin thought she might go for plucky best friend.

The girls never seemed to mind when their butts were pinched, or when they were tugged onto laps, or when masculine hands traveled somewhere they shouldn't. While Elin craved contact, she didn't crave a mauling, and she wouldn't be able to pretend otherwise. She would cry or freak out, and the patrons would be offended. She would lose her (probably substantial) tip and anger Thane. Therefore, it would be best for everyone if she stopped all potential groping attempts.

She drummed her fingernails against the mahogany counter meant to separate the employees from the clientele. The area had recently undergone repairs and now sparkled like new despite the dimness of the atmosphere. Alabaster walls were carved with intricate symbols. The marble floors were polished, and scattered throughout was all-new furniture.

Apparently, Kendra had tried to torch the entire building before Thane returned her to camp, but Adrian, Thane's very fierce head of security, had managed to contain the damage.

Customers would arrive at any moment. Paying customers! The myriad of Phoenix-kebabs outside had drawn more and more gawkers every night. A few had even asked to have their picture taken in "the little yard of horrors."

Don't think I'll ever get used to this world.

"Nervous?"

The gravelly voice shocked a gasp out of her, and she whipped around to face the intruder.

Adrian. A big mountain of a man she kinda sorta considered Neanderthal chic. He had a wide forehead and slightly overarching brows. A sharp, prominent nose. Stunningly lush lips. And a stubborn chin. He wasn't classically handsome by any means, but he was somehow all the more beautiful for it. Maybe because every inch of him screamed *male*.

He was immortal. He radiated too much power to be human, the waves of it stroking across her skin every time he neared, startling her. But she wasn't exactly sure what he was.

Should she try to use him for protection?

"Very," she finally replied. As strong as he was, he might belittle her for requesting aid. Or, like the Phoenix, he might turn her fears and weaknesses against her.

"No reason to be. Thane doesn't allow those under his care to be hurt without severe consequences. Which means, neither do I. Only a fool would strike at you."

"That's the problem. Alcohol creates fools. And I'm not like the other girls, able to defend myself against a roomful of sadistic man-sluts. Not that everyone here is sadistic," she rushed to add. "Or a slut." Crap! Her shift hadn't even begun, and she was already spewing verbal vomit. "They aren't. Really." And besides, how would Thane know what anyone did to her? There'd been no sign of him, or his two besties.

Not that she'd looked—around every corner.

Not that she'd waited, eager. Not that she'd gone to bed disappointed every single night, feeling as if she'd been abandoned by him. Which was silly! She barely knew him.

"People never forget *my* consequences, drunk or not," he said. "I've been told to take good care of you, and I will."

"Thank you. But who told you to take good care of me?" Had the absent Thane been thinking about her, sending orders on her behalf?

"Xerxes."

Oh. *Won't give in to any more disappointment.* Especially since there was no reason for the emotion! Xerxes and now Adrian were looking out for her. For a former slave, that was a dream come true.

"I have to warn you," she said. "I'm going to say the wrong thing tonight. Guys are going to assume my butt is part of their order, and I won't be able to help myself. Fights will break out, and the moment they do, I'm going to curl into a ball and suck my thumb."

His lips quirked at the corners. "I'll handle it."

Amusement? Really? "Won't my behavior drive customers away?" *And get me fired? Perhaps literally.*

Did Thane practice burning at the stake, too?

Adrian reached out, as if he meant to pat the top of her head, but he stopped himself just before contact. "Silly human. I recommend thinking before you speak."

Hey! Her questions were well thought out, thank you very much. "Insulting beast," she muttered.

A rusty laugh barked from him. "Or don't. I like your spirit."

From the corner of her eye, she spotted three Fae males entering the club, each with the pale hair and blue eyes quintessential to their race, dressed in colorful feathered tops and skintight pants.

As they selected a table in back, Adrian faded into the background, and Elin's nervousness returned, now jacked up several notches. Her insides were practically showering in acid-coated ice.

At last the band eased into their first song. A love song. Actually, a sex song, and sweet fancy, goose bumps broke out over every inch of her. The lead singer—what was his name?—had the voice of a born seducer.

"Son of a troll," Bellorie muttered, suddenly at her side. "The craptastic trio has arrived."

Savy appeared at her other side. "Don't be a hater. They're only craptastic to you—and everyone else. But there's no need for either of us to be subjected to that tonight. We have to throw our little E in headfirst, and this is the best way." Her gaze settled on Elin. "The Fae are regulars. They're also pretentious and infuriating. The most any of us has ever gotten out of them tip-wise is ten measly bucks. If you can get a penny more, I'll give you every jewel I earn tonight."

"Me, too," Bellorie said, clapping. "Oh, this is going to be fun. I love winning, and this is a sure thing. Like Chanel after a few drinks."

Elin rubbed mental hands together. Take their jewels? Yes, please. Her nest egg would start off with a bang.

"What do you want if I lose?" she asked. "Remember. I came here only with the dirty clothes on my back."

Savy's grin was evil. "If you lose, you have to serve those Fae for the rest of your stay. No exceptions."

"They're seriously that bad?"

"Yes," the girls said in unison.

"The tall one called me ugly," Bellorie said, her nose going in the air.

Jerkbag! "You're gorgeous. You're also on," Elin announced. Gathering her courage, she shuffled her way to the table. "Hey, ya'll." She offered her biggest and brightest plucky-best-friend smile. "I'm Elin, and I'm here to serve you tonight."

None of the males looked at her. They continued on with their conversation.

"The new king and queen want to do *what?* No, they must be stopped."

"Who can stop them? Kane is a Lord of the Underworld and Josephina is a drainer."

"Three words. Long. Distance. Rifle."

Please. Pretend I'm not even here. It'll be fun.

"I'd love to get you something to drink," she said.

Again, she was ignored.

Frustrated, she glanced over at the bar and caught Bellorie grinning like a loon. Elin stuck out her tongue.

Bellorie played show-and-tell with her middle finger.

Coughing to cover a laugh, Elin considered her next move. Put her head between the males closest to her, and risk becoming the night's entertainment? Or walk away, come back later, and risk losing her tip because of "slow service"? Finally, she placed her hand on the shoulder of the guy on her right.

He stiffened, then flicked her arm away with so much force she stumbled backward. "Touch and die, bar wench."

"Noted," she managed to squeak past the lump growing in her throat. *Run. Now.*

Victory. Jewels. Bakery.

She remained in place. A stroke of power against the back of her neck had her spinning—and facing Adrian's chest. She gulped, waiting for the end to come. When he didn't lash out at her for daring to touch a patron without permission, she turned back to the Fae and breathed a sigh of relief.

They were staring at Adrian with terror in their crystalline eyes.

"So, um, yeah. What can I get you to drink?" she asked.

The guy closest to her seemed to blink a thousand times before saying, "Ambrosia-laced whiskey."

She lifted her hand to write it down, only to recall pen and paper weren't allowed. They were "too human." She was to memorize every order and refill accordingly without being asked. "And you?"

"Ambrosia-laced vodka."

She remembered the stern warning Bellorie had given her only this morning. *Don't sample the ambrosia. It's immortal brew and you'll die.* "You?"

"Surprise me. And it had better be a good surprise."

Wonderful. "Of course. I wouldn't know how to do a bad surprise." She stepped back, expecting to bump into Adrian—except he was no longer behind her. Frowning, she returned to the bar. Bummer. Bellorie had wandered off.

She told the bartender what she needed. "Whatever you make for the third drink, put a rainbow-colored umbrella in it." That was a "good" surprise, right?

The tattooed hottie with pink hair glowered at her before filling three glasses. He did *not* add an umbrella.

O-kay. Note to self: *bartender is not one for idle chitchat...or suggestions.*

Chanel had mentioned his name was "effing McCadden," and he was a fallen Sent-One-slash-cold-blooded-murderer. Oh, and that he had a serious case of love ebola for the minor goddess of Death, whoever that was. He was also Xerxes's prisoner—and strangely enough, his friend—and he was not to be messed with.

She loaded up her tray. "How am I supposed to know which glass has which liquid?" Everything was black.

McCadden strode to the end of the bar, snubbing her. Wonderful. Just great! She turned, her gaze automatically dusting over the stage. A crowd had arrived, seemingly between one blink and another. Women now crowded the edge of the stage, throwing their panties at the band and begging for one night in "Merrick's" arms.

"The singer is Merrick, I take it," she said as Bellorie came up beside her to fill an order.

"Yes, indeed. He collects female hearts just so he can break them."

"That's sad."

"That's life."

"Well, it doesn't have to be *my* life." Elin carefully returned to the Fae, threading her way through the crowd without spilling a drop. Murmurs rose and blended, adding to the already chaotic kaleidoscope of noise.

"What took so long?" Whiskey demanded. Guess he'd gotten over his fear of Adrian.

A few minutes was "so long"? "The goodest surprises—" No way. No way she'd just said that. "I mean, the best surprises take time." She once again donned her biggest and brightest smile as she set the glasses in the center of the table. Let the males pick their own. "Is there anything else I can get you? A bowl of nuts?" *Your own knocked into your throats?*

Violence without bloodshed. She could deal.

Her wrist was grabbed, and thrust under the nose of Vodka. "You smell especially sweet. What race are you?"

Shut your big, fat mouth hole! she almost screamed as she searched for Adrian. Had he overheard? When she saw that he was across the room, oblivious, she yanked free of the Fae's hold. He was stronger than her, obviously, and could have held on, and she wouldn't have been able to do a thing about it, but he let her go.

"I'm, like, totally human." *Just drop it. Please, just drop it.*

Laugher met the pronouncement, and she nearly had a heart attack. These Grade A jerkwads could ruin her.

"Thane would never force his valued clientele to slum it with a lowly human," Whiskey said.

Going for calm and confident rather than scared and sickly, she arched a brow. "You know him so well, then? You chat with him regularly?"

He flinched, clearly embarrassed to be called out in front of his friends. Douchey Fae: 0. Elin: 1. And now, Subject Death Trap was closed.

Yeah, but the jewels...the bakery.

She'd lost the bet, no question, but she wasn't sorry. A dead girl couldn't live her dreams. "So...no nuts?" she asked, flashing another grin.

"I can't imagine Thane has plans to bed you." Surprise Me stroked his chin with long, lean fingers. "But that's the only reason someone like you would dare to speak to us in such a fashion."

His condescending tone annoyed her, but she managed to maintain her grin. If there was one lesson that had been hammered home while living with the Phoenix, it was to act as if she was too stupid to realize when she'd been insulted, even while she was dying inside.

"No, really, how well do you know him? Because I've been here less than a week, and I'd love to learn more about him."

Sadly, it was true.

Vodka rolled his eyes. "If you survive the entire week, I'll pledge my life to my new king and queen without a single qualm."

The three returned to their conversation.

Crisis averted.

Breathing a sigh of relief, she turned away with every intention of finding one of the girls and asking for a different table. *Throwing in the towel? Waving the white flag? Pathetic!*

All at once, the entire club went quiet, even the music seeming to fade into the background.

The reason why strode through the bar as if he owned it. Because he did.

Thane had arrived.

It was her first sighting since MOP, the Massacre of the Phoenix, and it utterly stole her breath. He wore a long robe made of brilliant white fabric that should have hidden his strength but somehow only accentuated every luscious swell of muscle he possessed. Innocent blond curls framed the wicked beauty of his face, the savage contrast enough to intrigue the deadest of hearts.

I'm not intrigued and I'm not affected. I'm not, dang it.

His electric blues scanned the sea of customers, only to stop abruptly on Elin. As if lit by a match, his expression heated.

For a moment, she wondered if he'd finally learned the truth about her. If he was going to arrest her in front of all these people and escort her to the Courtyard of Horrors. Tremors struck her like bolts of lightning. Then his gaze stroked over her scantily clad curves leisurely, as if he'd found something worth further study, and she shivered.

Um…was that *arousal* she'd seen?

Just like that, the world around her vanished. There was only Thane and mutual animal attraction. The air seemed to charge with molten electricity, and her neglected body cried out. *One touch. Just one.*

"Thane," she whispered, and his gaze jerked up to her face. The heat she'd seen before? Nothing compared to *this*. Fire that scorched, even from this distance.

She licked her suddenly tingling lips. A low growl sprang from him. He took a step toward her. She didn't mean to, but she took a step toward him. *One touch. Just one.* Then he stilled, not even seeming to breathe. His expression hardened, and his hands fisted at his sides.

He turned away, effectively dismissing her.

A heavy breath deflated her lungs. She was dismissed. And so freaking easily.

The sting of rejection jolted her back to awareness. She was in a club. A club filled with immortals—his club. People were watching her with avid curiosity now. People who had seen him seduce hundreds...perhaps thousands...of other women.

Elin raised her chin. *I didn't want him anyway.* One touch? Never.

"Gorgeous," a dragon-shifter gasped. He reached out and ghosted his fingertips along the curve of Thane's wing.

No fair, she thought with a longing she couldn't deny, even now.

Thane reacted immediately, snatching the guy's wrist and breaking it with a single squeeze. A pained howl scraped at her ears, making her cringe. Adrian appeared at the injured man's side, taking him by the scruff and hauling him out of the club.

The entire scene played out in three seconds, tops.

O-kay, then. Wings: off-limits.

And there was no reason to make a mental note of

that, since she'd already decided not to touch Thane, or to let him touch her, ever.

He resumed his walk through the club, stopping to address a table of Harpies. Elin couldn't make out the words that were spoken, but whatever he said after the introductions caused each of the females to gape. Had he issued a death threat? His expression was harsh, determined.

Then he held out his hand to the tallest and strongest at the table. A striking blonde.

Blondie willingly placed her fingers in his, and, ever the gentleman, he helped her stand.

Not a death threat, but a seduction. A lance of something hot branded the center of Elin's chest. Anger? Jealousy? A measure of both? Yeah. Nailed it.

Thane led the woman out of the bar.

To his special room?

That quickly? That easily?

Elin gripped her tray with so much force the board cracked down the center.

Startled, she peered down at the two jagged halves. She was *that* jealous? No, impossible. She didn't know the man, and certainly didn't want him for her own.

He didn't matter to her.

Honestly, he was nothing more than a means to an end. A *scary* means to an end, at that. Stupid Thane was welcome to his stupid Harpy and his stupid love life and his stupid room and his stupid pleasure.

She would forget him just as easily as he'd picked up that skanky Harpy.

Name-calling? *Who are you?* The blonde was probably as sweet as candy, a stay-at-home divorced mom just looking for a night of fun to give her self-esteem the boost it needed after her husband cheated on her with their next-door neighbor.

Buck up, Vale. You have Fae snobs to charm and jewels to win.

Charm. Right. Except, she'd already failed in that endeavor.

So…what else could she try?

What would your mother do?

Easy. Renlay would kill *everyone*.

Well, that wasn't going to work for Elin. There had to be another way.

As she thought it over, her eyes widened. There *was* another way. It might land her in serious trouble with Thane, but at the moment, she didn't exactly care.

Victory, here I come.

CHAPTER FIVE

THANE TUGGED ON his robe, his motions steady despite the aggravation attempting to choke him. The Harpy was asleep and unaware of his mood, thank the Most High. She would have panicked—or asked for round two. He wasn't in the mood to deal with either.

What was her name?

Not that he cared. It wasn't as if he would ever speak to her again.

He'd used her. She'd used him. Pleasure was had. The problem was, he wasn't satisfied.

Have you ever been?

He worked his jaw. Yes, of course. At least a little. For years, he'd brought his women here, to the bedroom across from his. It was where he'd kept Kendra.

She was the first, the only, woman ever to move in for longer than a few hours, and he'd allowed it only because she'd experienced no remorse after his depraved desires had been slaked. No matter how badly he'd frightened...and marred...her. No matter what horrible things he'd asked her to do to him.

A perfect union, at least on the surface. And yet, they had never actually fit, or balanced each other.

Same with the Harpy. While she possessed a measure of dark yearning, proved every time she'd run the tip of a blade over his skin, as demanded, and smiled as his blood welled, she hadn't satiated him. Not when he'd chained her, and she had struggled, her wrists and ankles chafing, her eyes tearing up—not just with fear, but with uncertain anticipation. Not when he'd shown her an array of weapons and told her slowly and quietly what he was going to do with them, and the tears had streamed down her cheeks in earnest. Not even when he'd put his words into action, and she had begged for mercy...and for more.

Her whimpers hadn't been sweet, sweet music, as he'd expected. Her fear hadn't fanned the flames of his passion, and her pain hadn't soothed the savage beast inside.

She hadn't given him anything he'd needed.

What did he need?

He thought he'd known.

He could take her again, harder, harsher, and finally, hopefully, exhaust himself, but he refused to bed the same woman twice. Never again would he risk enslavement.

Oh, he knew there were only a handful of females like Kendra, capable of enchaining through sex, and none that were not Phoenix. But what if the Harpy had Phoenix blood in her ancestry? How was a man to know?

Besides, why take the Harpy a second time when his body craved another woman?

The...*don't say it...ignore the desire, and it will go away*...human.

He had to bite back an aggravated snarl. He couldn't ignore—and he couldn't forget. Somehow, she had branded her image in his mind. *Her* name, he was suddenly desperate to know. He wished he'd confronted her, today, yesterday, every day, and drank in every word about her.

What was it about this female?

At the camp, she had looked at him with wild panic and even fear, and he'd hated every moment. He should have enjoyed that, as he did with other women, but no. He hadn't. Therefore, he shouldn't desire her. But earlier in the club he'd taken one look at her and hungered as if he had never eaten.

She was prettier than he remembered, and he'd somehow scented her from across the room. He'd had to fight the compulsion to close the distance between them, sweep her into his arms and carry her away to ravage her.

She had been dressed provocatively, yes, but that shouldn't have had any bearing on the situation. Since the opening of the club, his female employees had worn that barely-there uniform. It was like white noise to him—there, but hardly noticeable. And yet, on the human, he'd noticed.

Despite her fragile build, she had lush, ripe breasts made for a man's hands and dangerous curves made to cradle the hardest part of him. Her legs would fit perfectly around his hips, anchoring him as he plunged into her—

No!

Tomorrow, he would force her to wear a robe.

He no longer screwed the staff. He could always find a lover, but he couldn't always find a dedicated, trustworthy worker. And if he took the delicate human the way he liked, the only way he could, he would do more than panic and frighten her. He would harm her irrevocably. In body…and in mind.

He didn't like the thought of her alabaster skin blighted…or fear in her smoked-glass eyes.

How odd.

You could be gentle with her. You could—

No. He couldn't. He had tried that before, but it hadn't worked. He hadn't even been able to finish. Pain, he'd realized, wasn't just a desire; it was a need.

Although, he thought he might actually *like* seeing the human lost in the throes of passion. She would writhe underneath him, soft and warm and wet. He would spread her legs, and she wouldn't fight him, because she would want him just as desperately as he wanted her. He would relish the sight of her body, pliant and eager. He would kiss each of her freckles, then move over her, push inside her, going slowly at first, savoring every sensation, before increasing his tempo.

His shaft throbbed.

And what happens when your control slips, and you revert to habit?

He pushed the upsetting thought from his mind and focused his attention on the things around him. Though this room was smaller than his, it was far more luxurious. Overhead hung a chandelier boasting a bouquet of rose-shaped diamonds. The walls were sheets of the purest gold, so clear rainbow flecks appeared to be trapped inside. The bed was formed from intricately twisted metals, fit only for a queen…of the night. At both the headboard and footboard were rings for different types of shackles. Whatever he preferred to use during any given encounter.

The Harpy's breathy sigh sent him striding to the door. The chance for a cold, clean getaway grew slimmer by the moment.

"Don't want to…sleep with me?" she asked, her voice slurred by fatigue.

Too late.

He looked back. She was still naked and bound to the bed.

Thoughts he'd previously ignored rose. Why had she agreed to be here? He hadn't used charm, like he once had. He'd simply said, "For a few hours, I'll do things that will make you cry and demand you do the same to me. Only I won't cry. I'll curse you, and take you harder than you'll think you can bear. Are you in or out?" She'd agreed faster than any other woman ever had. Had needed no other prompting. With only the slightest encouragement, her friends would have agreed, too. They'd moaned, "Lucky," while she'd stood.

Perhaps he shouldn't try to analyze why. The answer would probably sadden him.

"Sleeping together wasn't part of our arrangement." He'd never spent an entire night with a woman, and he never would. Sleep left you vulnerable. And to have someone within striking distance? No. His dreams were far too violent, his reactions far too telling. He could kill his partner without realizing it.

"Mmm-kay. Chains?"

He returned to her and unfastened her ankle cuffs first, then her wrists, careful not to brush against her. She reached for him, her arm shaking. He backed up before contact could be made. How could he offer solace to someone else when he couldn't even offer it to himself?

With a sigh, she sagged on the mattress.

He pulled a diamond choker from the air pocket he always carried with him. A shelf of space that hovered between the spiritual and natural realm, opened and sustained by his energy, invisible to the rest of the world. He placed the bauble on the nightstand. "I thank you for your time."

"Matching earrings?" she asked, before her head lolled to the side and sleep once again claimed her.

He placed a pair of earrings beside the choker and left the room without another word. Bjorn and Xerxes waited for him in the antechamber they shared. The two were on the couch, sipping perfectly aged scotch.

"Thane, my friend, you look far from satisfied," Bjorn said. "In fact, you look like me."

The male only ever tolerated sex, using it to forget the past, but never quite succeeding.

"What he means is, you look like a savage," Xerxes reported.

To Xerxes, sex was a quest for comfort he'd never actually found. He vomited after every encounter, shaking from the effects of the intimacy.

"For once, looks are not deceiving." His head should be clear. His body should be relaxed. A certain dark-haired, gray-eyed barmaid should be exorcised from his mind.

Zero out of three wasn't acceptable.

"So…did anyone else notice the way our new barmaid stared at Merrick?" Xerxes asked, his tone sly.

Thane stiffened. The lead singer of Shame Spiral was a known heartbreaker. "Did she leave with him?"

"No," Bjorn said. Voice just as sly as Xerxes's, he added, "Why? Would you be upset if she had?"

Crossing his arms over his chest, Thane remained silent.

Clearly trying not to smile, Xerxes said, "What's next on the agenda?" taking mercy on him.

"The meeting with Zacharel." Their leader had sent a mental-o-gram this morning. *My cloud. Ten. Do not be late.*

It was time for Thane to be punished for his most recent sins...or kicked out of the skies. A cold sweat broke out over his skin, and he fought to level his breathing. *Can't be kicked out.*

"I must speak with Adrian before we go." And tell the male to never again invite Shame Spiral back. Their music had lost its appeal.

He tasted something bitter on his tongue and frowned.

"Will you be speaking to Adrian about the human girl?" Bjorn chuckled for the first time in weeks. "I saw the way *you* looked at her earlier."

Xerxes snickered. "Everyone saw."

"Do we need to settle this the old-fashioned way, boys?" Thane asked, one brow arched as he shook a fist in the air.

"You mean break-dance fighting?" Bjorn asked.

He nodded. "Exactly."

Both males laughed, easing his dark mood.

He moved into the private hallway guarded by three vampires he'd saved from human slayers centuries ago. Each nodded in acknowledgment as he stepped into an elevator built for large men with even larger wings.

The doors shut, and the box descended with a slight shake. A few seconds later, he was striding across the lowest level of the club, snaking a corner, entering the bar. All customers were gone. The lights were no longer dimmed but shining brightly, illuminating the gilded mirrors on every wall, the dark leather chairs scattered about, and the high-gloss tables.

Adrian the Frenzied, a berserker booted from his tribe for being *too* ferocious—as if there was truly such a thing—stood in the far corner, watching.... Thane followed the line of his fascinated gaze, and gritted his teeth. Watching the reflection of the new barmaid, who was in the process of wrapping a ruby choker around her neck and preening sweetly in a mirror. Multiple gold and silver bracelets clacked on her wrists, and diamonds winked from each of her fingers; she clearly liked the look of them.

Like a little girl playing dress-up for the first time.

Too adorable for words. An unfamiliar ache bloomed in his chest. Did Adrian feel something similar?

He scowled. Perhaps there *was* such a thing as too ferocious. Because just then, Thane would have ripped the male's face off—with his bare hands.

Who had given her such expensive pieces? An admirer? Merrick?

He stalked in front of Adrian, blocking his view. "You will take Savy and Chanel to my suite to help the Harpy dress and find her way out," Thane snapped. *Be calm. He's done nothing wrong.* "But first tell me about the human's jewels."

In a heartbeat of time, Adrian's expression changed from soft and amused to cold and hard. He found Thane's way of life deplorable, had never made a secret of it, and didn't like that the girl was on his radar.

Well, *Thane* didn't want her on *Adrian's* radar. The berserker possessed unnatural strength and had to be careful with everyone he encountered. From him, even immortals had trouble surviving something as simple as a pat on the back.

"The jewels," Thane prompted. If he mentioned Merrick...

"Bellorie and Savy made a bet with the human," Adrian said. "If she could get more than ten dollars from a trio of Fae, she would win their tips for the evening. In only an hour, she got far more."

She'd won a bet against two fierce competitors? Pride joined the ache in his chest, baffling him.

Pride? Why pride?

"She's wearing three months' worth of tips," he pointed out.

Adrian lifted his wide shoulders in a shrug. "Patrons were extremely generous tonight."

Why? Were males already trying to win the human's favors?

The ache intensified.

Adrian walked away.

"The girls are in the opposite direction," Thane informed him.

"I know. I must speak with Xerxes first."

"About?"

Adrian stopped, sighed. "He told me to inform him of any inappropriate advances made toward the human."

Thane's blood flashed ice-cold in less than a second. "Inappropriate advances were made?"

"In a sense. She was grabbed."

His budding rage fed off the ache, both growing exponentially. "Where? How?"

Adrian told him of the three Fae regulars who'd clasped her arm and sniffed her, then pushed her away.

It was something the other barmaids endured every

day. Something he had always overlooked and the girls had handled. Just then, he wanted to commit murder. "You will toss the trio over the edge of the cloud the next time they enter the bar."

Surprise darkened Adrian's navy eyes. "You risk war with their families."

"I have more stakes."

"I don't think—"

"This isn't a negotiation, Adrian. You have your orders."

The berserker gave a stiff nod.

No other employee would have dared to speak out of turn—or to delay the completion of his orders—but Adrian had more liberties than most, and they both knew it.

After Thane and his boys had physically recovered from the worst horrors of their imprisonment, they'd returned to the demon dungeon and freed the other prisoners trapped inside. Adrian had been among them, captured soon after his family had cut him off.

Thane stalked around the corner and came up behind the human. Her gaze met his in the glass, and she gasped, spinning to face him. She was prettier than he remembered. Prettier than a few hours ago, even. How was that possible?

From her silky fall of dark hair, perfect for fisting, to her wide, gray eyes that held a mixture of awe and fear, to the Cupid's-bow lips he would have given anything to have wrapped around his shaft, to the freckles dotting her skin.

How did she draw him in a way no one else ever had?

Differing shades of pink infused her cheeks, each one lovely, utterly captivating.

Would she look this way after climax?

He bit the inside of his cheek until he tasted blood. *Calm. Control.*

"What's your name?" he barked more harshly than he'd intended.

Panic flared in eyes that seemed to shadow with a thicker waft of smoke before she stared down at her feet, blocking her emotions. Her fear and panic actually *doused* his desire.

"I'm Elin."

E-lynn. Lovely. Delicate. Fitting. "And your last name," he said, consciously using a much gentler tone.

She shifted several inches away. "Uh, well, it's Vale."

Why the hesitation? Because she didn't want him to do any digging, find her family, and send her away?

An excellent idea. Finally the madness would stop.

Except, fury was like gasoline being poured over him, and dread was the match. Put her in the line of danger? No. Here, he could protect her. Here, he could watch over her the way she had watched over him at the Phoenix camp.

He owed her. Yes, that was the reason he sought to protect her, when he'd never done the same for another.

"Why did you help me?" he asked. "*How* did you help me?"

She blinked, seemingly surprised at his questions. "You were trapped, like me, and I didn't like it. I thought we could save each other." She nibbled on her bottom lip. "I stole Frost from Kendra."

"Frost?"

"A new medication that combats the effects of poison like hers."

He would have a supply of Frost delivered by the end of the day. "How did you manage to steal it?"

"I snuck into Kendra's tent while she was sleeping. And just so you know, it was a one-time thing. I won't steal anything from you, promise!"

Was that what her unease was about? "I'm not worried."

"Oh. Okay." Her shoulders sagged with relief.

"You have nothing to fear from me. I'm grateful to you, Elin," he said. "What you did for me..."

Her jaw dropped. "Uh, no sweat. Really. We're even."

He wished she had asked for a boon. He wanted to give her something, anything. "How did you get the Fae to tip you so well?" he asked, changing the subject. He dusted a fingertip along the edge of the ruby choker.

The flush returned to her cheeks, tantalizing him. *My human is sensitive to touch.*

No. *Not* my *human.*

"Not because I did to them what you supposedly did to the Harpy," she muttered.

The bravery was welcome. The attitude, not so much. He ran his tongue over his teeth. Someone told her of his sexual preferences.

That someone would die.

Who was he kidding? Everyone had probably talked.

The fact that she knows doesn't matter. You weren't going to seduce her. Her disgust is meaningless.

True. But still it bothered him. "No one is allowed to question my choice of partners—or my actions."

She met his gaze, unflinching. Her lids narrowed, her lashes almost fusing. "Gotcha. Won't happen again, sir." She gave him a jaunty salute.

Was she...mocking him? "Besides, what do you know of such things, hmm?"

"I know quite a bit about getting it on, thank you," she said, her tone prim. "But you're right. Who you do isn't any of my business."

Who, she'd said. Not *what.* She didn't know the particulars. His relief was palpable.

Living here, however, she would find out. And soon. Any ease she had with him would cease.

But what did she mean, she knew quite a bit about "getting it on"?

"Why did the Fae tip so well?" he repeated.

Clearly uneasy, she shifted from one foot to the other. "Well...you see...it's like this. I told them that you... well, that you had a few extra stakes and the stingiest people at the bar were going to be extended an invitation to join the Phoenix on the lawn."

He suddenly wanted to...grin? "You lied?"

"Never!" She crossed her arms, now defiant. "After everything I've witnessed, there's a good chance I'm right."

And now she won't back down. Fascinating.

"The girls made more money than ever," Adrian called. He hadn't yet moved from his perch. "But I'm not sure we'll have customers tomorrow."

Had Adrian taken Elin under his protection? Was he hoping to shield her? Even from Thane? Or did the male desire her, the way a normal man desired a woman?

The thought settled Thane, even as it angered him. Another defender would ensure she remained safe. But another admirer would try to tempt her into bed...and that, Thane would not allow. She needed to be focused on her job.

Yes. That was why.

He would deal with Adrian in a minute.

"Besides the Fae, has anyone given you any trouble?" Thane asked her.

Silence reigned as she again nibbled on her plump bottom lip.

Want to do that for myself. Want to nibble on other parts of her, too. No! He squared his shoulders, the feathers in his wings ruffling. "Elin?"

She...was staring at his wings, he realized. Curious about them? Wondering how soft they were? Everyone did. He curbed the urge to proudly flare them, to show her just how long and strong they were. To preen and impress her. Instead, he drew one forward, closer to her.

"Uh, you asked a question, I think," she said, watching the motion with wide eyes. "Yes. Yes, you did. And it was... Oh, yeah. For the most part, everyone has been really nice." As she spoke, she reached toward a patch of golden down. Just before contact, she swung both arms behind her back and kept them there.

He frowned, not liking such a reaction from her. It was as if she'd suddenly found the thought of touching him repugnant. "Feel the wing."

She vehemently shook her head. "No way."

"This isn't a debate." He never debated. He ordered. And expected. Using the muscles in his back, he caused the end of a wing to shake ever closer to her. "Feel." A command.

A command she did not heed. "Is this a trick?"

Why would— Ah. Realization dawned. She'd seen him break the dragon warrior's hand, and could only assume he would do the same to her.

"No trick. You have my permission; the shifter did

not. But you are not ever to touch another Sent One this way. Or any way. Not even Bjorn and Xerxes. Understand?"

"Yep. Copy that." Still she didn't touch him.

"I won't harm you, female. Feel," he demanded. "Now."

"Why?" she insisted.

Continuing to defy him. What a strange mix of bravery and fear she was.

"Well," she prompted.

Because he would discover his reaction to her was the same as his reaction to the Harpy in his bed—not that he'd allowed the Harpy to come into contact with his wings. As her skin had rubbed against his, he had remained distanced. Bored.

"Do it," he replied, ignoring Elin's question.

At long last, she obeyed.

Not the same, he realized immediately.

Trembling fingers stroked over his feathers in a single, innocent moment of communion, flooding him with sensations he'd never before experienced. Sultry heat arced through his wings, spread through his body. His blood crackled and fizzed with something akin to contentment. An impossible contentment. His shaft was filling, threatening to burst.

This was pleasure, he realized, dazed. Pleasure without a hint of pain.

His first true taste. Another impossibility. Yes? And yet, everything he'd felt before had been a weak dilution.

No. Surely not. He had this wrong.

He had to have this wrong.

No woman would affect him so powerfully with so little.

"Elin, you are human, yes?"

The color he'd so admired in her cheeks drained, and she smoothed several errant strands of hair behind her ear with a shaky hand. "Yes. Of course."

He tasted no lie.

"Why?"

"Doesn't matter," he grumbled. It was just her, then. *She* affected him.

His gaze homed in on her hands. Six jagged scars crisscrossed over the tops, the raised flesh red and angry, clearly from recent wounds. They must have come courtesy of one of the Phoenix.

Before he realized he'd moved, he took her by the wrists to bring her hands to the light. Not six scars, but eleven. Each was long and thick.

Hands were sensitive, layered with nerves. Oh, how she must have suffered.

"Who did this?" he demanded quietly.

She tugged from his grip and once again snaked her arms behind her back. Embarrassed?

He...mourned the loss of her warmth and softness.

It was irritating. Confusing.

And not to be tolerated.

"Who?" he insisted, determined to mete out punishment. And he didn't miss the irony. He, of all people, had no right to condemn another for causing a female pain.

She thought for a moment, shrugged. "It's not like I have any loyalty toward her. It was Kendra. After you brought her back to camp, but before she snuck out and returned with you."

Vile witch. Tonight, he would administer like for like to the princess. "Why did she do it?"

"I mouthed off."

Well, then, after Thane sliced up Kendra's hands, he would cut off her ears. Perhaps growing a new pair would help her appreciate the gift of listening to others.

It's almost time. Xerxes's voice drifted through his mind.

"I must go," he said, "but when I return we will speak." And he would force—*allow* Elin to touch his wing again. He would realize she affected him as little as everyone else, that the first contact had been a deviation.

She gazed up at him with dawning horror. "Speak about what?"

He wasn't used to being questioned but opted to indulge her. Just because. "You."

She backed away from him until her thighs hit the edge of the table. "Are you going to stake me?"

He frowned. "No. I have more questions for you."

"What kind of questions?"

"The kind that will help me get to know you better. You are my employee, after all."

"Oh." She released a heavy breath. "Okay, then."

What, she'd expected him to attack her? "I have told you before, kulta, I'm not going to harm you. I'm going to take care of you."

The admission startled her as much as it did him.

Him? Take care of a female? Something that went far beyond mere protection.

But even as it surprised him, it felt as natural as breathing.

"What does *kulta* mean?" she asked.

Honey. Baby. Darling. Precious. Any of those things. All of them. *Take your pick*.

Little wonder he'd never used the endearment before. He wasn't sure why he'd used it now.

He was the one to back away this time. Only, he didn't stop. As he strode from the room, he snapped, "Adrian, I don't recall telling you to wait before overseeing my orders. Go. Now."

CHAPTER SIX

FINALLY, ELIN COULD BREATHE.

Thane's presence somehow sucked the oxygen out of her lungs. He was just so much…man. Big and hard, undeniably dangerous, he soaked the atmosphere with the fiercest testosterone, making every woman in his vicinity downright giddy with an intoxicating rush of hormones, endorphins and chemicals.

Seriously. She'd wanted to have him for dinner. No crumb left behind.

She imagined him spread out on a buffet table. If he were a food, he would be a Grade A fillet, marinated in a rich sweet-and-tangy sauce—and sprinkled with enough cayenne pepper to burn just right.

No. No! Bad Elin. But…he'd looked at her with dark intent, only to touch her with tender kindness. He'd broken a man's wrist for grazing his wing, only to demand Elin caress it.

He was a bundle of contradictions. But then, so was she, both frightened of him *and* attracted to him. An attraction that would only get her in trouble. He held her future in his strong, snap-her-neck-with-a-single-flick-of-his-wrist hands.

Even still, there was no controlling her body's reactions to him. In his presence, wanton heat liquefied her bones. And her brain! She forgot who she was, who he was, saying "screw you" to the vast gulf between them and the danger he represented to her, focusing only on the things they could be doing to each other. Kissing, tasting. Licking. Touching. Stroking.

Devouring.

She shivered at the thought. Then she cursed.

These reckless desires meant nothing, changed nothing. Thane was her boss, and therefore off-limits. He was also a borderline sociopath with extra stakes, and he would hurt her the moment he learned of her origins. But the nail in the I-wanna-slice-of-that coffin, besides her vow to Bay? He was a blatant womanizer.

He and Blondie had clearly gone nuclear between the sheets. His hair had been tousled, the strands sticking out in spikes. There had been claw marks in his cheek and bite marks on his neck.

Elin ignored the pang in her chest.

He wasn't worth the mental anguish he would surely inflict on her. So, pursue him? Break her vow? Become one in a line of thousands? Lose her cash cow of a job, not to mention her new, blooming friendship with the other barmaids? No, thanks.

So, moving on. Elin donned the rest of the trinkets she'd won and headed to her room. She desperately needed a nap.

Bellorie was sprawled on her bed, wearing adorable flannel pj's and reading a book—*Decapitation For Idiots*—looking so normal Elin momentarily flashed back to college.

She'd attended the University of Arizona what seemed a lifetime ago, getting married when she was only six credits shy of a business-management degree, and deciding to take time off and finish later. After all, her best years were ahead of her.

Yeah. Right. *If "best years ahead" is the answer, then "things stupid people say" is the question.*

She'd moved out of the dorm, and into an apartment with Bay, but oh, how she'd missed the way her roommate used to stack pizza boxes in the corner. She'd enjoyed making art out of empty beer cans. There'd been a message board on the door and borrowed clothes from six different people on the floor. The clash of diverse styles and tastes should have been overwhelming, but they had been comforting. There'd been nothing to worry about but midterms and which party to crash.

This new bedroom provided the same whimsical variety. One of the beds seemed to be made from LEGO. Another had a huge stuffed panda as the headboard. The only side table had wooden human legs as the, well, legs, with fake vomit spilled on top. The reading chair was normal, but the ottoman in front of it was shaped like a turtle, with the head, arms and legs peeking out at the bottom.

"Hey," Elin said, noting the other girls hadn't yet arrived.

Dark eyes flipped up and landed on her. "Hey, yourself. You little hooker," the Harpy added with a sunny laugh. "Look at you, flaunting your prize so blatantly. I'm impressed."

"I know, right." She performed a twirl, knowing the diamonds, emeralds, sapphires and rubies sparkled in the light. "You jelly?"

"Beyond." A smiling Bellorie threw the book at her. Despite how fast and strong the girl was, Elin managed to jump out of the way in time. And it was a good thing she succeeded, because the corner of the hard-back lodged into the wall. Had that been her head…

Instant goner.

"Oops." Bellorie made a *my-bad* face. "For a minute there, I forget you're only human. But you're getting good at dodging. You might be a halfway decent member of Multiple Scorgasms after all."

Highly doubtful. Elin wasn't strong enough to lift the boulders, so she couldn't throw them. And if someone actually hit her with one of those death missiles, her internal organs would burst. Right now, she wasn't exactly sure what position she would play. Other than… bait? What she did know—she did not like the sport. It was far too violent and a trigger to the worst of her emotions.

"Oh, and just FYI," Bellorie added. "We play the Spinal Tappers this weekend, and the Rockzillas after that."

"Yay." Elin managed to pull off a convincing fist pump. "But are you sure I'm ready? Maybe I should ride the pine for those. You know, continue to learn through observation."

"Nah. You need to experience a true scorgasm of your own."

"I suppose." Renlay would have wanted her to play *so bad*. Her dad, a major adrenaline junkie, would have cheered like a madman. Bay would have had to drink a case of beer to calm his nerves. But all three of them would have been proud of her.

And…something was wrong, she thought with a frown.

What?

She'd thought of her family and—

Hadn't immediately remembered the deaths they'd faced. Hadn't cried.

Something wasn't wrong. Something was different. Why?

Before she could ponder the answer, a knock sounded at the door.

"Enter at your own peril," Bellorie called.

Adrian stepped inside, his size startling Elin all over again. "Where are Chanel and Savy?"

He must have followed directly behind her, and yet she hadn't heard him. *Gotta work on my awareness.*

"Chanel's on a blind date," Bellorie replied. "The guy had his eyes removed by his brother, or something like that. And Savy took off right after her shift. Don't know where. Octavia is out buying ice cream—not that you asked."

Dude! Why hadn't Octavia offered to bring Elin a scoop of double dark chocolate?

Adrian sighed. "Very well. I need you and Elin to come with me to help remove Thane's newest plaything."

No! First instinct—curiosity that did not need to be assuaged.

Yes! Second—physical preservation.

Mentally and emotionally, no good could come of seeing the kind of girl Thane preferred, up close and personal, after he'd had his big hands and sinful mouth all over her. Elin would not be jealous—not anymore, dang it!—but because of her silly attraction to him, she might begin to wonder what it would feel like to have the man's hands and mouth all over *her.* It would be better just to avoid all things Thane until her lustful feelings faded.

And they would.

They had to.

When she dated, she wanted nice. Normal.

Wait. No. She didn't want to date. She didn't want a man. Not even a so-called "normal" one. She wanted to be alone.

Right?

"I'm too tired," she said, risking castigation. She didn't have to force a yawn. It came on its own. "You two go on, have fun. Live it up. Send me a postcard, and all that jazz."

Bellorie rolled her eyes. "You're going, you little hussy, and that's final. This is a twofer job, and Adrian's not allowed to touch the opposite sex."

He wasn't? Why?

Elin glanced over at him, hoping he would offer an answer. He turned and stalked away, forcing her and Bellorie to follow. Asking Bellorie directly behind his back? Not cool. She would wait. Surely she would overhear someone talking about it.

Accidental cavesdropping? Very cool. All the kids were doing it nowadays.

The trek took longer than she anticipated, each new hallway more luxurious than the last, each set of stairs more elaborate and winding, until they reached a heavily guarded corridor leading to a pair of arching double doors. On the left side, iron was twisted in the shape of a tree. The branches bowed all the way to the right side, forming a canopy.

Those doors were pushed open for Adrian, splitting the tree, then held open for her and Bellorie. By strong, beautiful vamps. Or, as she'd started thinking of the race, bloodbarians.

As Elin bypassed the males, she tried not to care when they eyed her as if she would make a very tasty liquid snack, and all her neck lacked was a straw. Once inside the room—suite—she stopped and gaped. This was Thane's private wing? Because wow. The man certainly knew how to pamper himself. There were plush couches and chairs in jewel tones, with feathered pillows, a coffee table with the legs of a lion, and a dark wood floor draped by a snow-white rug. Plants and flowers decorated every corner.

"Don't you just want to rub up against everything and purr like a kitty?" Bellorie asked with a good-natured grin. "Although, I don't recommend you actually do it. Thane will know, and he'll be *tee-icked*."

"Listen to her. She came across the knowledge the hard way," Adrian said.

Bellorie nodded. "True story."

Even still, Elin couldn't stop herself from ghosting her fingertips along the softness of one of the couch pillows. Mistake! Her skin tingled and heated, desperate for more. A blush stained her cheeks. It wasn't a good sign that her attraction encompassed Thane's belongings.

"What did Thane do to you?" she asked. Over such a minor offense. "And how did he find out?" *So I can be doubly careful with my own secrets.*

"Aura, maybe? He keeps the hows to himself, so we can't circumvent his methods. And I was lucky. I only got an hour-long lecture. 'In some cultures, Harpy,'" the girl said, doing her best impression of Thane, "'they chop off hands for a crime such as yours, blah, blah, blah, this isn't a debate, blah, blah.'"

Elin laughed and cringed at the same time, and she was sure it looked as grotesque as it sounded.

"Since then," the girl continued, "I always blame a man for my crimes. I've been quite satisfied with the results."

They reached the first doorway down the longest hall. Bellorie let herself into the room, and Elin trailed behind reluctantly. Adrian waited outside. To avoid temptation?

The air smelled strongly of sex, and Elin's nose wrinkled. Her chest began to ache. She hadn't been prepared for this. Thane had smelled as luscious as always.

Forget him. More luxury greeted her. The kind she wouldn't have thought possible. Gemstones glittered on the walls, and silks and velvets covered the massive bed.

A bed currently in shambles, as if a massive earthquake had hit. Blondie occupied the center, her bruised and battered body coiled into a ball. Elin's breath caught as her hands curled into fists.

"Come on," Bellorie said, dragging her the rest of the way inside.

What, exactly, had Thane done to the girl? "Did he hurt…? Why would he…? What could he possibly…?" A full sentence refused to form. Whatever he'd done? Not sexy! Not bad-boy delish! Just wrong.

Dude. She understood the desire for fierce, wild passion. But this? This was beyond her realm of experience.

"They love it," Bellorie said, taking a tube of ointment from the top drawer of the nightstand and slathering the girl's chafed wrists and ankles. "He does nothing they don't beg for, I promise you."

How could she know for sure? Had she ever—

No, Elin thought, as little sparks of jealousy—couldn't

be jealousy—were immediately doused. He would have banned the barmaid from the club. Right?

Bellorie gave her a little push toward the closet. "Be a dear and grab a robe for our dearly departing guest."

Elin obeyed, amazed to find rack after rack of robes, all in different sizes, though each was smaller than anything Thane would be able to fit over his bulging wings and muscles. Which meant he bought these specifically for his women.

A bang-and-bail memento for the ladies to take home.

Her attraction to him took another major hit.

But…he couldn't be the same man who'd taken Elin's damaged hands in his and looked at them as if they were still somehow beautiful. As if he would like to burn to death the person responsible.

Possibility: *I saw only what I wanted to see.*

Disgusted with him, with herself, she handed the garment to Bellorie. The girl dressed the rousing Harpy and helped her stand, and Elin rushed to act as a second crutch.

"Wait. My jewelry," the Harpy rasped.

Bellorie swiped a diamond choker and a pair of earrings from the surface of the nightstand and stuffed them in a pocket of the robe. "All set."

He *paid* his lovers? To make what he did more palatable?

Attraction, almost completely gone.

Together they were able to haul the Harpy out of the room, down the hall, down an elevator, and through the club.

At the exit, the Harpy wavered on her feet. "Tell Thane…more…must have…"

"Sure, sure," Bellorie replied. "You want more of

him, will die if you don't have him. Got it. Problem is, sugar bear, and please know I'm saying this to be kind, he's already forgotten all about you."

As the doors closed, sealing the dazed Harpy outside, Bellorie pinned Elin with a regretful stare. "Told you. They love it. Every freaking time. It's only later that they start to hate him and lash out, but I suspect that's because they still want him."

Not me. Never me.

And yet, part of Elin mourned the loss of the Thane she'd hoped he was, the man she must have invented in her mind. The white knight. The charmer. The…hero.

Lesson learned: always look beyond the surface.

Slight problem, however. Her body still craved him. It didn't know the difference between good-for-Elin/bad-for-Elin. It operated solely on sensation.

Well, it would have to be controlled.

And there was one sure way to satisfy the worst of the cravings…with another male.

The thought hit her, and she shook her head. No. Definitely not.

Definitely yes, said a beguiling voice, a temptation that had brewed for days, waiting for the perfect moment to pounce. *Your entire being is waking up and remembering what it's like to be kissed and touched. Remembering…and hungering. You* need *a man.*

Elin flattened her hands over her now-rolling stomach. She hated this thought path. It was like forgiving herself for her part in Bay's death. Worse, it was like saying she'd suffered enough.

She hadn't, on either count.

Taking a lover doesn't have to mean anything more than scratching an itch.

No.

Maybe sex can be another type of self-inflicted punishment. Thane certainly seems to think so.

Okay, now temptation was hitting her where it hurt. *I deserve punishment.*

She gulped, imagining what would happen if she continued to do nothing. The tension in her body would build…and build…and build. She would cave and throw herself at someone—probably Thane.

No matter what, she was going to cave, wasn't she?

It would be better to take a lover now, while she had some sort of control…and could make herself hate it.

Yeah.

She drew in a deep breath, then slowly released it, the guilt winding cold, clammy arms around her, embracing her like an old friend…or the lover she was soon to take. Whom should she pick?

Someone like Bay? Gentle. Happy. Fun. But then, she would be giving this nameless, faceless guy what she was unable to give her dead husband. Affection and attention.

No. That wouldn't do.

She would have to pick someone hard and harsh.

Like…Thane?

No! He wasn't an option. He was the reason she was in this bind, yes, but he wasn't an option. She would have to pick someone *like* Thane. A patron of the bar, maybe.

Like Merrick, the heartbreaker, maybe.

Yes. Him.

He would do.

He would be perfect, actually.

So…the next time his band came to the bar…

She closed her eyes to ward off the oncoming flood of remorse. She was really going to do this. She was really going to climb in bed with another man.

I'm sorry, Bay. I love you, and I miss you so much. Once I've done it, once it's over, I'll never want to do it again. I can go back to the way things were.

THANE PEERED AT ZACHAREL, incredulous. "Let's make sure I understand you correctly. You aren't going to kick me from the heavens, and you aren't going to force me to free the Phoenix clan under my…care?"

"That's right."

Again, astonishment roared through him.

His leader stood at the edge of his home in the sky—a large cloud—his piercing green eyes scrutinizing the human world below. Wind whipped black locks of hair against his cheeks and around his shoulders. Gloriously golden wings arched proudly, a testament to his exalted place in their world.

In the heavens, there was a very clear hierarchy. The Most High. Clerici. The Elite Seven, Zacharel among them. Then everyone else.

To disobey Zacharel's edicts was to court ruin. Thane had known that. But he'd done it anyway. And he was to be…forgiven?

Now, he looked to Bjorn and Xerxes. Both were as baffled as he was.

"I know Clerici allows for vengeance," Zacharel said stiffly. "I also know it violates the Most High's code of ethics, and will have spiritual consequences for us all."

Yes. But the Most High wouldn't stop Clerici from doing what Clerici wanted to do—they all had free will.

Even still, every act against his rules edged a Sent One out from under his umbrella of protection.

"The Phoenix enslaved you," Zacharel continued, "and so you are now allowed to mete out death."

"I am." And he would. Over and over again.

His leader wasn't done. "And *I* am allowed to punish you."

Forgiven, yes, but not forgotten. "What will you do?"

Zacharel sighed. "Koldo was whipped when he enslaved his mother. What kind of leader would I be if I allowed another of my warriors—even if he is my second-in-command—to forgo the same?" He met Thane's gaze dead-on. "Therefore, you will receive a lash of the whip for every warrior being tortured on your front lawn."

That was to be a *punishment?* "Very well." He wouldn't let Zacharel know how much he enjoyed it. He would control his body's reaction. Somehow.

"You won't release them of your own volition?"

"No."

"Even though you rush headlong into disaster?"

Even though. One day, the king of the Firebirds would return to camp, find it deserted, hear of Thane's macabre courtyard, and come gunning for him. There would be a gruesome battle, for Ardeo's decree that Thane be spared from a deathblow would give way to vengeance. But Thane would not relinquish his captives, even then.

And everyone around you will be placed in the line of fire.

He didn't want to care. Wanted to glory in the same casual disregard he'd harbored before.

But…what if Bjorn or Xerxes were hurt? It would be his fault.

They are strong. They can protect themselves.

And what of Elin? The fragile human was now his responsibility. Unlike his friends, she would not recover if the Phoenix burned her alive. Their preferred method for eliminating someone of another race.

He worked two fingers over his jaw, the action so fierce he left welts behind. *She is nothing. Means nothing.*

A foul taste coated his tongue, and this time he knew what it was. An indication of a lie. Despite the fact that he hadn't spoken a word. Irritated, confused, he ground his molars. *She. Means. Nothing.*

The foul taste intensified.

"I will take the lash," he announced.

Zacharel's nod was grave. "Very well."

Leave us, he projected to Bjorn and Xerxes. He didn't want the two to see this. They'd witnessed enough of each other's torture.

Both shook their heads no. They would stay. They would watch. And they would support him.

"I played a part in this," Xerxes said. "I will take the lash, as well."

"As will I," Bjorn said.

"No."

"Yes," they said in unison.

Guilt rose. They weren't like him. They found no solace in pain, and had suffered too much already, when Thane had been unable to help them. Now, he couldn't let them take his deserved punishment—especially since they were utterly undeserving.

Don't do this, he pleaded. *Go.*

It's already done, Xerxes said with a determined shake of his wings.

Together until the end, Bjorn said, his rainbow eyes fierce.

In unison, his friends removed the top half of their robes, gave Zacharel their backs, and sank to their knees. Ready.

Thane closed his eyes. He should let the Phoenix go. He—

Couldn't.

Very well.

Hating himself, Thane followed suit. He spread his wings and wound them forward, around his arms and out of the way. He was lashed first, the leather biting into his wings, and then, when they were shredded, into his skin.

Any pleasure he felt was negated during Xerxes's turn, then Bjorn's. Neither displayed any type of reaction, but Thane couldn't help but cringe with every blow.

"Now. Business," Zacharel said after they had dressed. As if nothing had happened. He motioned to the cars driving along winding roads. Nothing more than ants on a hill beneath them. "A few days ago, William the Ever Randy's daughter, White, was killed by the same Phoenix responsible for slaying King Ardeo's beloved concubine."

Thane focused. William. An immortal of questionable origins. A male without allegiance or conscience. A man with unequaled power. Thane had always admired him. He lived his life the way Thane wished to live his. Without regrets.

"The killer's name was Petra," Zacharel continued. "I say was, because William and his three sons ensured she would not regenerate."

"How?"

"I'm not yet certain."

Still, an interesting bit of knowledge Thane stored away. When he finished with Kendra, he wanted to ensure she was unable to regenerate, as well.

"William's daughter, White…" Zacharel sighed.

She was the embodiment of subjection, and upon her death her spirit broke into millions of pieces, each like a bug, spreading throughout New York, infecting the humans unfortunate enough to be in the way. Their leader pushed the words inside their heads, perhaps not wanting the information floating away on the breeze to panic those who didn't yet know. *Demons used that subjection to their advantage and more easily possessed human bodies. Crime is now at an all-time high, and I have since learned from the Most High that one of the demons responsible for killing Germanus is using the violence as a cover, attempting to shield his whereabouts.*

What do you want us to do? Bjorn asked.

All members of an army could communicate this way. Meaning, all members of an army were bonded through mental highways. Thane had never liked it, had only ever wanted such a connection with Bjorn and Xerxes. Because if voice could travel those roadways, so could thoughts. Memories. No one had a right to his secrets.

Go to New York and hunt the demon, Zacharel said.

And we're, what? Xerxes replied. *Supposed to bust into random homes and businesses, and hope we get lucky?*

Thane scrubbed a hand down his face. *Did the Most High offer any specifics?*

A shake of Zacharel's dark head. "I can tell you that

evil always leaves a trail. Find the start of it, follow it, and then you will find the end of it."

He made it sound easy. Thane knew it wouldn't be. It never was. But he and his boys would persevere. They always did.

"Koldo, Axel, Malcolm, Magnus and Jamilla are already there, waiting for you."

Thane arched a brow. "Waiting?" The most impatient warriors of all time? "Rather than hunting?"

"I realized I made a mistake, sending my people to different locations. It thinned our efforts. So, from this moment forward, we will work together. We will concentrate on catching only one of the six demons responsible for killing Germanus. Once that's done, we will turn our efforts to a second, and so on."

The snowball effect. One victory would prime everyone for the next.

Wise.

Frowning, Zacharel tilted his head to the side. "Go. Go now. The others have been ambushed, and a battle is in progress."

CHAPTER SEVEN

METAL WHISTLED THROUGH the night-damp air. Determined footsteps from one, two…five different individuals echoed. Warrior footsteps, not the clacking of demon hooves. A hiss of pain sounded, followed by a grunt of satisfaction.

Thane dive-bombed the dark alley, straightening at the last moment to land on his feet in the middle of the violent battle. As he palmed a sword of fire, he snapped his wings into his sides, making room for Bjorn and Xerxes.

A quick glance revealed writhing shadows that cringed from the swords of fire the Sent Ones brandished. But the moment the Sent Ones became preoccupied with another opponent, those shadows struck, swiping out blackened claws.

Koldo fought with the cold calculation of a robot.

Axel fought as if he had no concern for his own life, leaving himself wide-open to counterattack, just to make a single kill.

Twins Magnus and Malcolm stood back-to-back. After Magnus injured the prey, Malcolm finished it off.

Jamilla was the wild card, unpredictable in her strikes, as if she strove to kill everything in her path.

Rage set a collision course with Thane. Detonation imminent. He'd encountered the shadows once before, a different sort of demon than the mundane type they usually battled—it had happened the night Kendra died with his dagger in her gut, which had strengthened the slave bond...the night Bjorn vanished. A single scratch could have devastating consequences.

Thane stepped forward, intending to help. His back burned; the wounds hadn't had time to heal.

Do not join the fray, and do not move from this point, Bjorn said inside his head.

Though it was an odd request, Thane acquiesced without hesitation. He trusted his friend with his life, *every* part of his life, whatever the circumstances.

Bjorn swept into the heart of the battle, only, instead of producing a sword, he spread his arms. The action said, *Look at me. You know who I am and what I can do. Obey me or suffer.* "Enough!"

The shadows reacted instantly and violently, shrieking and darting out of the way, out of Bjorn's reach, before disappearing altogether.

Last time, the creatures hadn't feared the warrior. *What* had changed? *Why* had it changed?

I shall return, Bjorn said, his tone tight with...something. *Worry not.* And then he, too, was gone.

Thane shared a look of concern and frustration with Xerxes. They wanted to act. They *needed* to act. Their best friend could be in serious trouble. But what could they do? So far, Thane had been unable to dig up any information about what had happened to Bjorn when he'd disappeared, what his current situation was, or even the creatures. What were they, exactly?

Even as he raged against the circumstances, he released his sword. The flames faded. "Was anyone injured?"

A chorus of "no" rang out.

"Dude! We've been fighting those shadows for, like, ever."

"More like five minutes," Thane interjected.

"Some of us a little more skillfully than others, but whatever," Axel continued, unaffected, his baby blues sparkling as he actually patted himself on the back. "Then Sgt. Buzzkill shows up, and it's over? What's up with that?"

Lips curling in a scowl, Thane approached the warrior with menace in every step. "Say that again. I dare you."

"Then Sgt. Buzzkill shows up—"

"No," Koldo said, cutting him off as Thane lunged. The warrior moved in front of Axel, acting as a living shield. "No."

Thane planted his feet and forced himself to remain in place. The two had been partnered on a few missions, and Axel had even saved Koldo's life, but that did not mean they were now as close as brothers. Why would Koldo do this?

A grinning Axel reached around the big guy's shoulder and flipped Thane off.

Koldo sighed.

Perhaps they *were* as close as brothers. An unlikely pairing, the usually silent, always withdrawn Koldo and the irritating, irreverent Axel, but not as unlikely as, say, a Sent One and a fragile human.

"I'm now heading this mission," Thane said. As Zacharel's second-in-command, it was only right. "Tell me everything I've missed."

Different degrees of anger, amusement and indifference met his announcement. Even still, he was obeyed without question. Their determination to remain in the skies, wings intact, was stronger than their emotions.

If only it were that easy for me.

What Thane learned: the nightclubs with the highest demon activity had been searched. So had the homes with the darkest auras. A handful of demons had been captured and tortured, but no new information had been gleaned.

The result: the Sent Ones were no closer to answers.

If you wanted a different result, you had to do something different.

If I were the incarnation of evil, and had just killed Germanus, the king of my greatest enemy, I would expect said enemy to come after me, determined to punish me. So, where would I hide?

First, Thane wouldn't hide. He wasn't a coward. But demons most definitely were.

Then again, demons were also braggarts.

So…which would prevail? The cowardice or the pride?

Pride. It almost always did. And pride would demand… what?

Ego stroking. Yes. If the demon couldn't brag about what he'd done in the skies, he would resort to bragging about what he'd done down here. Human accolades were better than none.

"The demon we're looking for has probably possessed a human in some kind of position of power. I want a list of the fifty most influential people in the area. I'm willing to bet someone has recently experienced a dark metamorphosis."

The anger, amusement and indifference shifted to intrigue.

"I'll do it," Jamilla said. Having been tortured by demons only a few months ago, she relished every chance to strike back. "I'll need at least twenty-four hours to go through our annals and put the list together."

The annals recorded every move every human ever made, every word ever spoken. But because free will always played a part, demonic influence wasn't mentioned with regards to the decisions made.

He nodded. "Koldo, talk to the rest of Zacharel's army. Send the soldiers out to watch over and protect as many citizens of New York as possible. Axel, talk to Clerici. Perhaps he can speak with the Most High and have angels dispatched, as well."

Both warriors nodded.

"Everyone is to come to the Downfall tomorrow night. We'll plan our next move then."

He waited until he received some sort of agreement from each of the warriors before flaring his wings and darting into the air.

A few seconds later, Xerxes was beside him. *I know you're worried despite Bjorn's words, as am I, but this has happened to him several times before. He'll be back at the club before nightfall.*

Thane released a breath he hadn't known he'd been holding. As usual, his friend had known the crux of his problem. *Does he suffer?*

He must, Xerxes answered honestly. *Upon his return, he reacts as he does after sex.*

Bjorn hated to be touched. That rarely stopped him from taking a lover—Thane often thought his friend hoped to prove something to himself—but he always ended up withdrawing into the darkness of his mind for days afterward.

Thane swallowed a curse as he landed on the roof of the club, a flat strip of smoked glass—like Elin's eyes—leading to his private wing. So badly he wished he could take Bjorn's place.

Bjorn had suffered so much already, and edged ever closer to his breaking point. Familiar helplessness battered against Thane's composure, guilt a noose around his neck, choking him.

"Cario," Xerxes suddenly roared. He jumped the ledge of the roof and arrowed through the night sky.

Thane searched and found the girl climbing the side of the building in an effort to sneak past one of the windows.

A few weeks ago, she had come to the club. A woman of questionable origins, like William the Ever Randy, and clearly powerful, with the ability to read others' thoughts. Thane had made a play for her. She had said no, but offered herself to Xerxes. Before the two could retire to the bedroom, she made the mistake of revealing what she'd gleaned from their thoughts.

It had enraged them all.

Thane had kicked her out and forbade her from returning. On her way out, she'd looked at Xerxes and said, "Remember me."

Now, she noticed Xerxes's approach and screeched, releasing the brick to fall down, down, down, hurtling toward the earth.

Xerxes followed, determined to catch her.

Poor girl. When he got his hands on her, he would interrogate her—to death. She kept coming back, and he wanted to know why.

Perhaps his questions would finally be met with answers.

Questions. Answers.

A reminder. Anticipation swept through Thane. He had his own interrogation to oversee, did he not?

UGH. SUMMONED BY the Big Cheese for their get-to-know-Elin chat.

She had just finished practicing with the Multiple Scorgasms. Three hours trapped inside the gym next door to Thane's club. Today, she had not only been taught the art of throwing boulders too heavy for her to lift at targets moving too quickly for her to see, she was also given her nickname. Bonka Donk.

Yeah. A real winner.

Savy was Black Cawk. Don't ask *anyone* why. The girls snickered every time they said the name, and Elin was afraid she would, as well. Chanel was Alcoballic. Bellorie was The Little Red Rocket That Could—Rocket for short. Octavia was Kobra Kai.

They were as serious about their nicknames as they were about their victories.

Adrian held open the double doors, his expression blank. Great. Would giving her a hint about Thane's mood have killed him? Elin reluctantly entered the sitting room. *I'm totally used to the luxury now. I won't gawk. I* won't.

"I'll be waiting in the hall when you are ready to return," Adrian said, and sealed her inside.

Thane relaxed at the edge of a backless couch, his blond curls surprisingly tamed. *I do* not *want to run my fingers through those curls.* The robe he wore was a brilliant white, almost blinding, and without a speck of dirt. *I do* not *want to peel the material from his body and feast on the muscles he displayed at camp.*

She wasn't attracted to him anymore.

Tension radiated from him, making him appear bigger, stronger. More aggressive.

I'm not intrigued by that.

I'm not drawn to him.

I'm scared. Right.

"Sit," he said.

Though she wanted to run—because she was scared, dang it—she forced herself to claim the chair across from him. Already the air seemed drenched in the most expensive champagne, with hints of cinnamon, making her head swim. And this close to Thane, the scents only intensified. Did they come from him?

She crossed her legs in a vain attempt to slow the warmth stirring in her core.

Would she always react to him?

No, please, no.

At least she was out of her skimpy uniform and in the world's most expensive pair of flannel pj's. Bellorie had sold the soft, snuggly outfit for a sapphire brooch, a ruby choker and an emerald bracelet. Parting with the jewels hurt. Bad. But there was no way she would have shown up for this meeting so scantily dressed, and she had no other clothes.

Tomorrow, she and the girls were going shopping. She could hardly wait.

Thane looked her over, his gaze hooded and sensual, but hiding his thoughts. He arched one golden brow. "You aren't curious about your surroundings?"

"Not really." Though she did like seeing him in his natural habitat. "Been here, searched everything already."

A terrible kind of stillness came over him. "You have." A statement, not a question.

Survival instincts flashed a yellow light inside her mind. *Proceed with caution.* "Well, yeah. I had to pass through to get to your—" She motioned to his bedroom with a wave of her hand. "Afternoon delight. But I didn't touch anything! Mostly."

A volcano of fury erupted in his eyes, startling her. "Adrian," he called in a quiet tone. And yet, she heard the promise of pain and suffering.

The male entered the room.

"Did you forget my orders?" Thane asked, still using that shudder-inducing tone.

What were his orders? What was going on here?

Head high, Adrian said, "I did not. Savy and Chanel were gone. Only Bellorie and Elin remained."

Uh-oh. Somehow, Elin had gotten him in trouble. "I was happy to help. Honest." *Liar.* "Well, honest-ish. Like I said, I didn't touch your stuff. Much. And I didn't break anything. For reals."

Thane ignored her, saying to Adrian, "Never again. Do you understand?"

She noticed he didn't bother with an "or else." But then, he mustn't need to.

Adrian nodded and backed from the room, shutting the door behind him.

"Never again what?" Elin asked. "Disobey you?"

"That, too."

"But he didn't."

"He did. And now, that line of conversation is over." A moment passed before Thane's features smoothed out, the sheen of rage falling away. He still managed to give off an uneasy vibe. Why? Because she'd seen his postcoital leftovers?

He stood, and her eyes widened as he approached her.

In her mind, the yellow light flashed again. Yellow. Yellow. Suddenly red. She stiffened. What was he going to do?

"I'm innocent!" she shouted.

"How many times must I reassure you?"

He merely sat on the coffee table in front of her, his knees caging her legs, and she breathed a sigh of relief. This wasn't so bad. Then he placed scabbed-over palms on the tops of her thighs. The contact electrified her, and she had to mask a gasp with a cough. And, oh, his champagne scent was even stronger now, making the ache so much worse.

"What happened to your hands?" she asked in an effort to distract herself.

"What was deserved."

O-kay. But why had he deserved to be cut? And did the wounds hurt him? Acting on impulse, she kissed the tip of her index finger and lightly pressed it on the angriest wound, as her mother used to do to her.

"There. They have to get better now."

He sat very still, his expression frozen.

It hit her then. What she'd done—and to whom she'd done it. She nearly erupted in flames of embarrassment. "Uh, I mean… Wow, look at the time. Maybe I should go?"

His lids dipped to half-mast. "Stay." As he peered at her, he ran his tongue over his lips. Then he moaned, as if he'd just tasted something sweet. The sight and sound were heady, hot enough to melt any woman's resolve—even hers. "And thank you," he said, whisper soft.

Not a rebuke. A total shocker. "You're welcome," she breathed.

A moment passed in silence, though her heartbeat echoed in her ears. Then, his gaze intently studying her face, he said, "How did you, a full human, come to live with the Phoenix?"

Full human.

She was right. He had no idea she was a halfling. And she had to keep it that way. "They killed my... my..." A lump grew in her throat. Sweat sheened her forehead, and a scream budded at the back of her throat.

Gently he cupped her cheeks, his thumbs brushing over her cheekbones. "This again."

The contact centered her—delighted her. "This?"

"The panic. Why?" he asked. "You truly are not in any danger."

She closed her eyes to gather strength, and said, "I was remembering when I *was* in danger. The Phoenix killed my husband and father, and enslaved me and my mother."

"You were married?" The words lashed like a whip. He released her as if he'd just found out she was a carrier for the worst disease ever. "How long?"

Okay. Not the bit of info she'd expected to garner a reaction. Why did her marital status even matter? "Yes, I was married. For the best three months of my life."

"Why?"

"Why?" she parroted. What kind of question was that?

"Why were they the best?"

"Because we loved each other." Why else? "He was

compassionate and caring, sweet and gentle, and the best thing to ever happen to me."

A sheet of displeasure glazed Thane's irises as he rubbed two fingers along the curve of his jaw.

Why displeasure?

"How old are you?" he asked.

"Twenty-one."

"So young." He reached out and pinched a lock of her hair, tickling her scalp. Guess she'd been cured of the disease. "How long were you with the Phoenix?"

She resisted the urge to pull away—and the stronger urge to lean closer. "A year."

"A year. Twelve months. Fifty-two weeks. Three hundred and sixty-five days. Quite a long time for someone of your species." His tone gentled, becoming achingly kind. "How many horrors did you suffer during that time?"

The moisture in her mouth dried. She wanted to tell him. Perhaps he would comfort her.

Comfort, she'd learned, was a commodity far more precious than sex.

Can't go there with him. "I don't want to talk about it," she croaked.

He sighed, nodded. "I understand."

He wasn't going to press? Another shocker. It made her want to open up, if only a little, about *something*. "We had an ally at camp for a few weeks. There was a girl, a Harpy. Neeka the Unwanted. Do you remember her?" She didn't wait for his response. "She was only there for a short time before another clan came and stole her away, but she was nice to me, and I heard she was nice to you during your short overlap. Word is, she even beat the fire out of Kendra—almost literally—when the princess paraded you around camp naked and—"

"What were your duties?" he interjected, his tone harsh.

Uh-oh. Had she made a critical mistake, replaying one of his more humiliating moments? "I didn't see it," she tried to assure him. "I just heard—"

"Duties," he snapped.

She gulped. "I cleaned. And I was the entertainment," she added bitterly.

"Explain."

No way. Even mentioning that aspect of her captivity had been a mistake.

On your hands and knees, dog. Now bark.

A dog doesn't use a toilet. Go here.

No bath for you this week. Dogs lick themselves clean.

"At first," she said, as if he hadn't spoken, "I was responsible for all the meals. Then they realized how much I enjoyed cooking, and made me stop."

He ran his tongue over his teeth. "You will cook for me."

By "me," she assumed he meant the entire bar. "Uh, no, I won't." *Stop arguing!* But she couldn't keep her lips clamped shut. "I'd love it, truly, but I have a feeling cooks don't make as much money as barmaids."

"Money again. Why are you so obsessed with it?"

To tell or not to tell?

Do you trust him not to sabotage you?

Well, yeah. He was cold and hard, but he wasn't cruel. Not to her, anyway. "One day I'm going to open my own bakery and call it Let Them Eat Cake. Or Happy Ever Afters. Or Bundt Dreams. I haven't decided yet. But no matter what, it's going to be glorious. People will come from all over the world to sample my amazing desserts."

His eyes gleamed with an emotion she couldn't name. "Tomorrow, before your shift, you will bake one of these amazing desserts for me."

Thanks for asking. "Sure. That I can do. For a price."

He looked ready to crack a smile. "How much?"

"Like…a hundred dollars?"

"Are you requesting advice or telling?"

"Telling?"

He covered his mouth with his hand, his eyes glittering. The smile had cracked! "Very well. A hundred dollars." His expression cleared. "What did you miss most while you were a captive?"

Subject changed. Got it. Without missing a beat, she said, "Besides my family? Food."

His brow furrowed with confusion. "Family. You said your mother was taken captive."

A wave of pain washed through her. "Yes. But four months ago, she died."

Everything about him softened. He tenderly cupped her jaw and grazed his thumb over her cheek. "I'm sorry for your loss, Elin."

Her chin began to tremble. *He's going to undo me.* She forced herself to nod.

Taking mercy on her, he said, "What kinds of food did you long for?"

"Every kind. The Phoenix only fed me scraps."

Annnd, the softness disappeared, anger taking its place. "Like for like," he muttered. He stood, walked to the phone beside the wet bar and placed a call, his voice so low she couldn't make out his words.

Even when he hung up, he remained in place, his

back to her. For several minutes, she played chicken with confusion—and the confusion won. What was going on?

A knock rattled the door.

"Enter," Thane called.

A large tray was wheeled into the room. The most divine scents wafted to her, and her mouth watered.

Elin hopped to her feet, the action involuntary, and rushed over. Breads, cheeses, fruits.

"All yours," Thane said, watching her intently.

"Really? Like, seriously? Because if so, you need to look away. Things are about to get weird." Waiting for him to reply would have taken too long. She attacked the food, a total savage, until there was nothing left.

Blimey. She moaned with keen satisfaction as she rubbed her belly. "Me and my new food baby thank you from the bottom of our cholesterol-filled hearts."

"Believe me, the pleasure was mine." The huskiness of his voice drew a blush to her cheeks.

"All I need now is an after-dinner scoop or twelve of chocolate-covered peanuts."

He motioned to the chair she'd vacated. "You like chocolate?"

"Almost more than breathing." Once she was in place, he reclaimed his perch on the coffee table. And leaned in closer. She gulped, unsure of him…or unsure of herself?

"Did you have a lover?" he asked, picking up their conversation as if it had never lagged.

I can do this.

She knew what he was asking. Was there a man out there among the courtyard throng she would try to free? "No. I promise you, no."

His gaze dipped to her lips, lingering. "Did you want one?" So silkily asked.

A shower of delicious shivers stole through her. Was he trying to seduce her? Because he was doing just that. The heat of his body tickled her skin. The sultriness of his scent pleased her nose. The rasp of his voice enchanted her ears.

"N-no," she said, gripping her pants to keep from reaching for him. *Not until I met you.*

Almost in a trance, he traced a fingertip along the scars on her palm, stopping at the pulse hammering in her wrist. Her insides tingled and burned. Her stomach quivered.

Feels so good.

"You have such a slender bone structure," he said quietly.

Her breathing was so shallow she worried it would just stop. This was not part of the plan—this was totally anti-plan. *Gotta get away from him.* "May I go now?" she practically squeaked.

He blinked into focus, shook his head. Then he stiffened, his ease with her vanishing, the stolen moment of tenderness broken. He straightened, severing contact. "Yes," he barked, and waved toward the door. "Go."

She didn't wait for him to change his mind, but popped to her feet and raced from the room without looking back.

CHAPTER EIGHT

XERXES BURST INTO the antechamber, stalked to the wet bar, and drained a three-finger shot of whiskey. Then another. And another. His dark temper churned under the surface of his pale, scarred skin.

"She got away, I take it," Thane said.

"Yes."

It was funny—in an appalling way. He'd been thinking that very thing for the past hour. *She got away.* But rather than Cario, his torment centered around Elin. He hadn't moved from the coffee table. Had sat there *aching.*

Aching because of her nearness—and absence.

Aching because her softness and warmth had been taken from him.

Aching because her soap-and-cherries scent had stayed with him.

A thousand times he'd almost jumped up and chased after her, the little human too pretty and fragile for her own good, a force greater than himself pulling at him, demanding he act. But he'd resisted. He didn't understand the things she made him feel. Obsession. Jealousy...

Her dedication to her dead husband...

Thane banged his fist against the coffee table, cracking the stone.

"I appreciate your anger on my behalf," Xerxes said drily.

"You're welcome," he replied, distracted.

How did Elin feel about him?

He knew she feared him. But he suspected—hoped—part of her wanted him. When he'd touched her, her breath had hitched and her cheeks had flushed. But in the end, the fear had won, and she'd scampered away.

For the best. He stared at the scabs on his hands. Today, he'd put his talent for causing pain to good use and punished Kendra for punishing Elin. The princess had fought back, especially when he'd gone for her ears. If Elin had seen him then...

Elin, who had used her finger to kiss him and make him better. Her fear would never fade.

It had to fade. Only then could he allow himself to have her.

You plan to take her now? Yes. No. If he were to get her in his bed, he would whip the sweetness out of her, and the thought disturbed him more now than ever.

Doesn't have to be that way. In her presence, his desire for pain untwisted from his desire for pleasure.

Why?

You know why. She suffered at the hands of the Phoenix. Suffered terribly—and enough.

"What happened?" he asked Xerxes. He had to get the girl out of his head.

"Now he talks to me." His friend settled on the couch. "I don't know. We were free-falling. Halfway down I caught her. She cupped my face, told me to remember, and vanished."

So. The girl could flash, moving from one location

to another with only a thought. Explained a lot. "Remember what?"

Xerxes met his gaze and quirked a brow.

Right. If he knew, he wouldn't be so frustrated.

"I see her, and I have to force myself to look away," the warrior said, rubbing the center of his chest. "But I do force myself, because looking at her brings grief. In my head, and in my heart."

Can't stand the thought of him grieving. "May I suggest knitting to help you forget your—"

Xerxes threw the glass at his head.

Chuckling, Thane easily dodged. "No? Then how about a walk through the courtyard?"

He led Xerxes to the courtyard, and they strolled along the walkway. The scent of blood, both old and fresh, saturated the air. Moans of agony created a symphony of horror. He couldn't summon a smile, even though the Phoenix deserved this and more.

Hate them.

But are you willing to fall from the skies for them?

Stiffening, he glanced at Xerxes. "Do you ever wonder what would have happened to you if you'd avoided capture by the demons?"

"All the time," his friend replied, swiping up a twig and snapping it in half. "I would be the man I was, happy, fulfilled, but I would be without you and Bjorn, and that's not okay with me."

A perfect example of finding beauty from ashes. The world could be a conniving harlot, as evil as a demon, but love would defeat her, every single time. Love never failed.

They reached the spot where Kendra was staked to the ground. But for the first time, Thane was not satisfied seeing her brought so low. He was treating her exactly as the demons had treated his friends.

Silly thought.

Frowning, he spread his wings and slowly crouched to one knee, meeting Kendra's gaze. She was thinner than she'd been at camp. Her cheekbones were gaunt. Limp strawberry-blond hair tangled around her head. Blood dripped from the holes where her ears should be. Cuts marred her lips, and dirt and blood streaked her naked skin. Every bit of exposed skin was blistered, some of it burned so badly it had blackened.

She was awake, lucid.

"Do you regret your treatment of me?" he asked, knowing she couldn't hear him.

Her eyes were wide, beseeching him. He could imagine the words she was trying to project at him, her throat too dry to let them form. *Thane, please. I never meant to enslave you, didn't realize what I was doing to you. It was an accident. A misunderstanding.*

No. She did not regret. She made excuses!

"Do you think the new king will come for you?" he asked, tracing his knuckles along her jawline. "Do you think he'll fight for you, the daughter of his beloved Malta? That he'll want you unharmed?" He paused for effect. "Think again. Ardeo will fight for the others, but not you. You're the niece of Malta's murderer."

As she tried to speak, incomprehensible sounds sprang from her. She began to struggle against the stakes, attempting to pull herself up and off. She only worsened her injuries.

He took a small bit of satisfaction from that. "What say you, Xerxes? Should I end her misery?"

"If you'd like her to repay you with a dagger, yes."

Grinning coldly, Thane straightened. "One day," he said to Kendra, "I'll tire of seeing you like this. One day, I might even let you go. But that day is not today."

SNAKING A CORNER, Elin ran into Thane. Literally ran into him, and almost dropped the cake she'd spent the past hour and a half baking. After leaving his suite, she'd needed a distraction, and gardening hadn't cut it, so she'd opted not to wait to wow him with her culinary genius.

His kitchen staff had protested—at first. Adrian had followed her there, and though he'd never said a word, his presence shut everyone up.

Mixing the ingredients, as she used to watch Bay do, had been as upsetting as it was gratifying.

Thane's strong arms banded around her to steady her. "Careful." He set her back a few feet and took the strawberry-vanilla confection from her hands.

Heat stained her cheeks. "Uh, sorry about that." Her body, the traitor, reacted to his nearness, as always, heating and tingling. "I was on a mission, and plowing forward without paying attention." Her gaze darted to Xerxes, who stood beside him. "Would you like to sample my dessert? I call it The Perfect Perfection. Trademark pending."

He looked at it, then at her. "I think I'll let Thane fall on this grena— I mean, let him have all of this one." Clearly fighting a grin, he stepped around her and ambled down the hallway.

Thane remained in place, as still as a statue. "You baked already?"

There were streaks of black on his face and hands.

Char? And what was with the bleak glaze in his eyes and the strain on his features?

"I did. And I know it's not much to look at." The middle had fallen the moment she'd pulled the pan from the oven, and then the top layer had shredded as she'd spread the icing. "But I'm certain it tastes divine."

"You didn't sample it yourself?"

"No." The last time Bay made one, he'd fed her by hand. Her heart couldn't take any more trips down memory lane. "You'll be the first," she said, eager to know his opinion. "Please."

"Certainly." He balanced the cake in one hand and pinched the edge with the other. His eyes widened as he chewed.

That was a good sign, right? "Well?"

"It's… Hmm." He swallowed with obvious effort. "This is what you're going to sell at your bakery?"

"Yes," she said, trying not to take a defensive tone.

"The best in the world?"

"Yes." She stomped her foot. "Why?"

He ignored the question, asking another of his own. "And you enjoy baking?"

"Well…yeah. It was my husband's favorite thing to do."

"I see." He pursed his lips. "And what was yours?"

"Well…" she repeated. "I liked to help him."

Lashes practically fused together, he said, "I'm sorry, Elin, but this is…" He stopped, thought for a moment, and sighed. "I've had worse."

A polite way of saying it sucked. "You hate it, don't you?"

"I…do. I'm sorry."

Her shoulders drooped. "At least you're honest." She

quickly rallied. "I'm out of practice, that's all." She snapped her fingers. "I know! I'll bake a few cakes a day and sell the slices to your customers. Soon, I'll do its name justice."

"I'm not sure—"

"I'll give you fifty percent of the profits," she rushed out. "And don't you dare say there won't be any profits. I'm not *that* bad."

"Very well." A gleam of pure calculation brightened his eyes. "We have a deal."

Why the calculation? "So, uh, yeah. Bellorie mentioned you had a library here." Wise to change the subject before he changed his mind. And wise to leave his presence, like, now. "Can you point me in the right direction? I want to check out a few books."

"You like to read?"

"Very much," she said.

One of his brows arched. "What type of books?"

Only, like, the best ever. "Romances."

"I have none of those."

"Oh," she said, trying not to pout.

"But I can get some," he added.

She perked up. "That would be awesome. Thank you. All right. Well. I guess this is good-night." She made to step around him, only to note the bleakness he'd sported earlier returning to his expression. A yearning to lighten his mood...his burden...or whatever it was that plagued him overshadowed her desire for escape. "Mr. Downfall, we need to relax you."

"And how do you suggest we do that?" His voice had changed, going low and husky.

With arousal? Attraction?

Please, no. She'd never be able to resist him then.

And if she couldn't resist him…goodbye, job. Goodbye, moneybags. Goodbye, new friends.

Goodbye, Thane.

"I'll show you." She handed the cake to the guard at
the end of the hall. "Do me a favor and throw this in the
trash. Do *yourself* a favor and never taste it." Then, in
front of Thane again, she held out her hand. When he
hesitated—why had his mood shifted so suddenly?—
she added, "Go on. Take it. This sweet little human isn't
leading you into an ambush, I promise."

Frowning, he curled his fingers around hers. There
was a shock through her system at the moment of contact, but it was expected. It had happened before. And
yet, she still trembled as she tugged him through the
building—or rather, the maze, as she'd begun calling
it—and to the backyard.

She never would have pictured a garden growing
from a cloud, but stranger things had happened, she
supposed.

"Sit," she commanded, waving toward the only bench.
The stone structure looked as if it had grown straight out
of the ground. Ivy clung to the legs, and a rose bloomed
just over the right corner.

He severed contact and sat. Those lovely wings
arched away from him, the gold-tipped ends brushing
over the ground. The sun cast golden beams directly on
him, paying tribute to his raw, masculine beauty, and
making him look as though he'd smuggled diamond
flecks in his pores.

"I didn't mean *on* the bench," she said with a grin,
"but *in front of* the bench."

His frown returned as he lowered to a crouch.

She knelt beside him. "Now, do you see this?" She

plucked a weed from the dirt. "It and everything like it are weeds. Weeds are bad. But those," she said, pointing to the flower stems, "those are good. Right now, bad is murdering good, so we've got to go to war and help."

Horror dawned on his features. "A fancy way of saying I am to…garden?" He shuddered.

"You'll be doing more than that, thank you. You'll be saving something beautiful."

He studied her. "Removing weeds is *that* important to you?"

"It's critical. And not just to me." *Drawing a parallel, Thane? Because you totally should. My hints aren't that subtle.*

Better question: *Are you drawing a parallel for yourself, Vale? Survivor's guilt is a big, thick weed with sharp thorns.*

Whatever.

As they worked, she tried not to notice the way Thane's muscles strained under his robe. She failed, and by the time they finished two hours later—the area around the bench cleared of weeds—all of Elin's girlie parts were desperate for attention.

Want him, they shouted.

Well, too bad. You can't have him.

But…but…he was so close…so beautiful…so obviously skilled with his hands. How easy it would be to lean into him and offer her mouth for the possession of his. She would lead at first, because he would be surprised, but then his desire would get the better of him and he would take over. He would taste her and touch her and urge her to her back. He would—

Blimey. Stop!

She cleared her throat. "While you're working, it's

hard to tell you've accomplished anything, right? All you can see are the things you have left to do. But then, suddenly, ta-da. This happens." The finished product. And it was better than she could have hoped. The colorful vines were thriving at long last.

He nodded, giving nothing away.

She anchored her fists on her hips. "Next time, would you rather I relax you by teaching you how to bake a cake?"

"So that there will be two of us capable of gagging my patrons? No."

The dryness of his tone drew a snort out of her. "See Mr. Serious tease Ms. Crocker," she mumbled, but inside, she rejoiced. Her plan had worked! The bleakness had left him. He actually sported an air of satisfaction in a job well done. "I'll improve. You just wait and see."

"Kulta, you couldn't get any worse."

She laughed with startling delight. "You never told me what *kulta* means."

His eyes glowed with a triumph she didn't understand. "I probably never will."

As if that would stop her from guessing. "'Witch'?"

"No."

"'Naughty girl'?"

"Not even close."

"'Honey bear sugar pop'?"

His smile was a slow bloom, revealing dimples that dazzled her.

She sputtered for a moment. "You…you… Thane, you have dimples." As if he didn't know! They were more adorable than a panda holding a baby kitten.

"I do?"

Wait. He *didn't* know? "You really do."

The dimples made another appearance. She shivered, suddenly aware that sweat had made her pj's cling to her skin. Her aching, tingling skin.

"Do you like dimples?" he asked.

Way too much. "Sure." She pushed to her feet, determined to put a little distance between them. "Well, I had better go and get my snooze on. You know how important beauty z's can be."

He opened his mouth, closed it. His gaze raked over her, and he scowled. "Go, then."

O-kay. Total mood shift. Again. For no reason!

She flicked her hair over one shoulder. "Just in case you missed it, the entire point of this exercise was to drive home the fact that everyone has weeds in their life. Including you. You need to yank them out—before it's too late."

THE NEXT EVENING, Thane had several boxes of chocolate delivered to Elin's room.

Of course, he immediately had to deal with sender's remorse. What was he doing? Courting her?

Hardly!

But he couldn't get her and her parting words out of his mind. What weeds did she have? He had to know.

He stomped through his suite, stripped when he entered the bathroom, and ducked under the shower spray.

His kind didn't need to bathe. Robes kept them clean from top to bottom, removing everything but a stain on the soul. Or, as Elin would say, the weeds. But there were times, like now, when he needed to feel the hot slide of water against his skin.

His entire world was being turned upside down.

Taunting Kendra yesterday might have given him

a measure of satisfaction—after the first burst of dis-content—but it hadn't lasted long, and guilt had taken its place. A guilt that had later proved to be kindling for the rage constantly brewing inside him, stoking it higher and hotter. Why should he feel guilty for doling out like for like?

Because Kendra, too, must have weeds?

He didn't want to think about that.

Instead, he pondered Elin, with her sweet smile and terrible cake.

She didn't know it, but she created desserts to keep her husband's memory alive, not because she enjoyed doing it, and certainly not because she had a talent for it. He grinned as he recalled the shock of having salted strawberries, eggshell, and an overload of vanilla on his tongue. He'd tried to hide his reaction, not wanting to hurt her feelings, but she'd been so good-natured about the whole thing, he'd just had to tease her.

Him. Teasing a female. It was inconceivable!

He only hoped she let go of her "dream" of baking while making countless desserts for the bar's patrons.

If—when—she did, he could put her in charge of the gardens. He could even help her. Shockingly enough, he'd liked having his hands in the dirt and the sun on his skin. Not so shockingly, he'd liked having a beauti-ful woman at his side, his muscles straining, his mind focused on a single goal.

What he hadn't liked was Elin's casual disregard af-terward. When she'd stood and announced she was leav-ing him, he'd wanted to curse. More and more, parting with her required an inner strength he didn't possess. And yet, she always seemed to do it with ease.

He shut off the water with more force than necessary,

then tugged on a new robe. The slam of a door caught his attention. He drew a sword of fire as he marched from the stall.

Bjorn, who had been absent longer than ever before, according to Xerxes, made it only a few feet away from the entrance before dropping to his knees and bowing his head. Thane dismissed the sword and rushed over. Xerxes was there a second later, and together, they helped their friend to his feet.

"Bathroom," Bjorn croaked.

Acting as crutches, they led him to where he wanted to go and eased him to the tiled floor. Bjorn crawled to the toilet and emptied the contents of his stomach, reminding Thane of Xerxes's reaction to a sexual encounter.

Thane held his hair out of the line of fire, hating the fact that there was nothing he could do to alleviate the male's discomfort. He met Xerxes's gaze. Did he look as bleak and grim as the warrior?

"What happens to you when you leave us?" Thane whispered.

Silence. Expected.

Xerxes washed Bjorn's face with a cool rag. "No matter what, we're here for you."

Again, silence.

Thane guided his friend to bed. A single, sharp breath stopped him from pulling up the covers.

"Wings," Bjorn said, and Thane helped the warrior to his stomach.

He smoothed dark locks of hair from the male's face, and looked over the white-gold wings. There was no sign of—

Foul play. There. A wound on each side of the thick,

corded arch, crusted with black, oozing a slight trickle of blood. As if clamps, or metal claws, had held him in place.

Rage returned in a flash. Wherever it was Bjorn went, he suffered. Something had to be done, and soon.

Together, Thane and Xerxes cleaned and bandaged him. They sat at his sides, talking about anything, everything, and absolutely nothing until some of the tension drained from the warrior.

"Do you remember the time you had to cloak your wings with an air pocket and walk through the streets of New York, visible to all as you tracked a demon-possessed heiress?" Xerxes said to Bjorn. "You were approached by three scouts hoping to make you the next supermodel. Had it been me, I would have had five scouts approach me. Scars are so this season."

The warrior's mouth twitched at one side.

"Maybe," Thane said. "But little-girl cherub curls and bad attitudes beat scars any day, which means I would have had ten scouts after me."

As they argued amicably about who was more attractive, Bjorn relaxed enough to drift off to sleep.

Thane and Xerxes shared a look rife with tension, all hint of good humor gone.

"I'll stay with him," Xerxes whispered. "I'll take care of him."

"As will I."

"No." Pale hair danced over the male's wide shoulders as he shook his head. "The other Sent Ones are due to arrive. You're needed downstairs."

His hands fisted. He wanted to protest. He couldn't. His friend was right.

He nodded stiffly. "Send for me if any problems arise."

"Of course."

He forced himself to walk away.

Despite Elin's threat to poor tippers, the bar was packed again tonight. The cacophony of voices quickly grated against his already frayed nerves, the female ones vying for his attention the worst of all.

"Thane! I heard you were hot, but, oh, baby, you're smoking."

"Sweet, it's Thane. Hey, Thane, look at me. Look at what I can do. I'm very bendy."

"Thane! Thane! I have five words for you. I'll. Let. You. Do. *Anything*."

If he walked away from this night without committing murder, he would consider it a win.

Thane stopped at Adrian's side. The berserker was on high alert as he watched the night's activities from his usual corner.

"I need the corner room." As he spoke, he searched the crowd for Elin.

She stood at a table of warlocks, her profile to him. *Luscious little human.* Her hair was twisted into a knot at the crown of her head, and she had flour on her cheeks. But her uniform looked smaller than before, and that wasn't okay.

Surely she was cold.

"She needs a robe," he told the berserker.

"I'll make sure she gets one."

She held up a cake as lopsided as the last one, doing her best to tempt the males to taste.

One of the warlocks was more interested in her body. He smoothed a hand over her backside.

Thane was halfway across the room, ready to push over the table and tear the warlock to shreds, before he realized what he was doing and reluctantly backtracked. If Elin wanted the warlock's attention, she could have it.

She better not want his attention.

He watched as she slapped the male's hand away and wagged her finger in his face. The warlock pouted, but didn't try anything further.

Thane forced himself to relax. "Has anyone bought one of her desserts?"

"Yes," Adrian replied. "And they've all demanded refunds, plus a little something extra for damages."

Not surprising. "Buy whatever she has left and put it on my table." If it would make her smile, he would eat every bite. And so would his troops. "For the rest of the night, she's to serve me, and only me."

The warrior blinked in amazement, but offered no commentary.

"Oh," Thane added, almost as an afterthought. Almost. "Remove the young warlock's hand."

"But, sir—"

"This isn't a debate. Are you becoming too soft, Ad? We both know he'll grow another one."

Adrian nodded. "And what do I cite as his crime?"

Thane thought for a moment. "He touched what's mine."

ELIN STEPPED INTO the secluded room located in the far corner of the bar, trying not to project her nervousness. Hiding her origins from Thane, Bjorn, Xerxes and all the patrons of the bar was one thing. Trying to hide her origins from a roomful of trained killers was quite another.

Sooner or later I'm going to be found out.

Her gaze sought Thane of its own accord. Strong, beautiful Thane, with the irresistible dimples. So badly she wanted to believe he wouldn't care about her mixed heritage, that he would protect her, whatever happened. And maybe that wasn't as vain a hope as she feared. The guy had sent her several boxes of chocolates. Who did that? A sweet, romantic man, that was who.

Of course, he'd pretended she didn't exist ever since, so...

Best behavior, Vale. No one will know. You've got this. She focused on his majorly hawt friends. And, wow. Just wow. No wonder Bellorie had practically foamed at the mouth with jealousy.

For a moment, Elin could only gawk.

There was a big—huge...huger even than Adrian, if *huger* was even a word—Viking with long dark hair and a thick black beard drawn together in the center by three little beads.

There was a set of twins, with a clear Asian heritage. One rocked out with a green Mohawk, tats and piercings, but the other was all business, with slicked-back hair and a clean-shaven jaw.

Then there was Voted Most Beautiful Man Ever to Live—if he hadn't been, he totally should be...and only if the sexy chocolate peddler known as Thane was taken out of the running. He had black hair and piercing blue eyes.

Had she found a better candidate than the love-'em-and-leave-'em Merrick?

"Nice fire-creepers you've got on your lawn," Most Beautiful said to Thane.

Fire-creepers. A derogatory name for Phoenix. Along

with flame-whore, hellmongrel, and grave-challenged. She had no love for the race and took no offense.

Thane gave a stiff nod before scooping a slice of her most recent confection onto several different plates. Would he like it? Or hate it?

Reviews had come in throughout the evening.

I've eaten tastier dirt.

My compliments to the chef. I didn't think anything was worse than my mother-in-law's dung-beetles casserole.

He would hate it.

Gah! Frustration threatened to overtake her, but she resisted it. Soon she would hit her groove, and everyone would eat their words—along with her desserts! She just had to keep at it.

The female sitting next to Thane smiled with cold delight before handing him a stack of papers. She had curly jet-black hair, dark flawless skin, and eyes of the most startling ocher. "The list is completed."

The list? What list? All the ways she wanted to make love with Thane?

Elin experienced a sudden urge to go alley cat on the girl. There would be hissing, biting and clawing.

Real mature, Vale.

"We'll devise a plan of attack after the drinks arrive," Thane replied.

My cue. "Uh, hey, everyone. I'm here to serve, so let's hear those orders."

His gaze finally met hers, desperately intent, and she shivered. For a moment, the rest of the world blurred. *Hate when this happens...because I love it so much.* She became hyperaware of her boss, could see his chest rising and falling with his breaths, could feel the heat radiating from him.

Her body responded instinctively. Her breasts began to ache, and her belly quivered. Her lungs constricted, and wave after wave of drugging warmth spilled through her veins, pooling between her legs. The air thinned, charging with excitement and anticipation.

Thane stood, his stance aggressive, his jaw clenched. He was pure testosterone and...need? As if he battled the urge to drag her away by the hair.

Did he want her? The way she wanted him?

Please, please, please.

No. Not please!

Someone chuckled. "O-kay. This is halfway to awkward."

Scowling, Thane tore his attention away from her and sat back down.

Good. That was good. She could breathe again. The only difference was, her skin was more sensitive...tingling, aching, as if she and Thane were back in that garden, sitting beside each other, within reach.

The stilted conversations she wished she'd tried to listen to instead of spacing out like a love-struck teenager had ceased, she realized. All eyes were glued to her.

"Where's your robe?" Thane asked.

So. He knew Adrian had tried to foist one off on her. "It's stuffed in a potted plant, where I'd like it to remain." A robe meant lower tips. "Now, then. What can I get you guys to drink?"

"How about a nice, tall glass of you, pretty girl," said Most Beautiful.

"Like I haven't heard that one before," she muttered.

"Ouch. Okay, I'll step up my game. Or not. I know that you noticed me," he continued smoothly. "Everyone does." A slow, seductive grin curved his sensuous mouth. It was an invitation to attend the party in his pants, no doubt about it. "Now the only question left to answer is what time you'd like to get off. Because I'll make sure it happens. Twice."

Yeah. She'd found a candidate. Teasing him, she said, "Okay, one arsenic, coming up."

A genuine laugh of amusement barked from him.

Most Beautiful liked death threats with his alcohol. Got it.

"I'll be coming back for you, female," he said. "I guarantee it."

Thane banged a hand against the tabletop, and a jagged crack formed in the center. Startled, Elin yelped. Uh-oh. Stupid girl! Had she really just threatened his friend the way she threatened regular customers? Plucky best friend hadn't worked. She'd had to go with homicidal sweetheart.

"I wasn't really going to feed him arsenic," she rushed out.

But Thane's gaze wasn't on her. It was on Most Beautiful. "Elin, send Savy in here, then have Adrian escort you to my suite."

Wait. What? "Uh, well—"

"No arguments," he snapped, still not glancing in her direction.

"Who said I was going to argue?" *I was. I so was.* Why did he want her to go to his suite? To punish her in private? She scanned the six occupants in the small, secluded room at the north corner of the bar, hoping for concrete answers. No longer did anyone pay her any heed. Everyone watched Thane with unabashed interest. "Fine. I'll do it." *I thought we were semi-friends, you jerk!* "But would it be okay if I gave the order to Bellorie instead?"

It was probably a million kinds of wrong to suggest a change. Probably? Ha. With Mr. No Debate, it was. More than that, warriors didn't like to be second-guessed. And Thane was more warrior than most!

But Bellorie was Elin's personal favorite, and the girl wanted in here so bad. And, really, Elin was already in trouble. What harm could a little more do?

Oh, crap. A little more trouble could equal a lot more pain. Like the time Kendra whipped her—and then threw her into a salt bath.

At last Thane faced her. Those electric blues practically vibrated with awareness, unnerving her. Making her feel naked rather than partially clothed.

Making her body crave all over again...

An unreadable light entered his eyes—something hard and hot. Carnal and dangerous. Rather than order her to bend over his lap and apologize while he spanked her, which she kind of expected, he nodded. "Send Bellorie."

Most Beautiful gaped at Thane. "Did you just change your orders? For an employee?"

Not waiting around to hear his reply, Elin rushed out and hunted her best girl. The bubbly Harpy was at the bar, loading a tray with drinks.

"You're up, Rocket," Elin told her. "Thane wants you serving his table tonight."

The redhead faced her, mouth agape. "Me? Really? Even though I tried to give Koldo a lap dance last time?"

Which one was Koldo? Most Beautiful? "Yep. Even though."

Bellorie jumped up and down with excitement. "This is gonna be the best night ever."

"Just be careful. Thane is in a snarly mood. Definitely don't threaten his friends."

"Please." Bellorie pulled a tube of bright red lipstick from her pocket. "I'm not in my early fifties anymore. I would never do anything as childish as threatening a Sent One."

Blimey. "How old are you?"

"One hundred and three luscious years." This was said as if the advanced age were perfectly normal. And up here, it totally was.

Just how old was Thane? Had he already lived a lifetime, like Bellorie? Or several lifetimes?

Either way, he would live several more. Maybe Elin would age more slowly than the average human. Maybe she wouldn't. She had no outward signs of being Phoenix, no fangs or claws. No ability to produce flames. No birthmarks. So, why would she have any internal signs, like eternal youth?

This was just another reason to stay away from Thane.

"So, where will you be while the sexiest males in the skies are falling madly, passionately in lust with me?" Bellorie asked, fluffing her hair and checking her appearance in the mirror over the bar.

Can't tell her. Just...can't. Pity—or worse, horror—would take over her features, and Elin would never find the courage to wait for Thane and the coming punishment, as ordered. A punishment she wouldn't accept peacefully!

"I'm taking care of something for Mr. Thane." Truth, without details. Friendship preserved. She gave the girl a little push toward the private room. "You better go before you make his crap list."

"Wouldn't be the first time, Bonka Donk." Grinning, Bellorie skipped away.

Elin reluctantly approached Adrian. He didn't look at her, but his posture did straighten the slightest degree. "You're supposed to escort me to Thane's stupid suite to await his stupid majesty's every stupid whim."

A moment passed. Then another. No response was forthcoming. At first, she didn't think he'd heard her. Then he stalked away from her and entered the private room. He exited a few minutes later, his expression granite hard and rougher than sandpaper. He bypassed Elin—still without a word. Whatever. She followed.

"So gracious," she tsked. "What did you say to him? Did you ask him if I was a dirty liar?"

There was a strained pause. Then, "I asked if he was sure that's what he wanted."

"And?"

"And, he threatened to stake me."

Ouch.

"I'm sorry for what's to come, human," he said, when finally they reached the suite. "I'd sneak you back to land if I thought it would make any difference. But he would follow, and neither of us would like what happened when he found you."

"That's not very comforting."

"At this point, there's nothing that will be."

She stepped past the doors. He returned to the hallway and shut the entrance in her face, sealing her inside, before she could demand details.

CHAPTER NINE

THANE STOOD AT the edge of the couch, peering down at a sleeping Elin. He would never tire of looking at her. Dark hair tumbled around her delicate shoulders. Long lashes cast shadows over the sweet definition of her cheekbones. Her freckles beckoned. Her soft lips parted as she released a breathy sigh. Of what did she dream?

And why did she continue to affect him so strongly— more strongly every day? Today his heart had sped into a wild beat at the first sight of her. Worse, sending her away had been torture.

He'd wanted so badly to go to her, but he'd left the meeting with the Sent Ones to speak to another group of males he... *Trusted* wasn't the right word. *Utilized upon occasion.* Yes. Better.

The Lords of the Underworld were immortal warriors possessed by the demons once locked inside Pandora's box, and, surprisingly enough, they were currently on the side of the Sent Ones, their would-be assassins. They fought the evil they hosted, rather than encouraging it, which made them worthy allies in the heavenly warriors' eyes.

Thane had asked about the shadow creatures now connected to Bjorn.

William had been there, pale and withdrawn, drinking and trying to forget the death of his daughter. "I know them," the male had said. "They were birthed in a realm unlike any other, dark without any hint of light. They are hive-minded. They have a queen, and they obey her without question. She is…" He shuddered. "If they're afraid of your soldier, then he's protected by her—or united with her. Either way, he'd be better off dead. And castrated."

Thane had fumed all the way home. He'd hoped to find a female in the bar and calm himself the only way he knew how—a plan he'd actually despised. But then he'd remembered his order to Elin and nearly mowed down his entire staff in an effort to reach her.

And here she was. Safe and sound.

Ripe enough to be plucked.

Her soap-and-cherries scent saturated every inch of the room. He'd always resented foreign fragrances on his things, but this…this he liked.

Elin was in an upright position, her head resting on the back of the couch. Had she fought her body's need for rest, only to succumb where she sat?

A small glass shard peeked from the top of a white-knuckled grip. Still frightened of him?

Careful not to wake her or cut her delicate skin, he pried the shard loose. Her skin was ice-cold, he noted, and frowned. With so little clothing, and no blanket, the air had chilled her.

He stalked to his bedroom—his, not the one he used for his women—and grabbed the softest blanket in his possession. Laughing male voices filtered through the crack underneath Bjorn's door as he strode back to the sitting room.

Thank the Most High. His friend had found some levity.

At the couch, he willed his robe to conform to his body and separate into a shirt and a pair of pants. Then he removed the shirt, wanting fewer barriers between the heat of his skin and Elin. He gathered her in his arms. *So light, so soft.* As trusting as a child, she snuggled her head in the hollow of his neck, seeking closer contact. He had to bite his tongue to silence a moan of pleasure.

Pleasure. Over *this*. What was wrong with him?

Reeling, he turned and eased onto the couch, settling the girl on his lap. He draped the blanket around her, cinching her in a cocoon of heat. Mistake! Her scent grew stronger. Her breath fanned over his chest, as erotic as a caress, and her hand fluttered over his shaft.

He hardened in an instant.

Resist her. Yes, he would resist her. Even as his body trembled with undeniable thrums of arousal. He would warm her up, wake her up, then escort her back to her room. *Then* he would find an appropriate woman to slake his desires.

Elin rubbed her cheek against his pectoral and purred, her mouth perilously close to his nipple.

Lick me. Taste me.

His arms tightened around her. He didn't want an appropriate woman. He wanted this one. But...

He imagined her chained and struggling.

He shuddered, more horrified than ever.

He imagined her crying and begging as he injured her, perhaps scarring her as Kendra had.

A shudder of revulsion shook him.

He imagined Elin standing behind him, using one of his plethora of tools to inflict pain on him, with delight in her eyes.

Cold sweat beaded over his skin.

He'd experienced this type of reaction before. With her. Only her. But it was beginning to spill over into other areas. Like every time he thought about the women he'd bedded, and how he'd never really known them. The kind of lives they'd led. Carefree...or as tormented as his own.

Had he heaped hurt on already hurting women? Crowded them with so many weeds they couldn't breathe?

The guilt...

He couldn't do the same to Elin. Couldn't add to her anguish. Wouldn't.

But he had to have her.

Take her, then. Gently. Maybe you'll like it. Maybe you won't. Either way...

Either way, she would be his.

And he could ensure she enjoyed it, whether or not he did. He could please her as much—or more—than her husband.

A dangerous thought, for she might want more from him.

A tempting thought, for that very reason.

If he found himself reverting to habit, as he feared he might, he would stop and walk away. He would leave her satisfied, but he *would* leave her.

Now, all he had to do was convince Elin.

ELIN WOKE UP GRADUALLY, several facts slowly pushing into her awareness. She was cozied up to a warm male body, and that warm male body didn't belong to the twenty-year-old Bay, who'd been lean, like a long-distance runner. It was too wide. Too hard. Too...everything. The male body *did* belong to Thane. She would recognize his dangerous champagne scent anywhere.

Confusion struck. How had she ended up in his arms? She remembered being shut up in his suite—*thanks, Adrian. Owe you one.* She remembered pacing, wondering what Thane planned to do to her, and yawning a few thousand times, despite her agitation. She remembered cursing the fact that she was missing a Multiple Scorgasms practice. The team might never forgive her. She remembered settling on the couch to conserve her energy. Then…nothing.

Now…Thane's strong hand stroked along the ridges of her spine, up and down, up and down, stopping every so often to play with strands of her hair. *Delicious.* Desire too long denied rolled through her, an unstoppable tidal wave. Consuming her. Drowning her. But, oh, what a way to go.

Here was everything she'd craved for the past year. Comfort. Contact. Connection. The three C's of enticement.

Thane wasn't a candidate for her bang and bail…but he was the only male she wanted.

Being with him will come at a terrible price.

Oh, yeah. Swallowing a moan that would have embarrassed her, she jolted upright. His arms, already banded around her, tightened before she could stand, locking her in place. *Ignore the rapturous feel of him.* Desperate, she cast her gaze over the room. The lights had been dimmed and now cast only the softest, most romantic glow. He hadn't moved her from the couch, but had slid in underneath her. Oh, criminy, why?

"Look at me, Elin," he demanded, the strain in his voice catching her by surprise.

Reluctantly she faced him—and then wished she hadn't. This close, she could see tension branching from eyes crackling with electricity, and a mouth set in a hard line. He looked wild, savage, capable of any dark deed…and yet she yearned to sink closer to him, to put her hands all over him, and feel his hands all over her.

"Are you going to punish me?" she asked. Nothing would toss her out of her amorous mood faster.

"Punish you?" His expression shuttered, then closed off entirely. "No. Why would you think that?"

"I threatened your friend with arsenic."

"That's right. You did. Thank you for the reminder."

She slapped the heel of her palm against her forehead. "How dumb can I be? Golden rule number one is never remind a boss of your mistakes. If he can't remember, you shouldn't, either."

"I liked that you threatened him. He deserved it." His gaze dropped to her lips. His eyelids seemed to grow heavier by the second, lack of emotion no longer a problem. He sizzled. "But that isn't what I wish to discuss."

Oh. "Then what?" she asked, relieved…confused.

He gave her a look so intense, so hot, it would be forever branded in her mind. "I thought I could stop it, but I can't."

Stop *it*. The attraction.

The need.

She knew that was what he meant, and heat pooled low in her belly.

Oh, no. No, no, no. One of them had to stay sane.

"You are wasted on a man's memory, kulta," Thane continued silkily, "and I'm not going to stand for it anymore."

Killing me... "You don't have to. I decided to be with someone," she whispered.

One corner of his mouth tilted up. "Me." It wasn't a question.

She hesitated, then admitted, "Actually, no." Maybe the truth would stop the madness.

He stiffened, and flames began to crackle in his eyes. Flames so wild, they were actually scary. "Who?"

The word was like a punch.

Should have kept my mouth shut. There was no way to make this better. *But that was what you wanted, right?* "Uh, well, uh, see. I was still deciding between some guy—you've probably never met him. I mean, yes, he's obviously been here, you hired him, but—"

"Hired. Adrian—no, I've seen you with him, and there was nothing sexual there. McCadden—no. He's in love with another." He paused, other names probably rolling through his mind. Then he narrowed his eyes, the fire raging brighter, and dug his fingers deeper into her flesh. "Merrick."

Her eyes widened. How had...? No way he could... Argh!

"That's not going to happen, Elin. You'll be with me." He lifted her by the waist and forced her to straddle him. "No other."

She struggled for a moment—and realized she was merely grinding her aching core against his erection. Her body settled, enthralled by the new position...while her heart careened into an uncontrollable beat. A mating rhythm.

He sucked in a breath. "It's better than I imagined."

"What is?" she breathed. But she already knew, because she thought so, too.

"Holding you like this."

"You imagined this?" He didn't just want her, she realized. He wanted her *desperately*. It was a heady thought.

"Many times."

"Me, too," she admitted softly, the words leaving her of their own accord.

His hands gripped her harder. "Say yes. Here. Now."

Yes, yes, a thousand times yes. *Touch me. Please.* But self-preservation proved stronger than primal instinct. "Yes to what, exactly?"

"To me. To us. I want to be with you, Elin. I want to do things to you. Things you would have never dreamed possible."

A low moan broke from her throat. *I want you to do those things to me, too.* "I…" Shivered with anticipation. "I can't," she forced herself to say. *Even though I'm willing to beg for it.* "I'm sorry."

His eyes hooded in challenge. "Don't be sorry." He kissed her neck, at the same time pressing his long, hard length more firmly against her core. Despite her claim, she tilted her hips toward him, deepening the contact, making it last longer. "Answer a question for me."

"Yes." The agreement felt good on her lips.

"You'll give yourself to another, but not to me?" His palms grazed the tips of her breasts. "Why? To punish me for the Harpy?"

Goose bumps broke out. "No." Maybe. "I…" *Take a time-out. Weigh the pros and cons.* "Want to give myself to you. I do." Forget the pros and cons. They had no time to form. Desire burned them away. Burned *her*.

He stilled. "What changed your mind?"

"It's what I've always wanted," she admitted, toying

with the ends of his hair. "I'm just not going to fight it anymore."

Triumph flared in his eyes. He nibbled on her earlobe, and reached down, cupping her between her legs. She gasped as a hot lance of pleasure speared her.

"You want me, and no one else?"

"No one else," she croaked. But once again self-preservation raised its head, forcing her to add, "I will go to first base with you *so* hard. But that's it."

And then I'll feel so guilty, I won't have to sleep with anyone. Ever.

Finally. Win/win.

Thane might have cracked a smile. He might not have. Either way, he was done with chitchat.

He grabbed her by the nape of her neck and pulled her to him, forcing her lips to meet his. Hard and un-yielding, he thrust his tongue inside her mouth. Tasting, demanding.

He dominated.

He mastered.

He owned.

When she mewled in rapture—*so good*—he gentled his hold and softened his thrusts, allowing her to learn him and savor. She melted against him, meeting his tongue with a plunge of her own.

"Yes," he rasped. "Like that." He sounded amazed.

She *felt* amazed. She met his tongue a second time, and it was like throwing gasoline-soaked logs on an already raging fire, the kiss instantly spinning out of control. Urgency overshadowed the desire to savor. They began to bite and lick at each other, his taste intoxicating her—dizzy with need—addicting her to his brand of tender aggression.

Don't want to ever let him go. Have to touch him. Everywhere at once. Fingers in his hair. Combing through his wings. Her nails scraping down his chest. Oh, sweet fire, her hands wrapped around his steel-hard length.

Greedy girl. One at a time. She started with his hair, sifting her fingers through the silky strands. He growled his approval as her passion forced her to tug a bit. Encouraged, she made her way to his ears, then down the taut muscles of his neck, before moving on to the down-soft feathers of his wings. So many sensations, each adding fuel to her scalding desire.

"Your freckles are delicious." He kissed her jaw, her throat, using tongue and teeth, and a fever flushed her skin, made her bones ache.

She loved it. Loved the heat and eroticism. How had she gone a year without a man? A year without pleasure and comfort. A year of dreaming and wishing and denying and suppressing. Now, every need she'd ever ignored came roaring to the surface. To touch and be touched. To give and to take. To live and to feel. Oh, to feel.

"Thane," she said, a command for more. She rubbed against Thane's erection, up and down, *sloooowly* at first, so slow and leisurely, easing herself into the riotous sensation, allowing her to savor, even while her mind demanded she hurry. Her neglected body could barely process its reactions to him. But raw, animal passion was driving her deeper and deeper into a world of carnality, making her desperate for some measure of relief, and she increased her speed.

"Incredible," he said, and never had she heard such a ragged tone.

Faster… "Yes." Her thoughts centered around three words: *more, now, need.* A little faster… Every point

of contact wrung a frantic gasp from her. Faster still…
"More."

"More than just first base?" His tone was teasing.

"Now!"

"With pleasure, kulta." He set her a few inches away, ending the sweet, sweet undulations.

"But…" She whimpered. "I need."

"And so you shall have." Going caveman, he ripped her shirt and bra away, and threw the material to the floor.

Yes!

He swallowed hard as he took in the sight of her. His thumbs circled her nipples, making them pucker, as he palmed her bare breasts. "So beautiful. Won't let myself mar them."

His absolute reverence nearly undid her, even as the words reverberated in her desire-fogged mind. *Mar them.* The punishment she deserved for betraying Bay. The thing she needed to stop herself from repeating this experience.

"Do it," she commanded.

He went still. "Do what?" The words were quiet, laced with menace.

How could she explain?

"What do you want, Elin? For me to throw you down? Sink inside you?"

Yes! No. Maybe. Ugh. Definitely yes.

"Because I don't think you truly want what I think you're trying to tell me you want," he finished.

Thoughts of elucidating her need to experience pain, to ease her guilt for feeling so overcome with lust for this man, vanished. Instead, a plea escaped. "Please.

I'm so close already. I just need to…have to… It's been so long."

His expression softened. "I'll take such good care of you, kulta." He gripped her backside and pulled her into his erection with one hand, while the other pressed into her stomach and urged her backward, until she sat at an incline on his thighs. He bent forward and sucked one of her nipples into his mouth, hard, harder, before flicking his tongue back and forth, easing the slight sting.

Slight, and yet sharp pleasure cut through her. She cried out. *More. Please, more.* He turned his attention to the other nipple, giving it the same treatment.

Desperation was making her frantic, and she tried to move against his shaft, to rub again, she had to rub, but she couldn't move her hips with his weight bearing down on her.

"Thane," she moaned. Never had she wanted a man—a climax—so much.

He lifted his head, his lips red, moist and kiss-swollen. His gaze met hers, his irises blazing with a hunger that was a mirror to her own.

All at once, he stood with her clutched against his chest, her legs wrapped around his hips, and turned toward the bedroom. The Room of Sweet, Sweet Horrors.

Reality pimp-slapped her. Just. Like. That. Not much time had passed since this man had banged another woman and left her a boneless heap on the bed. A boneless, *bruised* heap. The things he must have done to her…everything Elin thought she wanted. And yet, panic doused her wanton desperation and ruined her pleasure, memories of her captivity overtaking her. She felt as though she'd been drenched with dirty ice water.

What had she been thinking, kissing him? Begging him?

"No." Elin fought his hold. He frowned at her but allowed her to settle on her feet and back away from him. "No. We can't."

"No?" His hands fisted at his sides. "Not no."

"We can't," she repeated. "Please, understand."

"We *shouldn't*," he corrected coolly. "But we definitely *can*."

The evidence of his words was straining against his pants. Her body pleaded with her to agree. "Thane—"

"I wanted to stay away from you, kulta. I tried. I failed. Now…now I would like a chance with you."

A chance at a relationship? *Killing me all over again.*

"You liked what I was doing to you," he continued. "I could smell your arousal—I still can. If I were to feel between your legs, I know I would find you wet. Ready for me."

Treacherous heat bloomed in her cheeks. "It's true." Like she could really deny it.

"And still you say no?"

Do it. Confirm. "Correct." *Don't whimper.*

His eyes narrowed, but he said, "Let's talk about your concerns, then. Your…weeds?"

"No. Yes. Gah!" She breathed in and out with purpose, trying to calm her riotous pulse, and decided to start with the simplest problem. "I don't know you. Not really. And what I do know…"

He nodded stiffly. "You don't like."

The hurt in his eyes nearly buckled her knees. "I didn't mean it that way," she said. *Just say what you've been thinking. Let it out.* "Thane, when you sleep with women, you're done. Totally and completely done. You'll fire me to get rid of me. I've already been warned."

And if he slept with her and later found out what she was? He would feel betrayed, and punish her worse than the Phoenix in the courtyard.

He popped his jaw, but whether he was irritated with her or himself, she wasn't sure. "You have my word. You will not be fired."

Yes, but how would he treat her? As if she didn't exist? As if he wished she would leave? That might be exactly what her vow to Bay required, and might even help her continue to hide her origins, but wow, she was so tired of being the outcast. And what would happen if—when—Thane turned his attention to another woman? Perhaps even the very next day. Elin would have to watch, helpless to do anything about it.

Already the thought of him with anyone else turned her stomach, and they hadn't even slept together.

"What else?" he demanded.

Even talking about it was almost more than she could bear. Words made it real, rather than an action fueled only by passion. And stupidity. "I've never had a one-night stand, and while that's all I think I should allow with you, and all you'll probably want, I don't know how I'll react afterward. What if I…" she shuddered, saying, "cling?"

He rolled his shoulders, little ripples working through the feathers in his wings, mesmerizing her. "You will never hear me complain."

Her heart hitched at the words. Never *hear* him complain—which meant he could do it, just not when she was around.

"Would you prefer to have a commitment from me?" he asked.

No. Never! "Yes," she found herself saying. "I mean no." *Make up your stupid mind!* "I don't know. I promised myself I'd never do another commitment."

"No one-night stands. No commitments." His eyes narrowed. "You aren't leaving me any options."

That was the point. No options. No sex. "Maybe that's for the best."

"Maybe your promise deserves an amendment," he said quietly, almost menacingly.

"Like, in my heart I will always stay true to Bay, but my body is up for grabs?" *News flash. I already had a meeting with my board of directors and voted that one in, big guy.*

He arched a brow, all, *what do you think?*

She sighed. "Have you ever been a part of a committed relationship?"

"No," he admitted.

"Ever wanted to be?"

"No."

At least he was honest.

And why did any of this even matter? This wasn't a road she would travel. Was it?

He gently pinched her chin and forced her head to lift, her gaze to meet his. "Everything is different with you. Nothing is what I'm used to." He paused as she absorbed those wonderful, beautiful words. "But none of that compares with one fact. I want you, Elin." A flicker of unease flashed in his eyes—and of hope. "Do you want me? Because the answer is the only thing that matters right now."

His unease nearly undid her. He was *that* anxious to

hear her response? But it was the hope that sealed the deal. When it came to Thane, she was weak.

"I... Yes," she admitted softly. "Yes, Thane, I want you." Why couldn't she be that certain about everything else? "I think I proved that."

The hope intensified, only to fade in a blink. "Tell me, then. What is it, exactly, that you expect from me?"

Confused, she said, "What do you mean?"

"You saw the Harpy," he intoned, his voice going cold, hard. "She was shackled."

"Yes," she rasped.

"You saw her condition."

"Y-yes."

"That is what I've always needed. Absolute control... absolute pain."

"Always?"

He released a breath. "Until you."

What? she almost squeaked. What made her so special?

"But when I had you in my arms," he added, "you made it seem like you might actually desire a little pain and bondage."

She peered down at her feet, embarrassed. Did he have to be so frank? "You're saying you won't shackle me, even if it's what I claim to want."

"That's right. I won't."

That was good.

No, that was bad.

Actually, she didn't know what it was. "Why?" she asked. "And what about the other thing?"

"The desire simply isn't there. And I won't beat you, either." He reached out, traced his fingertips along her cheek. "You've had enough of that."

Yes, she had. And yet...

She wasn't sure what to think about any of this. "Has the desire ever been absent with another woman?"

"No."

"Because they didn't have a past like mine?"

A flash of guilt in his eyes, quickly gone. "I'm not sure. At the time, I didn't care to know. With you, though, I care. I crave every detail."

He cares. Why not tell him everything? Just put it all out there? He could get a peek at the overrun garden in her head. He might run.

What if he stays?

"You're correct about my wants. In part."

His brow furrowed. "Explain."

"At camp, I was slapped, pushed and whipped by the very people responsible for the death of my father and husband. I was called names, and treated like an animal. But that wasn't the worst of the abuse." She drew in a deep breath. Held...held... "They taunted me with details of my family's death. They wouldn't allow me to speak to my mother, or her to speak to me. But I should have risked punishment, and talked to her. She needed me, and I was too afraid to help her."

Emotion darkened his features. Emotions she couldn't read. "And now you think you deserve more pain?"

"Yes. But I also thought... I mean, if sex could be an experience I hated, I'd never again want to betray Bay."

He backed away from her, severing all contact, taking his wondrous heat.

"Thane?" she asked as a tear streamed down her cheek. *He's sickened by my acceptance of my fate. He considers me a coward—because I am.* "I'm sorry."

"You need to leave, Elin. Now."

"But—"

"Now," he roared.

She raced from the room.

CHAPTER TEN

HER TEAR…that one lone tear… *I'm gutted.* It brought Thane to his knees.

He'd known in that moment, as Elin left the suite, that a female's weeping would never again arouse him. He would always associate the action with his little human's soul-crushing anguish.

Elin is just like me. She thinks she deserves punishment, not pleasure.

Had his other women felt the same? He'd wondered before, but the truth had evaded him. Or maybe he hadn't wanted to face it. Now, the answer was clear, and undeniable. They had. He hadn't chosen females based on their exterior—tall, strong and stalwart. He'd chosen those with shadows in their eyes, because deep down he'd known they'd hoped to exorcise figurative demons, just as he had.

They'd all failed.

Thane punched a hole in the wall. Right now, he had to concentrate on Elin. His sweet mortal was in need of comfort he wasn't capable of giving. When she'd talked of her time with the Phoenix, his rage had been so great, he'd nearly stomped from the room to murder every man and woman in his courtyard.

Then Elin had listed her second reason for desiring pain. Even as she'd talked of commitments and clinging, she'd wanted to hate being with him, so that she would never again be tempted to betray her husband.

Her dead husband.

His hands curled into fists. If Thane were to harm her, even at her request, it would change her. It would dull her bright smile. Never again would she feel at ease enough to tease him. Never again would she bake him a cake or pull weeds in the garden with him. Never again would she speak so freely with him. She would flinch from him.

And if another man were to harm her...heaven and earth would tremble from the effects of Thane's wrath.

Have to prove she deserves good things. Have to make her crave good things.

He headed into town to buy chocolates and romance novels. Several hours ticked past as he selected the very best of both. A man devoted time to what mattered to him—to what he deemed worthy of his attention.

When he finished, he tracked down Merrick.

A man guarded what mattered to him.

Shame Spiral was performing at another bar that night. Bodies danced, and strobes flashed rainbow-colored lights in every direction.

Thane didn't bother pushing through the crowd. He flew above it and landed on the stage.

The moment he was noticed, the music stopped.

Thane locked eyes with a confused Merrick. "Stay away from the girl."

The male frowned and moved away from the mic, coming closer. "You'll have to be more specific. What girl?"

"The human. *My* human."

The confusion intensified. "I have no idea who you're talking about."

As if he hadn't noticed Elin. Only a blind man would pass by her—but he would backtrack when he caught hint of her scent. "Go near her, and I'll give you more of this." Thane hammered a fist into the Sent One's jaw.

Merrick's head whipped to the side, and he stumbled. Straightening, he narrowed his gaze on Thane. The other band members abandoned their instruments to flank their friend.

"I'll let you have that one," Merrick said, rubbing his jaw, "because there's a good chance I slept with her and forgot her."

"You didn't."

"You sure? Because it happens. A lot."

"Do you *want* me to kill you?"

Merrick shrugged. "There are worse ways to go."

How did you frighten a man like that?

Frustrated, Thane left.

At the Downfall, he plucked the fullest, brightest roses from the garden and arranged them in a diamond vase; the action soothed him.

The next morning, he had the gifts delivered to the kitchen, where Elin was busy baking.

This time, he included a note. It read, *I've never believed everything that happens is meant to be. Fathers and husbands aren't meant to be murdered, and mothers aren't meant to die in front of their children. But I do believe something good can come from something bad. You, Elin. You are my good. Give me a chance, and I'll prove it.*

LATER THAT EVENING Thane and his boys flew to Rathbone Industries in New York. They were systematically checking off names from their part of Jamilla's list. So far they'd come up empty.

Number seven was Ty Rathbone. Once lauded for his calm under the worst kind of pressure, now known for his violent temper. The switch had happened in mere moments, his closest friends had stated.

Demons were definitely involved. But was it one of Germanus's killers or just some minion?

Thane's wings glided seamlessly through the night-darkened sky. Wind cut through his hair. He rolled to avoid a flock of birds, even though he would have ghosted through. He was still in the spirit realm, the birds in the natural. Spirit and flesh were not solid to each other.

Your time with the human didn't go well, I take it, Bjorn said inside his mind. *Judging by the sounds I heard—no, I didn't eavesdrop, but, yes, you should be quieter—I expected you to be in a much better mood.*

The male had recovered from his time with the shadow demons, at least. *We ended...poorly.* And she had yet to respond to his gifts.

He should have been relieved, he supposed. Elin was kindling and salve, and he despised both. One pushed him past the limits of his control. The other made him crave the things he'd never before wanted. Connection. Communion. A future.

He would have blamed Kendra's poison, would have claimed it was still at work inside him, pushing him toward the human, but he'd consumed more Frost, and the fire for Elin wasn't even close to banked.

She spurned you? Xerxes asked, incredulous.

No.

I don't understand. What's the problem?

She wants what I give everyone else.

Xerxes frowned. *Again I have to ask. What's the problem?*

I want to give her more, he admitted.

Shock registered. *Can you?*

His hands fisted. Maybe. For her—probably.

For the first time in his existence, he'd lost himself in the beauty of a kiss, in the decadent taste and carnal touch of the female in his arms. In the breathy sounds she made and the way her heart careened out of control. He'd had no need for pain. Not to arouse him, and certainly not to keep him aroused.

Had Elin lost herself in him, too?

Had he turned her on as spectacularly as the husband used to do?

Jealousy struck, as vicious as a demon. Every festering wound hidden inside Thane suddenly stung as though doused in acid.

I can relocate her, Bjorn said. *Your torment will end and she will—*

No, he shouted, baffled by his vehemence. More gently, he added, *No. She stays at the club.* He wanted her within reach. Protected and…coddled.

Had they been in their suite, his boys would have regarded him oddly, he knew. He wasn't the type to fight to keep a female around.

Let me find you someone else, Xerxes requested.

I wish it were that simple. Now that he'd tasted Elin's sweetness, the thought of other women actually repulsed him.

Bjorn brushed the tip of his wing over Thane's. *A woman is a woman is a woman. Close your eyes, and they're all the same.*

A callous assertion—one he would have concurred with in the past. But now? Now he knew differently. *Elin has something other women do not.*

Both males were intrigued.

And that is? Xerxes asked.

Thane smiled without humor. *My trust.*

Their destination loomed ahead, effectively ending the conversation. Good. He studied the building. The base was five stories tall, and the steel tower above it forty-two. He swooped low, bypassed the walls and entered the atrium. There were two guards behind the reception desk. A man with a briefcase strutted out the doors. A female click-clacked over the tiled floor and entered the glass elevators. As the cart lifted, it ran through a waterfall.

Pretty, but not what caught his attention. In a spirit realm the humans could not see, a horde of viha, envexa, and picǎ stalked the lobby. Demons of anger, envy and unforgiveness. None of them were one of the six who'd slain Germanus; they weren't powerful enough. But they might *belong* to one of the six.

Twelve demons in total, ranging in sizes and shapes. Two were over six feet tall, but most were stooped over, gorilla-like, using both hands and feet to move forward. A few had horns—ivory towers, they were sometimes called—protruding from their scalps. A few had black, gnarled wings stretching from their backs. Some were covered in a mix of fur and scales. Some had antlers growing from shoulders and spine.

So ugly. Soon, so dead.

A battle of blood and bone was exactly what Thane needed to improve his mood. Grinning coldly, he held out his hand and summoned his sword of fire. Bjorn and Xerxes did the same.

One of the demons noticed the intruding Sent Ones and laughed. Not a typical reaction. The others stopped what they were doing and searched the lobby for the reason for the amusement. More laughter rang out before clawed footsteps echoed, the creatures racing away.

"Laughter," Xerxes said through clenched teeth, as befuddled as Thane.

"No time to give chase and interrogate. We'll have to catch them on our way out." Thane flared his wings and flew up, up, up the many stories, taking note of the types of demons on each floor. Para and grzech here. Fear and sickness. Slecht there. Maliciousness. More viha, envexa and picǎ.

The higher up the building, the more powerful the demons became, until Thane was certain he was seeing what the creatures of the ever-dark referred to as their "high lords." These supposed lords were only one position below the princes, the most powerful of all.

For demons, a prince was the equivalent of what a member of the Elite Seven was to a Sent One. Like Zacharel.

Thane had never fought one. He and his boys were the equivalent of a high lord, and as it was, he'd battled only a handful of those.

He stood in front of the bank of elevators and swept his gaze through Mr. Rathbone's lobby. Spacious, screaming with wealth. Several of Monet's best hung on the walls. Crystal vases perched on metal tables. A white leather couch formed a C in the far corner. Bloodred carpet draped the rosewood flooring. There were no prowling demons up here. Why?

He forced his robe to conform to his body and separate into different pieces. When the fabric darkened,
he was wearing an exquisitely tailored pin-striped suit.
He stepped into the natural realm. In the spirit realm,
Bjorn and Xerxes remained at his side, unseen to the
untrained eye.

A young, pretty receptionist tore her gaze from the
document she was pretending to type, while wiping her
watery eyes and nose—she'd been crying—and faced
him. Her jaw dropped. "Um…uh, hi. I mean, hello, and
welcome to Rathbone Industries."

"I will see Mr. Rathbone now." His tone left no room
for argument.

She gulped. "Do you have an appointment, Mr.…?"

Wasting time. He stalked away from her without
a word.

She called out a frantic, "Stop. Please."

He reached the far corner and entered a hallway that
led to several different conference rooms. He could
sense it. Left offered more doors. The right dead-
ended in a large corner office with frosted glass walls.
That one. Evil pricked at the back of his neck.

He opened the door.

A male, no more than twenty-five, sat at an ornate
cherrywood desk. He had dark hair, every strand in
place, and slate-gray eyes. His skin was deeply tanned.
His elbows were propped on the desk, his fingers drumming together as he waited. He'd known Sent Ones
had arrived.

"I've been expecting you," he said with an elegant
wave to indicate the chairs. "Please, sit."

Thane's first thought: not possessed, but influenced.
Demons possessed humans by entering their bodies

and controlling their minds from within. A human was influenced if a demon attached itself to his side, whispering into his ear to direct decisions. And right now a demon stood behind Mr. Rathbone's chair. A demon unlike any Thane had ever seen. Seven feet tall, at least, with skin that rivaled the brilliance of the world's most perfect diamond. A fall of white hair reached his waist.

Though Thane had never seen such a creature, he knew what it was.

Zacharel, he projected to his leader. *I believe we found one of the demons responsible for our king's death. But there's a problem. He's a prince.*

Leave. Now, came the immediate, panicked reply. *I'm gathering the Elite Seven.*

Thane had counted over two hundred demons in the building.

The odds were not in their favor.

Leave? We need answers, Thane said.

We need you alive, Zacharel snapped.

Very well. He would leave…soon.

He wasn't afraid. He wasn't intimidated. He was eager.

The demon stroked long, lean fingers through the human's dark hair, and the human smiled slowly, coldly. "Took you long enough to find me. I worried no matter how many clues I left you, you would fail."

The demon's mouth never moved, but those had been his words. So. The human wasn't merely influenced, but controlled. How? When the demon still lived outside his body?

A talent of all princes?

"Don't pretend you wanted to be found," Bjorn said, not needing to enter the natural realm to be seen by the demon. "Kind of defeats the purpose of hiding out, don't you think?"

No reaction from the prince.

But the human said, "I left clues because I was curious to know the warriors who would be sent to capture me. Now I know. I've seen. And you've seen. A new battle can begin. But, Sent Ones…you are wrong. So very wrong. You think I've been hiding, but the truth is, I've been amassing an army."

"Demons lie," Xerxes snapped.

Sometimes, though, they added a bit of truth to their lies, to make it harder to find the light in the dark.

"Yes," the human continued. "We do, but even we are capable of the occasional truth."

"Truth you use to mislead."

"Believe me…or not. I hardly care."

"Then why don't you skip ahead and tell us why you're here?" Bjorn said.

An easy nod. "Too long you have policed the skies and the land, as if you own them. No longer. My kind is taking back its world, and its people."

If the demons took over, chaos and death would reign.

"Is that why you killed Germanus?" Thane demanded. "To start a new war? To take what you think is yours?"

This time, the human remained quiet.

This time, the demon smiled slowly. "No. We killed your Germanus for fun."

The voice was all kinds of evil. Dark and twisted, a thousand screams hidden in the words—in the lie. With demons, there was always a purpose.

Then the prince and human vanished.

The prince had flashed, Thane realized, taking the human with him. An ability he and his boys did not possess.

A second later, the entire building began to shake.

It was the only warning they had—before the entire structure collapsed around them.

CHAPTER ELEVEN

ELIN MARVELED. "It's…it's…" Almost as cool as finding the chocolates, novels and roses in her room this morning. And Thane's note…oh, sweet fancy, his note.

Last night, the man had kicked her out of his room. And yet, the very next day he'd sent her a note that said, *You are my good.* What was up with him? Did he like her or not?

Either way, she wanted it to stop…*never stop*…but, oh, every time he did something nice for her, she fell a little deeper under his spell…and her fear of discovery intensified.

"Dude," Bellorie said "You're gawking, and it's taking attention away from me. In case you haven't figured it out, attention is my crack."

"News flash. I figured that out at meeting one. But we're in the clouds, and it's like Rodeo Drive meets the Middle Ages, and I'm a little overwhelmed."

The sun shone brightly, but it wasn't too hot. The sky was a clear baby-blue, such a tranquil shade. Winged men, women and creatures flew this way and that. Along the cobbled streets, immortals of every race manned booths, hawking their wares, while a plethora of potential buyers ambled past.

"Upper Class Immortal 101, by Professor Hotcakes," Bellorie said. "There are three different levels in the heavens. Thane's club is perched at the edge of the third, the lowest, which is known for its hedonism. We are now a mile from the Downfall, at an outdoor shopping center with vendors selling everything from waffles-on-a-stick to rides on the backs of enslaved…whatever, take your pick. Clothes optional. You can have *anything* if the price is right."

The other girls had shopped yesterday, as planned, but the Harpy had waited for Elin to return from her "errand" for Thane.

Her lips burned as she remembered the kiss. Her breasts ached. Her skin tingled. Carnal heat pooled between her legs.

Even though they'd put an end to things—hadn't they? That note… She craved him more than ever.

Why hadn't he sought her out to talk about things?

"So, where do you want to start?" Bellorie asked.

Elin pulled her mind out of the depressing gutter. "Clothes. That's where I want to start *and* finish." No reason to spend her precious money on anything else. Except maybe that door handle. It was shaped and colored like in a human hand. *Très* cool. The bedroom she shared with the girls could use a little of her personality.

But what if it really was a human hand? *Avoid the knob!*

"Excellent choice." Bellorie nodded. "I'm eager to see you out of the classic hobo style you arrived in." She led Elin down the street, shouldering people out of the way without preamble.

The air thickened with perfumes and desserts and… meat pies? Her mouth watered.

"Changed my mind," Elin said, clutching her rumbling stomach. "Let's start and end with food. Clothes can have the middle."

"Very well. But we gotta get you loaded with cash first."

After selling one of her necklaces, she consumed three meat pies, which were better than anything she'd ever tasted, except Thane, then two chocolate cupcakes and four peanut butter scones—better than even Thane. Maybe.

"Where do you put it?" Bellorie asked, gaze raking over her minimal curves.

"I guess we'll find out." She hadn't eaten like that in...ever.

"By the way. What you're currently tasting? That's real food. Whatever you're making at the club is...not."

Hey! "I'm getting better."

"Bonka Donk, you're getting worse. This morning's brownies can be used in our next dodge-boulder game."

Elin sighed. Baking wasn't as much fun as she remembered. Maybe it was time to reevaluate her life goals.

What madness is this? Bay had dreamed of opening a bakery, and now she was going to kill it the way the Phoenix had killed him? No! She had to do it, in his memory. His honor.

Especially since she had already betrayed him with Thane.

Despair danced at the edge of her mind, but she pulled a Bellorie and gave it the finger. This day would not be spoiled!

With Bellorie at her side, she talked and laughed as she spent the rest of her "go wild" money on a new wardrobe. She bought a couple of pairs of jeans, a pair of leather pants—what?—a dozen pretty tops, a few summer dresses, workout tanks and shorts, lingerie, pajamas, boots, tennis shoes, high heels and a robe.

"Everything will be delivered to the club by the end of the day," Bellorie had told her earlier.

She had protested. "No, I—" Or rather, she'd tried to protest.

"Can't carry it, you don't have the biceps," the girl had interjected. "And I'm not going to help because I need my pimp-hands free."

But she hated the thought of letting the prized items out of her sight, even for a few hours. *Mine, all mine.*

"Come on," Bellorie said now, tugging her from Vladmir's Closet. "Axel told me he has a booth today, and I don't want to miss him."

"Axel?"

"You met him last night, at Thane's table. Dark hair, piercing blue eyes."

Most Beautiful, the male she'd threatened with arsenic. Great.

His booth was at the end of the street, white scarves acting as walls and dancing in a gentle breeze. He offered no clothes, no foods, no jewels or furniture. He sat in the center of the empty stall, leaning back in a chair, his hands folded over his middle, his legs outstretched, his wings spread.

He grinned when he spotted them, his entire face lighting up and, somehow, making him more beautiful. "Well, well. If it isn't my favorite Harpy and Thane's favorite human. We weren't properly introduced, lovely. You're Elin. I'm Axel. And, don't worry. I know how this works. I tell you my name, and you say nothing—

because you've fainted." He paused for several dramatic seconds, waiting.

She fought the urge to roll her eyes.

His grin grew wider. "So how'd it go last night with Mr. Won'tsharemytoys?"

I am a strong, confident woman and I won't blush. "What are you selling?" she asked, ignoring his question.

"Blow jobs," he replied without missing a beat, and she blinked in surprise.

Bellorie didn't fight her urge—she did roll her eyes. "What he means is, he's willing to let women suck him off if they pay him with new and exciting weaponry."

"And there isn't a line?" Elin asked drily.

Unoffended, he patted his lap. "Take a seat and I'll show you why I'm offering such an exceptional deal."

The wicked gleam in his eyes... Yeah, she'd been right to view him as a candidate. He clearly knew his way around a female body. But only one man tempted her to plow full steam ahead, and Axel wasn't him. "No, thanks."

He shrugged, not even a little bit disappointed. "Your loss."

"So, the reason we're here..." Bellorie prompted. "You wanted information about William the Ever Randy, aka the Panty Melter, and I heard something last night. A Fae came into the bar, said William's daughter, some girl named White, was murdered in his realm by a Phoenix named Petra."

Petra. Kendra's aunt. According to gossip at the bar, the girl was dead. Like, never-coming-back dead. Someone must have eaten her heart—which meant she'd actually had one. Surprise, surprise.

Axel jolted upright, the teasing light extinguished from his eyes. "I knew that. But what else did you hear?"

"William the Panty Melter and his sons, Red, Green and Black, disappeared immediately afterward. William was later seen with the Lords of the Underworld, but the boys haven't been seen or heard from since."

Elin had no idea what they were talking about, and strolled to the booth to the left. Her gaze traced over the items for sale—jewelry—only to land on a big, strong Sent One. Merrick, she realized, the lead singer of Shame Spiral. Dark hair shagged around a face that had to be the epitome of beauty. Long, dark lashes shadowed eyes of the most luminous silver.

His only imperfection was the big bruise marring his jaw. He must have been in a fight.

Perfect. He was a brawler. He could be a candidate again, since Thane might have gone from hot-and-cold to permanently cold.

Forgetting the note?

No. Still just majorly confused about it.

Merrick grinned when he spotted her, the slow bloom of welcome unbelievably sexy. "I *do* remember you," he said, confusing her. He closed in on her. "You're the human, and I did *not* sleep with you."

"Uh. Correct." He smelled good. Like, really good. Dark, romantic and spicy, as if he'd just stepped out of *Arabian Nights*. But for some reason he did nothing for her hormones.

"I never realized Thane was the possessive type."

"I don't understand," she replied, her heart rate increasing at the sound of his name.

Merrick's grin widened. "He warned me away."

"From what?"

"You."

"Me?" She thumped her chest to make sure they were talking about the same "you."

"I don't know what gave him the impression I planned to make a move—"

Her moan stopped him. She did. She knew. She'd mentioned Merrick's name to Thane.

Merrick's eyes twinkled. "But you do, I see."

"Yes, and I'm sorry. So sorry. What did he do to you?" *And why am I aroused by the thought that Thane went fists of thunder on another guy?*

"Merrick," a whining female voice called before Elin could finish her reply. "I miss you already."

Merrick took Elin's hand, his eyes gleaming with amusement as he kissed her knuckles. "Make Thane beg you for it. The hardest battles have the sweetest victories." Then he was off.

His words, though seemingly delivered with an ulterior motive—that amusement did not bode well— haunted her long after. Make Thane beg for her? Yes, please. No. Bad Elin. But...she wanted to be a prize worth winning.

Make up your mind already! You want him, you don't, you want him again.

In an effort to distract herself, she walked to the next booth. Thousands of pelts greeted her. Some were from animals she recognized...some she didn't.

Thane wanted her all to himself?

Ugh. Don't go there, either. She picked up the most beautiful, a black and white in a mesmerizing pattern, with a shimmery inlay. Soft. Warm, as if it were an electric blanket. The card attached said it was made from the hair of a unicorn and griffin hybrid.

But seriously, Thane wanted her all to himself?

The owner spotted her. A six-foot-three Amazonian warrior woman.

Elin had no plans to buy. Her money went toward necessities—like heels and leather pants—or into savings. End of story. She glanced away, hoping to avoid a sales pitch. Her gaze caught on a sight she'd hoped to never see again, and she cried out with dismay.

There was Ardeo, the king of the Phoenix. Though he looked far different than she remembered, his dark hair standing on end, his hazel eyes bloodshot, and his once full cheeks now gaunt. Beside him was Orson, the second-in-command of the Firebird army.

The two males stalked down the row of shops determinedly, menace in every step. They scanned every booth, obviously searching for something—or someone.

Thane?

Or Elin?

What if they told Thane her secret?

Sickness gave birth to panic, both burning her chest. Part of her wanted to palm her glass shard and go to town on Orson's face, something, anything to punish him for his part in her father's and Bay's deaths. Part of her knew that would merely create more problems.

Whatever proves necessary, my darling, do it. Survive. Do not allow my sacrifice to be in vain.

Decision made. Elin threw the rest of her money at the Amazon and said, "I'll take the blanket. If that's not enough, contact Thane at the Downfall and he'll pay." *I hope.*

As she raced to Axel's booth—*use him for protection—*

she pulled the pelt around her, covering her hair and shielding most of her face and body.

For you, Momma. But deep down, Elin was ashamed by her behavior. There had to be a better way to save herself. A way that wouldn't trample on her self-respect.

"—invite to the Lords, no problem," Bellorie was saying. "Uh, what are you doing, Bonka Donk?"

"Hide me," Elin commanded, suddenly clammy. The Phoenix could ruin her in several different ways. "Don't talk to the warriors, okay? Don't talk to them, and don't listen to them. Send them away. Okay? Yes?"

Bellorie frowned at her.

Axel maintained his casual pose.

Neither understood the danger level.

Elin dropped to the Sent One's side, as if she was his slave, and bowed her head. Perfect timing. Two sets of scuffed leather boots came into view. Her heart thundered against her ribs, continually coming into contact with the heat of the panic—a match about to light and torch her.

Perhaps she was more Phoenix than human after all.

"You are a Sent One." Orson's voice. Deep. Harsh. Rough.

Making her shudder. With fear...and rage. *Can't fight a dragon before you fight a lion and bear.*

"Is this State the Obvious day?" Axel asked, and he sounded genuinely curious. "If so, I want a turn. You're ugly, and ridiculously stupid."

The Phoenix warrior sucked in a breath. "Watch your tongue, winger, or you'll lose it."

It was common knowledge Sent Ones were allowed to kill demons, and no one else. Unless, of course, they were being held against their will. Right now, Axel wasn't being held against his will. He was at a major disadvantage.

"We're here for Thane. Do you know him?" Orson demanded.

Why wasn't Ardeo speaking? He was king.

And what did they want with Thane? The captives? Probably. So...maybe, if Elin stayed out of sight, she wouldn't be mentioned and her secret would stay safe.

"Bellorie, darling," Axel said, checking his cuticles. "They're boring me."

"My reward?" she asked, confusing Elin.

"Double."

"Deal."

A second later, before Elin could even track the girl's movements from beneath the blanket, Bellorie jabbed her hand through Orson's chest, grabbed his heart, and jerked it out. The organ beat twice more before stopping.

The warrior collapsed on the ground, dead.

Blood dripped from between Bellorie's fingers.

Blood...blood...blood sprayed from her father's head as it rolled. Blood dripped from Bay's broken body as it slumped over the table. Blood smeared her mother's thighs as she clutched her dead baby.

Ice doused the heat inside Elin. A scream brewed in the back of her throat, quickly escaping. Another followed close on its heels—then another. Maybe Ardeo saw her face. Maybe he didn't. She didn't care anymore. Couldn't stop screaming as the king of the Phoenix swooped up his second-in-command and raced away, most likely hoping to get him somewhere safe so that he could regenerate.

"Quiet," Axel commanded.

She tried to obey, she really did, but the screams just kept coming. Blood…a pool of red…the scent of it in the air…old pennies. Familiar. Wafting from the two men she loved more than life. Then from her mother and only sibling—her precious baby brother.

Strong arms banded around her and lifted her off the ground. Elin fought with every bit of her strength, swinging her arms, kicking her legs. Biting. Scratching. She would act like a warrior and battle to the death. Screw survival at any cost!

The arms released her, and she fell; she must have been higher up than she'd realized, because she lost her breath when she landed, angry pains tearing through her side. And still the screams emerged, though they were softer now, mere rasps of broken breath.

"What's wrong with her?" she thought she heard Bellorie ask.

"I don't know, but I've summoned Thane," Axel replied, his tone grim.

"He won't come for a bottom-level employee. He—"

"Is already here."

Suddenly blond curls and electric blues consumed Elin's line of vision. Thane's beautiful face was streaked by soot. There were vivid cuts on his forehead and cheek, but at least the purity of his scent replaced the old pennies, and the heat of his body chased away the chill of panic.

"Elin, look at me."

Struggling to breathe, she focused on the beauty of him rather than the injuries.

"You're safe now. I need you to calm."

Have to make him understand. "Help me get it off. Please, Thane. Help me get it off." She realized she was sprawled flat on her back in the middle of the street, and Thane was crouched beside her, his wings wrapped around her, shielding her from the curiosity of others.

"What do you need me to get off you, kulta?"

"The...the blood." *Even hate the word.* "Get it off."

"I see no blood."

"It's there. I know it is. And I need it off. Please." She gasped. The blood had even spread to him. His wings... they were red. Everything was red!

"Kulta."

Hot tears streaked down her cheeks as she sagged into a panting, boneless puddle. *"Please."*

"Did someone harm you?" he asked, his tone so quiet she barely heard him.

"Please."

Frowning, he tenderly cleaned her face with strokes of his thumb. "All right. I'll take you home, and wash you."

"Hate to break up the party," Axel said, "but two Phoenix warriors were here looking for you, my man. They were pretty upset."

Panic hit Elin. If Thane hunted Ardeo and Orson... if the three had a little chat...

Her secret would not be a secret anymore.

Elin began to fight.

Hatred and determination fought for dominance in Thane's expression, but still he cooed softly to her, reassuring her that he was there, that he wasn't going anywhere. When finally she calmed, he said to Axel, "Take Bellorie to Xerxes, and tell the warrior of the Phoenix." He scooped Elin into his arms, cradled her close to his chest, and shot straight into the air.

CHAPTER TWELVE

THANE COULDN'T BELIEVE the day he'd had. He and his boys had almost died in the building collapse. If not for the Water of Life, they would have. Within seconds of taking a sip of the healing agent, their broken bones had mended, torn muscles had woven back together, and dry veins had replenished.

Once healed, they'd pulled the humans from the rubble, and fed each a drop of the Water, as well, ensuring no lives were lost. Unfortunately, news stations were now blasting the story of the three odd-looking males who'd "preformed one of the world's greatest miracles."

He was a bundle of emotions. Relieved the humans survived. Guilty for not following orders and thereby leading to the blast, and discovery. After all, a mistake that turned out well did not make it any less of a mistake. He was even worried. What would happen next?

What would Zacharel say? Would his leader reprimand him? Or finally kick him out?

Just then, Thane cared.

Without his strength, his wings, how would he protect Elin?

Back at the club, he had gone in search of her, thinking he would keep her by his side for the rest of the day, just in case the prince decided to attack on his home turf.

Lying to yourself? No. But massaging the truth? Definitely.

The truth, without any massaging: he'd wanted Elin in his bed, naked. He'd wanted his hands on her. His mouth on her. He'd wanted to thrust inside her and hear her cry his name.

As the Rathbone building had collapsed around him, his only thought had been this: he couldn't leave this world without having Elin in every way.

Elin, who hated blood and didn't realize his soul was soaked in it.

Now, he carried her through his suite and into the bathroom, placing her on the toilet lid. He sent Xerxes a mental command.

Relocate Bellorie. I don't want her at the club.

She'd caused this.

Did you sleep with her? Xerxes demanded, his shock evident.

No. Her presence offends me.

There was no more need to discuss. *Very well.*

Elin was silent, her mind probably somewhere else. The past, most likely.

Moving as swiftly as possible, he locked the doors and drew a steaming bath. She offered no protest as he stripped her and looked her over, searching for injuries. Her skin was pallid in places and flushed in others, her freckles stark. But her beautiful breasts, topped by little pink nipples, and her stomach, flat and soft, and her legs, long and lithe, were all unmarred.

"Elin," he said softly.

Finally, movement. She wrapped her arms around her middle—to warm herself against the chill in the air, or to at last shield herself from his view?—and he saw the beginning of a bruise on her right side.

He hissed in a breath. Elin…in pain…

His hands fisted as something inside him broke. Or finally yanked out some of the weeds. He remembered Elin's screams, her voice laced with fear and broken at the edges. The sound hadn't aroused him; that was no surprise it hadn't at camp, either. But it *had* tormented him. He would have done anything to make it stop.

He remembered the way some of his lovers had looked at him over the years—as he had once looked at his demon captors. What would he do if Elin ever looked at him that way?

Die, he realized. Some part of him would die. His last shred of decency, perhaps. He would be no better than the monsters he fought.

Are you any better now?

The thought jolted him. He was. Now. Finally. Before, he'd been dead. Choked by those weeds. Now he could breathe. He lived.

He crouched in front of Elin and traced his knuckles over the discoloration on her ribs. "Why do you have this, kulta?"

She kept her gaze on the tiled floor, saying softly, "I don't know. I mean, I fought Axel when he tried to pick me up and I fell, and it hurt. Maybe then?"

Axel had not protected Thane's treasure. He and Axel needed to have a chat.

Thane picked Elin up and settled her in the hot water. He perched at the edge of the tub, wondering if he should bathe her or just allow her to soak.

"Join me," she beseeched.

The words were soft, barely audible. Even still, they caused his entire world to shift.

"No, kulta." He would make the bath sexual rather than comforting, and she was too vulnerable right now. "You are not in a good place right now. Your decisions aren't—"

Haunted smoked-glass eyes found him and pierced all the way to his soul. "Please. I don't want to be alone."

My female should not have to beg for anything. "All right." *So easily swayed.* After a moment's hesitation, he removed his robe, steeling himself against the excruciating rapture to come, and climbed in behind her. Liquid heat lapped at his skin as he drew her between his legs and settled her against his chest.

Careful. He adjusted her position, or rather, tried to, but no matter her angle, his erection pressed against some part of her. He shuddered, fighting the urge to rub against her. *Can't...resist...* He had the most exquisite view of her body. A long strand of midnight hair clung to her dampened skin, the end wrapping around her pearled nipple. Droplets of water clung to the flat plane of her stomach.

"I'll clean you now." *Remain detached.* He soaped her from neck to waist. At first, he managed to keep his mind on other things. The meeting with Zacharel tomorrow, concerning his actions at Rathbone Industries.

Would he receive another whipping?

That led to thoughts of tracking the demon prince and dishing out a whipping of his own. All the while Elin remained still and quiet, but she was also soft and sweet, her scent rivaling all distractions, and it wasn't long before the tether on his resistance frayed, then split and he accidentally-on-purpose grazed her nipple with his knuckles.

She gave no reaction.

End this. He poured warm liquid over her stomach, washing away the suds.

"All done," he rasped.

"Thank you," she replied, her tone somewhat automated.

It was clear her memories still plagued her. Despite his own poor condition, he couldn't leave her like this.

Massaging her shoulders, he asked gently, "Why do you hate blood, kulta?" in an effort to purge the past.

Quiet, hesitant, she said, "The Phoenix burst into my parents' home on my twentieth birthday. My husband and I were there for a celebration dinner. It was just the four of us. Momma grabbed me and threw me under the table, and I was such a coward I stayed there while Daddy and Bay... They jumped to their feet to protect their women. The warriors decapitated Daddy and stabbed Bay. His body fell over the table, and his blood, it rained all over me. I screamed so much I permanently damaged my vocal cords."

Her words painted a truly horrific image. Thane squeezed his eyes shut in an effort to blank his mind. His heart clenched. He ached for the girl she'd been. So young. So vulnerable.

So tragic.

"You aren't a coward, kulta."

"I am," she said, dropping a fist into the water. "Today, when I saw Ardeo and Orson, I hid beside Axel rather than attack."

"And you were wise to do so, not cowardly. You are a human without training. You—"

"Have training," she interjected. "I've just never had the courage to apply it."

A human learning to defend herself against other humans was hardly training for defending herself against the beings populating his world. "Would you hide if Ardeo and Orson burst into this bathroom?"

"No. I'd attack!"

"Then you are already a changed person. You learned from your mistakes."

"That's…right." The knots in Elin's muscles smoothed out, and she relaxed against him—while he grew tenser by the second.

He could have roared with triumph. He'd helped her.

And maybe that was why, despite the horror of their conversation, his shaft remained as hard as a steel pipe, throbbing, urging him to arch into her at last and stroke against her cleft.

"Thank you, Thane," she said, trembling.

"Welcome." Did she sense the direction of his thoughts? Or had she finally realized she had a fully aroused male at her back?

"So…how did you find me?"

He wouldn't mention his search for her. The way he'd torn the club apart, more desperate to see her by the second. Or that Chanel had said Bellorie took her shopping and he had been airborne mere seconds later.

Along the way, Axel had spoken inside his mind. *Your human won't stop screaming. What would you like me to do with her?*

Protect her. I'm almost there. Thane had quickened his pace.

"Axel summoned me," he finally said. "Sent Ones can communicate telepathically."

"Oh. That's cool," she said, shifting restlessly in the water, as if beseeching him…for more.

You're misreading. He gritted his teeth.

Then she moved again…and again, seeming to deliberately stoke his desire. Soon, *she* was rubbing against *him*.

Thane flattened his big hand on her stomach to stop her. Instead, he spread his fingers, covering as much ground as possible, and encouraged her to move faster. He'd fought for control. He'd failed.

She arched into his touch. "Thane."

The neediness in her tone…

He stroked his pinkie at the apex of her thighs, edging ever closer to her sweet spot, letting pulse after pulse of sizzling desire leave him and seep into her. She moaned.

"Neither one of us is thinking clearly right now," he said. "Now is the time to stop."

Her head rolled against his shoulder as she released another moan. "I don't want to stop." She paused. "Do you?"

"I don't just crave you, kulta—I'm literally *starved* for you." He pushed himself against her so she would have no cause to doubt his words. "I would rather die than stop."

She shivered, the water rippling. "Will you use whips and chains on me?" She reached up and behind, threading her fingers through his hair.

"No." Never. "All I need is you." He licked the shell of her ear.

"But—"

"No buts." He pinched her chin and forced her head to angle toward his. Her eyes were at half-mast, her lips already parted and ready for his possession. Triumph surged through him. "When we're together, it will be you and me. No one else. Nothing else. Agree."

"Thane—"

"Agree, kulta."

A torturous pause. Then, "I agree. For now."

For now was good enough.

Leaning down, he pressed his mouth against hers. She opened immediately, as if she couldn't help herself, and he took full advantage, thrusting his tongue against hers. He demanded. He consumed. He devoured. Never had a female intoxicated him more.

He would give her everything. *Do* everything with her, things he'd never done with another. He would touch and taste every inch of her, then let her touch and taste every inch of him.

They would never be the same.

His water-slick hands moved to her beautiful breasts and cupped, kneaded. The water had fever-flushed her skin. Or maybe the intense heat radiating from him had done it. His palms burned so hotly he feared he would scorch her, but as he rolled her nipples between his fingers, she moaned and arched her hips, her arousal unfettered.

"Can't get enough of you, kulta, and I think, perhaps, you can't get enough of me, either." He kissed and licked a path down her neck. "Am I right?"

"Yes." She tilted her head to give him better access. As he sucked on her hammering pulse, she dug her nails into his scalp. "The things you make me feel. It's like poetry."

Such beautiful praise… Pressure built, driving him to rub against her with more force. He hissed at the rightness of the sensation. "Tell me what you need." His voice was nothing more than a growl. "I will do it. Will do anything."

"You. Your fingers."

His greedy gaze tracked a path down the center of her stomach, and his hands soon followed. He'd been with hundreds of women. He'd bitten, scratched and whipped, but he'd never touched one the way he was about to touch Elin. He'd always used external devices.

"Open for me."

She obeyed, spreading her knees as far as they would go.

"Good girl." He curled his fingers around her mound and moaned. She was hot enough to burn him.

"Thane," she gasped. "Yes. Like that. But inside."

His name on her lips…a throaty wisp…

He parted her, dipped a finger into the tight, silken warmth of her, and felt her clench around him. Utter. Perfection. He nearly came. A hoarse cry left her as he pulled out…and sank back in…again and again.

"Move on me." As he spoke, he urged her backside into a rocking rhythm against his shaft. Up and down, creating a dangerous friction…*so insanely good*…propelling him closer and closer to the edge of no return. "That's the way, kulta," he gritted.

Water lapped over the tub's rim only to return and stroke over his sensitized skin. Water that had not cooled in the slightest. Water that had only heated.

"Yes." She reached up to knead her breasts, just as he had done.

It was too much…not enough. He should close his eyes and allow himself to calm, simply enjoy the feel of her inner walls clamping around his thrusting finger. But the sight of her…so erotic… He couldn't look away, and his need for satisfaction continued to climb.

He battled the urge to grab her by the hips, lift her, and slam her down on his erection. That was what he needed. Her, surrounding him. Her, dripping on him. But he felt like a virgin, completely inexperienced and unsure. This was still so new to him. Pleasure without pain—without even the desire for pain. Being lost in a woman: her scent, the little moans escaping the back of her throat, the way she writhed against him. He didn't just want to please her. He *had* to please her. It was a need as necessary as breathing.

"Tell me how much you like this," he demanded.

"So much."

Rejoicing, he fed her a second finger and began to work them in and out of her.

Faster and faster. Harder.

Panting, she arched to take him deeper. The heel of his palm pressed against the heart of her need, and she cried out, those wet, wet walls squeezing at him almost as tightly as a fist.

"More. Please, more."

The sight of her, the sounds she made, both pushed him past all reason. He couldn't wait a minute longer. Had to finish her. Him. Now. Just like this. With his fingers still nestled inside her, he slammed his hips forward, rubbing the long, hard length of his shaft against her. Then he did it again. And again. Hard and fast. And again. Again. All the while he worked her with his fingers and palm.

"It's so good, baby. I'm so close," she rasped.

Baby. An endearment. From a woman. For him. It was as new as the pleasure—and just as intoxicating.

"Come," he commanded. "Come now. Let me feel you. See you." He thrust harder, higher, the heel of his hand pressing against her.

"Thane!" she screamed, her inner walls clenching on him, her entire body bowing. A rush of liquid heat spilled over his fingers.

The knowledge that he'd brought her to climax— the sensation of it—sent him over the edge at last. He roared as sublime satisfaction slammed into him, and came against her back. Came more forcefully than he ever would have imagined possible.

When the last of his shudders stopped, he collapsed against the tub and realized he had Elin in a death grip. He loosened his hold and withdrew his fingers.

In the light, those fingers gleamed. His mouth watered, wanting to taste. He licked his lips…and then the fingers. His eyes closed, and his head fell back. So deliciously sweet. How had he lived without it? Without *her?*

"Maybe we should wash my brain while we're here," she said, her voice breathless. "My thoughts are still very, very dirty."

"You want more, kulta? I'll give you more." Gladly. He kissed the base of her neck and grinned. "Your skin is so hot, your freckles little infernos."

"Hot?" She stiffened. She jolted upright, severing contact. "Um, I think I've had enough for one day. I'm gonna take off, okay, and I'm going to borrow your robe." Before he could reply, she rose and stepped out of the tub. As she pulled the white material over her head, she said, "Everyone will see and know, won't they? It'll be my first walk of shame."

Shame.

She felt ashamed of him, of what they'd done. Even though he hadn't hurt her.

Ice rained over him. He'd loved every moment together, and she had, too. And yet, the moment her desire was slaked, she regretted.

"I'm sorry." Elin raced to the door, only to pause with her hand on the knob. "I, uh, had fun. Thanks."

Thanks?

Why not leave a wad of cash on the sink? The sentiment was the same. He scowled.

When she actually made to leave, without another word, he stopped her with a barked, "I don't want you to vacate the club grounds again, Elin."

She turned to peer at him, aghast. "I'm a prisoner, then?"

Her cheeks were still flushed from her climax. A climax *he* had given her. Wet hair stuck to her cheeks. He wanted to hate her.

He couldn't hate her.

"You are to be protected."

"Is everyone else to be similarly protected?" she demanded.

A muscle ticked under his eye. He couldn't lie. But then, he'd had centuries to learn how to get around stating an untruth. "All *humans* are." What she didn't know: she was the first and last human ever to grace his club. "My enemies are out there, hunting, and you could be used against me."

She looked away from him, fingers twisting over the center of the robe, lifting its hem, revealing her calves… and the water droplets still clinging to her skin. "What are you going to do about Ardeo?"

"That will depend on the king."

"Maybe you should avoid him—"

"Enough." He wouldn't discuss strategies of war with her. They would only frighten her. "You had your fun. Go." *Before I close the distance, carry you to my room and take you the rest of the way.*

Just like before, she scurried off.

CHAPTER THIRTEEN

ELIN STEPPED INTO the hall with her shoulders folded in and her head bowed. She wasn't embarrassed of her relationship with Thane, and she didn't want to act as if she was, but part of her expected Thane to holler out a command for his guards to kill her.

He'd remarked on the temperature of her skin. As smart as he was, it was only a matter of time before he realized one plus one equaled Phoenix.

The vampires at his door noticed her departure, but they didn't comment, or try to grab her.

As she turned a corner, both relieved to have escaped detection and saddened by the abrupt end to such a sweet encounter, Adrian stepped from the shadows to follow her.

She wanted to drill him about Thane. What did he know about the male and his previous lovers? How long had they worked together? But she held her tongue. She didn't deserve answers. The hurt in Thane's eyes as she'd dressed… He'd looked as if she'd stabbed him.

I hurt him, my closest friend, and I'm not sure how.

Closest friend. The words echoed in her mind. Yeah. He was, she realized. He always came to her rescue. He always listened to her stories about her past and wanted to know more. He cared about her well-being. Just like she cared about his. She trusted him.

Just not with her origins.

Ugh. What a mess.

Her new clothes had been delivered, at least. Multiple boxes were piled on and around her bed. Sighing, she changed into a tank and shorts as quickly as possible and tucked Thane's robe under her pillow. She wasn't in the mood to answer questions about what had just happened.

First, she had to get things straight in her head.

What was clear: she'd discarded her make-it-hurt-so-the-cravings-will-stop-and-the-guilt-will-ease plan. Hadn't even given it a thought. She'd offered herself to Thane without reservation. He'd accepted. They'd gotten down and dirty without actually having sex. It had been a-maz-ing.

But now, without the haze of pleasure driving her, the guilt was worse.

She hadn't waited for love this time. Hadn't made Thane wait for marriage the way she'd made Bay wait, and Bay had worshipped her. To Thane, she was just a passing fancy. If that. And then, to add insult to injury, Bay hadn't even been her first thought when she'd come down from her mind-blowing orgasm. He'd been third.

First, she'd been wishing for a second go-round.

Second, fear had come. The more excited the Sent One had made her, the hotter she'd grown. Literally. Nothing like that had ever happened to her before, but she'd known the reason for it. Her Phoenix side.

What would happen when Thane realized the truth about her? Would he hate her? Yes. Stake her? Maybe. Kick her out? Definitely.

And, until then, what about his sexual needs?

Needs change, he'd said, and maybe his had—for

the moment. But what about later on? Would he want to hurt her *for pleasure?*

She shuddered. After the miracle of tub time, she didn't want to deal with whips and chains. She didn't want to compare her time with Thane to her time with the Phoenix, whether the treatment would alleviate her guilt or not.

No matter what way I look at this, he's not good for me. I should just stay away from him.

Well, that wouldn't be a problem, she was sure. At this point, he wanted nothing to do with her, guaranteed. After she'd thanked him for the happy ending, the hurt had left his eyes, leaving them cold, blank. His lips had thinned, and the muscles in his jaw had tightened.

It was an expression he'd shown to Kendra—just before he'd killed her. *Did I make him feel like a discarded he-slut?*

Disheartened, she made her way to the gym for dodge-boulder practice. She couldn't afford to miss another one.

Last time, the girls had tried to drill into her head the fact that she needed to aim low whenever she threw a stone. *If* she ever threw one. Not so low the intended victim could jump up and avoid being smacked, but just low enough that the missile couldn't be caught.

"—he really did," Savy was saying as she stretched to the left, then the right.

"What the eff! You lie," Chanel replied, bending down to touch her toes.

"I'll give you my favorite shifter pelt if I am, and you'll give me yours if I'm not. Deal?" Savy spotted Elin and grinned slowly.

Chanel rubbed her hands together. "Deal," she said.

Then, noticing Elin, she added, "Settle a bet for us, Bonka. Thane flew into the city to get you while you were having a meltdown, then carried you away in his arms. Yes or no."

Cue the embarrassment. Cheeks heating, she said, "Yes. But—"

A grinning, whooping Savy fist-pumped the air, cutting her off, and Chanel cursed.

The bet was about her. Great. "He was only there because the Phoenix king showed up," Elin added with gritted teeth. "You know how much he hates the Phoenix." *Bitter finish, Vale. Check yourself before you wreck yourself.*

The girls shared a look loaded with mirth.

"Oh, that's why?" Chanel said, her tone sly. "So, when he got there, he didn't go straight to you? He hunted the Phoenix king and put a stake through his effing heart?"

"Well, no, but I was screaming and drawing all kinds of unwanted attention and he—"

"Knocked you out to make you quit it," Savy said, just as sly. "Like he would have done to anyone else. Like I've *seen* him do to others."

"No." *He tenderly cared for me, and gave me an earth-shattering orgasm.* "What are you guys trying to say?" And was that hope dripping from her words? Was she *trying* to drive them into saying Thane thought she was special?

What could she do if they did? He'd just kicked her out of his bathroom.

Yeah, and you'd just pulled a bang and bail, rushing to get away from him the moment you got your some-some.

Yeah. He'd felt like a discarded he-slut.

Shame and regret curdled in her stomach. Emotions that had nothing to do with Bay. She owed Thane an apology. Big-time.

"You are too effing adorable for words, Bonka Donk." Chanel said, patting her on the cheek. "No wonder Thane wants a slice of you."

Well, he'd already gotten a slice. Body and, it seemed, soul.

THANE, BJORN AND XERXES stalked to the roof of the club and in unison shot into the brilliant afternoon sky.

Thane's wings glided up and down with an ease he didn't feel. The farther he flew from the club—from Elin—the tenser he became. Soon he would have to let her go, and he knew it. The more time he spent with her, the more he would want her, need her, have to have her. But he couldn't have her. Even if she stripped and climbed into his lap, he would never forget her shame. And over what? A few kisses? A wanton touch? A climax that had—what? Delighted every cell in her body? Betrayed her husband?

That one, he thought, the muscles in his back jerking. If not fully, at least in part. She had loved the man so much, she had vowed to stay true to him. And she had— until Thane. What if her shame had been self-directed?

Hope proved stronger than hurt, shattering the icy wall he'd tried to build against her allure. He wanted to return to the club and talk to her. Wanted to comfort her, and take comfort from her. They both had reservations about a relationship, but if they tried, they could work through them.

Thane, Xerxes snapped inside his head.

He blinked, realized he hadn't made a turn, and backtracked.

Distracted? Bjorn asked, clearly trying not to laugh.

Yes, he gritted.

May I suggest knitting? Xerxes's tone was sly, teasing. *It's very relaxing.*

No reason to suggest it. I'm already knitting a nightshirt—for your mother. Even teasing, he tasted the foulness of a lie, but he didn't care.

Mother jokes? Bjorn tsked. *How low the sophisticated Thane has fallen.*

I think he needs to fall a bit more. Xerxes rolled above Thane, clipping his wing and sending him plummeting several hundred feet before he caught himself.

Thane came up grinning. If he hadn't seen his destination looming straight ahead, he would have played air chicken with his friend, something they hadn't done in years.

He arrowed toward the cloud of smoke wafting from the center of the woodlands just outside Αμαρτία City, where Elin had shopped and Bellorie had killed one of the Phoenix. Roughly two hours had passed since then, and the warrior was clearly in the process of regenerating.

Thane reached the crest of the smoke and descended. Seeing the Phoenix, he hovered in the sky alongside his friends, remaining in the spirit realm, unseen to all but Sent Ones, angels, demons and the rare immortal, watching as the slain warrior burned atop a stone altar. Two other males stood beside him, chanting. One of the chanters was Kendra's husband, Ricker.

He'll expect to have a chat with me.

Very well.

Ardeo, the king, knelt in front of a campfire, his head bowed as he tugged at his hair. He cried "Malta" at the top of his lungs, over and over again. His sorrow was as fresh today as it had been the day of her death several weeks ago.

Eight of his best fighters were armed and spread out around him, peering into the trees, watching for any threat.

Thane floated to the ground.

"Dead or alive?" Bjorn asked, doing the same.

"Alive if possible." For two reasons. He wouldn't risk another punishment from Zacharel, and he didn't want any of these men regenerating and strengthening.

Together, he, Xerxes and Bjorn stepped into the natural realm, going from invisible to seen in less than a second. The Phoenix guarding Ardeo noticed and reacted instantly, unsheathing swords and spinning to face them—then marching forward.

Thane tucked his wings into his back and reached into his air pocket to withdraw a pair of short swords. When the warriors reached him, he sprang into the air, twisted and struck two from behind as they raced past the spot he'd just vacated. Both males tumbled to the grass face-first—each missing an arm. Twin howls of pain erupted.

Xerxes stood in place, letting his opponents come to him. He bent. He ducked. He swung. He kicked. He remained in a constant state of motion, delivering more hits than he received.

Bjorn zigzagged through the air, attacking and retreating.

Two of the bigger males struck Thane from behind, hacking at his wings. Hissing, Thane turned and swung his weapons in a wide arc. The tips sliced through skin and muscle, but not bone. The males had jumped back, avoiding more serious injuries. And when Thane swung a second time, both were ready and parried. Metal clanged against metal.

Ricker the War Ender shoved the pair out of the way. "I want my wife!" he roared, spittle spraying from his mouth. He raised his sword.

"Even though she preferred me?" Thane asked, genuinely curious.

Teeth bared, Ricker lunged at him. Thane shot into the air, then dropped behind the male and swung his sword. But the War Ender knew what he was about and spun, meeting Thane's blade. *Clang.*

He swung high. *Clang.*

He swung low. *Clang.*

He went low again. *Clang.*

Grinding his teeth, Thane slashed one of his swords toward Ricker's left, and as the warrior parried, sending the weapon flying, Thane stabbed at his right side with the other. Metal finally encountered flesh.

Ricker didn't react as expected. He pressed deeper into the blade. The tip slid from belly to back, allowing him to draw closer and closer to Thane. When they were chest to chest, Ricker raised a sword. With his free hand, Thane grabbed his wrist, stopping a strike. But Ricker raised his other sword, and this time Thane couldn't stop him. The blade sliced through his shoulder.

Pain. Pain he did not welcome.

For Elin, he had to stay strong.

"You think you have me?" Thane released Ricker's wrist, reached inside the air pocket and withdrew a dagger. He pushed the tip against the male's voice box, drawing a bead of blood. "You think wrong. I can do this all day."

"As can I." Ricker unsheathed a dagger from his waist and rested the cold steel against Thane's throat.

"Enough," Ardeo shouted. "Enough."

Ricker grunted with disapproval. "But, my king—"

"I said enough! He could have ended my people, but he didn't. I won't have him killed."

Hate blazed in Ricker's dark eyes as he jerked the sword out of Thane's shoulder. He backed away, Thane's blood-soaked weapon sliding out of his belly. Finally free, he bowed low to Ardeo, saying, "My apologies, Great King."

Bjorn and Xerxes stepped over the bodies of the men they'd fought, men now writhing in pain, to flank Thane's sides. They were, and always would be, united.

"You were looking for me," Thane said to Ardeo. "Here I am."

The king stood and stumbled over. He'd been drinking. The smell of liquor seeped from his pores. His eyes were fogged over and bloodshot, and his leathers were torn and stained with blood.

"My men want their precious women," the king said, his voice a slur and a sneer all at once.

Thane thought for a moment. As much as he desired eternal revenge against the entire Firebird clan—did he? Still?—he had a new enemy to contend with, and the prince would require all of his skill and attention.

Perhaps it was time to clear some more weeds.

"I will relinquish your women, and even your males," he said. "All but Kendra. Her, I keep." He no longer wanted to torture her eternally, he realized with no small measure of surprise, but he wasn't ready to give her up, either. "In return, you will leave the heavens and never return."

"My king," Ricker said, affronted. "Kendra is more than my wife. She is your consort's niece. Surely that means something to—"

"My concubine is dead, killed by her own family. The rest of them can rot," Ardeo spat. "Besides, your wife was poisoning you. You would have become her slave if I hadn't forced you to leave the camp with me. You would do well to send Thane a fruit basket in thanks for his part in your liberation."

Ricker nodded stiffly, but his eyes threw a new dagger of hatred at Thane.

Message received. This wasn't the end.

Ardeo looked to Thane. "Your terms are acceptable."

He tasted no lie.

"You must give us the halfling, as well." Orson, the one Bellorie had killed, tugged on a pair of pants as he closed the distance, his regeneration complete. A dark, twisted look had marred his face as he'd made the demand—one Thane knew well. He'd seen it in the mirrored walls of the Downfall, every time he'd gone in search of a lover.

"Halfling?" Thane asked.

"A female named Elin."

Elin. Thane's Elin. Rage clawed at him. *The warrior wants her. He wants what's mine.*

He dies.

Thane held out his hand to summon a sword of fire. Then the warrior's words penetrated the haze of jealousy, and his arm fell to his side.

Elin was a halfling? Half human, half...what? Phoenix? Captured because she was considered an abomination, never permitted to procreate—a practice the Phoenix were known for.

No. *No!* She was not a tricky, conniving Phoenix, able to enslave every male she bedded—able to enslave *him*.

But what if she was...

Emotion welled inside him. More rage. Disgust, sorrow and, worst of all, bone-crushing fear. If she was Phoenix, he would never again be able to touch her. Never again *see* her. She would no longer be welcomed in his club.

He would lose the sweetest part of his life.

Abruptly, the sorrow overshadowed all else, even the fear. He could feel a roar brewing at the back of his throat. Not knowing what else to do, he stepped into the spirit realm, where the Phoenix couldn't see or hear him, threw his head back and let the sound loose. His entire body shook with the force.

When he quieted, several rays of light managed to penetrate the darkness of his reaction. Elin screamed at the sight of blood. She baked terrible cakes, and enjoyed digging in the dirt. She laughed. She teased. She was nothing like Kendra and her fire-witch friends.

Thane began to calm.

Elin might be a halfling, but she certainly wasn't Phoenix. Her people were probably at war with the Phoenix. Yes. That fit. For all he knew, she was part banshee. That scream...

Completely reassured, he returned to the natural realm.

The Phoenix were in the process of demanding Xerxes and Bjorn go get him, wherever he'd gone, and his friends were in the process of standing still and quiet, arms crossed over their chests.

He wanted to rapid-fire different questions about Elin but didn't. Revealing vulnerability was foolish.

"The girl," Orson barked, jumping back into the conversation.

"Trust me. You don't want to travel that road," Bjorn told him.

"The only fork you'll come to," Xerxes added, "is the one leading to Pain and Destruction."

Orson ignored the males, saying, "Do you have her or not?"

Thane once again held out his hand, and this time, a sword of fire formed. The flames crackled menacingly. "With your words, you negate our deal. Therefore, I will offer you a new one. After I discover what each of your people did to my human—" *my halfling* "—I will mete out proper punishments. *Then* you may have your people back. If they regenerate."

"Dirty winger!" Orson spat.

"Let it be known," Thane said with absolutely zero inflection. Only cold, hard truth. "Hurt what's mine, touch what's mine, even desire what's mine, and suffer."

For a moment, Ardeo's eyes cleared of the fog. He peered at Thane with newfound respect. And envy.

"Very well," the king of the Phoenix said, giving up the battle to remain on his feet and plopping to the ground. "Your human was kind to me. Kind to my precious Malta. She is yours to do with as you please." His shoulders slumped. "As Malta was once mine."

The liquor wasn't ruining him, Thane realized—it was merely a symptom. The true culprit was grief. The man had finally gotten Malta in his bed—but she was killed a few days later. He'd tasted heaven, and then he'd lost it.

"Until we meet again." With a last warning look at the seething Orson, Thane flared his wings and returned to the sky.

Remove the prisoners from the stakes, and lock them in the cells, he projected. He would have liked to do it himself, but the time to face Zacharel for his part in the destruction of the Rathbone building had come. *I have an errand. I shouldn't be gone long.*

Bjorn and Xerxes didn't know about the meeting or what would be done to him, and that was the way he would keep it.

Consider it done, Xerxes said.

You don't have to worry— Bjorn stopped, hovering in the middle of a sun-drenched cloud. Thane and Xerxes had to backtrack. The warrior's face was pained. *I must go.* He glanced over his shoulder. *She's—* He pressed his lips together.

She? Thane looked but saw no evidence of…what? The shadow demons? Or had his friend been summoned by their queen?

I'm sorry, but I can say no more without breaking my vow. Bjorn, his features tormented, vanished.

Thane bit his tongue until he tasted blood. *The Lord of the Underworld, Lucien, has the ability to follow a person's spiritual trail,* he said to Xerxes. *After my errand, I'll hire him to follow Bjorn.*

Good plan.

Lucien was the keeper of the demon of Death, responsible for escorting certain souls to the hereafter. He was a good man. Honest. Honorable. Rules mattered to him.

"I'll see you soon." Thane branched to the right.

Xerxes called out, stopping him. "What about the girl?"

"She is to be protected at all costs." When he returned, he would talk to her. She would assure him of her ancestry.

All would be well.

CHAPTER FOURTEEN

ANOTHER WHIPPING, YES. That was what Thane expected. Or, finally, the end of his immortality. He would have begged for another change. Instead, when he came to rest at the edge of Zacharel's cloud, the leader of the Army of Disgrace was waiting for him. He cupped the back of Thane's neck and pressed their foreheads together, the wind blustering around them.

"You could have killed hundreds of humans," the Elite soldier said.

"I know. The prince—"

"Acted because you did not heed my order."

He gave a stiff nod. "I know that, too. I regret my actions."

Surprise whisked through eyes so green they could have been mistaken for emeralds. "Do you?"

"Yes." Arrogance had cost him a much-desired victory. Maybe more.

"I hope so. Because every decision you make affects more than your life," Zacharel said, black hair brushing his cheek. "It affects the lives of those who love and depend on you."

The words struck a very sensitive chord inside Thane. He knew his actions affected the lives of his loved ones. He'd chosen to stay at the building, and Bjorn and Xerxes almost died. Elin almost lost her protector. His club almost fell under new management. Immortals from all over the world would have made a bid for it.

"I have a new assignment for you," Zacharel said, and Thane realized with startling clarity that he would not be receiving punishment.

"Have you nothing more to say about Rathbone?" he demanded.

"No. You endangered lives, but you also saved them. Now, listen."

Dazed, he nodded. In that moment, he felt…loved by his leader. Accepted.

It was humbling.

"It's imperative that we diminish the prince's growing army." Determination pulsed from the warrior. "One of his many hordes has been found in New York. I'll send you the coordinates when you reach land."

He flexed his fingers with anticipation. "How was the horde found?"

"Maleah."

Maleah. Of course. A fallen Sent One. She monitored the world and its happenings, never resting. Once, she had been one of the most beloved members of the heavenly armies. Now she was determined to help the people she'd let down when she gave up her wings— for whatever reason. Speculation was rampant, but facts were few and far between.

Once, Thane had lusted for her. Now, he mentally placed the pale-haired gothic beauty next to the dark-haired, delicate Elin. There was no contest.

"Take the soldiers you need and kill the demons," Zacharel instructed. "Kill them all. Leave no minion standing."

Very well. No mercy. A policy he still excelled at.

Thane nodded, anticipation already slithering through him. "And if we come across the prince?" he asked.

"Summon me."

"All will be done as you have said." Unfortunately, his meeting with Lucien would have to wait.

As he dived from the cloud, he communicated with Magnus, Malcolm, Jamilla and Axel all at once, commanding their presence on the roof of another building owned by Rathbone Industries in Times Square. Now.

Zacharel gave him the coordinates he would need as he landed. Thane tucked his wings into his back and peered down at the colorful human world. The streets were crowded. Neon lights flashed. The atmosphere was thick with scents of food, perfume and exhaust. Voices chattered; cars honked. Some footsteps click-clacked. Some thumped.

He heard the warriors arrive behind him. He turned, told them what Zacharel had said and where they were going. The same anticipation he felt was mirrored in their expressions.

"I want one demon left alive," he announced. "Doesn't matter which one." Post-battle interrogations were always fun.

Nods of agreement met his words.

"Let's do this thing!" Axel said with a whoop.

In unison, the group leaped from the building and arrowed toward the ground below. Because the warriors were in the spirit realm, their bodies were like mist as they bypassed the road, the subway system, and entered a labyrinth of dark, dank, forgotten tunnels.

At the bottom, Thane solidified his body and palmed a sword of fire. The others did the same, and the flames acted as torches, casting golden light in every direction. The smell of sulfur stung his nostrils. Cackles echoed up ahead, but it was impossible to tell where they originated. The blood-splattered walls provided too many options.

Thane held up his free hand and signed the direction he wanted each warrior to go. The group split up, everyone snaking their assigned corner.

Alert, on guard, he raced forward, using his wings to propel him faster and faster despite the tight, cramped space. The voices grew louder. He heard humans now. Whimpering. Pleas for mercy that would never come. He gave up following the man-made tunnels and ghosted through the walls, the vibration of the sounds guiding his feet. But he took a wrong turn and ended up in an empty room.

Scowling, he tried again.

And again.

And again.

Finally, he cleared the mud and concrete and entered—

A hell on earth. A scene from his deepest nightmares.

At least thirty demons of every type congregated in a large room with crumbling stone walls, dilapidated wooden columns, and a floor swimming with dark, congealing blood.

Six humans were chained throughout. Two females, three males. One child. Thane's stomach twisted. He sent his warriors a mental map of his location.

He didn't understand this. The prince's demons were supposed to do anything necessary to possess certain humans. This went far beyond possession—it went far beyond depravity. Some of the creatures lounged in the blood, lapping at it. Some still tormented the humans, clawing at bits of exposed flesh and laughing.

Thane's sword illuminated every wicked act, and one by one the demons noticed and faced him. Maniacal glee gave way to fear in every glowing red eye as the Sent Ones entered and closed off every possible exit.

That was all he'd been waiting for.

"Now!" Thane shouted.

Chaos erupted.

The Sent Ones jolted into action, swords swinging with lethal purpose. The demons with wings tried to fly away, but Thane and Axel were having none of that and clipped the appendages before a single creature could leave the den of horrors.

Heads began to roll across the floor. Arms no longer attached to bodies flew through the chamber. Howls of pain rang out. Thane remained in constant motion, happily slicing, slicing, slicing at his enemy. No one could escape him.

"Someone do me a solid and try to make this difficult for me," Axel quipped. "Or am I just too good? Yeah. That one. I'm so good *I* couldn't beat me."

Magnus and Malcolm played hack and sack with a serp demon, punting the snakelike creature at each other—but only after removing another appendage each time. Soon, there was nothing left to punt.

Jamilla pinned an envexa to the ground and plucked out his eyes…then cut out his tongue…then ripped out his throat.

Thane stabbed a viha through the chest and moved toward his next target. Only there was a problem. There was only one demon left standing, and Axel was about to remove his head.

"Stop," Thane said, and surprisingly enough, the Sent One complied.

Thane stepped past him and backed the demon into a corner. It was one of the larger ones, with gnarled antlers extending from a misshapen head. Red skin matched its eyes—eyes nearly overshadowed by the protruding bones of its brow. It had no nose, merely holes for breathing. Its lips were thin, revealing teeth big and sharp enough to rival a great white.

A menacing snarl rose from it.

Thane smiled his coldest smile, then said to his warriors, "Take the humans to a safe place. Get them medical help, and assign a Joy Bringer to attend to each." Otherwise, the humans would crack, never be able to mentally heal. "I'll take care of the creature."

Again, he was met with obedience.

"Now...your turn. Allow me to help you shed a few pounds," Thane said, and promptly removed the demon's arms and legs, making it impossible for the creature to get away. Then he hauled his bounty to the Downfall's dungeon.

"Where's Adrian?" he asked the guards waiting in the doorway.

"Xerxes has him following the human girl."

Good.

As Thane marched down the corridors, the undernourished Phoenix trapped in the cells were too weak to do anything more than look at him and moan. When he reached the center alcove, he pinned the demon to the wall, directly across from Kendra. Once again she had a place of honor.

She had more energy than the others and hissed like an angry cat. "Release me, Thane. Now."

Still so high and mighty. Despite his newfound clarity and remorse, rage surfaced. He turned and gave her the cold smile he'd given the demon.

She trembled and pressed her lips together.

"Pay attention, Kendra, because you might be next." He pulled a dagger from the air pocket. The metal was already stained with blood. He faced the demon. "I don't know if you've heard, but I'm *very* good with knives... and my interrogations never stop until I have what I want."

ELIN HEARD THE newest round of agonized screams and flinched. How long had this been going on? She'd lost track several hours ago.

After practice—where, big shocker, Bonka Donk was declared an abject failure at the fine art of boulder tossing—Savy, Chanel and Octavia tried to distract her from the noise with a game of favor-poker. Boons were the currency, and Elin had lost every round. But the only boon the girls desired from her was to never again have to sample her desserts.

After that, they'd switched to strip poker, and even though she was down to her new bra and panties and highly embarrassed, she still wasn't distracted.

Apparently, Thane was in the dungeon "going native on a demon's ass."

"I'm done," she said, throwing her cards on the table.

Her announcement was met with boos from all three women. And more screams.

"Done? You can't be effing done."

"We just got started!"

"Are you seriously pussing out?"

Ignoring their questions, she asked one of her own. "Where's Bellorie?" She hadn't seen the girl since—

Never mind.

Chanel frowned. "You mean you don't know?"

Her stomach clenched. "Know what?"

"Thane banished her."

"What?" she gasped.

Octavia nodded. "It's true, petal. Axel brought her to the club. Xerxes told her she'd showed off her hodad and had to go. He watched as she packed her bags, then escorted her from the building. That's the *I done been exiled, ya'll* routine."

Just like that? "Okay, let's back up a little. What's a hodad?"

"Hands of death and destruction," Octavia explained.

But...Thane showed off his hodad every danged day. Why blame Bellorie for a single indiscretion?

Elin still wasn't a fan of violence and had trouble meshing the Bellorie she adored with the Bellorie who'd callously reached inside a man's chest to perform a heart amputation, but that didn't mean she was going to let this banishment thing happen without a fight.

Years ago, her father gave her sage advice. *Sometimes emotional terrain is too mountainous to run, Linnie, my girl. Sometimes you just have to walk it.*

In other words. Baby steps.

Step one. She would stop avoiding Thane. Step two. She would begin a new round of interaction with him. Step three. She would nag him until he returned Bellorie to the club.

"I'm going to talk to him," she said, standing and tugging on a fresh set of clothes. A pretty pink tee and a pair of hip-hugger jeans. She didn't bother with shoes.

"Uh, I wouldn't do that if I were you," Savy said. "*You'll* end up banished. Or worse. No one questions Thane when an order has been given. Not even his... whatever you are."

"Pet human," Octavia offered. Helpful, as always.

Chanel snorted. "I don't know how it happened, the lion and the lamb, but I think she's more than that." Her head tilted to the side as she pondered. "And I think he'll make an exception and do whatever she asks. He *did* rush to her side when there was nothing effing wrong with her."

"Excuse me," Elin huffed. "I was screaming, and practically catatonic."

"Maybe he rushed to her side because he needs her for some type of ransom." Savy spoke over her, drumming her nails against the table. "Or some kind of revenge against the Phoenix. Or, maybe he experienced a moment of insanity. Did you ever think of that? No offense," she said to Elin. "He just isn't the type to chase a woman. No matter how awelicious she is."

How could Elin take offense when she suddenly had the same suspicion? Why *did* he want her? Wait. She had to rephrase. Why did he *used to* want her?

"Maybe he's just a nicer guy than any of us realized," she muttered.

Of course, that was when the demon issued another blood-curdling scream.

Chanel and Octavia giggled like naughty schoolgirls.

"Care to make another wager?" Chanel asked Savy. "Double or nothing."

"Know when to hold 'em, know when to fold 'em." Elin strode out of the room. Adrian stood sentry just outside the door and quickly swept up beside her.

"Where are you headed, human?" he asked.

He made it sound like her humanity was a crime. Well, it wasn't. Just ask Thane. To him, it was the only thing that wasn't, and for once, she was going to use it to her advantage. She was going to stop worrying about being found out, and start taking charge of her life.

"I want to go to the dungeon. Be a dear and show me the way," she said, blinking her eyes in what she hoped was an innocent, flirtatious manner.

He tensed. He frowned. He shook his head. "No. Go back to your room."

She put her hands on her hips. "I heard Xerxes tell you to take me anywhere I asked. And I just asked to go to the dungeon."

"We both know he didn't actually mean you could go *anywhere.*"

"No, we both don't know that. He doesn't strike me as the type to say something he doesn't mean."

Adrian glared at her.

"So, what are we waiting for?" she insisted.

His glare darkened. "Perhaps it will do you some good to see the nature of the male you provoke." He led her into an elevator and pressed a series of buttons. Blue lights flashed over a small portion of the wall. The doors closed and the cart shook, carrying them down... down...down, before opening into an underground cavern with gray walls and a cracked stone floor.

Two vampires guarded an open doorway.

Unease pricked the back of Elin's neck. The screams were far louder here, and they echoed. Worse, a familiar scent of old pennies clung to her nose and sickened her stomach.

"Wait here," Adrian told her before motoring on, by-passing the guards.

The vamps gave her a once-over…no, make that a twice-over…and she pretended not to know they were sharpening mental forks and knives. She stared straight ahead. She could see bars, indicating a hallway of cells. She could even see fingers curled around some of the bars. The Phoenix were here? Xerxes had freed them from their stakes and escorted them inside, but she'd kind of thought it was for medical care or something.

Only an idiot wouldn't have realized it was for further torture.

"My lord," she heard Adrian say. "The human wishes to speak with you."

"The human has a name," she muttered.

"Tell her I'll summon her when I'm finished here."

She heard *pleasure* in Thane's voice. For her…or the job he was doing? Either way, the low cadence of his tone made her shiver.

"Very well," Adrian said. Footsteps resounded.

Oh, no. The last time she'd been forced to wait for Thane, nothing had been settled. "Thane Downfall," she called.

Tension crackled in the air. The footsteps retreated.

"She's here? You actually brought her down here?" Thane demanded, even as Kendra cried, "Help me, girl. You have to help me."

"Sure," Elin responded. "Here's a tip. Be nice to people, no matter how low their station. You never know when they'll be in charge of yours." Not that she was in any way in charge. Still. Truth was truth.

"You should have known better," Thane growled, and she figured he was talking to Adrian.

Was Thane going to punish him, too? She tried to step forward, intending to go in, but the vampires moved in her path.

"He did nothing wrong," she said, speaking past the shoulders of the vampires now watching her with unabashed awe. "Your dearest friend Xerxes told him to take me wherever I asked to go. So, here we are. Now, listen. I want Bellorie brought back immediately. We need her for the Multiple Scorgasms." And heck, as long as she was making demands... "And I want the screaming to stop. It's screwing with my nerves."

Like you have any right to make demands.

"Please," she added, and slapped her hands together in the center of her chest in a classic begging stance, even though he couldn't see her. "With an extra sweet cherry on top."

Another pause.

"Bellorie shall return before the next shift," Thane said tightly, "and screams will not be heard again."

"Thank you, thank you, a thousand times thank you, Thane! Seriously!"

"Help," Kendra shouted.

A rustle of clothing. A grunt. A gurgle. Then muttering voices, too hushed to decipher.

A cold sweat broke out over Elin's skin, and she trembled. What had just happened?

Adrian stalked past the guards. His facial features were expressionless and cold. He didn't glance in her direction as he spat a single word at the vampires. A word she didn't understand.

She made to follow him, but one of the guards grabbed her by the wrist, halting her.

She tried to jerk away, but he held steady.

"Release her, or lose the hand," a harsh voice whipped out, and the vise grip instantly fell away.

Elin's gaze returned to the cells—and collided with Thane's.

CHAPTER FIFTEEN

THANE STRUGGLED TO rein in his temper. At any moment, Elin could race around a corner and witness the horror of his actions. If she saw that side of him…if she screamed…

He burned the demon and all of its severed parts, destroying the evidence. He'd gotten the answers he'd sought anyway. He now knew the prince was a fallen angel named Malice, once a soldier in the Most High's army. Unlike demons—spirits that inhabited the earth long before humans—the prince had a corporal body, and therefore couldn't possess someone else's.

When Sent Ones fell, they lost all power. The same held true for the angels, but they could gain power through acts of evil and spiritual theft, basically siphoning it from others.

Like any living being, the prince had weaknesses. However, Thane had yet to learn what they were.

Pride?

Hatred?

Malice's endgame? The destruction of mankind. Both to punish the Most High for banishing the fallen angels from the highest level of heaven, and to try to steal all the power he felt he'd been denied.

To start, Malice and his five cohorts had struck at

Germanus—ripping out the root—but there would be others.

Malice's next move? Unknown.

When Kendra continued her pleas for help, Thane took a page from Jamilla's book of attack and removed the girl's tongue. There was no way he would let her receive aid from the very girl she'd beaten and scarred, and as soft as Elin's heart was, she might very well ask him to release her.

He might very well say yes.

Now, guilt was heavy on his shoulders. "I'm willing to look past the surface to the reasons, and fully accept my share of the blame for the horrors of our relationship, but I will not tolerate bad behavior."

Her narrowed gaze sizzled at him, even as blood leaked from the corners of her mouth.

"Do not speak to my human again," he told her.

After sending Adrian to find Bellorie, Thane stepped out to see Elin. Only to watch a guard grip her fragile wrist.

No one touched her but Thane. Anyone tried...they died.

When did you become so possessive of a female?
When I encountered this one, apparently.

He met her smoked-glass gaze and remembered Orson's use of the word *halfling. Please, don't be Phoenix.*

He closed the distance. Perhaps he should send her away for a few hours. He was always seething with intensity after battle or torture, and he'd just come from both. If he went about this next encounter the wrong way, he would scare her. But she lifted her chin with brave determination, surprising him, and a deep sexual awareness cut through his fury and fear.

He couldn't send her away.

For a moment, he saw her as she'd been in the tub. Naked. Flushed with heat and arousal, nipples turgid, stomach quivering, legs parted for his fingers. Even now his shaft readied for her, growing long, thick and hard.

Not yet.

A tremor rocked her, as if her body reacted to his of its own accord.

"Are you cold?" he asked, just in case. "I will have a robe fetched for you—"

"I'm not cold."

Did she hunger for his touch? His taste? He would give anything to know.

"I'm, uh, sorry I interrupted your murder session." She reached for him but balled her hand just before contact and dropped her arm to her side. "You, uh, seem to really be enjoying it." Her gaze landed on the bulge between his legs, before darting away.

He clenched his jaw. "I didn't enjoy it the way you're thinking."

"Hey, no judgment," she said, palms out in a gesture of innocence.

"Elin. I'm aroused, yes, but it's for you."

Her eyes widened, some of the smoke replaced by crackling flames. "Oh."

That was all he got?

"Yes. Well." She cleared her throat. "Do you have to torture the Phoenix? Can't you let them go?"

"I wasn't torturing a Phoenix," he said. "But I will. Soon. An eye for an eye—"

"Puts you in a never-ending cycle of violence, yes," she interjected. "They'll retaliate, then you'll retaliate again, and so on and so forth." She sighed. "Look, I know I didn't have any right—"

"You have every right," he said, and knew he'd just shocked the listening vampires. But it was true. Why deny it? Things were different with Elin. Things had always been different. He liked that she'd sought him out, expecting him to fix her problems. He even liked the scolding she'd just given him—maybe because she was right.

She nibbled on her bottom lip, as though unsure. Of his reaction? As if he would harm her? "Really?"

He nodded. Then, with his eyes still locked on Elin, he snapped, "Leave us" at the vampires.

The pair rushed to the elevator without delay, disappearing behind the doors. He wouldn't take Elin to his suite until she felt safe with him. Because, when he got her alone—anywhere other than here—he would pounce on her. He knew it.

"I don't know if I'll ever get used to this world," she remarked.

As if he would allow her to leave it. "You will." A command he expected to be obeyed.

She shrugged. "Does it affect you emotionally, to torture others?"

No one had ever asked him such a question, and he wasn't quite sure how to respond. He'd been a young lad of three when the gold striations had appeared in his wings, informing him and everyone who looked at him of his warrior status. At the age of five, he'd left the only home he'd ever known to begin his training.

At ten, he'd made his first demon kill.

Elin reached out and twined her fingers with his. Her

skin was warm and soft, though calloused. The freely offered contact—the comfort of it—stunned him.

"Never mind," she said. "You don't have to answer."

He did anyway, desperate to prolong the connection. "Demons are evil, with nothing good in them. With them, and the centuries of our battles, I regret nothing."

Her head tilted to the side as she studied him. "How old are you?"

"Old."

"Over two hundred?"

"Yes."

A gasp. "Over three hundred?"

"Yes. Let me save you some time. I am a little over a thousand."

"Wow. That's, like, really old."

"Just as I said."

"No, Grandpa. You left out the *really.*"

His lips twitched at the corners. She'd teased him; she wasn't afraid of him. "Come. We have much more to discuss."

He ushered her into the elevator. When the doors closed, sealing them inside, the scent of her filled the confined space and enveloped him; he could almost taste the cherry flavor he knew was embedded in her skin. His body ached.

He didn't want to wait to pounce.

He pushed a button and stopped the elevator before it reached the upper floor.

He turned to her and leaned against the railing. Whatever she saw in his expression made her gulp. She backed away from him, trying to move out of reach, but he caught her by the wrist and tugged her close, between his spread legs.

"Whatever you're thinking," she said, breathless, "take another route."

"But I like these thoughts." He leaned down to run his hands up the backs of her thighs, cup her bottom and squeeze, making her gasp. Then he pinned her against the railing and braced his palms beside her temples. He wanted so badly to rub the hardest part of him against the softest part of her and barely managed to hold himself still. "Tell me. Are you ashamed of what we did in the tub?"

"Ashamed? No." Her gaze held his, unflinching, letting him see the fire banked in those smoked-glass eyes. "But…"

"But?" he insisted, suddenly hating the word. "Why did you run?"

"A lot of reasons," she hedged.

"Start with one. We'll work from there."

"Okay, fine. Number one, guilt. I'd just betrayed my husband."

As he'd suspected. Confirmation was sweet. "Was the male—"

"Bay."

"Was he cruel? Would he want you to remain alone?"

"Noooo," she admitted, drawing out the word. "But that doesn't change anything."

The tenderness in her expression roused his jealous side. A side he hadn't known he possessed until he'd met her. "So…you would honor his memory…but not his wishes?"

Her lashes practically fused as she glared up at him.

He didn't want her angry; he wanted her pliant. *So let's try this another way.* "You attended parties as a couple?"

"Yes."

"You had fun. Laughed."

"Yes," she repeated, her head tilting with confusion.

"I bet he adored your laughter." *I do.*

"Ah, okay. I see where you're going with this. I should live my life the way he'd like. Carefree."

"Weedless."

She pursed her lips. "What about you?" She waved her hand to indicate the club behind the elevator doors. "I know you're some bigwig billionaire sky mogul, but what do you do for fun?"

He thought for a moment. "I don't. As one of the strongest fighters of my race, I fight. I've always fought."

Her fingers abandoned his robe to twirl the curls at his nape. Even better. "Poor Thane. You've never had time to play?"

Every muscle in his body clenched. "I seem to remember playing earlier today."

She sucked in a breath. Apprehension—and desire—danced through her eyes.

"That was a lot of fun," he whispered. "I'd like to do it again."

She gulped. "All right," she finally said, her voice going low and husky. "Let's play."

A sense of triumph flared. "Yes. Let's." He arched his hips, grinding his erection between her legs, and she moaned. "We'll play Elin, May I."

Her breaths came more heavily as she nodded.

"Elin, may I kiss you?"

She nodded again, her eyes wide, and he lowered his head. But he didn't press his mouth against hers. Not yet. He hovered above her, breathing her in, drinking in her mounting arousal—and letting her drink in his.

She braced her hands on his shoulders, waiting. "Thane. I'm ready. I'm not even going to make you beg for it."

"You want me to beg for it?" He knew how temptation worked. Knew it was better to chip away at resistance a bit at a time. A taste here. A nibble there. Until the first true craving hit...and it was too late to stop. "Because I will."

A tremor rocked her.

"May I cup your breasts? Please."

"Y-yes," she agreed softly.

"May I spread your legs and stroke myself against you?" Her mind might want to stay true to her dead husband, but her body did not. "May I bring you to climax?"

Her next exhalation came fast and shallow. *"Please."*

Such a sweet capitulation. But still he didn't rush into action. He grazed the tip of his nose against hers, and gave her the barest of kisses.

She tensed, eager for more, only to deflate a moment thereafter. "Are you having fun?" she gritted.

"Yes." At last he traced his tongue around the seam of her lips. "Do you like my game?"

She fisted his hair so tightly, several strands pulled free. "No. You've asked, you've received permission, but you haven't taken."

He nuzzled her cheek. "And you want me to take?"

"Yes!"

"Me. Only me?"

"Yes!"

"When?"

"Now!"

Such vehemence. He couldn't resist.

Thane kicked her legs apart. As he pressed his lips against hers, thrusting his tongue deep, he cupped her breasts, her nipples already hard little buds. He ground his erection between her legs, giving her everything he'd promised in one fell swoop.

Everything but the climax.

Soon...

His tongue changed tempo, to one his body matched, thrusting against her...thrusting...faster and faster... harder and harder... Groan after groan left her, each needier than the last.

He fisted her hair and kicked her legs farther apart, and when her body dropped, he was there to catch her with another thrust, hitting her sweet spot with more fervor.

She clung to him. She clutched at him.

When her climax came, it was swift and brutal, just the way he'd wanted it to be, and she cried out. Though he was panting, practically on fire for her, he moved away from her, severing all contact. Her knees almost buckled, and he had to stop himself from reaching for her.

The more she hungered, the more she would seek him. And the less likely she would be to leave him when it was over.

"My resistance is so weak," she grumbled, smoothing the hair from her damp forehead.

"Or my persuasion is so strong."

Her grin was slow, but it melted the ice that had managed to meld to his heart. "Yes. Let's blame you. But what about your needs?" Her gaze lowered to his shaft. "What about *that?*"

Hot arousal continued to pump through him, clam-

oring for release. And though he was almost blind with
need, he wasn't giving in. Not yet. "You'll take care of
me, kulta. Don't worry. Just not here, and not now."

She trailed her fingertips down his length, the
whisper-soft caress making it twitch in response, and
making him sweat. "How will I take care of you?
Where? When?"

He met her gaze. "The first time, you'll use your
mouth, and we'll be in my suite."

A tremor nearly knocked her off her feet. "And the
second time?"

"With your body, bent over the couch."

Another tremor shook her. "When?" Her voice was
breathy. "When do I get to do those things?"

She was so warm…so willing…so difficult to resist.
"After we chat."

"But we've been chatting," she complained.

Yes, but he had a very important question to ask her.

He punched a button on the console, allowing the
elevator to continue its rise, to stop and open its doors.
He ushered her to his suite, careful not to brush against
her. One more moment of contact, and he was certain
he would forget his purpose.

Bjorn lounged on the couch.

Something inside of Thane eased at the sight of his
friend…only to tense back up when he noticed the
male's condition—pale skin, haunted eyes, hair sticking out in spikes, and lips cut from being chewed.

"I'm well," Bjorn said, noting his reaction. "Don't
worry."

"I see you've brought us tonight's entertainment,"
Xerxes piped up. At the wet bar, he poured amber liquid into a glass.

Thane's most primal instincts balked. They had shared women in the past, but they wouldn't be sharing this one. "She's mine, and mine alone."

"Actually," she said, her chin going up. "I'm my own. I'm funny that way."

Xerxes hid a smile behind the ambrosia-laced whiskey.

A tray of food rested on the coffee table, Thane saw. The fruits, cheeses, and breads he always kept on hand, now mixed with the chocolates he'd added to the order. He sat in the chair, the food within reach, and dragged Elin into his lap.

"Eat," he commanded her.

She struggled against him, reckless in her bid for freedom.

He tightened his hold and said, "Enough, kulta. This is happening."

"No, it's not. I'm not going to have a snack while leaning against your erection," she finally gritted out. "Okay? All right?"

"Not okay. Not all right. You caused it." Far from embarrassed, he gripped her hips and yanked. When she gasped, he wound his arms around her, using them as shackles, locking her in place. "The more you move, the bigger the problem is going to get."

She stilled instantly. He wanted to laugh.

Darling human. What was she doing to his staid world?

Both Bjorn and Xerxes watched the entire exchange with unabashed interest.

"Thane Downfall," Elin said in a mother-to-child tone. "Did you just make a penis joke?"

"Joke? I spoke true."

She shook her head in exasperation. "Gotta baby-step it," she whispered. And before he had time to question what that meant, she added, "So...how did this bromance begin?" motioning to the three of them. "Oh, chocolate!" Finally, she'd noticed. She selected—every piece.

"In tragedy," Xerxes said.

"Oh." She melted against Thane, as if to shield him from further harm, and consumed her treats. "I'm sorry. I was expecting something epically bromantic."

Thane kissed her temple. "Something beautiful bloomed from something evil. It *was* epic."

She relaxed, and he realized the chocolate was already gone. "Beauty from ashes. That's nice."

"If only that were always the case," Bjorn muttered, breaking his heart.

"It will be today," Thane said. "Elin is going to tell us everything that was done to her in the Phoenix camp, and we are going to punish those responsible."

She stiffened all over again. "I gave you a few details already."

"Not enough."

"Well, I don't want to give you any others."

"In this case, your wants do not matter. You will be avenged whether you'd like to be or not."

Quietly she said, "Baby step, baby step." Then, with more volume, she added, "Believe me, I have been. Those stakes took care of business."

"For me. Not for you."

Sighing, she patted his thigh. "I think it's really sweet that you want to brutalize people on my behalf, I really do, but I'm going to take a pass on this one, and that's final."

Final? Hardly.

"Here's what's going to happen," he said. "I've seen your naked body and know all your scars. I can guess the types of beatings and whippings you were forced to endure. The same beatings and whippings will be meted out against every Phoenix waiting in my cells, even those who were kind to you. If any were. You can either tell me what I want to know, and I can release the innocents, or they can all suffer the same fate."

She twisted to meet his gaze. "You wouldn't."

"If you believe that, you don't know me very well."

"Oh!" she growled, clutching the collar of his robe. "You make me so mad at times. But guess what? I won't be intimidated. I decline both options and offer you another. Go screw yourself."

He wrapped his fingers around her throat, drawing her deeper against his chest, and placing her ear at his mouth. "I'll decline that one, and give you another. Tell me you are half human, half Phoenix, and I'll let you leave with every single one of the warriors *now*."

CHAPTER SIXTEEN

ELIN DID HER best impersonation of a Popsicle and froze. *Red alert, red alert. The worst has happened.*

Thane hadn't sounded angry. He'd sounded desperate. Nothing like the man who'd kissed her so passionately in the elevator. Deep down, she knew this was far, far worse. As strong a warrior as he was, he wouldn't be happy with the person who'd made him vulnerable.

"Let's shelve this conversation until Muesday, May 32nd, at thirteen p.m.," she said.

"Elin," he snapped. "Answer."

Panic choked her. If she admitted the truth, he really would send her away with the Phoenix, back to Orson. Once again, she would be forced to serve the people responsible for the deaths of her loved ones. Once again, her life goals would be placed on hold. Even if she no longer knew what those goals were. This—all of the sweetness and romance and wanton touches—would end. But she couldn't lie. He'd know. Besides, she wasn't going to play the part of coward any longer.

"I never hurt you," she said, her tone soft. She had given him everything. Given—not cajoled, as Merrick had suggested. Because, the singer had it wrong. Not every victory was sweetest after a battle. Some victories were better as gifts.

He stiffened. Now anger oozed from him as he said,

"Tell me you are part banshee, or even chimera. Shifter, vampire, Drakon. Cetea, gorgon. Minotaur. Hydra. Siren, laelaps, sphinx. Or any other of a thousand different races. Tell me!"

Tears burned the backs of her eyes. "I want to. I do. But I…can't. I'm so sorry, Thane."

He flung her off his lap, and as she stumbled to her hands and knees, he stood with lethal grace.

"You are Phoenix?" he demanded, practically spitting fire at her.

Won't cower. Not this time. She popped to her feet, the glass shard she'd never thrown out now palmed and outstretched. At the ready. "Yes, I am."

Accept it. Accept me. Don't turn me into an outcast again.

More than that, she didn't want to lose Playful Elevator Thane. Or even Protective Killer Thane. She'd tried to resist him. Not with a lot of effort, but still. She'd tried. And she'd failed. She hadn't just added an amendment to her vow, she'd broken it, utterly shattered it, and there was no going back. Now, she wanted a chance to enjoy the results.

His eyes narrowed, and she was suddenly glad she couldn't hear the thoughts tumbling through his mind. "You deceived me. You talked to me about yanking weeds, yet all along, *you* are a weed."

Disappointment struck her. A sense of betrayal bloomed, accompanied by defensiveness. "I kept the truth to myself, and quite wisely, too. I didn't tell you because I didn't want to be staked. Can you really blame me?"

With a single, skilled swipe of his hand, he batted the glass out of her grip, leaving her weaponless. He advanced on her, saying, "Can you enslave, like Kendra?"

"No!" His electric gaze was as sharp as blades, mentally slashing her to ribbons. Still Elin held her ground. "And if I could, I never would. Her actions disgusted me."

"You expect me to believe you?" he roared down at her. "You, the liar."

"Yes, I absolutely expect you to believe me. You Sent Ones can taste lies, right? So you should know I'm telling the truth. *Right?*"

His scowl darkened. "You could be unaware that you're poisoning me."

"Kendra was always aware. She bragged about being able to control just how much her victims received. And if that's not enough for you, think about this. My husband was never mindless, and I did him *so good,* over and over again."

The jab only made him angrier. His chest brushed against hers, and she was horrified to note how tight her nipples became for him, eager for more contact. "You used me, helped me at camp so that I would help you."

"Well, duh. I told you that already."

"You never desired me. This whole time, you've been seducing me. To get what you want—money!"

Seducing him? *For money?* "First, what has that got to do with the Phoenix? Second, you are *such* a douche. I did want you. Did. Past tense. Your money was just a bonus. Money I earned, by the way. *May I* remind you that I refused payment for making out with you. And while we're at it, *may I* remind you that I ran away from you before intercourse occurred and I didn't come back begging for more? That was you."

Thane raised his hand, as if he meant to strike her or grab her and shake her. Or grab her and haul her the rest of the way into his body and finish what he'd started in the elevator. Instead, he dropped it and backed away from her.

At the door, he turned, giving her his back. "I'll return in an hour," he said to his friends. "I want her gone."

"Thane—" Xerxes said.

She'd forgotten about their audience.

"This isn't a debate. Release the Phoenix. All but Kendra. When they leave my cloud, Elin goes with them." He slammed into the hall, vanishing from view.

Elin remained in place, trying not to cry while panting with…relief. Yes. Relief. He hadn't staked her or ordered it done. Also, he hadn't banged her, but he'd definitely bailed. And, okay, it hurt just as much as she'd always known it would. Actually, it hurt worse. She wanted to curl into a ball and sob.

Thane had abandoned her.

Thane was disgusted by her.

Thane was giving her back to his enemy—to *her* enemy.

"I…I'll go pack my things," she said to no one in particular. *And then I'll run away before I can be escorted to the Phoenix.* Surely she could pay someone in the city to fly her home.

Home. Where was home? She didn't have one.

"I purchased every item with tip money," she added, just in case they thought to deny her. "Tip money I earned fair and square. I won't pack anything that isn't mine."

The red-eyed Sent One moved in front of her, blocking her path to the door. He was just as tall as Thane, just as muscled, but while Thane had once looked at her with tenderness, this one never had and didn't start now.

I'm about to go swimming in a crap storm, aren't I?

"I'm going to create a mental bond with you, female."

Uh. What? "No, thanks."

"Xerxes." A frowning Bjorn sidled up to the warrior's side. "He won't like it."

"Not at first."

"Maybe not ever."

"But one day, he'll thank me for it "

"Someone clue me in before I have a coronary," she demanded. "What kind of mental bond? Why do you want it? What will it do to me? Not that it matters. My answer isn't going to change."

"Unfortunately, I'm not giving you a choice." He flattened his hands against her temples, his fingers spearing through her hair. "I'll be able to send my thoughts into your mind, and you'll be able to send yours into mine. We can communicate without ever having to speak a word, no matter the distance between us."

Too much to process. "No."

"Yes. Creating this bond with non–Sent Ones is an ability only Thane, Bjorn and myself possess. A gift we received from the Most High after our time in the... Just after. This way, you can summon me if ever you get into trouble."

"No," she insisted.

"Consider it an honor. We've never done this for anyone else."

"I don't want to stay in contact with you." Once she left the club, she would be gone for good. There would be no looking back. No wishing for what could have been.

"This is in your best interest," he said, ignoring her protest.

She tried to wiggle from his grip, but he held steady. "Let me go, you winged behemoth, before I do something—" The rest of the sentence died in her mouth.

Jagged pain ripped through her, and she groaned. Was that a hammer slamming its way through her skull and cerebral cortex?

Light flashed across her mind, then scenes from her past played in Technicolor. Her mother, clutching her dead baby to her chest, gasping out, *his name...Amil, means hope....* She'd given him a name when he'd never even taken a breath.

Her father's head rolling past her, stopping. His dulled gaze peering at Elin as she trembled under the table.

Bay, falling, landing in a contorted heap in front of her.

"You're so vulnerable...so open," the warrior gritted. "At least *try* to block me from your memories."

Try? How?

The Phoenix calling her hateful names, hurting her, degrading her. Peeling away her pride day by day.

She gritted her teeth and imagined shoving Xerxes away. It did no good. Her back bowed as pain, oh, the pain, consumed her. What she'd felt before? Nothing compared to this. A loud ringing erupted in her ears. A sheet of endless black fell over her eyes.

She was dying. She had to be dying.

Elin. Elin, sweetheart, you're not dying. I need you to open your eyes.

No, the pain—

Is fading. I've left your mind.

Realizing he was correct, that the hammer had stopped pounding, she fluttered open her eyelids. Xerxes and Bjorn watched her with concern and curiosity—and now, Xerxes's expression was heartbreakingly soft.

"Don't *ever* do that again," she spat, barely quelling the urge to slap him.

He sighed. "I give you my word. I will never again invade your thoughts without an invitation."

"Good. Because I'll be issuing an invitation in *never!*" She didn't like his voice in her head. The words whispered through her, a wind she could feel in every cell. A foreign invasion. Unwelcome in every way.

"Very well," he said. "But if ever you need me, simply think of me and project your words at the image. I will hear and I will find you." He offered his hand, palm up. "Now, would you like to return to Arizona?"

"Without the Phoenix?"

"Without the Phoenix."

"On my own?" she asked, just to be clear.

He nodded.

Her gaze swept through the suite, taking one last look at the luxury Thane enjoyed. Luxury she could have shared with him, if only his hatred hadn't gotten in the way. Her heart hardened. "Yes. I'm ready."

THANE DARTED THROUGH the evening sky at a furious, reckless pace. Wind slapped at him. His muscles burned. He welcomed the pain.

Elin was Phoenix. Half human, half soulless flame-eater. Sex with her could have enthralled him. Ruined him. He could have become mindless all over again.

Very few creatures possess the ability, and none who are weakened by human blood. You know this.

Didn't matter. It wasn't worth the risk. She affected him more than anyone else ever had, and had from minute one. She could be the exception.

Then why didn't you taste a lie when she spoke about her husband?

Enough! He wanted to pluck out the rational part of his brain and watch it splatter on the surface of the earth. He didn't like how out of control Elin made him feel— and hated that he actually yearned to spin out of control again. With her. Only with her. He didn't want to remember that he'd felt only jealousy at her pointed mention of once sleeping with another man, followed closely by humiliation that he had once fallen prey to Kendra.

Elin knew his feelings about her race, and yet she still let him kiss her. Let him touch her. Bring her to climax twice—and even experience his own.

What, she was just supposed to confess and accept your ruge as her due?

Another unwelcome observation. Another he ignored, plodding ahead with his ranting. She could have been planning to aid the Phoenix all along.

Please.

Why else would she refuse to give him the names of those who had hurt her? Because she hadn't actually been hurt!

Or, because she despises the sight of blood, isn't used to violence, and wanted to prevent more.

Thane rolled to the left to avoid hitting a flock of birds. What did he know about the girl, beyond any shadow of doubt?

She smelled of cherries. She tasted of them, too. She was soft to the touch and melted when he approached.

Sometimes she looked at him with equal parts awe and apprehension. Sometimes she looked at him with insatiable hunger.

She had scars on her hands and back. Scars he should have kissed when he'd had the chance. She grew more beautiful every time he looked at her.

She had two different smiles. One she gave to the Downfall's patrons. He'd been treated to it during his meeting with the Sent Ones. And then there was the one she'd given to him in the elevator. The first was sort of mechanical, definitely forced. The other was soft and sweet, loaded with promise.

What do you know about her, besides the physical?

She was a startling combination of attitude, kindness, and wit. Oh, was she amusing. Who else wanted to open a bakery when her culinary dishes tasted like cardboard—at best? Who else offered to go to first base *so hard?* Or teased him about playing games?

She'd missed Bellorie, a female who had caused her untold horror. She had found a demon's screams too much to bear. She was merciful.

He remembered the hurt in her eyes after he'd pushed her off his lap. He remembered the way she'd bravely withstood his shouts of accusation, refusing to back down even though he could have ended her life with a flick of his wrist. She was sensitive, and she was brave.

She wasn't going to survive with the Phoenix. Not this time. The warrior Orson—the one who'd had that twisted gleam in his eyes when he'd insisted the halfling be returned—wanted her for sinister purposes. He would break her.

He imagined Elin chained to the male's bed. Her face battered and swollen, marked by tears. Her skin black-and-blue with bruises. He imagined her cries for help going unheeded—or worse, being met with laughter. He imagined her spirit broken, her sparkle forever extinguished.

The thoughts utterly shredded him.

He'd made a huge mistake, hadn't he.

Elin wasn't a weed. She was a rose. And one day, when he stood at the end of his life and looked back, he was going to regret his actions this day. More than anything else he'd ever done. He felt the knowledge in every cell in his body.

He didn't bother slowing his momentum. He simply dived and twisted, heading back in the direction he'd come.

Keep Elin at the club, he projected to both Xerxes and Bjorn.

A tense pause razed his nerves. Then, *I'm sorry, my friend,* Xerxes said, *but it's too late for that.*

Is she with the Phoenix? No. Please, no.

She isn't. I dropped her off at her human home.

Thane's fault. All his fault. She was alone, without any means of protection. But at least she wasn't with the Phoenix. He was glad his friend had more sense than he. *Where?*

Xerxes rattled off the address. *There's something you should know.*

More? *Tell me.*

You won't like it.

He wouldn't groan. *Tell me anyway.*

Very well. I...bonded with her. I can speak inside her mind, and she can speak into mine.

A violent wave of possessiveness surfaced, and he

had to swallow a mouthful of threats. Only Thane should have the privilege. Even if he didn't deserve it. *Why?*

I knew you'd want her back, and I wanted to keep a line of communication open.

Wise. But *he* should have been the one to do it. Foolish Thane. *Thank you, my friend.*

That's not all. I saw into her memories, Thane. They're bad. Really bad.

NIGHT HAD FINALLY FALLEN.

Elin nearly broke down when Xerxes deposited her on her parents' old doorstep. The four-bedroom spread in the valley, with the gorgeous red mountains in the backyard, brought back the best—and worst—memories. She decided *not* to ask the new owners for a tour, and left.

She trudged four miles to the strip and pawned one of her bracelets. Though the diamond band was worth thousands, she only got five hundred. A hose job, but whatever. Because she was without any type of ID, she was unable to rent a car. Or rent a room. No one was gonna fall for the old "the dog ate it" excuse. But thanks to the daily paper she purchased from the convenience store across the road, she had been able to call people selling cars. Problem was, most of the sellers either hadn't answered or had already sold their vehicles.

What was she going to do?

New life goal: come up with new life goals.

Without a coat, she was cold. Her shoulders ached from lugging around a ten-thousand-pound bag filled with clothes and jewels. Needing a quick rest, she leaned against a shadowed wall in the alley between two buildings crying out for major repair, and sipped the hot chocolate she'd purchased with the paper.

Maybe it was a good thing she was without any ID. The entire world might think she'd killed her father and Bay, and abducted her mother. Her name might come with media attention she couldn't afford. Ugh. From now on, she was off grid. Anything to keep the Phoenix from finding her. Heck, anything to keep Thane from finding her.

As if he'd really look. Prejudiced winger! He had to go and ruin everything.

From the corner of her eye, she noticed the shifting of certain shadows. Heart pounding, she turned to watch more intently. A moment passed. Then another. All remained still.

No. Not true. A snakelike creature peeked from behind a trash bin. She said snake*like* because the thing had gnarled antlers rising from its head, and its fangs were so long they almost scraped the ground. As it opened its mouth to unfurl its forked tongue, she saw there was *another* set of teeth in back.

Elin straightened and backed away from it. Glowing red eyes followed her.

Another snakelike creature emerged from the shadows. Then another. And another. Each one focused on her, slithering closer.

What the heck *were* those things?

"The prince would like to ssspeak with you," the one closest to her said. "Preferably alive."

The others chortled.

Keep a cool head.

Use someone. Who? Xerxes? No. *You've cut ties, remember?* And there was no way she would throw innocents in the path of these…things.

She dropped her chocolate, and, as the liquid gushed

out, she ran, her bag slamming against her side, slowing her down. Dang it. Money or escape? She couldn't have both.

She released the handle and, without the weight, picked up speed.

Even still, the chortles pursued her...and closed in.

CHAPTER SEVENTEEN

Xerxes, she's NOT HERE.

Frantic, Thane checked the entire house, misting through the walls. Two human adults and two human children were inside, but not Elin.

Try this location. The warrior rattled off another address.

Even more frantic now, Thane darted across the night sky. The apartment was close to the college, and young partygoers were spilling from the building. He performed the same visual sweep, scanning every face in every room. Still no sign of Elin.

Not here, either.

Where was she? At this late hour, demon activity was always heavy. But here, it was heavier than usual. At least thirty viha, ten envexa, fifteen pică, and forty slecht slithered over the walls, searching for potential prey. Whispers meant to elicit whatever emotion the creatures fed upon soon rose. Any humans who responded drew the notice of other demons.

Any other time, Thane would have shot into battle. Now, he just wanted to find Elin. He'd misjudged her terribly. She might be part Phoenix, but she wasn't evil. In fact, she had reason to hate the Phoenix more than he did.

She'd told him about the murder of her father and

husband, but not the abuse her mother had suffered. Chained in a tent, given to multiple warriors every day, until she became pregnant. Then Elin was forced to witness her death—and the death of her babe—while she was tied up, unable to reach her, unable to help, forbidden from speaking.

Afterward, Elin was denied the right to mourn.

She had been utterly friendless. Trapped. Scorned, mocked. Beaten far worse than he'd suspected. Treated like an animal. And yet, knowing she could be treated far worse if she were caught, she'd helped Thane escape the camp. And then, when she finally had begun to feel safe, he—her protector—dumped her on the floor and threatened her.

He was so ashamed.

I've tried to initiate contact, Xerxes said, *but I can't get through her mental shield.*

Impossible. She couldn't have learned to block so quickly. Not as open as Xerxes claimed she was, and not against a centuries-old warrior. So, a block must have formed on its own. And there were only two ways that could have happened. Through fear…or through pain.

Bust through the shield, he commanded.

I would cause her untold anguish. Perhaps even permanent damage.

There's a chance she's already suffering. And he couldn't make it stop if he couldn't find her.

True, but I told her I would never use force.

And a Sent One would not go back on his word.

Thane had to do this on his own, then. As he darted through the town, staying low enough to see every face he passed but high enough to cover more than a block at a time, he tried to calm his raging emotions. He noticed hordes of demons headed in the same direction. Racing, really. Laughing, excited.

Clearly, they were on the hunt.

Dread filled him. Demons could scent Sent Ones, a single whiff causing the demons to scurry away in fear. But there was an exception. When the demons realized the scent was mixed with a human's. After what had happened in the elevator, Thane's scent was most definitely all over Elin.

He followed the trail to a little park at the edge of town—

And that was when he saw her.

His heart withered, forever useless. The demons had cornered her atop a child's wooden fort. A pile of rocks rested at her feet, and she tossed what she could. The strength of her fear gave the demons the strength they needed to materialize. From spirit, unable to touch her, to tangible...able to *destroy* her.

Claws had already shredded her jeans and left her calves bleeding. Fangs had already punctured her neck and arms. Her eyes were glazed, and she was wavering, about ready to tumble over.

A war cry burst from Thane. He shot toward the ground. The demons were too frenzied to notice him. He summoned a sword of fire the moment he landed and began hacking through the masses. Flesh sizzled. Heads rolled.

A heavy weight on his back. Fire-tipped claws digging into his neck.

Thane slammed his sword overhead, then tilted it back, the flames pressing against the spine of whichever demon had thought it would be a good idea to jump on him. The weight fell away, and Thane swung the sword forward, from left to right, right to left, his motions never ceasing.

Demon after demon died.

He spread his wings and rose to the same height as the fort, maneuvering his big body in front of Elin. "Put your arms around my neck," he commanded, killing the four demons that dared edge too close.

He expected resistance. But she must have been more afraid of the demons than she was of him, because she obeyed without hesitation. He shot into the air. Higher. Higher still. He wanted her safe and well more than he wanted to kill the enemy.

"Can't...hold..."

Her hands fell away from him, and she plummeted, screaming. Thane switched directions, his heart leaping into his throat. He caught her just before she hit the ground and jerked her against his chest, leveling out, then angling up, once again moving away from the grasping demons. Tremors racked her small body.

"I'm sorry," he said. "This is my fault."

"Yes. A-all y-your fault," she agreed with chattering teeth.

"I'll make it up—"

"Sh-shut up," she whispered. "Just...shut up. Don't want to...talk right now."

Very well. When he reached the club, he carried her straight to his private suite. But the moment he realized he was headed toward the room where he'd once kept Kendra, the room where he'd had sex with the Harpy, he paused.

He didn't want Elin in the same bed Kendra and the Harpy had used. He didn't want Elin in the same bed he'd taken countless females. *Hurt* countless females.

Didn't want her to look at the shackles and think about what he might have done to her. Especially now, while she was cut and bleeding. So, he had three options. Take her to her own room and leave her with the barmaids, put her on his couch, or put her in *his* bed, where no other female had ever been.

He put her in his bed. And he liked that she was there, he realized.

He looked her over. She was in worse condition than he'd suspected. The cuts were deep. Bone deep. Black already oozed from them, indicating a poison had been injected. If left untreated, she would die the worst of deaths.

My fault. All my fault.

Working swiftly, he removed from the air pocket his last vial of Water of Life, and forced a mouthful of the clear liquid down her throat. She coughed and sputtered, and then her entire body bowed, a high-pitched scream ripping from her.

His chest constricted with another bout of self-hatred and guilt. "The pain will pass, kulta, I promise you," he said, brushing his fingertips across her fevered brow. "The Water is fighting the toxin inside you, helping you heal. Sometimes it hurts more than receiving the injuries. Just a few seconds more and... There, see? The pain is already fading."

She sagged against the mattress, her skin glistening with perspiration. Watching him warily, she reached up with a trembling hand and pushed a damp lock of hair from her brow.

He couldn't stop himself from cupping the back of her neck, lifting her head and lowering his. "I'm sorry," he said, and kissed her. He had to make her understand.

"I'm so sorry." He kissed her again. She stiffened and bit at him, but he never ceased his apologies. He had to win her forgiveness. "I've never been so sorry in my life."

"Enough."

Another kiss. "Please," he said, willing to beg.

"No." Scowling, she pushed at him. "Stop that. Right now."

He straightened but didn't leave her side.

"That's not happening. That part of our relationship is over." She wiped her mouth with the back of her hand, as if she'd encountered something foul.

Words could be weapons, as powerful as actions, and hers were a direct hit. *I earned that and more.*

"I don't want to be here," she said, and tried to sit up.

"Too bad." *Gentle, gentle.* "You're here, and I'd like you to stay."

"No way. I'm leaving. But I'm not leaving with the Phoenix, and if you try and make me I'll scream until your head explodes."

"You're staying," he said. "And the Phoenix are already gone." He held her down with pressure on her shoulders, peering at her intently. "Close your eyes."

"No, I—"

"Do it, Elin. Please. I'm not going to hurt you."

She huffed and puffed at him, only to finish with, "Why do I need to close my eyes?"

"I don't want you to see…." The blood. "Just do it. Please."

Comprehension dawned, and her shudder rattled the bed. She closed her eyes.

"Don't open them until you have permission."

Her lips pursed. "I'm not one of your sex-slave girls in chains, nor am I your employee. If you missed the memo,

I quit after I was thrown out. So, you don't get to tell me what to do anymore. And FYI, I'm only doing this because you got me away from those…those…creatures."

"Demons," he said. "They were demons, and I'm proud of you for fighting them to the best of your ability."

"Well, you can take your pride and shove it." She laughed bitterly, but the laugh quickly turned into a sob. When she calmed, she sighed, and it was clear she was racing from one emotional extreme to the other. "Even a dog fights when it's cornered."

"No. Some run. But you aren't a dog. You aren't an animal. You're…precious."

At first, she gave no reaction. Then she slapped him. Hard. "How dare you say that to me!"

"Why?" He hated the sting. Hated what had driven her to such violence. "It's true."

"It's not! I'm not precious to you. I'm disposable. I'm tainted."

"No." What a fool he was. He'd once relished pain, and considered whips and chains the height of exquisite punishment. But this…this was pain. And the blunt instrument delivering it was regret. He'd lost a prize worth more than gold. He'd lost Elin's trust. "You're precious," he insisted.

"Well, I think you suck," she huffed, "and kind words aren't going to change my opinion."

"You're right. No, you don't need to accuse me of lying. I have never lied to you, and I won't start now." His voice was soft, as if he hoped to soothe a frightened kitten from a tree. "I do suck. What happened shows *my* worthlessness, not yours."

Silent, she looked away from him.

He tried to ignore his hurt. *Surely I'm bleeding inside.* He stalked into the bathroom to wet a rag with warm water. He cleaned the blood from her skin. Her expression softened, he noticed, and he took heart. He was also pleased to note the worst of her injuries had already knitted together. The only lasting wounds she'd have to deal with were the ones left in her mind. Those, however, he couldn't heal for her.

She cleared her throat, and when she next spoke, the anger was gone. "Why did the demons come after me? I mean, they mentioned some kind of prince, but—"

"Prince?" The fiend had clearly made his first move. The fiend would pay.

"Yes. And even though, according to you, I'm some kind of moneygrubbing gold digger, I actually have no desire to be a princess."

The tidal wave of guilt was inescapable. "You aren't a gold digger. And the demons struck at you merely to strike at me," he said. He draped one of his robes over her body, knowing it would clean her clothing. "You may look now."

Her lashes fluttered open. Looking anywhere but at him, she said, "Nothing's changed. I'm still the dreaded enemy. So why did you help me?"

"You are not my enemy. I reacted poorly to your origins—"

"Poorly? Ha!" she interjected. "That's the understatement of the year."

He continued as if she hadn't spoken. "And I will never be able to articulate how sorry I am. It was wrong of me to blame you for the sins of another woman."

She opened her mouth, closed it. Her gaze landed on

the robe covering her, and she sighed. She eased to a sitting position, her head bowed, and her knees drawn up.

A position of shame.

One he knew well. One he'd vowed never to be in again, and yet, he'd driven another person to it.

He was the one who should be ashamed. "I am so sorry, kulta."

"Fine. Apology accepted. You're forgiven. And you're not worthless," she added grudgingly. "*I* can be reasonable and let go of resentment."

She wanted to mean those words. He could tell. But she wasn't quite there yet. "Are you cold? Hungry? Is there anything you need? Anything I can get for you?"

Eyes narrowed with suspicion, she nodded. "My bag of clothing and jewels, if you can find it. They're mine. I earned them. Although, someone's probably picked it up by now. Dang it. Oh," she added, clearly speaking as thoughts came to her, "before I go back, I'll need a new ID."

Go back? "I told you. I want you to stay here, at the club. Where we can be…friends. I need help with the rest of my weeds."

"No, absolutely not," she replied with a shake of her head. "I've realized I don't like being dependent on you. Because, let's face it, Thane. At any moment you could change your mind about blaming me, and then where would I be? Staked to the courtyard?"

"I won't. I will *never* hurt you."

"I've heard that before." Fatigue settled over her features. "I'm glad you believe that, I am, but it's time I was responsible for myself."

He had to fight a wave of despair. Her precious trust was ruined, and all because of him. "Stay. Please." *Beg-*

ging again? For friendship? He just… He couldn't stand the thought of her out there, alone, defenseless. In danger. Or, worse, in lust with another man. "Work here, or not. Either way, you'll be safe."

Again she denied him, shaking her head.

Stubborn female. He studied her, trying to figure out his next move. The length of her hair spilled over his pillows, a dark cloud—he liked that. Smoked-glass eyes that had once sparkled up at him were now guarded—he didn't like that.

"I will get your new ID," he said. "However, it could take several weeks. Maybe even months." *Because I don't plan to begin the process anytime soon.* Meanwhile, he would do everything within his power to rebuild her faith in him. After a while, she would want to stay. Surely. "You can make more money while you wait."

She pinched the bridge of her nose and sighed. "Okay," she finally said with a nod. "I'll work here while I wait. I'll be able to build another nest egg, at least."

"Yes. A nest egg. Exactly." He sifted a lock of her hair between his fingers, marveling over the softness. "I'll make sure you have the best tables."

"No. No special treatment. The girls shouldn't be overlooked just to appease your guilt." She yanked the strands away from his grip and threw her legs over the other side of the bed, rising across from him, putting as much distance between them as possible.

The robe fell to the floor, pooling at her feet. Thankfully, the material had done its job, leaving her bloodstain free.

"I'm going to my room," she said, once again unwilling to meet his gaze.

He fisted the sheet to keep from reaching for her. "You may have this one for the duration of your stay."

She eyed the undecorated walls, the sparseness of the furnishings. Hurt bathed her expression.

Hurt? Over *this?* An offer he'd never made to another female.

"No, thank you," she said, lifting her chin. "I like staying with the girls."

Another rejection. One he should have expected. But the clenching in his chest returned, sharper, stronger than before. "Bellorie should arrive in an hour, just in time for tonight's shift, as promised."

"Thank you." Head high, she strode from the room.

THANE WAS WATCHING HER.

What was she going to do with that man?

Two weeks had passed since the demon attack. Both weeks, Thane had sent her a basket of chocolates, a vase of roses, and a box of books. Each gift had come with an "I'm sorry" card. Even though he'd already begged for her forgiveness. Which had been nice, she could now admit, and completely out of his ice-king character.

He sat at a table next to a horribly scarred but seriously rocking warrior she'd heard him call "Lucien," the two locked in a heated conversation about a missing warrior named Torin, a girl named Cameo trapped in some type of rod, time delays, Bjorn and shadows.

Not that Elin had been eavesdropping…more than a little… Okay, a lot.

Through it all, the Sent One's attention returned to her again and again. And he seemed to grow angrier by the second.

As if he had any reason to be angry with her!

She, however, had every right to be angry with him. He had men following her everywhere she went. And let's not forget the "we can be friends" line he'd dished, and yet she, the lowly human-slash-disgusting-Phoenix, wasn't worthy of staying in his precious sex room. Instead, he'd offered to put her up in what amounted to a prison cell. Stark and empty and devoid of any of the luxury he was only too happy to heap on his other lovers.

And yet…

He'd battled demons for her and taken care of her, feeding her some kind of healing liquid. Then he'd tenderly cleaned every drop of blood from her, so that she wouldn't show her cray-cray side. He'd apologized for treating her cruelly, and she was certain he'd meant it. He'd invited her to stay in his home for the rest of her life.

Leaving him on that bed, without throwing herself into his arms, had been the hardest thing she'd ever done. But she wasn't falling under his sexy-sexy-boom-boom enchantment a second time.

New life goals: resist Thane, make bank, open a shelter for immortal halfings, and hire a chef to feed them.

That way, people like her would always have somewhere to go.

"Elin," Thane called, jolting her out of her thoughts.

Not good for the first goal. The sound of his voice still had the power to make her shiver.

She dragged her feet to his table. "What?"

The scarred man smiled at her before standing and leaving the club. Thane remained in his seat, peering at her; she thought she saw longing in the soulful depths of his ocean-blue eyes. Longing her body responded to, her nipples puckering…her stomach quivering.

"You look beautiful," he said, a husky edge to his tone, making her shiver all over again. "You always look beautiful."

"Thank you." *What you need, Vale, is distance.* "Is that all, boss man? Because I'm, like, superbusy."

Not necessarily a lie. Pondering all things Thane was demanding work.

He frowned. "No. That's not all."

"Well, too bad," she said, and the people at the table next to his gasped at her daring. Obviously, eavesdropping was the special du jour. "I'm taking off anyway."

She turned away, but he latched on to her wrist, keeping her in place. The point of contact burned in the most delicious way, and she experienced her third shiver. Something had to be wrong with her.

"Are you cold?" he asked. "I can have a robe fetched."

Why did he always want to give her a robe? "I'm fine." *Can't let his concern screw with my emotions.*

A pause, as if he searched for the right words to say. Then, "Has anyone given you any trouble?"

"Yes." She glanced over her shoulder, saying, "I'm looking at him right now. Let go."

Another gasp from the neighboring table.

A muscle twitched below Thane's eye, but he released her wrist.

Why am I striking at him like this?

But then, she already knew the answer. The nicer he was to her, the harder it was to remain detached from him. She had to provoke his temper.

"I'm sorry, okay, but I'm gonna go now," she said, and walked away. Her knees knocked all the way to the bar. One of her customers flagged her down, and she rushed over.

"Yes? May I help you?"

May I.

The words got stuck in her head, reminding her of the erotic game she and Thane had played in the elevator; she…freaking…shivered.

Rather than place a drink order, the female, a siren, said, "I heard Thane rescued you from a Phoenix camp."

"You shouldn't believe everything you hear." *Rescued* was not the word Elin would use. Not anymore.

"Hmm" was the reply. Somehow, the brunette managed to put a wealth of disapproval in that one sound. "Well, I'm much prettier than you, so I should have no trouble getting him to rescue me from my orgasmless situation."

The ensuing scratch of jealousy left a raw, angry wound in Elin's chest.

Jealousy? No! She refused to feel it.

She killed a nasty reply. *I'm better than this.*

No, actually, she wasn't better. She offered the girl a double-birded salute. Then, donning an expression she'd often seen on Bellorie, she said, "News flash. No one's prettier than me." And it felt good.

The girl hissed at her.

"You want a go at me?"

Before the girl could reply, two wolf-shifters jumped to their feet at the table to her left, chairs skidding backward as they growled obscenities at each other. Both males looked ready to fight each other to the death.

Get in line.

Adrian walked over and casually announced, "There's a new house rule. Shed blood inside the building, and get staked immediately. Who wants to be first?"

The males glared at each other but eased back into their chairs.

The girl wilted in her seat, now unwilling to spar with Elin.

The Harpies at the table across from the shifters—well, well, Blondie had come back for more Thane-and-chains time—groaned with disappointment.

"What are we supposed to do for fun now?"

"Why can't we shed blood? Huh, huh? Tell!"

Yeah. Why? Because… Oh, no. Had Thane put the rule in place for *her*?

He must have. There was no other explanation.

Beautiful warmth spread through Elin's entire body. *Not going to fall under his enchantment, remember?*

But she should definitely be nicer to him.

Maybe it was even time to baby-step again. He wasn't a bad guy. He'd just made a bad choice. A really, really bad choice. One she'd said she'd forgiven him for. *Am I all talk, or am I action, too?*

Action. Definitely action.

Feeling lighter than she had since the start of her shift, she skipped to the bar to gather another round of drinks. She watched as Thane rose. She had a smile waiting just for him, but he never looked her way.

The sirens began to act upset over the "close call" with the shifters. He sauntered to their table and offered what might have been a few words of comfort. The girls thrilled at his attention.

Thane leaned down and kissed Prettier on the cheek.

Somehow, Elin managed to maintain a neutral expression. He was making out with someone right in front of her? Forget the baby steps. She'd give him one giant kick.

He held out his hand; Prettier twined her fingers with his and stood.

He was going to... Oh! How dare he!

Bellorie approached Elin's side, her gaze following the same path. "Oh, Bonka. I'm so sorry."

He's not mine. He wasn't ever mine. "It's fine. I'm honestly fine. And *I'm* sorry you were sent away."

Bellorie gave her a small smile. "You keep saying that, and I keep telling you it wasn't your fault. Axel told me Thane is fighting his feelings for you, and that makes him volatile and unstable. Axel also told me we have to treat him like a wounded animal if we have any hope of surviving."

"Clearly Axel is an idiot. Thane does *not* have feelings for me. Obviously." Elin gestured to the display of pure male hobaggery taking place before their eyes. "Now, be quiet. I'm trying to listen to their conversation."

"When did you become so bossy?" Bellorie grumbled.

"Today. Now, hush it."

Thane and the girl were close enough to hear...would pass her at any moment.... *Can't attack. Really can't attack.* Besides, after her spanking in Arizona, Elin had no desire to ever fight again.

"Told you," the girl muttered, flicking her dark hair over her shoulder and giving Elin a proud smirk.

Thane noticed and stopped in his tracks. "What did you tell her?" he asked the siren.

"Oh, uh..." The girl stumbled for a response, perhaps knowing she wouldn't get away with a lie. "Hmm. Did I tell her something?"

Here, let me help you with your memory problem.

"She said she's prettier than me, and she would have no trouble getting you to nail her. Looks like she was right. But then, you aren't exactly a man with discriminating tastes, are you?"

An insult to Thane…and herself. Ouch. She'd do better next time.

He dropped his hand from the siren as if he'd just discovered she liked to bathe in toxic waste and said, "You need to leave. Now."

"No, I—"

"This isn't a debate," he said. "Leave."

Hated hearing that before. Kinda sorta love it now.

"Surely you don't mean—" the girl continued.

"You disrespect my human, you leave," Thane snapped.

Funny. Thane had been about to go off and have sex with a siren, disrespecting Elin far more than mere words ever could.

"You don't talk to her like that," he continued. "Do you understand?" He spun, shouting, "That goes for all of you. Forget, and you die."

"Does that go for you?" Elin muttered.

His gaze swung to her and narrowed. She turned her back and walked away.

CHAPTER EIGHTEEN

THANE'S DARK EMOTIONS wound more tightly around his heart with every day that passed.

Two weeks ago, Lucien had agreed to track Bjorn's spiritual trail, hoping to discover every location the Sent One had visited lately, but the trail was so twisted, so tangled, he'd said when they met again today, he'd made little progress.

Malice was hiding somewhere, but Thane had found no trace of him.

Kendra's tongue had grown back, and she'd taken to calling him "My Slave" just to remind him of her hold over him. He had resorted to violence. If Elin found out, she would be upset.

Elin...who was avoiding him.

Thane was failing at everything lately.

He'd thought taking another lover would douse his craving for the human—halfling. But when he'd chosen the siren and she had spoken to Elin with such smug derision, irritation had overwhelmed him. The siren was lucky to have left the club alive.

Afterward, Elin had walked away from him, dismissing him, and he'd stomped to his suite. Alone. He'd paced. He'd pondered. And he'd realized *he* had disrespected her in ways the siren never could.

Now, days later, he didn't know what to do. He just wanted to stop hurting.

He sent Adrian shopping for new uniforms for all the girls. Long-sleeved. Midriff draped by extra pleats of material. Pants. Maybe that would help. The less he saw of her, the less he would want her. Right?

"Thane Downfall!"

His brow puckered with confusion, even as his blood heated with awareness. That sounded like Elin's voice, only muffled. And only she called him by that silly name.

He jerked open the doors to his suite, and sure enough, there she was, trying to push her way past the guards. Arousal and anger battled for supremacy; at the same time, the tension that had been building inside of him since their first meeting cranked up another level. He needed some kind of release. Soon.

"Is something wrong?" he asked.

Her gaze met his, only to skitter away. Afraid of him now?

Disappointment overshadowed both the arousal and anger.

"Yes," she said, "there's something wrong, and I'd like to talk to you about it. In private. If your majesty's imperial guard would be so kind as to let me pass…"

No, not afraid. Livid. That, he could deal with. He motioned her inside. As she bypassed the vampires and Thane, he found himself leaning down to take in more of her cherries scent.

Catching the action, she sent him a scathing glance.

He silently dared her to comment. An apology would have been a lie.

When she was settled on the couch, he quietly said

to the males, "I will tell you only once. Elin doesn't need an invitation. When she wants to see me, let her through immediately." A concession he'd never made for another.

A concession he shouldn't have made for her.

A concession he wouldn't take back.

He shut the door and faced Elin, then crossed his arms over his chest. He was shirtless, and her gaze chased the motion, lingering on the cords of his strength. She might as well have licked his nipples, so strongly did his body react.

"Elin," he said, stepping toward her.

She blinked rapidly, and blushed. "I thought I was a guest rather than a prisoner—until I found out I'm not allowed to leave without your majesty's exalted permission," she said, her tone dripping with annoyance.

He stilled, not letting himself close the rest of the distance. "The day you saw the Phoenix king, I told you leaving the club was no longer permitted."

Jumping to her feet, she said, "And that's exactly why I don't want to stay here any longer than necessary."

Still hoping to leave him. *Shouldn't punch a wall. Must display a modicum of decorum.* Hating—loving—the way her breasts had bounced with her movements, the way her skin had flushed to a rosy pink, he said, "I'll allow you to leave…if you take an escort. And before you reject the demand or complain, try to remember that you are a half human among full-blooded immortals. You are breakable. They are not."

Her features softened. "I get that you're trying to protect me, and I appreciate the effort, but I'll be with Bellorie. She's tougher than any of your men."

"Even the toughest soldiers require backup," he insisted.

"I don't care." A stomp of her foot. "I need a break. Your men have been following me everywhere. I expect one of them to burst into the bathroom the next time I'm doing my business. I can't take it anymore."

He ran his tongue over his teeth. "Where do you want to go?"

"The dodge-boulder game a few clouds over. I missed the last two, and that isn't fair to my team."

"You're actually going to play? Even though you haven't improved?" He knew, because he'd watched her practice on more than one occasion.

Her eyes narrowed, but she nodded.

"There will be blood. *Lots* of blood."

She shuddered but said, "No big deal. The girls have been working with me to get over the fear."

Should have been me. I should have worked with her. Instead, he'd tried to wrap her in a protective bubble, he realized. He'd avoided her, giving her space. A mistake, on both counts. Time to rectify. "If you get hurt, I will be very displeased."

"I'm strangely okay with that."

Seeing no other way, he said, "Very well." Anything else would alienate her completely. "I'll allow you to leave without an armed escort."

She brightened, and his heart actually skipped a beat. *Gorgeous girl.* "Thank you, Thane."

"*If* you allow me to establish a link with you," he finished.

The brightness dulled. "No. I don't want to link with you. Your majesty," she added, just to be difficult, he was sure.

He used to taunt Zacharel this way. Had his leader found it as aggravating as Thane did?

"You will link with me anyway," he said, "so that you can reach me if there's any trouble."

"I can reach Xerxes."

The reminder angered him. "You shut him out."

She gave another stomp of her foot. "So? What makes you think I won't be able to shut you out, too?"

"Unlike my friend, I won't let you." He would cut through her shields if she tried.

Wrong of him? Yes. Going to stop him? No. Her safety came first. Always.

"My answer is no," she huffed. Her pique added luscious color to her cheeks.

"This isn't a debate."

"Gah! You and that phrase. Just so you know, you're both beyond annoying."

Someone had a sassy mouth today.

He stepped into her personal space, and she gulped.

"This is *not* happening," she said. "I'm not giving permission."

"I'm not asking." Her nearness...her scent...her beauty...her temper... It was one punch of lust after another. But...more than that. He admired her. She knew he could destroy her in a physical altercation, and yet she charged at him anyway, demanding her way.

He placed his hands at her temples, such soft, warm skin. She tensed at the moment of contact, but still he closed his eyes.

"I don't want a bond with you," she croaked.

"Elin," he said, smiling for the first time in weeks. "I can taste your lie." And never had he been so pleased.

Through the connection of flesh against flesh, he

swept himself into her mind. He caught a memory-flash of her laughing up at her husband. A male of average height, with dark hair, dark eyes, and a classically handsome face. Her eyes were filled with love and tenderness.

Then a flash of the warrior Orson, calloused hands gripping her shoulders, shaking her.

The images burned away, there one moment, gone the next, mental flames leaving nothing but ash. She was blocking him. Intrepid human. But she was too late. The bond was in place.

Thane broke contact and jolted back, creating distance.

"If you encounter any problems or threats," he said, "just think of me. Reach for me with your mind as you would reach for me with your hand. I will do the rest."

"I know," she grumbled. "Xerxes explained how it's done."

Jealousy struck—and struck hard. He breathed in and out with deliberate slowness, hoping to calm. He stoked his desires, instead. The scent of cherries roused his deepest hunger.

"I'm gonna go now," she said with a tremor, and backed away. Could she sense the change in him?

"Not yet." He cupped her shoulders, stopping her. "There's one more thing you need to do."

Her gaze got caught on his, and they peered at each other, silent, for a long time. The air seemed to thicken, as if they'd just stepped into a sultry midnight bayou. She began to pant. Her pupils dilated.

He rejoiced.

"What?" she finally asked, breathless. "What do I need to do?"

"This." He yanked her against his body and kissed her.

He didn't start soft, and he didn't ease her into it. He thrust his tongue hard and demanded entrance. Surprised—or willing—she opened. He took full advantage, thrusting again and again, taking her mouth the way he wanted to take her body.

She melted against him and moaned his name. *Want him. Want him so much. Can't fight this. Don't want to fight it anymore.*

Her voice drifted through his mind, snapping what little remained of Thane's control. He devoured her mouth, sucking, biting and thrusting. Basking in all that was Elin. Little mewls escaped the back of her throat.

He cupped her under the thighs and lifted her, fitting her core against his erection. "Tell me what to do, and I'll do it," he whispered. "Anything." *Just don't leave me.*

She gasped, as if she'd heard the words he hadn't spoken. Maybe she had. He was past the point of caring. All that mattered was what came next. Her needs and his ability to meet them.

A moment passed; she stopped kissing him. He ground his teeth. She wiggled free from his grip, stood, and stepped away from him. He ground his teeth harder. When the back of her knees hit the coffee table, she met his piercing stare. It wasn't regret that he saw—but passion. She licked her lips…and he began to hope. Slowly, so blessedly slow, she stripped from the waist down.

Lust like he'd never known hit him, and it *hurt*. But it was the best kind of hurt. She wasn't leaving him.

He drank in her beauty, trembling with the need to touch her.

Steady. Wait for her direction.

Gaze hooded, she moved around the table, eased onto the couch, and slowly spread her legs. She crooked a finger at him. "Come here."

A willing slave, he closed the distance, shoving the coffee table out of the way and breaking its legs. He knelt in front of her. With his hands on her knees, he forced her to spread her legs even wider. He fought to retain composure.

Mine. She's mine. That's mine.

He'd never tasted a woman—not the way he was currently thinking. He knew some men hated the act, and some loved it. He knew some tolerated it the same way some women tolerated sex, willing to do it to please a partner, but not necessarily enjoying it.

Now, in a daze, almost desperate, fueled by desire, he lowered his head. Hovered, still waiting. "Elin?"

"Do it. Put your mouth on me."

He slooowly tasted her. His eyes closed, and he savored the feminine flavors that instantly drugged and addicted him. "More," he said. He took another taste, and another, until he was lapping at her...indulging.

Her exhalations turned shallow. "Yes," she moaned, hips writhing, seeking more of him. "Don't stop. Please, don't stop."

Would rather die.

"Die. Yes, I'll die if you don't take me all the way."

He reached up to knead her breasts, but she took one of his hands and sucked a finger into her hot, sweet mouth. He felt the suction all the way to his sac, and jerked, rubbing his erection into the couch. When he next licked her, he was frantic, flicking the tip of his tongue over the little bundle of nerves at her apex, again and again, and she cried out.

"More," she said, and sucked him harder.

He slid lower, to her entrance, and thrust his tongue in and out, in and out, mimicking the motions of sex. He was so hard he feared he would burst at any second.

"Thane." She anchored her feet at the edge of the couch and undulated against his mouth. He returned to the bundle of nerves, flicking, flicking, and slid two fingers deep inside her. She was so warm and wet the glide was easy. "Yes!"

My woman likes this. He sucked on her, using the same rhythm as his fingers, and she began to buck against him. Faster and faster. The sounds she made became incomprehensible. It was exquisite nonsense... until she grabbed him by the hair and screamed his name, her inner walls clenching on him.

He was still kissing her when her body stopped twitching. Still kissing her when she sagged against the couch, spent and boneless.

Still kissing her when she stopped sucking his finger and gave him a little push.

Though he wasn't nearly done with her, he lifted his head. As she watched, he licked his mouth, taking in the rest of her essence. Nothing was left behind. Each little bit was a reward.

She straightened. Expression bright with contentment, she reached out and rubbed her palm over his aching shaft.

He almost spilled. He definitely moaned. "Harder."

"No. I'm going to leave you with this," she whispered raggedly, "and you're not going to do anything about it. That's your punishment for sending me away."

Punishment. Pain.

But the best kind...

He would not be injured. She would not be injured. Guilt would never enter the equation.

It was…perfect.

He nodded slowly, eager to play her game. "I will not touch it."

She placed a soft kiss on his lips. "Maybe I'll see you later."

"Count on it." She stood, stepped around him, and clothed herself before leaving the room without another word.

ELIN STOOD BEHIND the out-of-bounds line and tried not to tremble. The Fang Bangers waited on the other side of the court, ready for the gun to fire and signal the start of the game. The team was made up of six women, with two substitutes on the sidelines. Each was a vampire.

"Hey, hemogoblins," Savy called. "How does it feel to know you'll be leaving the gym in pieces?"

Every member of the Fang Bangers hissed at her. One even growled, "Go ahead and start singing, fat lady songbird. This game is already over."

Between the two teams were six huge boulders Elin would never be able to lift. Thane was right. She hadn't improved.

Why am I even here?

Answer: because the girls asked her, and she couldn't say no.

The "rules" raced through her mind.

The first rule of dodge boulder: there were no rules. Kidding! If a boulder was thrown at her, and she caught it, the thrower was benched, but there was no such thing as an illegal shot. Someone could nail her in the head or the groin, and she would be out. Literally. Causing someone to experience a physical death for five seconds or more added ten points to her team's score—immortals would revive. There were no breaks (other than bones) and no time-outs. No penalty flags. The game would last until an entire team was out.

Basically, it was dodgeball on a steady diet of steroids and growth hormone.

This is gonna hurt, so bad.

Boom!

In the opening rush, every player converged in the center of the basketball court to claim a boulder. Except Elin. *Have to play to my strengths.* Aka survival. Dodging thousand-pound missiles equaled survival. She hung back and waited.

Her heart drummed in a wild rhythm, and sweat trickled down her spine. Loud cheers scraped at her ears. The surrounding stands were filled to capacity with immortals of every race, a sea of faces grinning with relish. Everyone was foaming at the mouth, eager to witness the first splat.

For a moment, Elin thought she felt Thane's gaze upon her. Only he could heat her skin with a look, and melt her bones, and make her tremble. But there was no way he'd come here to watch her play. Not after she'd taken her pleasure and left him without his own, hard and desperate. She'd just thought…hoped… Well, it didn't matter now. He was probably ticked. The sensation of being visually caressed must have sprung from their new connection. A connection she hadn't wanted! Already she was too aware of him. She needed distance, not a chain that bound them.

Concentrate.

Good idea, and none too soon. One of the boulders

acted as a heat-seeking missile, heading straight for her. Elin danced out of its path at the last second, barely avoiding a meet-and-greet with her internal organs.

Bellorie ran past her, a huge silver rock clutched to her chest. "Plan Hurt Some Biatches, Bonka Donk! It's a go!"

That was right. Plan A: Stay close to Bellorie, but not so close Elin would be hidden. Taunt and tease the other players, drawing their wrath, and thereby making them forget the Harpy was nearby.

As Elin closed in at Bellorie's left, Chanel tossed a boulder at one of the vamps, knocking the girl in the jaw. Impact threw her down, and she was unable to catch the stone before it hit the ground. Blood poured from her now-misshapen mouth.

Sickness churned in Elin's stomach, but she somehow managed to breathe past it. She hadn't lied to Thane. The girls *had* been working with her to help her overcome her fear. But by "working with her" she meant they'd talked about it nonstop, all while taking turns cutting their hands, and shoving the pooling crimson in her face. Immersion therapy, they'd called it.

As she'd watched their wounds weave back together, she'd realized blood wasn't always accompanied by pain and death. Blood could be…life.

I can do this. Elin spread her arms to make herself seem like a wider target and called, "Hey, vampyra. You're so ugly, the doctor slapped *your mom* the day you were born." Okay, so that wasn't the best trash talk, but it did the trick.

"My mom is gorgeous!" The vampire flashed very long, very sharp fangs before hurtling a rock at her. As

Elin ducked, Bellorie tossed her own rock, nailing the girl in the shoulder. Out!

Grinning, Bellorie gave Elin a high five.

Okay, this was getting fun.

After they took out another player in the same manner—only four to go!—the Fang Bangers caught on and decided to take Elin out for good. One boulder after another launched her way. Blimey! There was no way to dodge them all. Then Octavia was there, catching one, Chanel was there, catching another. Bellorie and Savy were too far away. The last stone was closing in quick…

She had a choice. Dodge, and keep the game going. Or catch, and end it, ensuring victory.

She opened her arms, and—

Crack. Elin's body skidding backward as her sternum and ribs howled. She lost her breath. *Oh, the pain!* Catching had been a mistake. A huge mistake.

When she stilled, she tried to focus. Stars swam through her vision.

The crowd was eerily quiet.

Then a celebration bomb detonated, and cheers erupted.

"You did it!" Bellorie screamed.

Meaning…they'd won, she realized. They'd really won! Adrenaline kicked in, dulling the pain.

The girls pulled the boulder from her kung-fu grip and jerked her to her feet. She winced as they hugged and kissed her and lifted her above their heads.

A sense of triumph flooded her. Triumph and relief. She'd helped her friends. And they really were. They were her friends. She wasn't an outcast. Wasn't considered a lowly slave. She was an equal, and she was liked.

Laughing, uncaring about the sting in her chest, she

pumped her arms in the air. Then she found herself peering into the familiar crystalline gaze of a spectator and lost her breath all over again. Thane *had* come to her game. And he was grinning, those scrumptious dimples on full display.

CHAPTER NINETEEN

ELIN DOWNED ANOTHER shot of "Legspreader." That was what Bellorie had called the drink, anyway. It was sweet at first, but had a bitter aftershock, and oh, wow, it packed a powerful punch. Like a boulder, she thought with a grin.

After checking her out and declaring her sternum and ribs hadn't shattered into a million little pieces, the girls had taken her to Inferno, a nightclub—Thane's biggest competition—to celebrate their massive victory.

"Because of me," she shouted with a laugh.

Beside her, Bellorie rolled her eyes.

Music thumped through the air. Lights were dimmed, creating a shadowy atmosphere. Smoke wafted, and bodies crowded...danced. Elin would have joined them, but she was currently too chummy with dizziness, and the black-and-white tiled floor wasn't helping.

Bellorie patted her on the shoulder, and despite feeling numbed out, Elin grimaced. Her sternum and ribs weren't broken, but there *was* a size-jumbotron bruise on her chest.

Jumbotron. Like Thane's penis.

She snickered.

Maybe she needed to admit to him that she'd seen Thane Jr. at the Phoenix camp, and that, like a few of the romance-novel heroines she loved to read about, she didn't think it would fit inside her. Then he would be determined to prove that it would, and she could at last have her wicked way with him.

Brilliant!

Because, here it was, flat out. They had chemistry. The kind that caused explosions. She had no idea why one element reacted to another, and she didn't care. They just did. She was done fighting a losing battle. She wanted him. He wanted her. Why not try out a resextionship?

As he'd said, Bay would tell her to move on and be happy.

Somehow, Thane's touch made her happy.

"So proud of you, Bonka Donk," Bellorie said.

"Me, too," she replied with a nod. "It's got to be the best plan ever to be planned."

"Plan?"

"Yep. Maybe even as soon as tonight I'll be riding the jumbotron."

"You are *so* weird."

"Thank you."

"Welcome," Bellorie said with a nod that made her dizzier.

Thane would be supereasy to seduce. He wasn't even mad at her! He must have understood what she'd hoped to accomplish by leaving him turned on— meeting every single one of his needs, even the darker ones, without actually harming him, or herself. Whether he denied having those needs or not.

"Last season, we lost to the Deep Fryers, a group of Phoenix," Savy said. The girls stood around a small, circular table. "The ladies have since dropped out of the league due to fear of staking, and that really sucks, because a rematch would have been so cool. With Elin as bait, we could have stolen victory—and their boyfriends."

"Woo-hoo!"

"Well, next up we play four Sent Ones," Chanel said, flipping her hair over one shoulder. "The Knock Knocks. They're part of Thane's army. And don't ever strike up a conversation with them. They'll say, *we're the Knock Knocks,* and you'll think you're being hilarious by saying, *who's there,* and they'll say, *the girls that are gonna eff you up.* Well, *we* are gonna eff *them* up."

"I'm gonna be playing with jailhouse rules, ya'll," Octavia said, raising her glass.

Uh-oh. "Won't Thane have a problem with us beating the faces off his fellow soldiers?"

The girls whooped with glee, and she frowned. She'd asked a serious question. Hadn't she?

"Hells yeah, we're gonna beat their faces off," Savy shouted, and downed another shot. "They are gonna hurt so bad!"

This was the perfect conversation opener with Thane, Elin thought. Exactly what she needed to kick off a discussion about his penis. She closed her eyes, concentrating, and mentally reached out to him.

Are you gonna stake the Scorgasms when we cream the Knock Knocks? she asked.

Silence.

Had she failed?

Hello, kulta. His voice was pure eroticism as it whispered through her, touching every cell. She yelped. *Have you been drinking to celebrate your victory?*

Yes.

And how many have you had?

Only six—teen. No bigs. In college, I could out-drink anyone. So...where are you, and what are you doing? Better question: What are you wearing?

I was fighting demons. Now I'm in the air, flying. And I'm wearing a robe.

Robes are for girls.

I agree. You should wear one from now on. I like the easy access they provide to all my favorite parts.

Liquid heat pooled between her legs. *Can I ask you a question?*

You just did, he replied.

Har-har.

Ask.

She...forgot what she'd planned to say. So, she went with the one she'd wondered about for weeks: *Why can't Adrian touch a female?*

Why do you care? This time, there was a bit of bite to his tone.

Curiosity only.

Then I will assuage it. He killed his last two lovers.

Oh. Talk about a bummer.

Quite.

So...why did he kill? How?

He's too strong. An accidental mauling.

Both times?

"Elin," Bellorie said, her tone odd. "You must listen to me."

"Not yet," she muttered. Things were about to get interesting.

"Now."

Hold on, she said to Thane, finally remembering what she'd wanted to talk to him about. *But don't go*

*away because I have a very important revelation about
your penis.*

At first, he offered no response. Then he rasped,
*I'm still aching, kulta. Are you going to do something
about it?*

Yes! But all she said was *Time will tell.*

Tease.

I'm not sure how it happened, but, yes.

Another pause before he said, *I like it.*

Denying the urge to twirl Sound-of-Music-style, Elin
blinked open her eyes and faced her friend.

Bellorie's expression registered, and she frowned.
The girl looked…off. Relaxed, yes, but also emotion-
less as she waved to the male standing beside her. He
was tall and wide, stacked with muscle, and, okay, he
was quite handsome. But thousands of tiny snakes slithered from his scalp, like living strands of hair, and that
was a…mild deterrent.

"You must dance with him," Bellorie finished.

Elin, Thane said, exasperated, and she jolted.

She extended her index finger to Bellorie and the
male. "One sec."

Question, she said to Thane. *What kind of creature
has snakes for hair?*

A gorgon.

*Oh, that's right. Momma told me. But aren't all gor-
gons female?*

*Mostly. But every century, a new male is born. He
becomes king. Why?*

*Well, I believe I'm looking at this year's contender
for the crown.*

You will walk away from him, Thane said, his voice
now flat. *Immediately.*

Why? Her mother had told her…what? That male gorgons wielded some sort of special power? Yes! That was it. But what power? Something about…hypnosis?

"Elin," Bellorie said again. "You must dance with him."

Yup, definitely hypnosis. Her friend was in a daze, and as Elin met the gorgon's gaze, intending to tell him to take a hike, her mind shut down.

"Female. Dance. Now," he said, his voice low, quiet. Formidable in a way that left her defenseless.

Defenseless? *No. Not me.* Not anymore. But she couldn't look away from him, couldn't think of anything but him…and his arms wrapped around her. His eyes were golden, with striations of emerald. They were beautiful eyes. Freaky eyes. His pupils were nothing more than a thin black line that stretched from the top of his irises to the bottom.

And the snakes… They were currently focused on her, peering through her skin and muscle and into her soul.

She—

Would dance. Yes, she thought, as every muscle in her body went lax. That was an amazing idea.

The male led her out to the dance floor. Stalwart arms wrapped around her, just as she'd imagined, holding her close, guiding her into a sensual sway. The scent of sandalwood wafted to her nostrils. It was nice, but… wrong.

All of this was wrong.

"Kiss me," the gorgon commanded.

"No, I—"

"You will kiss me." He and his snakes stared at her.

No, she said again. Or tried to. She couldn't work the denial past her lips.

His mouth pressed into hers, and she stiffened. He lifted his head to peer at her again. "You will like it."

When he came down for another peck, she somehow found the strength to turn away. She wasn't attracted to this man. Was she?

The music stopped abruptly. Laughter and chatter died. Silence reigned. As the crowd quickly parted, the gorgon straightened, widening the distance between them. He and his creepy snakes at last looked away, and Elin jolted into awareness, her mind suddenly whirling with a single question.

What. The. Crap?

Thane strode through the center of the crowd, and her knees almost buckled with relief—and instant, undeniable arousal. The male was a fantasy made flesh, and every desire she'd ever experienced for him came rushing back. Kiss. Taste. Touch.

Devour.

But he zeroed in on the gorgon, a murderous rage pulsing from him. When the two males were mere inches apart, Thane didn't bother with words. He tugged Elin behind him and punched Gorgodude in the grille.

She gasped at the sheer display of violence, but she wasn't horrified. She was, well, kind of turned on.

The creature fell to the floor, and Thane jumped on him, straddling his shoulders and pinning him down.

Then Thane went jackhammer, whaling, throwing one savage punch after another.

The gorgon never managed to engage a counterattack. Or a defense. Thane beat at him until he passed out.

"Thane," Elin said, surprised at the huskiness of her

voice. A voice that somehow penetrated his rage. "Forget him. Concentrate on me. I need you."

He stopped abruptly, stood, and rounded on her.

Sweet mercy. His expression was pure aggression. He crossed his arms over his chest, an aggressive move. He braced his legs apart, an aggressive stance. But at least the blood on his skin and robe disappeared.

"You need me?" His tone was more than aggressive. It was hedonistic. Practically an invitation. One she accepted.

Elin launched into his arms and wrapped her legs around his waist.

"You're a barbarian. Let's make out," she said. And maybe her new nickname should be Octopussy, because her hands were everywhere, all over his wings, stroking the feathers, sifting through the ultrasoft down. "You just stand there and look pretty, and I'll do the bulk of the work."

"Uh, Elin," Belloric said, coming up beside her. "You might want to zip your lips. Your mouth is making promises your body won't want you to keep."

"What did she drink?" Thane asked, his lips quirked at the corners.

"Legspreader," she and Bellorie answered in unison.

His gaze had never left her and now gobbled her up. "You're never drinking that again, unless you're with me."

"Because it makes me handsy?" she asked, leaning closer to nibble on his earlobe.

"And bossy. But I like this side of you. I like *all* sides of you."

My man is sweet. "Even the Phoenix side?"

He tensed.

Answer: no. *Won't let myself be hurt over that.* Baby steps.

He kissed the shell of her ear and whispered, "I believe there's something you wanted to tell me about my penis."

Lost in a world where only Thane existed, she admitted, "Well, I've thought about it a lot today." She toyed with the ends of his hair. "I saw it while we were at camp together, and I felt it while we were in the tub, and it's so big, and it's pierced, and I want to flick my tongue over the piercing, and you practically promised me I could and you never lie and, oh, I'm boning this up again, aren't I?"

"You're certainly boning *me* up," he muttered. "Let's go home."

He darted into the air, and the bottom dropped out of her stomach. He soared through the building—*through it!*—then the sky, with her clutched tightly to his chest. Stars glowed brightly, winking from the sea of black velvet. And the moon... The perfect strobe light for a worldwide party.

"Gorgeous," she said.

"Yes. But I want you to look at me," he commanded, and she was helpless to obey. "A human could die after sixteen Legspreaders. Do not drink so much ever again."

As strands of her hair slapped at her, she rubbed her nose against his. "Guess my other half came in handy today, huh?"

He glared at her.

"Fine, whatever. I won't drink so much ever again."

He nuzzled her neck, drawing a groan from deep in her throat. "Good girl."

Her eyes closed as she savored the sensations. "Mmm, that feels amazing."

"*My* lips, or will anyone's do tonight?"

"Yours. Only yours. How many times do I have to tell you?"

"As many as it takes." He sucked on the wild thump of her pulse, and a lance of nearly unbearable pleasure shot through her. "Gorgons can hypnotize with a glance. Never again look one in the eye."

Took her a moment to look past her desire and concentrate on his words. "But you did. You looked him in the eye."

"My mind isn't...right."

"What do you mean?"

He sighed. "You said it yourself. It's full of weeds. Not as many as before, but some are still there. After Kendra..."

"Oh...oh, Thane."

"I'm more guarded than ever, which means it will be difficult for anyone to hypnotize me. But somehow," he added softly, "you have managed it."

She cupped his jaw and forced him to meet her gaze. "Another romantic proclamation. What am I going to do with you, baby cakes?"

"I know what I would like you to do," he muttered.

"Does it involve rolling around naked?"

"Several times. But, Elin? In the spirit of honesty, I have to warn you. I'm not romantic."

"Are you kidding? Multiple times you've sent me books and flowers and chocolates. And your note! Do you remember your note? I almost died from romantic-overload when I read it."

He looked boyish and shy as he asked, "So romantic-overload is a good thing?"

Her heart clenched. "Very. It's like a Valentine's Day parade in my heart."

He straightened out, keeping her snuggled against him. "We're here." A second later, he came to rest on the roof of the Downfall so gently there was barely a jolt.

"To your room!" she commanded.

He moved forward at a swift pace, bypassing the vampires and double doors. The hallway seemed to stretch for miles, but he finally entered the suite...and the barren room he'd taken her to last time.

She pouted. "Why do you keep bringing me here? Why aren't I good enough for the fancy hobag room?"

"Good enough?" He tenderly placed her on the mattress. "Elin, that room isn't good enough for *you*. This one is mine, and I have never shared it with another."

"Oh." He'd just given her the best. Response. Ever. "I'm special, then?"

"Beyond." He settled beside her and tucked a strand of hair behind her ear. "You arouse me, amuse me, anger me, frustrate me, challenge me, and did I mention you arouse me?"

She almost melted. Almost. "But can I satisfy you?" she asked, putting the rest of her fears out there. "What do you do to them, your lovers? Besides chain them up and, I'm guessing, spank."

A blank mask covered his features. "Be specific with your questions."

"Do you hit?"

"Did I. Yes. Sometimes."

"And that arouses you?"

"Aroused. Past tense. I think it eased something in me, and *that* aroused me."

"But you could have hit other men instead. Like you did with the gorgon."

"Yes. I'm a skilled fighter, and I enjoy that, too, but it comes with a different kind of satisfaction. A muted version, like tasting a cake—that someone other than you baked—instead of eating the entire thing. More than that, it can get me into trouble. My opponents tend to…die."

Oh. "Yes. That's best to avoid. So…will you get into trouble for the gorgon?"

"No. He'll survive. Barely."

Good. But back to what she really wanted to know. "Did you maim them?"

Strain pulled his body taut, making her think of a rubber band ready to snap. "Nothing permanent," he admitted quietly.

So, yes. He had. But because they were immortals, they'd healed. "Forgive my curiosity. I'm just having a hard time understanding the pleasure in pain." When Elin had been looking for a bang-and-bail candidate, and she'd considered letting Thane hurt her, she hadn't actually expected to feel pleasure. "Especially when it springs from an angry pain."

"I wasn't angry when I did it."

"I disagree. I think you did it because you were *seething* with anger over something."

He frowned.

"But we don't have to discuss that now," she rushed to say. "I'm more interested in whether or not your desires have changed again. Do you now want to hurt me?"

His relief was palpable, his determination so strong it vibrated from him. "No."

"Do you want to chain me?"

"No."

"But not too long ago, you wanted to do those things to the siren."

Guilt replaced the relief in his eyes. "I brought this on myself. I really did. The past is colliding with the present, trying to make a mess of my future." He breathed in, out. "She was a last-ditch effort to forget you, and I'm so sorry I took things so far. But I swear to you, I didn't want her, and nothing like that will ever happen again. You are the only woman I desire."

If he doesn't stop, I'm going to do more than fall under his enchantment. Feeling suddenly bashful, she fiddled with the collar of his robe. "Then what do you want to do with me?"

"Tomorrow, I'll show you," he said, husky promise in his voice.

She tried to pull him down for a kiss. "Show me now, too."

He resisted, gently breaking her hold. "No, kulta. Not now."

But…why not? To leave her hungry, the way she'd left him? "We only have a limited time together, and I want us to make the most of every second of it."

He went still, not even seeming to breathe. "Limited time?"

"Yeah. You're getting me an ID, remember, and I'm going to go back to the human world, where I'll have a semi-human life. I've even got new goals! I've abandoned my bakery plan, because let's be serious, that was never going to work, and now plan to help others, halflings just like me. No one will ever be unwanted again." It was going to be legend—wait for it—dary.

So, why is a sense of depression settling over my shoulders?

It wasn't. That was an alcohol-soaked imagination only.

"You won't consider staying with me?" he asked quietly.

"No, but I'll consider stripping you," she replied, trying again to pull him on top of her.

Though his electric blues glowed with an odd mix of anger and yearning, he once again resisted. "You need to rest, kulta."

The sense of depression took root and grew. If he desired her even half as much as she desired him, he would be inside her right now. "Thane."

"I won't take you like this. Sleep, Elin," he commanded—and walked away, leaving her alone.

CHAPTER TWENTY

ELIN SAT UP with a jolt. Disoriented, she scanned her surroundings. Spacious bedroom, barren walls. A window with bright morning light slanting through. Very little furniture. A bed—empty, except for her.

Thane's room. One he'd never shared with another female. And apparently hadn't actually shared with her. Where was he?

Memories of her drunken behavior came back in a rush, and she groaned, burying her head in her hands. She'd asked Thane to be her lover, and he'd agreed. Hadn't he? But then, he'd left her, saying he refused to take her, anger clearly riding him.

Did he still want her?

Maybe not. Did *she* still want *him?*

She pictured his smoldering eyes and his wicked smile. Those glorious wings. Those smoking-hot abs. The jumbotron.

*And s*he didn't have to rack her brain for his other admirable attributes. Strength. Sweetness that seemed to be reserved for her, and her alone. Intelligence. Resourcefulness. Protective instincts. A vulnerability he tried to hide but couldn't. A fierce savagery both on and off the battlefield.

So, did she really need to think about it? No.

Elin still wanted Thane. Badly.

Determined to find him, she threw her legs over the mattress and stood. Steadiness wasn't a problem. Not once, in all of her years, had she ever experienced a hangover. No matter how much she'd drunk. Besides a slight twinge in her temples, she was fine today, too. She padded to the bathroom, where she planned to wash away last night's funk, and stripped. Thane must have anticipated her needs because he'd left a toothbrush, soaps, and toiletries, as well as clean clothing he must have taken from her room.

Had he personally picked the items or had he sent someone else to do it?

After a quick shower and blow-dry, she tugged on the clothes. A white T-shirt, paired with hip-hugging jeans and a matching bra-and-panty set. In red, with peekaboo lace. Well, she now had the answer to her question. Thane had picked. The bright color of the bra showed through the shirt, something a man wouldn't have considered. Or maybe he'd chosen accordingly, for that exact reason.

"Why did you dress?"

The smoky voice came from behind her. Blood heating, she whipped around. Her heart almost stopped. Thane stood in the doorway, a tower of beauty and menace— Wait, menace? Yes, she realized. A fire blazed in his eyes, evidence of a ruffled temper.

She wasn't afraid.

His beautiful white-and-gold wings were tucked into his back, a glimmering robe draping his muscled frame. His blond curls stuck out in spikes, as if he'd plowed his hands through again and again.

"You…" she said, tremors of desire laying siege to her. "The outfit was—"

"For later. After."

Her heart sped into a too-fast beat. "But you refused me last night."

"You were drunk, and that's not the way I want you. Strip," he ordered softly.

Sweet fancy. He wasn't worked into a temper. He seethed with sexual need.

But…but…this was happening *now?* "I," she began, unsure what she planned to say.

Apparently that was enough. He stalked toward her, every inch the predator. For once, she was happy to be the prey. His mouth crashed against hers, his tongue thrusting inside with a savage intensity that took her from simmer to boil in a single heartbeat.

Her mind tried to play catch-up with her body. Yes, this was happening. No, they weren't going to stop this time. They were going all the way. It was going to be wild, earthy, and animalistic.

"I told you I wouldn't hurt you, and I won't." He nipped his way to her neck, his breath warm and his tongue hot. "But I can't give you gentle, Elin. Not this time. I'm too desperate. I've waited too long. For weeks I've thought about how I'll take you, how you'll feel and look and sound. And last night was the worst. Or the best. I need to be inside you." As he spoke, he walked forward, urging her backward until she hit the bathroom wall.

Brick behind her, a mountain of muscle in front.

"I don't want gentle." She wound her arms around him, her fingers tangling in his hair. "I just want you."

"Then you'll have me." He ripped at the waist of her jeans. Down went the denim. "Step out of them."

Cool air stroked her skin as she obeyed.

A man on a mission, he straightened and yanked the shirt over her head. With a few flicks of his wrist, he had a thick hunk of her hair wrapped around his fist, tilting her head. He claimed her lips.

She suspected his control tugged at a very thin leash. Never had he dominated her quite so intently, but she found that she didn't mind. Actually enjoyed it. Beyond enjoyed. Tension coiled deep in her belly, ready to spring at any moment.

"Thane," she gasped, and when he bit softly at her, another bolt of pleasure shot through her.

How can you enjoy this? How can you betray Bay?

Surprise had her wrenching away from Thane's kiss. Guilt tried to flood her, but she resisted. Where had those thoughts come from? "I'm sorry. I'm sorry. It's just…"

He cupped her jaw. "Look at me, kulta."

Struggling to catch her breath, she met his gaze. Desire had sharpened his features, hooded his eyes and reddened his kiss-swollen lips. "It's just you and me. Here and now. This moment."

That's right. There wasn't room for unwanted emotions.

"There you are," he said, and lowered his head. This time, despite his warning, despite her claim to want otherwise, he was gentle, easing her into the passion. His tongue rolled against hers, tasting her, taming her. She melted against him, bones suddenly soft and liquid.

"Who are you with?" he asked.

"You. Thane."

"That's right."

She traced her fingers over the arch of his wings. He tilted the tips toward her and stroked her calves. Tantalizing her. Making her ache. Need overwhelmed her. Goose bumps broke out over her skin.

He cupped her breasts, kneaded. Her nipples beaded as he swiped them with the pads of his thumbs.

"Thane." The lazy seduction was almost more than she could bear. "Take off the robe. I have to have skin against skin."

Her urgency must have been contagious; he responded quickly, jerking at the collar of the robe. The material gaped from his body and whooshed to the floor, leaving him completely bare.

Oh, bless me. He was utterly magnificent. The ripples and cords of muscle were bronzed to perfection. The majestic width of his shoulders made her feel sheltered, protected. And his shaft wasn't just pierced in one place, she realized with amazement, but *twelve* places. Silver bars formed a glorious line from head to base.

"You're not going to fit," she rasped, and almost grinned. Almost.

"I'll fit," he said, determined.

THANE BASKED IN the admiration and awe shining in Elin's eyes, and in the reverential thoughts he could hear. *Magnificent. Perfection. Majestic. Glorious.*

Only a few heated whispers separated them as he met her perusal with his own. Her beauty never failed to astound him, but it wasn't what fed his desire. It was her. All that she was. His need no longer revolved around what, but who. He needed *her* touch. *Her* taste. *Her* breathy moans. *Her* heat. *Her* wet. Her…everything.

"My poor kulta," he cooed, tracing a fingertip down the center of her chest and the massive black-and-blue bruise already in the process of fading; she was healing faster than a human should be able to. He'd never thought to rejoice in her Phoenix heritage, but that was exactly what he did. "Had the boulder done any more damage, I would have beat it into dust."

Her laugh was husky with desire, a caress that enthralled. "Sweet talker."

No. Truth talker. He'd liked watching her play. He'd liked her bravery in the face of opponents far stronger than herself. He'd especially liked her unwillingness to back down. But the enjoyment he'd taken from her reactions could not compare to his determination to protect and defend her.

"You have me naked," he said. "Now what?"

"Now, you give me what you've been promising."

"That's right." He lowered his head and pressed a light kiss between her breasts, then at the top of the bruise. The contact drew a husky moan from her. He licked his way to her nipple, nudging her bra to the side with his chin.

Pretty, perfect rosebuds greeted him.

He sucked. She whimpered.

"My new favorite toys," he murmured.

"Yes. Yours," she agreed, reaching between their bodies to fist his shaft. "But this—this is all mine."

He bit down, gently, so gently, though he was already fighting for control. With their bond, he could feel thrums of her emotion. She was as desperate for him as he was for her, and the knowledge affected him as surely as her touch.

Not going to last, he thought.

You must. This was going to last.

And last.

And when it was over, she would know she belonged to him. Belonged *with* him.

Nothing else was acceptable.

ELIN SLICKED HER THUMB over the tip of Thane's erection, grazing the moist head, before turning her attention to the barbells underneath. Groaning, Thane thrust into her clasp. He anchored his hard hands on her waist, his grip intractable, and sucked on her nipple with so much force she cried out.

"Softer?" he whispered.

"No. Please, no."

With a yank, he ripped apart her bra's center clasp, freeing her beasts completely. His mouth trailed moist kisses to her other nipple, and when he reached it, he flicked out his tongue, back and forth, back and forth, lancing arrows of pleasure through Elin's entire body. Smooth lips, caressing; white-hot tongue, searing.

Her arousal moved to the edge of a cliff and jumped, and suddenly, everything was amplified. The sensations. The heat. The emotions. And it scared her. The more he gave, the more she wanted to take. Her hips arched toward him of their own accord, seeking contact, pressure, something. *Anything.*

"Thane." His name was a gasp of need.

"Is this what you hunger for, kulta?" He removed her hand from his shaft and pinned her arm above her head. Then he ground his erection between her legs, her panties a hated barrier.

"Yes. Get inside me," she commanded.

"Not yet. You hunger, but you aren't starved." He pinned her other arm, keeping both wrists manacled by a single hand, forcing her back to arch and her breasts to lift for him. An incarnation of bondage, and yet, she loved it. Loved how vulnerable the position left her— for him, and only him. Loved that every part of her was made available to his mouth and his hands and his body.

"I'm starved. I promise. I'm starved." Was that desperate tone really hers?

He traced a burning path down her stomach. "There are a thousand different things I want to do to you," he said, and kicked her legs apart. "This is only the beginning."

"But I'm already dying for the ending."

"Let me help you enjoy the journey." He thrust a finger deep inside her, and she whimpered. "So wet already," he praised. "Do you know how happy it makes me to have this honey all to myself?" At her ear, he whispered, "I remember how good it tastes. I'll never forget."

Even his words aroused her, making her insides throb and melt. "Couch," she managed, remembering the way he'd once hoped to take her.

"No. You're too tight for me to take bent over like that."

Dizzy with need, she said, "Let me do the other thing, then. Free my hands. I'll drop to my knees and—"

His moan cut her off. "One day. Soon." He nipped at her lips. "Today, I'm going to penetrate you slow, and I'm going to penetrate you deep. I can't do that if you suck me off."

She could feel the tension banked inside him, the unequaled power, and reveled in it, understanding instinctively what he was trying to tell her. This first time was important. It would set a precedent. If she didn't love it, he would never forgive himself, and wouldn't take her again.

"Whatever we do, baby, it's going to blow my mind and—"

His lips were on her before she could finish her sentence. He kissed her, deep and hard—and at the same time fed her a second finger, scissoring the two. Stretching her, burning. But, oh, the pleasure overrode any pain. She devoured his mouth. A kiss of tongue and teeth, taking, giving, taking some more.

In. Out. Those fingers possessed her. "How long has it been for you?" he rasped through clenched teeth. In. Out.

"Over a year." She could barely get the words out. The tension constricted, threatening to snap. The burn was no longer about discomfort, but all about pleasure. His hands were hot, so wonderfully hot. Twin flames, only making her hotter. Any second, she would erupt. "The heat...too much."

"Never felt it before?"

"No."

"Don't be sorry." Purring his approval, he licked the seam of her lips. "Don't fight it, kulta. Let it happen or you'll hurt yourself."

Let *what* happen? Maybe...maybe the heat wasn't coming from his hands. Maybe it came from inside her. Sweat trickled on her brow, the back of her neck.

In. Out. Slow. Torturous. The heel of his palm ground against her, where she needed him most, creating the sweetest agony. In. Out.

He licked the cord between her neck and shoulder, and she tilted her head to give him better access. Access he took, biting down. Not enough to hurt but just enough to make her muscles clench in reaction—and the moment she clenched, he thrust in a third finger.

Just like that, she shattered into a million pieces. Pieces that melted. She shouted, then moaned, then shouted again as her body put itself back together and once again became swept up in sensation, every nerve she possessed acting like a live wire, buzzing.

"Gorgeous," he rasped. "Elin, I need you. Now. Tell me you're ready."

She blinked open her eyes, unsure when she'd closed them. Tension mixed with raw, animal need tightened his features. His skin was flushed by a dark fever that had only one cure.

"I'm ready," she panted.

He ripped away her panties and hefted her off the ground. "Wrap your legs around me."

She did, opening herself to his invasion. He gripped the base of his erection and placed the tip at her entrance.

"I know you can take it." He inserted an inch. It was wider than his fingers, and she was instantly stretched, so wet he was able to slide in another few inches. Her heart drummed a wild beat in her chest. "You feel so good, kulta. So sweet." Another inch. Sweat trickled from his brow. "Soon I'll be so deep inside you, you won't be able to breathe without me feeling it."

"Thane," she moaned. She tangled her hands in his hair, drawing him forward for another kiss. As their tongues dueled, he conquered another inch, and the discomfort ceased to matter. She needed him. Needed all of him. The ecstasy and the pain. "Do it. Give me everything."

He didn't require further prompting. With one forceful shove, he surged the rest of the way in, filling her up. She cried out—and in the sound, she heard contentment and bliss, things she'd never thought to feel again. And she did feel them. With him. Because they were one. He was part of her now. His body a live wire against hers, pulse after pulse of energy flowing from him and into her.

The knowledge teased her mind, *pleased* her mind. Almost as much as it pleased her body.

He stepped back and spun, taking her with him, staying inside her. The action jostled her, causing his length to rub against her already sensitized inner walls, and she gasped. He sat down, his back against the tub, so that she straddled him. It was a position of control—for her. A position she doubted he'd ever before allowed.

"Ride me. Take me the way you want me."

A sense of power claimed her. Power and more pleasure. Always more pleasure. He was a fountain of it, and she drank greedily.

"Thank you," she said, praying he understood. She braced her weight on her knees and lifted…hovered for several seconds, letting the sweet, sweet agony build… then slammed back down.

He hissed, as though the sensations were too much, and yet, he also lifted his hips, sending his length deeper, intensifying what they felt as his piercings stroked her inner walls. What had begun as a whisper of ecstasy soon became a roar, the barbells hitting her just right. Again and again and again.

"Come here," he rasped. "I'm not done with your mouth." He didn't wait for her compliance, but reached up and cupped her nape, drawing her down to him. His tongue found hers, and the two rolled together. "Can't ever get enough of you."

He pinched her throbbing nipples, heat following an invisible chain to her core, driving her up…up…then all the way back down. As she rose again, he curled into her, exchanging his fingers for his mouth, flicking his tongue over each bud. It was too much. Too much…but not enough…and she trembled almost uncontrollably as she slid back down.

"Still starved, kulta?"

"Yes, oh, yes."

"Can't allow that." He reached between their bodies and thumbed her center.

The heat ruptured, becoming a thousand starbursts inside her, and she threw back her head with a satisfied cry. As her body shuddered, her thighs clenched his waist, probably bruising him, and only when the blazes at last diminished, allowing her to breathe and still, did she ease up and sag against him.

He remained rock-hard inside her.

"Not done yet." He pulled out of her long enough to turn her, placing her on her hands and knees before him. She was ready for it. He was clearly desperate for it. He pushed back inside her, filling her up, those barbells hitting her in new places and revving her back up in an instant.

She looked over her shoulder, her gaze drawn to him. Suddenly she was struck by the undeniable beauty he radiated. His head was thrown back. His eyes were closed, and his lips parted. He was lost in her, in the pleasure they were creating together.

Her heart swelled with bliss.

His breathing was heavy as he took what he wanted—

and gave her the same. Sating them both with the raw, visceral desire he could no longer control. It was what he'd feared, but exactly what she'd needed most.

"Yes!" she shouted. "More, please, more."

He thrust harder, and faster, and she exulted in every point of contact. It was…it was… Her thoughts derailed as she shattered all over again, clenching around him.

This time, he followed her, roaring as he thrust a final time.

He collapsed on top of her. As weak as she currently was, she lost her balance and fell into the floor. But just before contact, he pulled from her and rolled, taking the brunt of the impact. He cradled her in his arms, giving them both a moment to breathe.

When her heartbeat finally calmed, he cleaned her, picked her up, and carried her to bed. She wanted to bask in the afterglow with him, and talk—probably to the point of annoyance. She couldn't summon the energy.

Though she'd never thought to be happy again, she was. And the man she'd once thought was nothing more than bang-and-bail material was responsible.

Miracles really did happen.

ALMOST TEN CENTURIES' worth of habits completely broken?

It should be impossible, Thane thought. But then, he hadn't known what he'd been missing. Ecstasy without the horror of guilt.

It was wonderful.

It was terrible.

The entire course of his life had just shifted, and he wasn't sure how to proceed.

Perhaps Elin sensed the change in his mood. From satisfied to uncertain. She roused from her relaxed state, mumbling, "When did you get the piercings? And why did you get them? Seems so unlike you."

Hoping to distract him? "About fifty years ago. I did it for the pain, which was very like me at one time." He paused. "Can you feel them inside you?"

"Yes," she admitted shyly, pushing damp hair from her brow.

"Did you like them?"

Her gaze briefly met his. "So much it scares me."

Perhaps he was not alone in this. Perhaps she was just as confused.

He locked his hands behind his head. His palms were still burning. At first, he'd thought the heat came directly from Elin. And most of it had. Even though she was a halfling with latent immortal abilities, her temperature would always rise with her arousal. The more stimulated she was, the hotter she would become.

Terrible of him, but he liked that she'd given him something she hadn't given the husband.

But the heat had also come from him, he realized now, shocked to see the soft, azure glow her skin possessed. His essentia had finally sprung free.

The chemical seeped from the pores of Sent Ones, allowing them to mark their territory and warn other predators away. *Like dogs.* Seemed appropriate.

Some Sent Ones produced it from birth. Some developed it after reaching immortality. Others required a life-changing event to trigger its release. He must be among the latter, because Elin had certainly changed his life, and this was the first time he'd ever seen evidence of it.

He'd thought he would have a choice in the matter, when finally the day came, but this had happened unbidden. Yes, he was thrilled to have branded Elin. She was his. But he was also uneasy. The timing was off. They hadn't settled their future. She hadn't promised to stay, was still determined to leave him.

"You tensed," she said, the uncertainty in her tone making his chest ache.

Ache? Him?

Who was he?

She gulped. "Regrets already?" she asked, hesitant.

He couldn't give her the truth. Because, in a way, he *did* regret. She was it for him. His one. His only. What they'd done had strengthened the bond between them. And yet, still he could lose her.

"What of you?" he croaked. "Do you have regrets?"

Silence greeted him.

Silence filled with a growing sense of inner torment.

"You just answered my question with another question," she said. "I may be a few peas short of a casserole, but I'm smart enough to know what that means. You do regret. You just don't have the balls to say it."

"Elin—"

"I think…I think I'm going to my room now. No, don't try to stop me." She gave a bitter laugh. "Or were you going to tell me to hurry?"

He'd offended her, offended her badly, and hated himself for it. "You don't understand."

"Sure I do." She lumbered to her feet, wobbled as she dressed. She looked down at him, and whatever she saw upset her further, because she sniffled, as though fighting tears. "Let's just take a breather from each other, okay, and in a few days we'll decide where we want to go from here."

He reached for her, frantic to draw her back into the fold of his arms, but she sidestepped him. Footsteps sounded, and then he was alone in the bathroom.

He scrubbed a hand down his face, remembering the day, not so long ago, when he'd left the Harpy in bed. She had wanted comfort from him, and he had paid her instead. Left her. Made her feel this way?

He was utterly unworthy of affection.

Of course Elin regretted what they'd done.

He should return her to her world. She could live the life she planned.

He closed his eyes, shook his head. Elin had done more than shift the course of his life. She'd changed him, and it was no longer pain he was addicted to, but pleasure. Not just the best sex of his life, but her. Her very presence. He wouldn't be able to survive without her.

For better or worse, he had to keep her.

CHAPTER TWENTY-ONE

What kind of weird world have I entered?

First, Elin knew she should be ashamed of herself. She'd slept with the man who'd once tossed her to the curb.

Hello. He also saved me from demons.

Whatever. The man had tensed up moments after the deed was done, dismissing her with a body language she'd had no trouble deciphering, making her feel utterly disposable.

Maybe it was as startling to him as it was to me, and he needed a moment to come to terms with what he was feeling.

Whatever! Rational thought sucked.

So, moving on.

Afterward, her roommates had pestered her for details about her overnight visit with Thane. That had been expected, but Elin had admitted to nothing. How could she answer the girls when she couldn't even answer herself? She was a mass of confusion.

What hadn't been expected? The way her customers treated her during her evening shift.

Men and women stared at her as if she had grown horns and a tail. But when she asked for drink orders, she was politely refused.

No, no, more than one patron had said. *Let me get you a drink.*

"I give up," she said, tossing her tray on the bar. "I can't figure out what's going on."

"It's the essentia," a voice said from beside her.

She pivoted and looked up, up, up at Xerxes. White hair shagged around a face she'd come to think of as hauntingly beautiful. His eyes glowed such a bright red she had trouble holding his stare. But, oh, the poor thing. He had more scars today. His cheek and neck were covered in short, straight, raised lines.

How had he gotten them?

Maybe it was the bond between them, but she now had a soft spot for the guy. Or, maybe it was the fact that he'd watched out for her, even when Thane hadn't wanted him to. A memory that no longer cut at her, she realized. She truly *had* forgiven Thane.

"The e-what-a?"

"Essentia is the Sent One equivalent of a beware-of-dog sign."

She looked down at herself, at the matronly uniform Thane now made the girls wear, with not an inch of skin exposed below their necks. "I don't see anything."

"Because you cannot see into the spirit realm. You are aglow with cerulean, Thane's color. And as pretty as it is, it's also dangerous—to others. Like an electric fence. A single touch can kill."

She had blue skin? Really? "I could literally fry people with a touch?" she demanded, sickened by the thought. Just this morning she'd given Bellorie a hug!

"No. You misunderstand. You won't. But Thane will. He considers you his. More so than this bar, even. If you are insulted, he will be angry. If you are harmed, he will be uncontrollable with fury."

Wait just a second. Thane 100 percent, no questions asked considered Elin his woman? Like, she wasn't just a fun bedtime buddy?

But…if that was true, why hadn't he told her how he felt? Or, hey, why hadn't he asked her if it was okay to use her skin as a coloring pad?

Maybe I should have stayed and talked to him like a big girl.

She just hadn't wanted to have to deal with the sting of rejection so soon after the most amazing climax(es) of her life—or before fury had time to bubble up.

Fury? Yes, she realized. If Thane wasn't so sexy and seductive, she could have resisted him and avoided all this drama. But noooo. He was, and she'd succumbed, and she. Did. Not. Like. It.

But what scalded most? Like a junkie, she just wanted more of him.

Gah! It was all Thane's fault.

Ridiculous logic, but she didn't care. She had been battling a million different emotions—upset, hope, anger, regret, sadness, happiness, yearning. Everything was trapped inside her, waiting for an outlet. Thane and his essentia now had a bull's-eye pinned to their backs.

"Where is Thane?" she demanded.

"Why?" Xerxes asked.

"He and I need to schedule a shouting match." She threw her apron on top of her tray. "Plus, I'm not staying down here while I'm glowing like toxic waste. Everyone's treating me like a china-doll-slash-grim-reaper."

"Other women would consider that a blessing."

Maybe she would, too. One day.

That day was not today.

"Thane," she prompted.

"He's not here, but he left orders for you. Follow me." A demand Xerxes clearly expected to be obeyed.

Suck it, she projected. "What kind of orders?"

He was grinning as he turned and stalked away. Sighing, Elin raced after him. She trailed him through the mass of customers jumping out of his way…who stared at her with that comical mix of awe and fear.

"You never answered my first question," she said to the wide expanse of Xerxes's back. "Where is Thane?"

"Demon slaying. Hunting a prince. Take your pick."

"Great, but that doesn't answer my question, either. I didn't ask what he was doing," she said, now worried for him. Ugh. *Stop that.* The warrior could take care of himself. Those demons were as good as dead.

"I could ask him for you."

"No. Don't bother." No need to distract him. Especially when she could ask him herself. "How long will the essentia last?"

"A few days."

"Oh. Okay. That's not so bad."

"But I'm sure you'll receive a new dose later today."

A shiver of anticipation caused goose bumps to break out over her entire body. *Traitor!* She wanted to deny that she'd let Thane back into her good graces—and her bed—but who was she kidding?

"Yeah, well." She cleared her throat. "Can humans see it? The glow, I mean."

"Not to my knowledge. Why?"

"Just curious."

They left the building, the sun setting, the air cool, and walked to a structure she'd never noticed before.

It was to the right of the gym where she and the girls practiced, and heavily guarded, surrounded by huge, thick clouds.

"What is this place?" she asked, a bit uneasy. And exactly how many females had been escorted here? "Wait. Am I in trouble?"

"In trouble? You?" Xerxes rolled his eyes. "I have a feeling you could burn the place down, and the worst that would happen would be a spanking both you and Thane would enjoy. As for the place, you will find out." He nodded, and the guards posted at the only entrance moved aside.

He entered, and she stayed close to his heels, her booted feet thumping against a clear, glittery stone she'd only ever seen in Thane's bang-and-bail room. "Amazing."

"It's pure gold, which is usually only found in the upper level of the heavens. But this was a gift to Thane from the Most High," he explained.

"A gift for what?"

"Exemplary service. At one time, Thane fought a demon high lord and forty of his minions. The battle lasted thirty-two days. He refused to back down until he'd removed every horned head, saving a human family from destruction."

Wow. He was more stubborn than she'd realized. Fiercer, too. "Has there ever been a battle he hasn't won?"

"Yes. One."

He said no more.

She took the hint. Discussion over.

A maze of multiple hallways loomed ahead, not a single detail different no matter which way she glanced.

There seemed to be a thousand doorways, with a thousand guards, all with the same face. A beautiful face, at that. Pale hair, black eyes. Blade-sharp cheekbones, and a prizefighter's chin. How Xerxes knew where to go, she wasn't sure, but not once did he hesitate to make a turn.

Finally, he came to a doorway—like all the others—and stopped. He fired off a string of words in a language she didn't understand, and the guard stepped aside.

Her heart pounded as she followed him through the opening…into a bona fide treasure room. She gasped. This was something she might find in a king's castle. There were piles of gold and jewels. There was furniture—ancient but well built, with intricately carved designs. Some pieces were even gilded. Some were chiseled from ebony, some from ivory.

"You are to choose whatever you want," Xerxes instructed, and she gasped again.

Payment for services rendered? "No way." They'd talked about it, and Thane had agreed. No money would exchange hands.

"It's for your bedroom."

"My bedroom?" she asked, confused.

"Yes. The one next to Thane's. You are to decorate it as you see fit."

"I see." She wasn't sure whether she should rejoice or cry. Thane still wanted her, but he didn't want her to share his bedroom. They were to have sex, but no cuddles. "So this is like a royal IKEA, huh?"

"If I knew what that meant, I'm sure I would agree."

Do it. Ask what you really want to ask. "Has he ever done this for another woman?"

"No. You are the first. And, I'm sure, the last."

Well, there was that. So, scratch crying. Grinning,

she wandered through the massive chamber. She traced her fingertips over pieces that belonged in a museum, wishing she knew their history. "Have you? Brought a woman here, I mean?"

"No."

"Why not?"

"Haven't ever cared enough."

Stated so casually, it was kind of sad. "What's your story, Zerk? Love gone wrong? Betrayal? Heartbreak? Or have you simply not found the right girl?"

"Do you enjoy horror movies?" he asked, throwing her for a loop.

"No. They give me the creeps."

"Then you would not enjoy my story."

THANE SLICKED HIS SWORD across the demon's neck so deeply he severed its spine. Another fiend dived for him—this one from behind, the whoosh of air a dead giveaway—but he spun and slashed, and it died just like its friend.

Finally, after a long search and many battles with minions, he'd found the prince. The male perched on a swing in the center of a children's playground, merely watching him now, and Thane knew why. The creature was studying him, scrutinizing his habits as he took out more minions. He was smiling a big, white-toothed smile of glee.

The bright, warm day had tempted over fifteen little boys and girls to come play. They were everywhere. *Demons* were everywhere, in the spirit realm and thus unseen by the children and their parents. The danger unknown to them, but still very real.

Thane needed help. He couldn't fight the minions

and protect the children *and* capture the prince—not that he would attempt to do the last without checking in with his leader. Lesson learned. But he also couldn't bring himself to summon his boys. Xerxes was guarding Elin, and Bjorn…wasn't yet right.

Zacharel, he projected. *I've found the prince, but I can't leave him. He's with a horde of minions and they are surrounding a park filled with human children.* He rattled off the location.

You were right to stay. The response was immediate. *I'm on my way.*

Thane spun left, right, felling a demon with each motion, his swords in constant swing, gliding gracefully through the air. There went a horn. And…bye-bye, arm. So long, wing.

A whoosh at his side. He turned, swords at the ready. Zacharel's dark hair and green gaze registered.

Thane glanced at the prince to gauge his reaction to one of the Elite Seven—but he was gone. And now, the demons were running away.

Cowards.

Zacharel looked him over, searching for injury, finding none. "That wasn't exactly the ending I was hoping for, but I suppose I should have expected it. How did you find him?"

"Took your advice. I've been working with Lucien on another task. He was in the area and wasn't busy, so I had him follow the spirit trail of evil."

"Lucien? Where is he now?"

"I'm not sure. My guess is, he was summoned to escort a human spirit to the hereafter." A summons he was physically unable to resist.

"And how long have you been fighting?"

"Here? No more than fifteen minutes." But there had been other battles, each leading to the park, where the prince had been waiting, oh, so casually.

"Fifteen minutes, and yet there are countless demon bodies littering the ground, floating on a sea of blood teeming with parts."

He shrugged. "I enjoy my job."

"Yes, I know. You did well." Zacharel patted him on the shoulder. "Just know, a demon prince will watch, study, wait, and attack in little ways to weaken and distract. Then, when he thinks you are at your lowest, he will swoop in and lay waste."

An insidious tactic.

Thane would have to stay on alert.

"Go home, rest," his boss continued. "You're of no use to me tired. I'll gather the rest of the Elite to hunt the prince's newest spirit trail. If we find him, you'll be needed."

He frowned. "I thought I wasn't to approach him."

"Not on your own, no. But we'll need all the help we can get when the time comes."

"I'll be ready." Thane spread his wings and shot into the sky, anticipation buzzing through him. For the first time, he had something—someone—to go home to. He couldn't wait to see Elin's things in his suite.

She was upset with him, and he couldn't blame her. Yesterday, she'd asked him a question—do you regret what happened—and he'd refused to answer. A mistake on his part. He should have talked to her. She would have understood. She would have helped him see the truth.

As it was, he'd had to discover it on his own in the light of the new day. He did *not* regret what had hap-

pened. How could he? In every way, she made him a
better man. Rather, fear had colored his perception. He
needed her, now and forever, and couldn't deal with the
thought of losing her—ever.

*I'll romance her. Send her another note. She'll for-
give me.*

She has to forgive me.

He reached the club and went straight to the suite. He
looked for a notepad and pencil and frowned. Nothing
had changed. There were no feminine pillows or books
strewn across the coffee table. Bjorn and Xerxes were
in the sitting room, talking over each other.

"—illogical little baggage," Xerxes grumbled.

"Calling her names now?" Bjorn tsked. "That's likely
to get you staked."

"Worth it," the warrior replied in a singsong voice.

"Where is Elin?" Thane asked, and both men faced
him.

They were very obviously trying not to grin.

"I'm almost embarrassed for you," Xerxes said. "A
female is your first thought, not your best friends."

"I *am* embarrassed for him," Bjorn said. "Thane, my
man, I'd rather see you in a pink dress and heels than
whipped like this."

"Just wait until it's your turn." They'd crumble like
Elin's cookies.

Xerxes propped his feet on the new coffee table.
One without broken legs. "You've met me, right? I'm
un-whippable."

Thane rolled his eyes. "The girl?"

"Not…here," Xerxes said.

What did that mean? Frown deepening, Thane stalked
into the room he'd emptied and cleaned for the girl. He'd

even taken out the walls and put new ones in. But Elin had failed to fill it with the furniture of her choosing.

"She's in her room," Bjorn offered helpfully. "The one with the other barmaids."

"*This* is her room," he gritted.

Xerxes finally gave up the battle to hide his mirth and smiled. "I'll let you convince her of that. The only things she took from the treasure room were armbands. Five of them. Because, I quote, 'the Multiple Scorgasms will look so freaking awesome with matching Wonder Woman bangles.'"

Should have known she'd fight me on this. New plan: make amends first, *then* uproot her. "Did she say anything?"

"Only that she would discuss her reasons for declining with you, and only you."

CHAPTER TWENTY-TWO

ELIN WAS LOST in the most amazingly erotic dream one moment, Thane slowly stripping her and kissing every inch of skin as he exposed it, and a nightmare the next, where Thane was actually looming over her, fury shining in his eyes.

"Get up," he snapped. Then more gently added, "Please."

She jolted upright, discombobulated for several seconds. Little details began to crystalize. Nightmare Thane was real. Sunlight slanted through the window to illuminate him like a rock star onstage at a sold-out concert. The girls were wide-awake and watching him unabashedly from their bunks.

"Is something wrong?" Elin asked, smoothing the hair from her face.

"You aren't where you belong," he said, and leaned down to scoop her up fireman-style, draping her over his strong shoulder. "I know I handled things poorly after...just after, and I'm sorry. But you have to admit I wasn't in my right mind. You had just ridden the intelligence right out of me."

No way. No way he'd just said that.

"I do not regret what happened," he said.

"He-man in the house!" Savy called. "Whooo, whooo."

"What, what," Octavia sang. "Bonka's about to get her a little some-some, ya'll."

Can't laugh. As her man straightened, she beat at his back. "Thane No Middle Name Downfall. Put me down this instant!"

He strode out of the room. The last thing she saw was Bellorie giggling as if she'd just downed an entire keg of beer.

"You wanted to be lovers. We are lovers. You wanted all of me, I gave you all of me. Good and bad. You wanted space, I gave you space. Now, we do what I want."

Caveman Thane was a major turn-on. Maybe it was the heat in his voice. Or the tight coil of muscle pressed against her, but Elin practically burst into flames. Just. Like. That.

"I see you like this idea," he said, and, oh, the cocky bugger sounded smug. "Your temperature rose ten degrees in less than a second."

Stupid Phoenix trait. "So what? What are you going to do about it?"

He stepped into the waiting elevator. When the doors closed, he smoothed her down the hard length of his body. A full-frontal assault ensued, his erection catching between her legs for several sublime moments.

With his arms banded around her waist, he said, "We will discuss my plans after you tell me why you aren't in your new room."

"Well," she hedged, toying with the collar of his robe. "For starters, I'm mad at you."

"This, I know," he said. "But I apologized, and you accepted."

"I did *not* accept," she protested.

He kissed her, soft and sweet. "Then I beg you, accept. I won't survive otherwise."

Her lips tingled from the contact, and her insides tingled from the words. "Fine," she said on a sigh. "I accept. I forgive you for how you acted after I rode you all the way to Stupid Town. But you've got another crime to answer for."

"Tell me, and I'll fix it."

"Okay. You essentiaed all over me without a word of warning."

"Not by choice," he said.

Wait. Hold everything. He hadn't wanted to brand her? Well, well. What do you know. There was a new sheriff in town, and his name was Disappointment.

She'd never really been upset about the essentia, she realized. She'd been hurt by Thane's possible regret and looking for an outlet.

Trying not to sound whiny, she said, "So you didn't want everyone to know I'm currently your favorite flavor of girl-cream?"

He cupped her cheeks and dusted his thumbs over her lips. "Kulta, I want to shout it to the world."

The doors opened before she could stutter out a response—Mr. Romantic strikes again! Thane guided her out, the guards nodding at him as he passed. The guards also avoided glancing in her direction. Was that a big no-no now? Inside the suite, she expected to find Xerxes and Bjorn, but the males were absent.

"This is why I will never succumb to a female's wiles for more than a single night," Bjorn had said after she'd explained she wouldn't be switching rooms.

"She's part Phoenix," Xerxes had replied. "She obviously likes to play with fire."

Har-har.

"Sit," Thane said now. "And we will discuss the room situation."

Ugh. She didn't want to discuss the room situation. Because, even though she'd forgiven him, no good could come from semi–moving in with him. The more she allowed him into her life, the harder it would be to leave him. "I'm only going to be here for a few weeks, right?"

His eyes narrowed.

"Right," she continued. She eased onto the couch. "There's no reason to go to so much trouble for me."

He sat beside her, lifted her, and placed her on his lap, forcing her to straddle him. "I'll decide the amount of trouble you're worth."

Okay, that was kind of (seriously) sweet. And her new position was kind of (out of this world) hot. "Yes, well, we're supposed to be booty-calling each other," she said, lazily grinding on him, making him gasp, "and, yes, I turned a noun into a verb. We aren't supposed to be living with each other."

He sifted his fingers through her hair, stopped at her nape and fisted. "Living together makes it easier to booty-call."

A laugh bubbled up, but it emerged as a moan of pleasure. "You lived with Kendra, and look what happened to her."

"You aren't trying to enslave me."

"That wasn't what you said last week."

He stiffened. "I *knew* I wasn't forgiven for that, either."

She nipped his bottom lip between her teeth. "You, the king of grudges, are one to talk. But, yes, you *are* forgiven. I mean that with every fiber of my being."

Lowering her voice to a seductive whisper, she added, "I already had my revenge, remember?"

The pulse in his neck thumped harder, faster.

"But, Thane…I still think it'll be better if, from now on, we are friends rather than lovers." Better, but probably impossible.

His eyes narrowed. "Better for whom?"

"Me. You. I'll be leaving soon, and—"

He cut her off, saying, "We will be friends *and* lovers, and that's final."

"Deal."

His eyes narrowed. "You just talked me around to exactly what you wanted all along, didn't you?" Before she could reply, he added, "So you will let me inside your body, but you will not live with me?"

"That about sums it up, yes."

He stood, and her legs glided to the floor. The look he gave her…lightning unleashed, fully charged, making her tingle and ache and heat another ten degrees.

"You want sex, nothing more?"

No. "Yes." Oh, she didn't know.

"Very well," he said tightly. "Ask, and you shall receive." He picked her up and carried her to his room— where he promptly dumped her on the bed. She would have bounced upon impact, but he was on her before she could, his lips claiming hers in a savage kiss. Tongue thrusting. Mouth demanding. Stealing her breath and filling her lungs with his own. Sweeping her up into a haze of need, hunger…obsession.

Giving her a taste of what she could have—and then taking it away.

She moaned in disappointment as he tempered the

kiss, exchanging raw passion for cold calculation. His tongue began to move with slow deliberation, as if he was no longer fueled by emotion. As if he cared nothing for her response, only for his own satisfaction.

"Do you like this?" He reached between their bodies and gave her breasts a perfunctory squeeze, then slid his hand lower and cupped her between her legs— without stroking the center of her need. Just held her, as if she were property. "Is it everything you hoped?"

The actions left her strangely hollow.

"Th-Thane?" she asked, unsure.

He lifted his head and stared down at her. His eyes were emptied of emotion, as well. "Quiet. My women aren't allowed to speak."

Hurt pierced her. "Then why did you ask me those questions?"

"Does it matter? And why are you complaining, anyway? This is what you wanted."

She knew he was manipulating her, and wanted to be angry. But anger proved impossible. She'd clearly hurt him with her insistence, treated him as little more than a few-weeks-stand. "Yes, but I just thought—"

"I know what you thought." He shut her up with another kiss. A slow, cold kiss.

She beat at his shoulders…his gorgeous shoulders, hard and strong and hot…then thought *screw it,* and yanked his robe—no, his shirt—over his head. Bare skin. Yes. Her nails scraped over his pecs, his nipples, and he hissed his approval.

"Give me what you gave me before," she demanded.

"All?" he snarled. "Everything?"

"Yes. Okay. Yes." She yanked him down for another kiss, and this time, she took control. She thrust her tongue deep and hard, and it wasn't long before he responded, taking over. Giving her deeper. Harder. Her shirt received the same treatment as his, leaving her in her bra, but he made quick work of that, too, freeing her breasts from confinement.

As he kissed and licked his way to her ear, his big hands kneaded her and his thumbs brushed over her nipples. There was nothing perfunctory about it.

"Like this," she said, and cried his name when he moved to the hammering pulse in her neck and sucked.

He wrenched from her and sat up, panting as he stared down at her. At her eyes, heavy and hooded. At her lips, parted and moist. Wanting. Maybe swollen. At her chest, heaving with the force of her breathing. At her belly, quivering.

"Are you sure this is what you want?" he demanded.

"Yes!" She scraped her nails over the glorious cords of strength lining his stomach—and the goody trail of golden hair that led to the glistening tip of his shaft now peeking so proudly from the waist of his pants.

He pried her legs apart, creating the perfect cradle.

He eased on top of her, rubbing against her, sparking a dizzying kind of friction. Fire streamed through her, scorching everything in its path.

"It's good," she moaned.

"It can be better." As he divided his attention between her nipples, kissing, flicking his tongue back and forth, she thrashed her head, getting lost in the rapturous sensations.

She was pulled as tight as a bow, her back arching involuntarily. She slid her hands under his wings. The muscles in his back were flexed, hard. Hers for the taking.

He glided his knuckles down her stomach, under her shorts. His hand was so big the tie at the waist ripped. Just before his fingers slid underneath her panties, he stopped.

"Hands burning," he rasped.

Oh, yes. They were. The heat absorbed into her skin, infused her cells, and lit her up. "I know."

"It's the essentia."

His strained tone... What was he trying to tell her? She couldn't—

Duh. Lightbulb. Essentia. The way he marked her.

She had complained about it. Now he didn't think he should touch her and definitely wouldn't mark her without permission.

Foolish girl! "I was wrong. I want it. I need it. Please, Thane." She moaned in desperation. "Put it on every inch of me."

He shook his head. "I don't claim casual conquests, Elin."

She froze, her chest rising and falling in quick succession. Dang it. He had a point. She could have hot, with emotional ties, or she could have cold, with emotional safety. "I...I don't want to be casual."

"You'll move into the suite?"

"Yes."

Just like that, his control snapped. He was on her a second later, marking her face, her neck, her breasts and stomach. When he reached the open waist of her shorts, he tunneled his fingers beneath her panties. She tensed, waiting for the blissful moment when— Ah! That! He massaged the center of her need. The heat of him, the knowledge that she now had his essentia there... *I might finally go up in flames.* Her hips writhed, following his motions to prolong the contact.

He wedged a finger in deep, and she cried out, bucking into the slide, sending him even deeper.

"You were made just for me, kulta."

Like you were made just for me.

A thought to be dissected later.

So close to climax. "Please," she said, still chasing the sensation with her hips.

Another finger joined the play as the heel of his hand pressed where she needed him most. He stretched her, delighted her. And yet, she still didn't fall over the edge.

"Not enough, is it, kulta?"

Can't quite catch my breath. Little noises were breaking from her throat. Whimpers, maybe. The pleasure was so strong it bordered on pain. She clutched at his shoulders, trying to force him to put more of his weight on her.

"So hot. So tight and wet," he said. His eyes were utterly ravaged with a desperation she'd only ever seen on wounded animals. It was empowering to know his feelings matched hers. "Can't wait. Have to have all of you."

"Yes."

He jolted upright, tore at the fly of his pants. He didn't bother pulling them down. With one hand, he gripped his shaft at the base. With the other he tugged off her shorts. Her panties were still in place. He shoved them out of the way, then positioned himself and slammed home.

There was no inching his way in this time. He took. He took everything. She climaxed with his third mighty thrust, shouting his name, her inner walls locking down on his length. Guttural sounds left him as he pulled back…back…then slammed back in. After that, there was no such thing as control, even shredded control. He thrust fast and hard, again and again, creating a punishing rhythm that swept her up in another sea of pleasure, nearly drowning her.

"Again, kulta," he commanded.

Yes. Yes. Already another orgasm was building, her blood heating. She scraped her nails through his hair and tugged his head down for another scorching kiss, devouring him, feeding him every bit of her passion.

There was an unquenchable need inside her. A need to consume, as well as provide.

"Getting close," he rasped. "Take more?"

"Give it to me."

He stretched his arms over her, grabbing the headboard. Holding on to it, he was able to pull himself deeper into her, with more force. She wound her legs around him, lifting her waist to take the brunt of his hammering aggression. The bed moved with his next thrust…and his next, until it was hitting the wall with a bang. Bang. Bang.

With his next inward glide, her body surrendered to the pleasure. She shot into another climax, clenching tighter on him, shouting his name. And just when she thought she was about to come down from the high, he lowered his head and bit into the cord between neck and shoulder, just the way she liked, and she soared all over again.

This time, he followed her. Roaring, he plunged with all of his might, and buried deep, shuddered against her, over and over, until he collapsed on top of her.

His weight held her in place, but she didn't mind.

"Not getting away this time," he rasped.

Trembling, she wrapped her arms around him. "There's nowhere else I'd rather be." And it scared her, how true that was.

CHAPTER TWENTY-THREE

THANE HAD NEVER experienced such contentment.

He was loath to let Elin out of his sight or the tight clench of his embrace, but he couldn't risk having her near while he slept. The nightmares… He had to take her to the other—

No. He didn't. Her room was currently without a bed. Without *any* furniture. He'd emptied it out, creating a fresh canvas for Elin to paint however she wished.

But she hadn't. She'd denied him in every way…until he'd pleasured her into accepting.

They would decorate the other room tomorrow. Tonight, he would hold her, as he wanted. He wouldn't allow himself to sleep.

"Am I glowing?" she asked, rubbing her leg against his.

"Yes." He didn't mention just how bright…or just how satisfied he felt about it.

"Good," she said, surprising him.

Delighting him.

"Thane," she began softly. "Are we seeing other people while we're messing around?"

"Did I not make that clear? No. I'm not, and you most definitely are not." He would kill anyone foolish enough to touch what so obviously belonged to him.

"I hope you hear yourself," she admonished. "The words *most definitely* extend to you, too, you know."

He curled his arm around her head, asserting the barest pressure on her jaw to hold her in place, to force her to look at him. "I hear myself, but do you hear me?" he said, and when she tried to speak again, he added, "You had your turn. Now it's mine." She had let him inside her body. Now she would let him inside her mind.

Her heart rate increased, and he wasn't sure if that boded well or ill.

He continued anyway, saying, "The pleasure I experience with you is worth *dying* for. Nothing and no one compares. I've never had it before, and won't give it up. Not for any reason. Do you understand?" *I'll keep you all the days of your life. Nothing and no one will separate us. Not even you.*

Her little nails curled into his chest. "I understand you sound totally gaga for me." She rolled to her stomach, half draping him, and rested her cheek on her upraised palm, giving him a wicked grin full of promise.

His body responded. His body always responded to her. But the conversation was too important to pause. "I am more than gaga."

"That's nice."

He pursed his lips. "I'd like to hear you say I'm more than a booty call to you."

She opened her mouth to do just that—he was sure of it—only to frown. "We've got a major problem. We have differing life spans. In a few years, I could have gray hair!"

"And you will look lovely. But you aren't fully human, and we aren't sure how you'll age. Or even if you will. You've begun to exhibit a few Phoenix traits."

"Yes, but—"

"But nothing. You burn when you are aroused, and you healed unnaturally fast from the boulder game. I suspect both abilities activated with the death of your family. Sometimes a traumatic event will do that for a halfling."

"I didn't burn in the Phoenix camp."

"You weren't aroused while you were there. And I suspect you would have died in that camp if you hadn't healed supernaturally fast from the punishments."

"Good point."

"Perhaps, over the years, other latent traits will emerge."

She thought for a moment, nodded. "You're right."

"I usually am."

"Ha-ha," she said drily. "We'll see if you're such a funny man the day I have to start wearing diapers."

He barked out a laugh, surprising them both.

She kicked off the covers and sat up, then crossed her legs. "We have to get you to do that more often."

Laugh? "I agree. I hereby task you with the job. Every day from now on."

She quirked a brow. "Does the job pay well?"

"Very." He traced a fingertip between her breasts. This was his first taste of domestic life, and he loved it. A male…a woman…united. A *family*. "An orgasm for every laugh."

Another smile made an appearance—only to fall. "What if you meet someone else and fall in love? What if you want to get married Sent-One-style, to someone of your own race, and start a family?" She gasped. "Thane, we've never used protection."

Needing to feel her against him, he forced her to

stretch out alongside him. "First, when I said no woman could compare to you, I meant it. That goes for every woman I will meet in the future. Only a foolish male would wed someone else when he already has the best. Second, Phoenix are only fertile two times a year, and," he added before she could remind him of her humanity, "I can sense when that occurs." He paused. "Do you want children?" Had she planned to make one with her husband?

"One day. Not for several years, though. What about you?"

"To be honest, I've never thought about it." Until now. He flattened his hand on her belly, imagined her growing big with *his* child. His shaft stirred. "Yes," he rasped. "One day." With her. Only with her.

They lapsed into silence. He toyed with the ends of her hair, and though she seemed to grow tenser by the second, she yawned.

"What's wrong?"

"I should really go back to my room," she said.

"You don't have a bed."

"I know, smarty. I meant, go back to the girls."

He stiffened. "You said you'd move in with me."

"But I didn't say when." Her entire body began to tremble. "I really should go. Like, now. Please."

She tried to tug from him, but he held firm. Something warm and wet splashed on his chest. He patted the area and brought his fingers into the light streaming in from the bathroom. Tears?

"What is this?" he asked gently.

A floodgate opened, and she sobbed against him, her entire body heaving. "I'm looking forward to a future without Bay."

He held her for what seemed an eternity, smoothing his hands through her hair, along her spine. When finally she calmed, he pinched her chin, forcing her to face him. Tears had caught in her lashes. Her eyes were swollen, her skin splotched with red. *Fragile right now. Proceed with care.*

An inexplicable need to make it better flooded him. "How are you planning a future without him? He has never left your heart. He goes on the journey with you." And Thane was still a bit jealous, he realized, but with Elin safe in his arms, the emotion was muted. He could share her, for the male had helped make her what she was.

She sniffled. "That's so beautiful."

"And true."

She traced a finger over his lips. "You are a good man, Thane— What *is* your last name?"

"I don't have one. Up here, we have designations. Xerxes the Cruel and Unusual. Bjorn the Last True Dread."

"Those are kind of creepy, but, okay. I can roll. Before she cut ties with her clan, my mother was Renlay the Deathtax Collector, and my bedtime stories were of her exploits."

"Did she tell you why she left the Phoenix?"

"Yes. My dad. Eric Wahlström. He lived in Harrogate at the time, and she was crazy in lust at her first sighting of him. Which must have been strange, because you have never seen a more mismatched pair. She was wild; he was proper. She was loud; he was quiet. But even still, he fell for her, and she had her wicked way with him. Afterward, she thought she'd be able to forget him."

He could hear the affection in her tone, knew she'd adored the man. "But she didn't."

"No. She didn't. She kept going back to him, and one day she realized she had to make a choice. Him or her clan. Mixed relationships aren't encouraged but aren't forbidden, as long as they're with someone of an equally strong or stronger race. Humans, as I'm sure you know, are a big, fat no-no. It's okay to take one as a lover, but never a mate. She chose him, and I was born a year later. I spent the first ten years of my life in Harrogate."

"That explains the accent."

"I do not have an accent. Once we moved to Arizona, and all the little kids made fun of the bloody Brit," she said, using the same mocking tone the kids must have used with her, "I feared my mother would slay them all. So, I learned how to blend in."

He might have slayed them all, too. "It's slight, but it's there." His voice dipped as he added, "It only comes out when you're aroused."

She chuckled. "You are racking up all kinds of rewards." She kissed the pulse at the base of his neck. "So, backtracking. You are Thane the...what?"

"Thane of the Three."

"Oh. Well, that's kind of anticlimactic."

"Disappointed?"

"Kind of. Sorry to tell you this, but I think you need a new one."

He was her man. He wanted her proud of him. "Most people assume the three refers to Xerxes and Bjorn, but I had the name before I knew the men." He added, "The three actually refers to the ways I kill. Dead. Deader. And purged from all eternity."

"I don't know whether to be scared...or pleased."

"I vote for pleased."

"My mother would have voted for pleased, too," she said.

He grinned almost shyly. "Do you think your mother would have liked me?"

"There are the dimples I adore," she said, brightening.

She adored them, and so he would make sure she saw them. Often. "Your mother," he prompted, anxious to know.

"She wouldn't have liked you."

He didn't allow his hurt to show.

"She would have loved you," Elin added.

Another grin—another flash of the dimples, he was sure. The word *loved* echoed in his mind. As if he were worthy of such an emotion.

He wasn't. *But I can* make *myself.*
I will.

DARK CURSES CUT through the air.

Thane's rage-infused voice roused Elin from a deep, peaceful sleep. She blinked open her eyes, and saw that he was thrashing on his side of the bed, the covers kicked off and bunched at his feet.

As he hurtled more curses, he clawed at his chest. His nails scraped away skin, like shovels scraped away dirt. His fingers burrowed in the open grooves. As if… as if…

Her stomach twisted. "Thane." She gently patted his cheek. "Wake up, baby."

His arm shot up. His fingers wrapped around her neck and squeezed. Squeezed so tightly she couldn't breathe. Couldn't even wheeze.

She latched on to his wrist and tugged—but he was so strong, he didn't budge. He only squeezed that much harder.

Pain…then light-headedness…

Was this the way she would die?

In a last-ditch effort to free herself, she batted at his face.

Weakness…

Her fingers ended up in his mouth, and for whatever reason, that snapped him to his senses. He blinked, shook his head.

His gaze met hers, and widened with horror.

He released her as if he'd just discovered she was nuclear waste, panting, "Elin, Elin. I'm so sorry."

She sagged against him.

He held on to her as she sucked in mouthful after mouthful of air. He even tightened his hold, as though she was a life raft amid a fierce storm—as though he feared she would run off at any moment.

Not nuclear waste after all.

His heartbeat thundered against her chest. "I'm so sorry," he repeated.

"It's okay, baby," she said, petting him. "You didn't do any permanent damage." A few weeks ago, a choking coupled with the sight of torn flesh would have sent her into a screaming fit. But honestly? She wasn't the person she used to be. She was the girl her mother had always hoped she'd be.

She didn't need to use anyone for anything. She was strong, in both mind and body. Proof: she had battled crazed demons. She had gone toe-to-toe with a team of adrenaline-junkie vampyras and purposely stood in the way of raining boulders.

A little suffocation? Whatevs.

A full-body tremor rocked him. "I could have... I shouldn't have stayed here...should have left you alone. I didn't mean to fall asleep."

Lightbulb. He hadn't wanted to share a room with her because he suffered frequent, and violent, nightmares. Inside her, a well of tenderness bubbled over. "I'm glad I'm here." The thought of him dealing with this alone nearly broke her heart.

"Tell me," she said. "About the dream."

He stiffened but replied, "Not a dream."

Then... "A memory?"

He released her and climbed from the bed. Naked, he stalked to the closet and withdrew a robe. No, two robes. After he dressed, he pulled her upright and tugged the other one over her head, tenderly freeing her hair before fitting her arms through the sleeves.

So...conversations about the nightmare/memories were a no-go. Got it. And it kind of hurt, after everything they'd already shared. But at least he'd gifted her with a robe from his personal stash rather than forcing her to wear something from the skank parade.

Meow. *Jealous, anyone?*

Why was she so upset, anyway? He was only giving her more of what she'd originally asked for. Sex without entanglement.

Yeah, but that wasn't what *he* had pushed for or what they had ultimately agreed on. They were part of a full-on commitment now, and he would just have to live with the consequences.

"Thane." She clasped on to his wrists, maintaining a physical connection with him. "Talk to me."

He wouldn't meet her gaze.

"You can trust me. I'll never share your secrets."

He lifted her hands to his mouth, kissed the knuckles on both. "We are going to the treasure chest, and you are going to pick the furniture you want for your room. I know you don't want to stay there, but you're going to do it anyway."

Strike one. But okay. She could tackle this from a different angle and launch a sneak attack via the room situation. Without the hurt of rejection, thinking he didn't want her in his personal space because she meant so little, she was touched that he wanted her so close to him. But three things bothered her. One, the nightmares. He shouldn't have to suffer alone. And he did suffer. The torment in his eyes... *Poor Thane.* Two, the terrible memories he'd created in the other room. Although, it might be time to make new memories in there. And three, the condition of his bedroom. He wanted to keep her in luxury and deprive himself. Why?

Complicated immortal. Far more than she'd ever expected. He punished his enemies without mercy—perhaps this was a punishment to himself. But for what?

Whatever the problem, whatever he'd done or not done, she only wanted good things for him from now on.

"All right," she said. "We can go to the treasure chest, and I will pick out things for the other room."

Relief bathed his expression. He smiled at her, baring those beautiful dimples.

Now, to go in for the kill. "But," she added, and he stiffened again. "I get to decorate this room, as well."

He opened his mouth, probably to protest.

"I have a feeling I'll be spending a lot of time in here, and I want to be comfortable." She was already comfortable, but she was beginning to think he would put her needs, and even her wants, above his own.

The thought…charmed her. Humbled her. Terrified her.

How was she supposed to deal with something like that?

After a few minutes of clear internal debate, he nodded. "Very well. Both rooms."

CHAPTER TWENTY-FOUR

THANE WAS UTTERLY ENTHRALLED.

Elin took her role as decorator very seriously. She'd made him find a notepad and a pen to keep track of her ideas and plans. Now, as she prowled through the massive chamber, her brow furrowed with concentration. Sometimes she paused to chew on the end of the pen and ponder, sometimes to write down instructions. She seemed to be on a life-and-death mission, and even had conversations with herself.

Should I put this here? Or there?

Neither. I like the dresser with the stained glass better.

Dang it, what would the Property Brothers pick?

His eyes narrowed. Who were the Property Brothers to her?

Surrounded as she was by untold wealth, priceless and colorful jewels, and precious antiques, all while wearing his white robe, she was like a queen of old.

One hour passed. Two.

He said not a word. He wasn't interested in rushing her. There was joy and peace in watching her.

Another hour passed.

"Thane," she said, her voice husky with promise— the same tone she used whenever he was inside her.

He shook his wings. "Yes, Elin."

With her back to him, dark hair flowing freely, she glanced over her shoulder and grinned slowly...wickedly. The strength of his reaction to her no longer shocked him. His muscles knotted. His blood heated. His need grew. *She's made for me. Mine.*

"I won't know if this is the bed of my dreams until I test it." As she spoke, she brushed the robe from her shoulders.... The material pooled on the floor, leaving her gloriously naked.

The sight of her proved to be his undoing. Need raged as he drank her in. The elegant line of her back. The two indentations above her buttocks. The graceful length of her legs.

She turned, facing him fully, and he was treated to a full-frontal assault.

His mouth went dry.

She eased onto the mattress, sitting, planting her feet on the floor—and widening her knees.

She was a seductress. A temptress.

"Come to me," she beseeched.

He walked toward her, as if in a daze, discarding his robe along the way. When he reached her, he made to drop to his knees. She placed her hands on his hips, stopping him.

"Stay just...like...this." She flashed him another wicked smile as *she* dropped to her knees.

He was already hard as steel but stiffened further with anticipation. Then her mouth descended on him. Searing heat. Dizzying suction. He almost spilled but managed to hold back—*have to have more of this.* He leaned over and braced his hands on the bed. Over and over she worked him. Up and down. Up and down. Taking him deep, deeper, so amazingly deep.

When he realized her fingers were playing between her legs, revving up her own desires, he began to rock into her, and couldn't stop himself. Control? Ceded to her or shredded—he wasn't sure which. Though he tried to be gentle, so gentle, not wanting to gag her or hurt her. But the gentleness didn't last long. Her tongue stroked him, and he rocked harder. Harder still. But even that wasn't enough. He had to have more.

Muscles knotted further.... The heat...oh, the heat... combined with the suction and tongue swirls and the knowledge of just who was responsible for his pleasure... The pressure inside him broke, opening the floodgates. He roared, loud and long, his climax shooting through him. He straightened to cup Elin's cheeks, to hold her to him as he gave her every drop.

She shuddered with the force of her own climax. And when she stilled, had to swallow a groan. He was sensitive now, every sensation almost too much. Their eyes met.

Shaking, he helped her stand.

"I was out of practice, but good, yeah?" she said with a grin. Her eyes sparkled, like stars in a night-dark sky.

"No words," he croaked, and felt her grin widen against his chest. "Wait. Maybe one. Grateful."

"To me or to Bay?"

The husband had taught her that nifty little skill? "Both." Thane couldn't manage a single thrum of jealousy this time. Elin might have learned from the male, but for the rest of her life, Thane would be the one to reap the benefits.

Two words snagged his attention. *Her life.*

How much longer did she have?

He'd told her not to worry. Worry did no good. Ultimately, it helped nothing and destroyed everything. But it never hurt to be prepared. How could he ensure an eternity with Elin? By making her fully immortal.

How could he make her fully immortal?

Thane knew a little about the ways of the Phoenix. Immortality came with the first death. However old the warrior was when he—or she—died the first time. That was the age the warrior forever stayed. Babies, toddlers and preteens rarely regenerated.

Elin was twenty-one. She was still a little young. And the fact that she was diluted with human blood...

He would have given anything for her to be a full-Phoenix, he realized. Absolutely anything.

He helped her dress before tugging a robe over his head. "We never actually tested the bed."

"Close enough." She wagged her eyebrows at him, then her shoulders. "I now know I gots to have it."

Humor restored, he said, "You have what you need from here?"

"Yes. But be warned. You are going to be so completely gobsmacked when you see the finished rooms."

He had no doubt. She thrived at everything she did. "There are errands I must run, but Adrian will be at your disposal, and he will make sure all of your selections are moved wherever you want them."

She pouted for a moment. "I'm not thrilled with the idea of forcing Adrian to do my bidding. Why can't you do it? Where are you going?"

"I have a meeting with my leader."

"The Most High?"

"Two spots lower on the totem. A Sent One by the name of Zacharel."

"You're not in trouble, are you?"

"No," he said. "Why? What would you do if I was?"

"Go with you and throw my pimp-hand around. No one punishes my man but me."

My man.

She'd just verbally claimed him. Grinning, he picked her up and swung her around. "Thank you. The thought is enough."

She laughed, and he laughed, and it was a carefree moment forever branded in his heart.

When he set her down, she said, "Oh, and here's another warning. I plan to invite the girls into your suite."

He liked the other girls, respected them, even, but didn't relish spending his time with them. However, they were dear to Elin, and he wouldn't keep her from them; so, for her, he would learn to deal. "Very well."

"Wait. I'm not sure you understand. They're going to touch everything and drink everything in your wet bar, and you won't be able to lecture them or punish them."

"I understand."

Rising on her tiptoes, she placed a soft, sweet kiss on his chin. "Don't worry. I won't let them inside your room. That's just for you. And sometimes me."

There at the end, her voice had taken on a fierceness he'd never heard from her. He liked it and what it implied. If necessary, she would fight for her place in his life.

She would fight for him.

"Only you and me," he agreed.

ELIN WORKED LIKE a madwoman, determined to get everything done before Thane returned. She also worked her friends to the bone, including Adrian. No longer did she feel quite so bad about forcing people to do her bidding.

This was for Thane. *Anything goes.*

But the berserker bailed the moment all the furniture was in place. Chanel, Octavia and Savy bailed soon after that, muttering about "bridezilla without the bride." As if! Elin was the sweetest person on earth, thank you.

Just not in the skies.

Now it was just a matter of putting the vases, bowls and jewels in their appropriate places. Had to be perfect.

Throughout the day, Thane kept her informed of his whereabouts, sending private whispers through her mind. Every time, she stopped whatever she was doing and grinned.

Bellorie dubbed it "sickening."

So far, Thane had visited with his leader, Zacharel, and talked with Lucien. Now, he was with a group of Sent Ones, including Bjorn and Xerxes, out hunting the demon prince.

"I'm thinking about having portraits commissioned," she said as she filled one of the crystal bowls with eight rubies the size of her fist. Should she add a few sapphires for effect? Or maybe string beads of ebony from the side?

"Excellent idea," Bellorie said, settling atop the new bed in the room formerly known as Bang and Bail Central. "You should totally dress up as the queen of the castle and hang portraits of yourself in every room of the club, proving you outshine every woman but, of course, me."

"Of course." And it wasn't a terrible idea, actually. A bold declaration that Thane was taken, and biatches better beware. Not that Elin wanted to be *that* girl. If she couldn't trust Thane, she didn't need to be with him. But still. Letting her portrait-gaze follow every female in the bar appealed greatly. "For right now, I should probably concentrate on portraits of Thane, Bjorn and Xerxes."

"Sure, sure," Bellorie said with a nod. "But there's one little problem. They'd never sit still for more than a few minutes."

Thane might, if Elin asked nicely. The man seemed so eager to please her. In fact, she'd never been so pampered, and she loved it. But she wanted him to feel pampered, too.

"I'll have to find a painter good enough to work from a few glances."

Bellorie thought for a moment. "Well, I have a friend, Anya the Great and Terrible, aka the minor goddess of Anarchy. She's getting hitched to that scarred dude Lucien. Remember him? Anyhoodles, all you have to do is tell her exactly who—whom?—you want painted, and she can have something created within the hour. I don't know how she does it, and I won't ask."

"How much would she charge?"

"Usually she likes souls, but since you're my bestie, I'm sure she'd give you a discount. Shall I call her?"

I'm her bestie? Elin grinned so wide her cheeks hurt. "Yes, please."

Bellorie drew her cell from her pocket and dialed the number. Elin listened to the one-sided conversation with interest.

"Your talents are needed....Yeah, yeah, long time no speaky....Listen, Thane has a girlfriend now....I know, weird, right....Yeah, the paintings, like you did for the Lords of the Underworld....Perfection....Sure, sure, but I want my girl Bonka to have a few as queen as the castle....Okay, I'll find out." She put her hand over the mouthpiece and said to Elin, "In payment, she wants to be bartender and karaoke host tonight."

That was all? "Done!" Thane wouldn't mind. Surely he wouldn't. Free labor. And what harm could one female do?

Bellorie removed her hand and said, "It's on like Donkey Kong."

The call ended after a high-pitched "woo-hoo."

Clapping, Elin jumped up and down. "This is going to be so beyond amazing! When did she think she could have everything ready?"

"Five minutes."

What! "How?" It should be impossible, even for an immortal.

"Don't ask, remember? She always makes you regret it. Also...don't pull the happiness trigger just yet." Bellorie nibbled on her bottom lip. "Whatever she shows you, you have to love it. Gush, compliment her excessively, whatever it takes. Really lay it on thick. Never seen anything so magnificent, blah, blah, blah. Otherwise, she will make you a member of her portrait-of-the-month club and send you a new one every four weeks—and you will want to gouge out your own eyes, then scrub your brain with bleach to erase the memory."

Unfazed, Elin said, "This Anya sounds just like my mother. Trust me, we'll get along just fine."

Bellorie cringed. "I'm suddenly thinking this was a huge mistake. If she hurts you, Thane will go butcher block on her. If Thane goes butcher block on her, Lucien will declare war against the Sent Ones. If Lucien declares war against the Sent Ones, Bjorn and Xerxes will slaughter the Lords of the Underworld to protect their boy. The world will bleed. Oh, look. Cookies!" She skipped to the tray of food in the corner of the room.

No matter what, I'll be on my best behavior. Elin hoped to make Thane's life better, not worse.

A daunting task, she knew, because he would resist. She would be poking at his wounds, pulling back centuries-old scabs. But she was up for the challenge. Look how far she'd come already! He considered her a welcome part of his day…and night.

"I can totally tell you didn't bake these," Bellorie said, holding up one of the cookies, crumbs raining down. "You know how? Because they're delicious."

Elin rolled her eyes. "Enough about my terrible cooking."

"If you can't handle the heat, don't turn on the oven. No, seriously. *Please,* don't ever turn on the oven."

She snorted.

Bellorie waved her over. "Come on. You've got to try these."

Feeling lighter than she had in weeks, Elin skipped to her friend. Life was absolutely perfect.

CHAPTER TWENTY-FIVE

A MISSION LIKE all the rest. Productive yet unsatisfying. Thane and the other Sent Ones had killed over two dozen demons, but the prince remained at bay, as always, and now Thane had to wonder where the fiend was and what he was doing…what he was planning.

Nothing good, that much was certain.

A sense of impending doom had taken up residence upon Thane's shoulders.

Finished for the night, he, Bjorn and Xerxes entered the club and, in unison, drew up short. The Downfall had been transformed. From elegant debauchery to down-and-dirty sorority. Neon signs silently shouted Ladies' Night! Free Beer! from all over the walls.

In the corner was a booth with a poster overhead. It read Reward for Info Leading to Cameo's Freedom and Torin's Return.

Cameo, the keeper of Misery. A Lord/Lady of the Underworld. Currently trapped inside a powerful spear.

Lucien had been a help to Thane, on Bjorn's behalf. A favor was now owed.

He would send Elandra to research the spear. She was a part of Zacharel's army Thane usually tried to avoid, but she knew more about ancient weapons than anyone else.

As for Torin, the keeper of Disease, he wasn't sure

where to begin. But Axel would know. That boy could find anything, anywhere.

Anya, Lucien's blonde and beautiful fiancée, manned the bar, pouring drinks without any rhyme or reason, mixing liquors that didn't belong together, making a huge mess, and teaching Elin how to do the same. But obviously the two were having a blast.

Elin's grin was huge. "I'm calling this one the Barking Kitty Toadstool," she shouted as she held up a glass of glowing pink liquid. "You can suck it, Anya. There's no way your Mooing Zebra Bird Perch can compare."

A chorus of "hoorah" met the pronouncement, and Elin drained every drop.

"Do another," someone shouted. "Only, make it spank Anya even harder!"

Anya threw a knife at the speaker, and if not for the girl's quick reflexes, the goddess would have taken out her eye.

"Can't," Elin said with a shake of her head. "I promised the old ball and chain I'd never do sixteen shots in a single night ever again, and I never break my promises."

"So, do seventeen, you idiot!" someone else instructed.

"Woo-hoo," a thousand girls seemed to yell at once, and Elin nodded, as if they were extremely wise.

There were no male patrons. Maybe because there was another sign proclaiming all men would be castrated on sight. A group of female gorgons stood on tables singing.... He wasn't sure what the butchered song was supposed to be.

"I'm both awed and horrified," Bjorn said.

"I fear for my precious," Xerxes said, cupping his hands between his legs. "But I must admit, I love what your Elin has done with the place. The decor is absolutely stunning."

Nothing from the treasure chest had been used. Only clothing. Bras dangled from the new signs, and underwear swung from the chandeliers.

"Mmm, the man-meat has arrived," a woman said. Soft fingers sifted through Thane's wings, and he swung around to confront the culprit. "Yeah, baby. Yeah. Momma's got a ferocious appetite tonight. She's not gonna stop eating until she's devoured every crumb."

"Hey! No touching!" Elin shrieked, and suddenly she was between Thane and the female—Kaia, a Harpy dating Strider, the keeper of Defeat and a fierce Lord of the Underworld. Elin must have dived over the counter and skidded across the tile. "He's mine."

His chest puffed with pride. She'd just claimed him a second time. And this time, she'd done it in front of witnesses.

But he'd forgotten to warn her. Never challenge a Harpy. Unless you were prepared to lose a limb—and all of your internal organs.

"News flash, little flame." Kaia the Wing Shredder was a redheaded beauty with a mile-long nasty streak. "I done did the touching. So, what are you gonna do about it, huh?"

"I'm going to break your fingers—then your face," Elin proclaimed.

Thane was about to throw the fragile human behind him and say goodbye to his friendship with the Lords when Kaia grinned and nodded. "That's better, Bonka Donk. A whole lot better."

Elin returned her grin. "I know, right. I'm such a badass it's scary."

The two high-fived.

"But seriously," Elin said, wagging a finger at the Harpy. "Thane. Off-limits. No exceptions."

"Okay, okay." Kaia held up her hands, all innocence. "I'll save my love taps for our dodge-boulder game."

Elin threw her arms around Thane and gave him a hug. "Oh, baby, did I tell you the good news? The girl-friends, consorts, wives—whatever!—of the Lords of the Underworld just joined the National Dodge Boulder League."

Kaia drummed her fire-engine-red claws together. "All we're missing for total domination is a supercool team name."

"Just call yourselves what the Scorgasms do," Elin suggested helpfully. "'Losers.'"

Kaia hissed.

"I heard that!" Anya prepared to launch another knife, this time at Elin.

Comments from surrounding immortals—and eaves-droppers—came in quick.

"Oh, no, she didn't."

"Oh, sweet hairy goodness, our little Bonka Donk is already laying down the smack."

"Fight. Fight. Fight."

Enough. Thane cupped Elin's cheeks and forced her attention to turn to him. "Are you having fun?"

"Dude! So much!" She threaded her fingers through his hair, and just like that, the rest of the world faded from his awareness. "What about you?"

"Now I am." In her presence, he felt lighter, even free, as if invisible chains had at last fallen away from him.

"Wait till you see the rooms," she said, twirling

strands of his hair. "You're going to love them so hard, you'll probably make a baby together."

"As long as you're happy, I'm happy."

"I am." She kissed his chin and beamed up at him. "It's like I ordered you from a catalog. Like I said, I'll take *that* gorgeous face, and *that* sexy body, now add a dash of sweetness and a smidgen of protectiveness, and, okay, yeah, just go ahead and dip him in raging lust."

He grinned. "There are no changes you would make to me?"

"Nope. Not a single one."

"So I'm perfect?"

"For me," she whispered, a ragged edge to her tone. "You're perfect for me. But what about you? Would you change something about me?"

Reeling from her admission, he said, "You are flawless." *Except for your expiration date.* He frowned at the unwelcome thought.

Must do something. Soon.

Problem was, he was still without a solution. All he knew was that he wouldn't be killing her in an attempt for immortal regeneration.

He thought about the two males in the Army of Disgrace with human wives.

Zacharel's woman, Annabelle, had been marked by a demon as a teenager, part of her soul stolen. The warrior had had to cleanse the evil and patch her soul with a piece of his own, twining their life spans.

That wasn't feasible with Elin. Her soul was intact. Koldo's woman had bonded to the River of Life, becoming a Sent One.

No one knew how she'd initiated the bonding.

Perhaps Thane would supply Elin with a fresh vial

of the Water every day. At the very least, it would slow her aging.

Under Germanus's reign, all Sent Ones had been forced to endure a severe whipping and give up something beloved to acquire a single vial of the Water. Now, Clerici offered the Water freely, but there was a line of Sent Ones waiting to approach the shore, and it was at least three years long, making it even more difficult to get.

Perhaps someone could be bribed to give up a space at the front of the line.

"I have a surprise for you," Elin said, returning his attention to her. "The most wonderful, amazing surprise in the history of…ever."

One of his brows rose in question. "Is it you, naked in my bed?"

"No. It's better."

"There is *nothing* better than that."

I'VE GOT A new life goal, Elin thought. Thane had stepped into the bar, and in a flash of intuition, she'd known she'd been born to make him happy. Not just to help him heal. Not just to amuse and delight him. But to usher in true happiness.

"Take me to the suite," she whispered, and nibbled on his earlobe. "I'll show you."

He stalked forward, dragging her with him. Girls moaned about losing "the best worst bartender of all time" and it made her eyes a wee bit misty. She was accepted here, even liked, and totally appreciated for her amazing talents.

"You guys come, too," she called over her shoulder, pinning Bjorn and Xerxes with an I-mean-business stare. "You have to see this."

They blinked in surprise but followed.

"Don't forget to tell me the verdict," Anya called.

Elin flashed her a thumbs-up.

Inside the suite, trepidation nearly got the better of her, but she pointed to the far wall. "There."

Thane looked, tensed. His expression gave nothing away.

Every nerve in her body suddenly felt exposed, raw.

"Well," she said, glancing over Bjorn and Xerxes. They were just as unreadable. "What do you think?"

Silence.

Not even crickets dared chirp.

She peered at the painting Anya had brought, trying to see the artwork as the warriors must. It was a nearly life-size canvas, with Thane in the center, and Bjorn and Xerxes flanking him. A position she'd seen firsthand. Thane's wings were stretched out behind the others, and it was difficult to tell where his ended and theirs began, because theirs were flared, as well. All three males were weaponless, but then, they didn't need weapons. *They* were weapons.

They were shirtless, their fierce muscles on display, their skin splattered with spots of crimson. Unfortunately, they wore pants. The material was white and kind of loose, like the bottom of a robe. Behind them was absolute destruction. Blood dripped. The bodies of demons lay in pieces.

"If you don't like it—" she said.

"I don't like it," Thane interjected.

Oh. Her shoulders drooped. She'd been so certain

he'd go gaga, the way she had. The violent images had barely even registered.

"I love it," he added.

Oh! Such relief. "I had a few others made, and—"

"Where?" he rushed out. "I want to see."

"Your room."

He dragged forward and shouldered his way inside. Then he gaped. This time, changes were everywhere. From the massive sleigh bed, to the gold-inlaid dresser, to the nightstands made entirely from jade. The walls were peppered with photographed portraits of, well, her.

Embarrassment heated her cheeks as Bjorn and Xerxes filed in behind her, determined to see what else she'd done.

Anya had taken one look at her and snapped her fingers. "I know just the thing," she'd said, and commanded Bellorie to fetch her Canon. Then she'd proceeded to direct Elin to "make love to the camera"…"make hate to the camera"…"make a thousand babies with the camera." Yeah. Weirdest twenty minutes ever.

But Elin had grinned and posed, and scowled and posed, and laughed and posed. And now, the photos of her face and all its many emotions stared at her from every direction of the room.

"This…" Thane said, his voice thick with…what?

"I can take them down."

"No!" he growled. Then more softly repeated, "No. These are even better than the painting. I'll never want to leave the room."

"Tell me you have a sister, Elin," Bjorn said. "I'll be whipped. I don't ca—" Abruptly, he went quiet.

She turned to look at him, saw that he'd paled. "What's wrong?"

His haunted gaze met Thane's before moving to Xerxes. "It's happening again. I'm being summoned, and must—"

He was gone. There one moment, vanished the next, with no time to even finish his sentence.

Thane said only one word. "Lucien."

A few seconds later, as if Lucien had been waiting for a summons, the scarred warrior appeared in the hallway. "If you expect me to pay Anya's bar tab—"

"Bjorn. Now," Thane gritted, and the warrior nodded grimly.

Like Bjorn, Lucien vanished.

"What's going on?" Elin asked.

Xerxes stomped into the sitting room to pour himself a drink.

Thane gave Elin a gentle push toward the front door. "Go back to the party, kulta."

"No." He was upset. He needed her. "I'm staying with you."

"Elin—"

"Thane." She pushed him onto the couch and climbed onto his lap, snuggling close while being careful not to give Xerxes a peep show. She wasn't wearing panties. "Tell me."

Her beautiful Sent One enfolded her in his arms and buried his nose in her hair, inhaling. "Shadow demons are forcing Bjorn to go somewhere. We don't know where, and until we do, we can't help him. Lucien is tracking him."

"And you wanted me to leave because…"

"Because my concern will make me…edgy. I may not be nice to you."

Silly rabbit. "You don't always have to be nice to

me." He would have to guard every word, every action, and that kind of sounded like torture. "You only ever have to be yourself. I can deal."

He exhaled, his breath tickling her hair over her brow. "Now who's the one who says romantic things?"

An hour passed. Then two. And Thane *did* become grouchy. She distracted him to the best of her ability with stories of her childhood. The embarrassment of having her mother come to her elementary school to speak at career day—and teaching the kids how to gut a fish. The time her best friend from junior high stayed the night and her parents walked out of the bathroom in towels. Obviously, they'd just showered together. Gross!

Both Thane and Xerxes listened and even cracked a smile. But the tension never left them.

A little before the third hour came to a close, the scarred Lord returned. He was pallid, his eyes—one brown, one blue—glazed with horrors no man should ever have to see.

Thane set Elin aside and jumped to his feet. "Did you find him? Can you take us to him?"

Without a word, the warrior stumbled to the wet bar. He didn't bother with a glass, just drank straight from the whiskey bottle. When he'd drained half the contents, he turned to the men, wiped his mouth with the back of his hand.

"Tell us," Thane commanded.

"Your friend is… No, I can't take you to him. I don't know where he is. I was able to track him, but once there, I had a hard time finding my way out. I couldn't go back the way I'd come, because his trail had already gone cold and twisted, like before. But I saw him. I saw what she does to him."

She?

"You were right, Thane," the warrior said. "The queen is responsible. She's protecting him—because she's wed to him."

CHAPTER TWENTY-SIX

THANE REELED.

After Lucien dropped the marriage bombshell, he went into detail about everything he'd seen.

Bjorn, bound to a rocky wall, helpless as a dark shadow approached. Obviously the queen. And when she reached him, the center of her darkness opened like a mouth, revealing an even blacker gloom. She enveloped him, until there was no sign of him.

What was she doing to him? Tormenting him? Violating him?

Knowing Bjorn would return soon and that he would not want Elin to witness his plight, Thane escorted her to her room. There was a bed now. A big, beautiful one, with four posters and designs carved into each.

"Thank you for what you did today. *Everything* you did. But it will be best if Bjorn doesn't see you." He explained the gist of the situation. "He won't be…right when he returns."

She clutched the collar of his robe. "What can I do to help?"

So determined. Another quality to admire about her. "Just stay in here and rest. I'll see you in the morning."

She sighed. "Okay."

Even though Thane needed her with him, her mere

presence soothing him, he forced himself to kiss her brow and shut her inside.

He spent the next few hours pacing in the sitting room alongside Xerxes. Finally, though, Bjorn returned, and he was as out of sorts as every time before. Pale, withdrawn. Trembling. Nauseous.

Acting as crutches, they led him into the bathroom. After he vomited the contents of his stomach, they cleaned him up and got him settled into bed.

There had to be a way to save him from such a terrible sentence.

Bjorn rolled to his side and curled into a ball, his arms drawn tight around his middle.

"We know where you go, and we can guess the horrors being done to you," Thane said. "We'll figure out how to save you."

Bjorn closed his eyes, the length of his lashes casting menacing shadows over his cheeks. "She knew Lucien found me," he said, his voice devoid of emotion. "She released me from my vow of silence so that I could tell you nothing can be done. She will never cut my ties to her."

"We can make her," Thane gritted. "Every demon has its weakness."

"No. The shadows are not demons, though are often mistaken as such. They are Sine Lumine. Evil, yes. Depraved. That, too. They hunger for life."

"They...feed off you?" Xerxes exclaimed.

Shame colored the warrior's ashen face. "Only the queen does, and only a little at a time. The longer I live, the stronger she'll become."

"What does she take?" Thane demanded, horrified on his behalf.

Bjorn closed his eyes. "My…soul."

All right. That was bad, but not insurmountable. His soul could be renewed with the Water of Life. *Have to get more.* For Elin *and* for Bjorn.

"Where's your vial?" he asked.

"Doesn't matter. It's empty."

To Thane, and Thane alone, Xerxes said, *Mine is out, too.*

Thane had a few drops, nothing more.

That would work for today, but not for the next visit. Which might come sooner than expected. The queen seemed to be summoning him more and more frequently.

Reaching into his air pocket, Thane projected to Xerxes, *I'm going to go to every Sent One I know and try to buy their vials. After that, I'll bribe people waiting in the line to approach the River. For now, give him whatever he needs of this.* He handed over what remained of his vial.

Xerxes accepted with a nod.

"We won't stop until you are free of the queen," he said to Bjorn. "This is my vow to you."

His friend shook his head. "No. I don't want you caught in this."

"Too bad. It's done." He strode from the bedroom. With only a backward look to Elin's door, he shot out of the building and into the night sky.

He decided to go with bribery of strangers first— less complicated—and stopped at the Temple of Sol, Clerici's home. The line to reach the River of Life was longer than he remembered. Wrap-around-the-world-several-times longer.

Amid glares and rebukes, he flew to the front, the

gate, and stopped beside the female who would be allowed inside as soon as the Sent One on the other side left. He tried to buy her spot, and every spot within a mile behind her. No go. He would have threatened—and even killed—but like everyone else, he'd heard the mandate. To use force to obtain a place in line was to lose all rights to the Water. Forever.

How could he have known getting the Water would be more difficult once the whippings stopped?

He faced the crowd. Head held high, he announced, "I am Thane of the Three, and I'm looking to buy the Water of Life, however much or little you'll sell me. I'm based at the Downfall. Once you have the Water, come find me and I will buy it—whatever your price."

Knowing there was nothing else he could do here, he went to Zacharel's cloud. His leader had no more. He went to Koldo. The warrior had no more. He went to Magnus and Malcolm, but the brothers claimed they needed it for their own life-and-death purposes.

Though he wanted to, he did not argue with them.

Jamilla offered half a bottle for one hundred demons' heads. To which he agreed, as long as he could pay in some type of installment plan. They decided on twenty-five a week for four weeks.

Next he tried the female Sent Ones Elin would be battling at her next dodge-boulder game: Charlotte, Elandra, Malak and Ronen. The four were famous for their plans, schemes and troublemaking.

Their goal: to become the supreme leaders of the world and throw a "truly legit kegger."

They were out.

He returned to the club, coming in from sky level, the sun bright and shining. He gave Bjorn the vial he'd gotten from Jamilla, and took the elevator to the main floor to meet with Adrian. The berserker had summoned him.

The building was emptied of guests—though on his way in, he'd noticed the courtyard was littered with sleeping female bodies, drunken snores echoing.

Adrian stepped from the bar, claiming his attention. "You have a visitor. It's Ardeo," he said, and motioned to the king of the Phoenix.

The male was on the other side of the room, already halfway to bombed.

Thane approached him warily. "Did your people reach you?"

Without glancing up from his nearly empty glass, Ardeo nodded. "They did. Came to thank you."

"No thanks needed. A bargain was struck. I merely kept my end."

The Phoenix king kicked the seat across from him, a command for Thane to sit.

Orders? In my own house? No. Thane crossed his arms over his chest. "Anything else?"

Ardeo shrugged, drained the few droplets in the glass, and stood. Swayed. "I spoke to a mutual acquaintance of ours," he said, the words slurred. He patted Thane on the shoulder. "He sends his regards."

A sharp pain cut through Thane's stomach. Literally.

His brow furrowed with confusion as he glanced down. A blade had been shoved all the way to his spine.

Ardeo removed it, blood coating his hand. "My apologies. Malice said he would bring Malta back if I weakened you. Whatever the price, I have to have her back." The blade clattered to the floor.

Thane stumbled back, clutching the wound to stem the flow of blood.

Adrian rushed over to block the only exit and await orders.

"Fallen angels lie," Thane gritted to the king.

Expression sad, Ardeo nodded. "I know. But I was willing to risk it."

"Then bear the consequences. Do it," Thane commanded Adrian.

In a blink, the berserker seemed to grow and expand several inches. The color of his face changed, from bronzed to almost crimson. His eyes darkened to black, overtaking even the whites. He moved so fast, he was nothing more than a blur. One moment the king had four limbs and a head, the next…he didn't.

Blood sprayed from opened arteries. The pieces and the torso thumped to the floor.

Adrian returned to his spot, his heavy panting the only evidence that he'd been the one to strike.

With a shaky hand, Thane reached into his air pocket for the vial of Water. Gone. With Bjorn. *Can't ever regret that.* But now he wouldn't heal nearly as fast.

"Lock the king's parts in the dungeon, just in case he regenerates. Then take however long you need to calm."

Adrian's nod was clipped. He carried the pieces out of the room.

Thane, Elin shouted inside his head. *He's here. Orson is here.*

Ignoring his pain, his weakness, he darted in the air, leaving the natural realm for the spiritual and misting through the walls. *I'm coming, kulta.*

I'm in your bedroom, not mine.

I'm almost there. He reached the top floor, stumbling as he landed. Demons swarmed the entire area, blocking him from the entrance to his room. Xerxes and a fully healed Bjorn were in the sitting area, fighting for their lives.

The blood of demons splattered the walls. Gnarled limbs littered the floor.

Thane summoned a sword of fire and pushed forward, hacking at the enemy along the way. But the more he fought, the less he could ignore the weakness caused by the gash. He was slower than usual, and several demons were able to swipe him with claws. Soon, his lack of speed allowed gleeful opponents to trap him in an ever-tightening circle, unable to gain any new ground and get to Elin.

He remembered Orson and his twisted desire for her. Desperation and fear, coupled with the wildest rage of his life, flooded him.

Hold him off, Elin, he commanded. *I've been delayed. Do whatever you have to do to survive. Do you hear me?*

There was no reply.

He wanted to command a response from her, but didn't want to distract her. As he debated what to do, a demon scratched at him. He sliced through the offending arm. As the limb fell, another creature reached for him, poking at his injury and laughing. Thane cringed. But still he fought with all his might, willing to endure anything to reach his woman.

ELIN HADN'T STAYED in her bedroom. She'd crossed the bathroom in secret and camped inside Thane's, knowing he would be fragile after dealing with Bjorn. She'd been determined to wait for him, no matter how long it took. She would comfort him and give him whatever he needed, even if he didn't know he needed it.

The first thing she'd done was stretch out on the bed, and read the copy of *Dodge Boulder: A True Alpha Dog Story* Bellorie had loaned her. But she must have fallen asleep, because the next thing she knew, a hard hand had settled on her shoulder and was shaking her, rattling her brain against her skull. Her eyelids had popped open—and Orson's smug, smiling face had come into view.

Now she scrambled to the other side of the bed.

The warrior laughed as he withdrew a small dagger. "Your reaction cuts to the quick, girl. It truly does."

Thane expected her to hold him off, and she didn't have to wonder why. It sounded like World War III beyond the door.

"Stay away from me," she spat at Orson.

"Or what? You'll call me a terrible name?" Smiling evilly, he looked around the room. His every action was unhurried, as if he knew a secret she didn't. "I see you've made yourself at home here with the Sent One. And you're warming his bed, too, despite his reputation for cutting and running after only one night. What must you be doing to please him?"

"You'll never know." This male had taunted her for an entire year. A few times, he'd yanked her into a darkened corner and kissed her, squeezing her breasts and promising—threatening—to do more. Her fear of him had been absolute. But no longer. For the first time, she would fight back.

"Want to bet?" Quick as a blink, he dived across the bed in a bid to grab her.

Prepared for such a move, she darted out of the way and rushed to the dresser where she'd stored a few weapons she'd found in the treasure room, hoping to surprise Thane. She grabbed the first thing she touched in the top drawer. A pair of gold knuckles. Suckwad! But, okay, fine. They'd have to do.

Hot air brushed her back. Orson was closing in. No time to waste. She turned and swung, nailing him in the cheek. The bone instantly cracked—and the gold knuckles did something she wasn't expecting. On impact, they released sharp, motorized spikes, slashing through the cracks in the bone.

Roaring, Orson batted at her. His fist collided with her skull, and though she saw stars, she held on. He tried to jerk away from her, but the motions only increased the speed of the spikes, one digging so deep and so far up it... Gah! Thank the Most High she'd been inoculated against violence. Orson's eye popped from his head and rolled to the floor, and all he could do was watch with the other one, horrified.

Elin slid her fingers from the gold knuckles, but still the weapon remained attached to his face.

"You little whore!" He swung a meaty fist at her.

Oh, the pain! There was another explosion of stars across her vision as the taste of copper coated her tongue and caused her stomach to flip-flop.

Took worse hits at the last dodge-boulder practice. The knowledge empowered her. Grinning coldly, she climbed to her feet. Surprised, Orson glared at her with his one good eye.

"Is that the best you've got?" she taunted. "Because I'm suddenly wondering why I feared you *at all*."

Huffing and puffing with indignation, he stomped toward her. Again, he swung a fist. This time she was prepared and went low, avoiding impact. As she came up, she slid her fingers back through the golden knuckles and jerked with all of her might. Bone and metal finally separated.

He grunted, spittle dripping from his mouth. Then he punched her in the stomach. Air abandoned her lungs, and she hunched over. A vulnerable position. One he used to his advantage, hitting the back of her head. She collapsed to her knees, gagging as acid raced up her throat.

"Yield to me."

Not now, not ever. Elin crawled to her hands and knees and swung up a fist, smashing the golden knuckles into his crotch.

His high-pitched squeal rang out. Stumbling backward, he yanked at the spikes now embedded in his scrotum. The backs of his knees caught on the mattress and he fell.

She swiped up the dagger he dropped, and without pausing to consider her actions, or what her feelings would be when everything was said and done, she stabbed him in the stomach, once, twice, three times. Blood spurted. Warm blood. Warm blood all over her hands.

She staggered away from him.

As he lay panting, dying, he glared over at her. "I'll come back," he choked out. "I'll come back and repay the favor. You have my word. Only, I'll make you watch me kill your lover first."

Teeth bared in a scowl, she waved the dagger at him. "If you think you're tougher than Thane, you're dumber than you look. And trust me. You look dumber than a box of rocks. Now, I'll leave you to your death." She opened the door, intending to go out and help Thane however she could.

A horde of demons shoved their way inside the room, pushing her aside.

The creatures converged on Orson, as if they'd scented his blood and nothing else would suffice. They began eating his flesh…muscle…bone. He fought as best he could, but as weak as he was, it did him no good. He lost his other eye. He lost his throat, his heart, his intestines.

He became an all-you-can-eat buffet.

Breath wheezed through her nose. Elin knew Orson would never regenerate. Not from this.

When there was nothing but Orson's spleen—not as tasty?—glowing red eyes lifted and focused on Elin…

Heart drumming erratically, she backed away slowly. "I'm sour. Probably bitter. I suggest you wait for someone sweet," she said. "It'll be better for your digestion. Honest."

The creatures advanced on her.

CHAPTER TWENTY-SEVEN

No matter how many demons Thane and the others killed, the number of opponents only grew. There were simply too many of them. Big, little. Countless hordes of every type.

Without question, this was a planned attack, and all the prince's doing. Ardeo had weakened him just before the army of demon minions attacked, all for the prince's benefit. It was a strike meant to end him. And if that failed, a strike meant to disable him.

The more Thane fought, the more blood and strength he hemorrhaged. There wasn't time or opportunity for one of his boys to feed him Water. A single moment of inactivity or distraction was certain death.

Claws swiped at him. Fangs snapped at him. Poisoned horns and antlers slashed in his direction. All he could do was swing the sword of fire back and forward, left and right, remaining in constant motion to keep the creatures from making contact.

We can't continue this way, Xerxes projected.

I can lead them away from the club, Thane replied. *You can get everyone to safety.*

Some of the demons may follow you. But every single one of them? No.

True. If the numbers kept growing, he would be leaving his loved ones here to be slaughtered.

Zacharel, he said to his leader. *I'm in trouble.* He explained the situation.

I'm too far away to help. Zacharel's unemotional tone was oddly comforting. *But I'll send the others.*

Help is on the way, he told Xerxes and Bjorn. Thankfully, neither asked him if he believed that help would arrive in time.

With a flick of his wrist, Thane removed the head of the demon closest to him—and caught a glimpse of Elin in the hallway, fighting six monkeylike demons on her own.

Little details hit him like bullets. Her only weapon was a dagger. Crimson stained her hands. Blood. Hers? Cuts and abrasions littered her arms. Her clothing—a tank and shorts—was torn.

One of the demons grabbed her by the hair and jerked her to the floor. When she landed, she kicked him in the stomach, punting him across the room. Another creature dived on top of her, but she punched him in the face, preventing him from biting her.

Rage returned some of the strength he'd lost. Thane battled his way toward her with new fervor, mowing down everything in his path. Though she remained on her back, she continued to fight with surprising ferocity, grabbing a demon by the horn and holding him still while she whaled—and while the other demons gnawed on her stomach and legs.

No one hurts my woman.

Fury coursed through his veins, making him insane with bloodlust as he stomped over. Quick as lightning, he ripped an arm off one of the culprits—and stuffed it inside the mouth of another. He—

Froze. Right along with everyone else in the room.

A horrible quiet descended, the air thickening, as if boiling water was being poured throughout. His gaze met Elin's. He saw pain. He saw confusion. He saw determination.

What's happening? she asked.

Don't know, he replied. *Are you all right?*

I will be.

Thane kicked a demon off her. The thickened air slowed his movements and tempered his strength, but he accomplished his goal. The rest of the creatures fell away from her, moving just as slowly as he had, as she struggled to sit up. With great effort he managed to crouch beside her and urge her back down before covering her with his wings.

I've never experienced anything like this. Until I know it's safe, you will stay here.

I'm not sure I—

Her words were cut off.

The demons looked as if they were shrieking as they ran out of the hall, and maybe they reached the exit. Maybe they didn't. A horrible darkness covered the entire expanse. A darkness devoid of even the smallest pinpricks of light. It brought helplessness. It brought emptiness. Thane's senses were suddenly switched off. There was nothing, no one. Except absolute, utter aloneness.

His skin crawled, and his mind screamed—*Elin, have to protect Elin.* He attempted to drape his body across hers, but couldn't move an inch. His muscles were like iron, his skin like stone.

Just when he thought he could take no more, that he would surely go insane, the darkness lifted. He blinked to focus. The first thing he noticed: the demons were dead. All of them. Motionless, mutilated bodies covered the blood-splattered floor.

What had just happened?

He was panting, he realized. And sweating. Blood leaked from his eyes and ears.

If *he* was this bad… "Elin!" He snapped his wings behind his back, and there she was, just as he'd left her. She had no new injuries, and she was still conscious.

His relief was so fervent he could taste it.

"Oh, baby," she said, sitting up to wipe the blood from his face, showing no reaction to it, the carnage of the past few hours having been so much worse. "Are you okay? I tried to talk to you, tried to move, but couldn't. It was awful."

He loved when she called him "baby." "I'm…" He couldn't lie. He wasn't well, wasn't even sure how he was still upright.

"That was her," Bjorn said, racing over. "The queen. My…wife." He cringed as the last word left him. "She tried to take out one of my most trusted allies, to make me helpless against her. You received a mere taste of her darkness."

What Bjorn experienced was *worse?*

"If that was your wife," Elin said, with a shudder, "I don't think marriage counseling is going to help."

Bjorn cracked the barest hint of a smile.

Thane's eyesight dimmed, and the room spun.

Crouched as he was, his weight became too much. He tried to tilt to his side and succeeded, but tilted too much. He fell, a sharp pain shooting through his side when he landed.

"Thane," Elin said. She sounded concerned, but far away.

Want her near.

He reached for her but ended up thumping Bjorn on the chest. "Elin."

"I'm here, baby. I'm here. Let Bjorn help you, okay?"

His arm flopped to the floor. Strong hands cupped his shoulder and pushed him to his back. His lips were pried open.

"Here," a female voice he recognized said. "The other half of the bottle, for a hundred more heads." Cool water dribbled down his throat. The pains sharpened further, agonizing him as the healing properties in the Water mended torn muscle and flesh.

"—you promise?" Elin was saying, what seemed an eternity later. "If you're wrong and he doesn't recover, I'll find a way to go fire-creeper and burn you alive."

She worried for him and obviously cared for him, if she was threatening lives. Could she even...love him?

He'd never wanted the emotion from a lover. The very thought of it had repulsed him. But he wanted hers, he realized. More than he'd ever wanted anything. If she loved him, she would never leave him.

"Yes. He will live," Xerxes said.

Xerxes had survived the attack, too. Thank the Most High.

Thane blinked, trying to focus.

"See? He's coming around now," Bjorn said.

"Thane," she croaked. She loomed over him. "Don't ever scare me like that again."

He met her gaze and noticed the tears wetting her lashes. As he reached up to brush them away, she leaned down to kiss him.

Though he wanted to stay where he was and savor this moment, he sat up. His boys stood in the hallway, watching him. Jamilla—the voice he'd recognized—was gone. Pulling Elin against him, he said, "We have to move everyone out of the club. It's not safe for them here…. If we have any survivors?" His chest clenched at the thought of losing any of his employees.

They were his people.

He guarded what was his.

"Adrian was just here," Xerxes said, his expression grim. "The other Sent Ones arrived just before Bjorn's shadow woman. They're all fine. Ricker, Kendra's husband, must have hidden in the club when Ardeo came in, because he broke into the dungeon and escaped with her and the king."

"Oh, Thane," Elin said. "Your revenge…"

"I don't care about that," he said, and meant it.

Xerxes held up his hand, a request for quiet. "There's something you both need to know. Chanel… She didn't make it."

"What!" Elin gasped out, trying to stand. "No. Not Chanel. She's strong. She'll pull through."

"No. Not this time." Xerxes shook his head. "The creatures devoured… They took… No."

Thane tightened his hold on Elin. At first, she fought him. Then a sob left her and she sagged against him. Tears stung his eyes as she clung to him, pouring out her misery. The other girls must be overcome with sorrow, as well. The five had been as tight a unit as he, Xerxes and Bjorn.

"I'm sorry, kulta."

"I didn't even get to say goodbye."

"I know," he said softly. "I know."

One way or another, the prince would pay for this.

ELIN CRIED SO MUCH and so hard her eyes swelled and her tear ducts clogged. Her nose stuffed up, and her throat burned, the tissues raw. She wanted to comfort her friends, but everyone had been split up. Something about making it more difficult for the prince to get a lock. Whatever. She didn't care.

Xerxes took Bellorie and McCadden. Bjorn took Octavia. Adrian took Savy.

Thane flew Elin to a home he kept on a deserted island. A true paradise, with palm trees, lush foliage and a white-sand beach. It was surely the Most High's most beautiful handiwork. Crystal clear water lapped at the shore and frothed. The scent of coconut and orchids drifted on a gentle breeze. Birds soared overhead, the sun glowing bright orange and pink on the horizon.

She spent the first day at the shore, her toes deep in the sand as she sobbed. Thane spent the day sending mental orders to Axel and Elandra, helping to map out strategies for the Lords of the Underworld, as well as to other Sent Ones in a bid to find the prince. At least, that was what she thought she heard him say in the few moments she was calm.

Elin spent the second day at the shore, her toes deep in the sand as she sniffled. Thane spent it communicating with Zacharel, explaining what was going on, the reports that had come in, and gaining permission for every move he planned to make. Later, he told her that he would never again risk getting into trouble and losing his wings. His homes.

His woman.

Elin spent the third day at the shore, her toes deep in the sand as she watched the world continue on, as if nothing had happened. As if it hadn't lost a precious gift. Thane watched her, silent.

On the fourth day, Thane sat beside her, waiting for her to speak.

"There's so much death in the world," she finally said.

"Yes. You've seen much in your short years. And the longer you live, the more you'll see."

And one day, if they stayed together, he would see hers. Or, in an ironic twist of fate, would she, the half human, see *his?* The thought shattered her. "Does it ever get easier?"

"I wish, but…no. No, it doesn't."

Brutal honesty. As always. A trait she loved, even when it hurt.

Still, her chin trembled as she fought the urge to scream. To scream and never stop. To rant and rail. To curse. This wasn't fair. Chanel was —had been—a good person. A *great* person. Sweet, charming. Fun.

"Who killed her?" Elin croaked. "The demons or the Phoenix or the shadows?"

"The demons. Bellorie was with her and saw it happen."

Poor Bellorie. She would have to live with the horrific images of her friend's murder for the rest of her long life. And maybe she'd have to live with a dash of survivor's guilt, too. Elin knew what that was like.

I want to hug her. I need to cry with her.

"I know we haven't talked about the future," she said. "I know I've told you again and again that I'm going back to the human world."

He tensed.

"But I'm not. I'm staying with you. Now and always. I want to make sure nothing like this ever happens again." The violence... Well, she could obviously handle it now. She'd fought demons. She'd attacked Orson and survived. She'd watched his body be consumed without blinking. "And," she added, "I want you. To be with you. Totally and completely." He'd won her trust, and she refused to dish pretenses. Life could be cut short at any moment. Why live without her heart's desire?

He breathed a sigh of relief. "I didn't want you to go. I...never worked on your ID," he admitted. "Elin, I'm sorry, but I wanted you with me, and put no effort into the task."

Tricky Sent One. "I should be mad. Later, when things have calmed down, I'll probably punish you."

"And I will accept it as my due." He nudged her with his shoulder. "Perhaps I shouldn't admit this, but if it's anything like the last punishment, I'll enjoy it."

"You might be the first male in this world or any other to say that—and mean it. But I'm glad you do." Chest aching, she leaned against him. "What happens now?"

He sighed. "Now, we recover." His expression darkened before he said, "Then we go to war."

CHAPTER TWENTY-EIGHT

THANE KEPT ELIN on the island for a week. His home sat right on the beach, with glass walls peering into the sunrise. There was very little furniture, but what was there was luxurious. His favorite piece was the massive bed with the wispy canopy falling over the sides. When the material was parted, there was a direct ocean view.

All Sent Ones kept multiple homes all over the world, because they never knew where they would be stationed. He even had an underground residence, a place he used to fly the lovers he knew he would be particularly rough with, so nobody could hear their screams.

Time to sell it. That part of his life was over.

He'd kept in contact with his boys and knew everyone was safe. Mourning Chanel's passing, but safe. He'd pampered Elin in every way he knew how to. He'd made love to her. Gently. Hard. Looong. Quick. He'd stayed in her bed all night and tried to remain awake, unwilling to risk a nightmare, but she had caught on and seduced him into a coma of pleasure. Nary a nightmare to be had.

He'd fed her by hand. He'd tried to tempt her to swim with him, but she'd claimed to have an ironclad deal with the sharks. She stayed out of the water, and they didn't bite her.

Today, he thought, *I make Elin smile.*

He missed her smiles. And he could help her with her guilt.

As sunlight streamed into the room, he scooped her from the bed. She was warm, soft and naked.

"Hey," she said groggily, blinking rapidly. She had spent more time sleeping than anything else, and it was time to force her to play.

He shouldered his way past the glass doors. Sand squished between his toes as he walked. Balmy air caressed his bare skin.

"Hey, someone is going to see us," she said, fully awake now. "Take me in, before I pop a serious cap in your arse."

He loved the way her accent thickened with her emotions. "We're the only two people on the island. No one will see us." He continued his march toward the water.

"I don't care. Whatever you're planning, I'm out." She began to squirm against his grip. "Let me go. Right this second, Thane Downfall!"

"Oh, I'll let you go. Don't worry." Cool water lapped at his feet.

"Thane! Remember my deal with the sharks!"

"They wouldn't dare sue you for breach of contract. Not while I'm around." When the water reached the middle of his thighs, he gave her a quick squeeze and kissed her temple. "I would never do anything to hurt you. You know that, yes?"

She relaxed against him. "Yes. Of course."

"Good." He gave her a wicked grin—and tossed her in.

She screamed and flailed. On impact, water splashed. She sank like a stone. Then, a few seconds later, she came up sputtering. "You wretch!"

Adorable female. Wet hair clung to her face and neck. Droplets slithered down her cheeks.

"Payback is going to hurt, Mr. Never Getting Laid Again," she gritted, swimming toward him. "That's your new last name, by the way."

He dived underwater and to the left before she could get a handle on him. But she followed him, and when he came up for air she was behind him, her hands on his shoulders, shoving him back down.

As he broke the surface a second time, he latched on to her wrists and yanked her around until her breasts were smashed against his chest. She exhaled sharply. And so did he, the beauty of her striking him as forcefully as a fist. The sun paid her nothing but tribute, turning her skin a lovely gold, showing hints of red in her dark hair.

A grin lifted the corners of her lips...only to fall a second later.

"Chanel is in your heart," he said. "Just like Bay. Moving on doesn't mean you love them any less, or that you didn't love them enough, and it isn't something that should plague you with guilt. Be stronger than your emotions, kulta. Don't let them define you."

She frowned. "Love is an emotion. There's nothing stronger."

"Love is more than an emotion. It's a choice. Feeling love is one thing. Showing love is quite another."

"And in this case, the way to show love is...what?"

"Give. Always give, I'm learning. Time. Patience. Mercy. In this case, give Bay and Chanel what they would have wanted for you. Happiness."

Her lashes fused together for several seconds, but when she opened them, her expression sparkled in a way he hadn't seen all week. Pretty color stained her cheeks, and he almost shouted with relief.

"You're right," she said on a wispy catch of breath.

"I believe we've had this conversation before. I'm *always* right."

She rolled her eyes. "Correction. You're always right…when you agree with me."

His lips twitched at the corners as he pulled her closer. She wrapped her legs around his waist, putting their bodies in the perfect position for penetration. Desire hardened his shaft.

Leaning down, lips hovering just over his, she whispered, "Are you getting naughty ideas, Mr. Probably Getting Laid Again?"

"Many."

"Well, then…too bad." She pushed away from him, severing contact.

He opened his mouth to protest…until he saw her smile. He'd done it. He'd made her smile, just as he'd hoped. And it was far more beautiful than he remembered, nearly unmanning him.

"If you want me," she said, her voice low and husky, "you're going to have to pay the ginormous toll."

"Charging fees now?"

"Absolutely. You've met me, right? I likes me some money."

He waved his hand with regal authority. "I'm listening. You may continue."

She swam a circle around him, as though marking her territory…or she was a predator who'd just spotted the tastiest of prey. "Tell me about the Sent Ones," she said. "I know so little about your kind."

"Your price is information?" he asked, incredulous.

"Exactly."

He feigned disappointment, even as he rejoiced. The more she wanted to know, the more she cared. "You know about angels, I'm sure. Well, Sent Ones and angels are very much alike."

"And you can both fall?"

"Yes. Though, when a Sent One falls, he loses his immortality. When an angel falls, he becomes the epitome of evil."

"Like the demons we fought?"

"No. Demons were living in your world long before humans. Long before dinosaurs, even. The fallen angels came much later. And I doubt you've ever encountered one before. Many are now chained deep in the earth's core."

Clearly intrigued, she said, "So the demons… They consider the world their home turf?"

"Yes. And humans their toys."

"And you Sent Ones are supposed to…what?"

"Police them. Hunt them. Kill them."

"And the angels…"

"Do the same, but they are servants of the Most High, meant to assist us."

"That's cool. If *cool* is the new word for *white-hot*."

"Why, Ms. Vale," he said, and tsked. He was the one to circle her this time. "Does power excite you?"

"Maybe a little," she admitted, pinching two of her fingers together. "What other differences are there?"

"While angels are created beings, Sent Ones are born."

"So you have parents?"

"I *had* parents."

"You mean…"

He nodded. "My mother was killed by demons, and afterward, my father wasted away."

A tinge of sadness returned to her eyes. "I'm sorry. How old were you when this happened?"

"Six."

"Just a baby. What happened to you?"

"I had already been sent to train as a warrior. My life wasn't disrupted at all." Not in the physical sense. He'd hardly known his parents, but still he'd mourned their loss. "My life didn't change until a hundred years ago, when I was locked in a demon prison."

"Xerxes said you've won all battles but one." She said this hesitantly, as if she expected him to shy away from the topic. "Was he referring to your time in the dungeon?"

She was his woman. He would share everything with her, even his past. And he would trust her to like him—*please, love me*—anyway. He fingered the ring of scars at his neck. "No. Even though we were tortured, I consider the experience a win, as we eventually killed our captors. What he refers to is a battle I lost…against myself. Bjorn, Xerxes and I had just escaped imprisonment, and I wanted to feel something physical. I… slit my own throat. Xerxes and Bjorn used the Water of Life to heal me. I was angry, so I slit my throat a second time. They were out of Water, and had to doctor me back to health. Every day of my recovery, I saw anguish in their eyes and it affected me. They'd suffered enough. I asked the Most High to leave the scars around my neck as a reminder that I wasn't alone, that others relied on me, and He granted my request."

"Oh, Thane."

He continued. If he stopped, he might never start again. "The dungeon changed us."

"How did you end up there?"

"I was captured when I was sent on a mission. They chained me in a cell and later brought in Bjorn and Xerxes. Things were done to them…horrible things they survived only because they are immortal. But me… me the demons left alone, and I never understood why until much later."

"Why?" she asked softly.

"They were feeding off my guilt, fury and hopelessness."

Her eyes widened. "Though you try to hide it, you feel more deeply than the average person. That explains so much."

He dunked under the water for a moment, cooling his face. "I was forced to watch, desperate to help the males but unable. I wanted so badly to hurt the demons and, barring that, wanted so badly for the demons to hurt me in their stead."

Her hand fluttered over her heart, as if she sought to dampen a sudden pain. "How did you escape?"

"I struggled so forcefully against my bonds, I broke both of the wrist and ankle cuffs. I also broke my wrists and ankles, and dislocated both my shoulders, but I somehow found the strength to unhook Bjorn from overhead and yank Xerxes from the wall. By the time the demons returned to us, we had healed. We were able to fight."

"Oh, Thane. What you endured… I'm so sorry."

He reached out, brushed away one of her tears. "No sadness or sorrow. Not for me. The experience broke me, yes. But the pieces were eventually welded back together, making me stronger than I would have been otherwise. And now I have Xerxes and Bjorn. Something beautiful from something dark."

"Beauty from ashes," she said, the words she'd given him once before. She propelled into his chest, splashing water into his mouth as she enfolded him in her arms. "But, Thane?"

Peering into her eyes caused the most exquisite ache. "Yes, Elin."

"You also have me."

ELIN TOTALLY GOT Thane's need to hurt and be hurt now. His past had shaped him, and what he'd been denied had become what he desired most, somehow becoming entangled with the most passionate part of his life. Sex.

All of her insecurities and reservations about that part of his life died in that moment.

"If those urges ever return—" she said.

"They won't."

"You don't know that. So, as I was saying. If those urges ever return, come to me. Let's talk about it. Let me be the one to satisfy you. I'm not afraid anymore," she added when he opened his mouth to protest. "Not even a little."

His features softened with adoration. "It isn't just about your fear. It's about my abhorrence of the idea of harming the one I'm meant to protect…of marring the woman I cherish most."

She knew her smile was laced with every dream and secret fantasy she'd ever had. "I'm sure there are ways to do it that won't truly harm me."

His eyelids went heavy. "Yes. I can punish you the way you punish me."

Her nipples puckered as she rubbed against him. "I'm looking forward to it. But right now, I'm more interested in giving you a severe tongue-lashing...."

THANE CLUTCHED ELIN to his chest. She'd given him a tongue-lashing all right...and like the warrior he was, he'd somehow found the strength to endure.

Wicked, wild woman. She pushed him to heights he'd never imagined possible.

The "punishment" session had taken place in bed hours ago, and they had yet to leave.

"I would like to discuss the future," she said now, straddling his waist.

He nodded, encouraging her to continue.

"I told you I want to stay with you, and I meant it. But I don't want to stay as your employee. I want to stay as your equal. And, yes, I know you're stronger. I'm not foolish. I know you have wealth, and I come with nothing. But I want to be your woman, and—"

"I agree," he rushed out. She was giving him the words he craved more than life. He would have promised the moon and stars.

She grinned. "You didn't even hear the rest of what I had to say."

"I don't need to. I want you, now and always. I'll do whatever it takes to keep you."

"Well, good, because it means exclusivity, open lines of communication, trust, girls' night at the bar every other Friday, and sleeping with me every night. And for the record, 'sleeping' does not mean lying awake and holding me."

"Elin—"

"No. You said you'd agree to anything, and this is

what I'm asking. Let me help you with your nightmares. I've done a good job so far, right?"

"At the cost of your own rest."

"Rest, shmest. If you'll let me, I'll scare your bad dreams away. I mean, really. Have you *seen* my new biceps? They are sick."

If by "sick" she meant "on life support," then yes. His woman was delicate, and there was nothing wrong with that—in fact, there was everything right with it. "Agreed." Whatever she wanted, he would give her. Even that. Because she was right—being with her was helping tamp down the nightmares. He had never imagined such a thing possible, but there were many things he would have denied…until Elin had made the impossible possible. "But I will need a concession from you."

Triumphant, she leaned down and nibbled on his earlobe. He almost lost track of his thoughts. Almost.

"I love you, Elin," he admitted, tangling his hands in her hair. "I love you more than any man has ever loved a woman."

Gasping, she jolted upright. Her eyes were wide with shock. "What did you say?"

"I love you." She owned his heart. His soul. And he couldn't regret their loss. They were safer than they'd ever been. "You had me from the start, when you bravely aided my escape from a common enemy. You became my brightest light. My sweetest hope. And now that you've addicted me to all that you are, I can't give you up. I *won't* give you up. We're in this together from now on."

Tears welled in her eyes.

He rolled her over, pinning her with his weight, and kissed the salty droplets away. "And now, the concession," he continued. "When I find a way to make you fully immortal, and I will, you will do what's necessary. Whatever it is."

"But—"

"No buts." He cupped her face, gave her a little shake. This was too important. "You will. I would rather die than lose you." Over the past few days, his sense of doom had only grown. Now, when things were finally right between him and the woman holding his heart, it was making him desperate. "And, Elin? That's exactly what will happen. If ever you leave me, whatever the reason, I won't be able to move on. I don't care what I've told you about overcoming your loss of Bay."

"But I'll want you to—"

"No," he said again. "Without you, I have nothing. Without you, I want nothing."

Overcome by the need to possess her, here, now, and always, he spread his burning hands over every inch of her. Staking his claim. Leaving his mark. "You are mine," he said. "I won't lose you."

"I'm yours. And you're mine. I won't lose you, either," she gasped, urging his head down for a kiss. "Not to anything."

"Not ever," he agreed.

CHAPTER TWENTY-NINE

SHE HADN'T TOLD THANE she loved him, Elin realized.

She wanted to tell him. She really did. Because she knew deep down that the man owned her heart every bit as much as she owned his. But guilt kept the words trapped inside her.

She was already giving him everything Bay had lost. How could she give him those precious words, too? Especially when, in Thane's arms, she was happier than she'd ever been.

"You ready, kulta?" He came up behind her and wrapped his strong arms around her waist, flattening his pleasure-giving hands on her belly, and kissing the hollow of her neck.

The time to leave the island and meet up with the others had arrived. Thane's injury was completely healed. Elin's sense of despondency had lifted. They had a demon prince to hunt, and a Phoenix king to spank. Not necessarily in that order.

"Ready." She turned in his embrace to anchor her arms around his neck, careful not to pull at the feathers in his majestic wings.

A rare few Phoenix had wings, though the appendages formed from smoke and were the color of the darkest night. She'd never craved a pair of her own. Until now. To keep pace with Thane…to be his equal in *some-*

thing. Oh, she knew she'd told him she wanted to be treated as his equal, but she also knew it would be an act, nothing more.

Gently, he chucked her on the chin. "What's this?"

Always he guessed her mood correctly and sensed the slightest change. *Am I that predictable—or is he just that aware of me?*

She told him her thoughts, leaving nothing out. She'd demanded his trust, and she would give her own. He was her man. He would never use her vulnerabilities against her.

"Elin, of the two of us, you hold more power. Never doubt that."

She blinked in astonishment. Of all the things he could have said, that hadn't been on the list of possibilities. Because he couldn't lie! So…those earth-shattering words were true to him.

"Sorry, baby, but I'm doubting," she admitted. "I don't understand."

"I told you. You own me. I'm yours. All that I have been. All that I am. All that I will ever be. Your happiness is mine. Your fury is mine. And your needs will be met *before* mine. I love you, and to me, that means placing you first and giving to you what I will never give to another. Power over me."

Trembling, she pressed her forehead against his chest. "Thank you."

Tell him. Tell him right now.

Just…can't.

She fisted his robe. "The things you say to me…"

"Come straight from the heart you revived."

"See! Like that!" She straightened and met his earnest gaze. "They're beautiful. Like poetry. And what do I give you in return?" Nothing but trouble!

His expression was infinitely tender. "You give me what I've never had before. Peace."

"How? I'm just…me."

"A puzzle without its final piece is never complete. I am a puzzle, and you are my piece." His eyes sparked with mischief as he added, "I am a rose, and you are my thorn."

She snorted. "Thorns aren't just annoying. They are there to protect the rose, you know."

"I know."

"So…stoic Thane just admitted his ladybird is one badass chick?"

"He did."

"Well, that's gonna get him laid *so hard* later."

He barked out a laugh. With a single flap of his wings, he shot in the air, and Elin tightened her hold on him. The higher they glided, the cooler the air became, but pressed against Thane she never grew cold. When he leveled out, pressure kept her body flat against him, practically bonding them. Wind whipped at her hair, and the strands slapped at her cheeks.

Hours passed before they reached their destination. A castle Bjorn kept in the third level of the heavens, about twenty miles from the Downfall. She gaped at the grand stone stairway outside, with flowers blooming on both sides, leading to something straight out of a fairy tale. Outer walls slightly darker than the clouds surrounded them, with sapphire steeples and stained-glass windows.

"You like?" Thane asked after setting her down and taking her hand.

"The word *like* makes a mockery of the enormity of my feelings. I want to marry it."

He smiled. "There is a similar castle for sale on the other side of the world. No one has bought it, because it's become overrun by trolls. But with only a phone call, it can be ours."

Ours? Ours! As in, living together for real? Her brows winged up. "Question. Why aren't you making that call *right now?*"

He chuckled, and it was such a beautiful sound. Rusty, but beautiful.

"What?" she said with mock fury and a stomp of her foot. "Forget what I said that day of the demon attack. Every girl dreams of being a princess at some point or another."

"You'll have to settle for queen of my heart."

Sappy male.

My male.

"Deal."

At the massive double doors, Thane didn't bother to knock. He pushed his way in. The foyer had a domed ceiling, gilded walls with carved swirling designs, and a marble floor.

Footsteps echoed beyond the hallway, getting closer by the second.

Then Bellorie was racing around a corner and barreling toward her. Elin let go of Thane to meet her in the middle. They hugged and they cried, and all the while she felt her man's gaze on her back, watching over her.

He's got it bad for me.

Thank the Most High, because I've got it bad for him.

She had to nut up and tell him how she felt about him—that was all there was to it. *I love you, Thane.*

With every ounce of my being. Boom. Done. Just like that. The feeling was all-consuming, disconcerting. And yet, somehow empowering. Being with him didn't take away from her relationship with Bay. Being with him reminded her that happy endings were possible. That she never again had to be alone, or an outcast. Thane accepted her for all that she was. He adored her. And he needed her.

Bay, sweet boy that he'd been, had never needed her. They had been two wholes coexisting alongside each other rather than two halves that made up a whole, each necessary for the other's survival.

Thane...she couldn't breathe without.

"You're the last to arrive, Bonka Donk," Bellorie said with a sniffle. "We were worried about you when we clearly shouldn't have been, because, girl, you are glowing like a night-light with Mr. Taken One's essentia. Far brighter than before...which makes me wonder what the two of you have been doing."

She blushed. Not because she was embarrassed for being Thane's woman—she was beyond proud—but because everyone would know what they'd been doing together. *Like they didn't already know. FYI, your satisfied smile is a dead giveaway, too.*

"So, anyway, we're holding a ladies-only memorial outside." Bellorie peeked over Elin's shoulder. "Thane, every henhouse could use a cock. Want to be ours?"

Don't laugh. Elin glanced back at him. He gave her a soft smile and waved her on. "Go without me. I need to confer with the other—men."

Elin blew him a kiss.

He caught it in the air and said, "I'll miss you."

The fact that he could utter those words in front of

an audience, and not care, melted her. "I'll miss you, too." So freaking bad.

"Gag," Bellorie said, pulling Elin along. "Be mushy on your own time."

As quickly as the girl dragged her, Elin had no chance to admire the castle and its interior—every piece of furniture had to have been built by unicorns while living inside a rainbow, because, wow. Talk about magical!

The backyard had a large garden teeming with sweet-smelling flowers and lush green vines, everything shrouded by a thin, glittering veil of mist—and were those fairies buzzing about?

Not full-grown Fae, like Chanel, but small, about the size of her index finger, and—

Chanel.

Threads of remorse wove a tapestry inside her. A tapestry of memories. Chanel's bright smile. Her adorable giggle. Her killer instinct on the field of boulder battle.

Octavia and Savy each held a bottle of clear liquid. It had to be the most potent alcohol of all time, judging by the smell of it. Bellorie grabbed the two bottles waiting at their feet and handed one to Elin.

"To effing Chanel!"

Everyone raised a bottle before taking a swig.

Elin coughed and choked the burning flames down. "What is this crap? Moonshine?"

"Better," Octavia said. "Moonshine from Tartarus. You know, the prison for immortals. I've got a friend on the inside. Well, the part still standing, that is."

So. She was drinking alcohol that had been mixed in some immortal's toilet. Awesome.

"I keep expecting Chanel to pop out and say 'gotcha, I'm still alive, suckas,'" Savy admitted.

"Wouldn't that be just like the little hooker? Make us mourn and cry and talk about her, just for grins and giggles." Smiling, Bellorie scanned the yard. "Come out, come out, wherever you are."

They waited.

When Chanel failed to appear, Bellorie's smile faded. "The world won't be the same without her."

"No. It won't." This was nice. Elin had never had this before. Camaraderie after a loss. After the deaths of her husband and father, she had been a slave, and emotional outbursts had not been tolerated. Sobbing into her thin blanket at night had been her only solace. With her mother and newborn brother, same deal. "I'll never forget her smart mouth. I like to think she gave some of that sass to me."

"Hear, hear," Bellorie said, and again raised her bottle. She drained half the contents. "I know she wouldn't want a sober person at her memorial. She was sweet like that."

"For you, Alcoballic." Elin drank. Thankfully, the more she drank, the smoother the liquid went down.

Within the hour, everyone was laughing and sharing their favorite stories about the girl. Elin almost peed her pants when Savy told hers, talking casually about Chanel tripping and landing face-first in some random immortal's lap. He'd just smiled, patted her on top of her head, and told her that his balls needed a moment to recover before she attempted another blow job.

They spent the next half hour guessing his identity,

and Elin was just certain she was right. Alex Pettyfer. He had to be some type of immortal, right?

Speaking of eye candy, she wondered where Thane was, what he was doing.

Probably still with his boys, she decided, planning his—their—war. *I'm in this with him. All the way.* Though she had no idea what to do about the prince, she had an idea about Ardeo.

If you want a man's attention, her mother once said, *find out what he loves most...and take it away. Guaranteed, he'll dog your every step from that moment on.*

Ardeo wanted Malta. It would be cruel to pretend the woman had somehow regenerated and was now in their clutches, but he'd written the rules of this war when he stabbed Thane, and those rules were quite simple: anything goes.

One mention of Malta's name, and he would come running...straight into a trap.

"—even listening?" Bellorie asked, and she blinked into focus. "She's got it bad, ya'll. Love has done gone and fried her brain."

It had. It really had. "What'd I miss?"

"The best story ever about how I'm going to march into the realm of the Fae and decapitate everyone I come across! Chanel would have wanted her entire race slaughtered for kicking her out. I just know it."

Savy shook her head and made a cutting motion over her throat.

"Why did they kick her out, anyway?" Elin asked.

Savy groaned.

"For being too wonderful," Bellorie said, ignoring

her. "But back to my war plans. I'll wear black spandex, of course, like a true ninja, and—"

Octavia waved her fists in the air and shouted, "Why me?"

Elin covered a giggle with the back of her hand, then sat back and listened to Bellorie wax on and on about the clothes she would wear, the weapons she would use, and the history books that would need to be written about her exploits.

Never would Elin have guessed that she'd find herself in such a situation. Sorrowful but comforting. Sad but sweet. This wasn't the life she'd once envisioned for herself, but dang if it wasn't better.

CHAPTER THIRTY

THANE EXITED THE BATHROOM with a towel wrapped around his waist. He and the boys had decided on a plan of action, to be carried out later today. Find Ardeo. Track him. Follow him to the prince. Perhaps the two would set up a meeting so the prince could reward Ardeo for stabbing Thane. If not, Ardeo would find a way to reach the prince. The Phoenix king believed the fallen angel could bring Malta back to life; he wouldn't rest until he was proved wrong.

After that, the Army of Disgrace would go in with the Elite Seven, weapons blazing, and capture the prince. Interrogate the prince. Find the other princes responsible for Germanus's death.

Then they would execute the final part of their plan. Kill. Them. All.

The only thing in question was what to do with Elin. Where would she be safest?

Thane's blood heated when he spotted her lounging in the center of the bed.

She was already naked.

She grinned when his gaze met hers. A truly wicked grin, like none she'd ever given him. He wasn't sure what to think.

"What are you waiting for, gorgeous?" she asked throatily, tracing a fingertip between her breasts. "I'm ready for you. I want to be chained and taken so hard I'll feel you for weeks."

Chained?

He frowned. Something was wrong with her.

The alcohol must be at work. Her behavior always underwent a shift when she drank.

He strode to the edge of the bed. She leaned up and tried to tug away the towel, but he held firm to the material and sat beside her.

"Kulta," he said gently.

"Kulta?" There was a flash of...something...in her eyes, but it was so quickly masked he couldn't identify it. "Don't you want me?" she asked with a pout. "Because I want you, and I don't want to wait."

"I do want you." Desire for her always simmered underneath his skin. Right now, concern proved stronger. "What's the matter? Did someone say something to hurt you?"

"What would you do if someone did hurt me?" she asked silkily.

"Avenge you." Brutally.

She blinked with surprise. "Why?"

"Because I love you." *You know this.*

Know what? she asked, the words wafting through his mind.

His confusion intensified. *That I love you.*

Of course I do, but I will never tire of hearing the words.

Even as her voice filled his head, her eyes narrowed. "Prove it. Prove you love me," she said, planting a series of kisses across his throat.

The stroke of her tongue was hotter than usual. Her lips were firmer than usual, and her scent was all wrong.

She didn't smell like alcohol as she had earlier when he'd checked on her; but even more tellingly, her scent was missing the cherries.

And…the essentia had faded from her skin completely, he realized.

Suspicions danced through him.

This wasn't Elin. This *couldn't* be Elin.

He pinched her chin and held her face steady for his concentrated scrutiny. Smoked-glass eyes without any hint of warmth. They were wells of cold, hard determination, and the pupils were not dilated. Her delicate cheeks lacked the warm flush of arousal. Another sign of cold, hard determination.

The truth settled, and rage sparked.

This was Kendra.

Somehow, she'd removed her slave bands. Somehow, she'd found him. And now, she was trying to trick him into bedding her, so that she could enslave him all over again. That was how she'd gotten him last time. Eight times she'd come to him as a different woman, and eight times he'd spilled inside her, binding his soul tighter and tighter to hers.

Every fiber of his being longed to lash out, to hurt her in some way. But this time, he didn't react according to emotion. He was a different man, and he wouldn't make the same mistakes.

He breathed deeply, in and out, releasing the rage and concentrating on the regret he'd experienced every time he'd thought of his past.

What kind of life had Kendra led? What had brought her to this moment?

If he hurt her today, she would only want to hurt him another day, and then he would want to hurt her, and so on and so forth, and it would become an endless cycle of pain and remorse.

It was time to break the cycle.

Not knowing what else to do, he stood and stalked to the closet.

"What are you doing?" she demanded, unable to hide her irritation.

"What do you think?" He turned and held up four links of chains. "You wanted to be chained, did you not?"

At last, arousal came. He smelled it on her, and that saddened him. "Yes."

"Lie back," he commanded.

Instantly she obeyed, placing her arms over her head and spreading her legs. Goose bumps broke out over her skin as he clamped the metal on her wrists and ankles. A master at bondage, he had no problem anchoring the shackles to a bed not made for that type of activity.

Standing at the side of the bed, peering down at her, he sighed. He would talk, and she would listen. Hopefully he would get through to her.

"You overplayed your hand this time…Kendra."

He expected her to erupt in defense, or spill more lies. Instead, she returned his grin. "Did I?"

A gasp from the doorway had him turning.

Bjorn stood there—with Elin at his side. "Uh, I came to tell you I obtained a vial of Water," he said, holding the small, clear container up. "But we can discuss it later. I'll just take Elin—"

"No." Elin's skin paled. Betrayal colored her eyes. "I told you to come to me with anything, that I'd do anything to ensure your needs were met, and you said okay. You even said your tastes had changed," she rasped, the words rushed, as if she wanted to hold them inside but couldn't. "You said you were done with this."

"Well, he lied," Kendra responded, and she no longer looked like Elin. Or even like herself. Her hair was blond, her face that of a stranger.

Elin backed away.

"This isn't what it looks like," Thane said, desperate to make her understand.

She gave a bitter laugh. "Do me a favor and save your explanation for the next girl you're looking to fool." She pivoted on her heel and ran.

"Elin!"

Thane stepped forward, intending to chase after her. A single thought stopped him: he would have to restrain her to force her to listen to him, and restraining her would remind her of the chains, and he would do anything to make her forget what she'd just seen.

Kendra laughed. "Poor Thane. He finally falls for a woman, but she wants nothing to do with him."

He gritted his teeth. He'd tried to do a good deed, and this was how he ended up?

Kulta, he projected. *I need you to listen to me.*

Too bad. I need you to shut up.

Elin, I promise you. What happened wasn't sexual. Kendra was pretending to be you, but I realized her game and chained her up.

This time, she offered no response.

He tried again. Again, there was no response.

She'd blocked him. Probably hadn't heard a word of his explanation.

"Go after her," he commanded Bjorn. "Guard her. I'll take over as soon as I'm done here."

As the warrior rushed off, Thane turned his full, seething attention to Kendra.

Despite the implied threat—and his murderous expression—she gave another gleeful grin.

Calm. Just because you began poorly doesn't mean you have to end that way.

"You should have stayed away," he told her, his voice low. "I was done with my vengeance."

"Well," she snapped, "I wasn't done with *mine*."

"It will cost you. Because I will not allow you to leave until you understand the consequences of harming what's mine."

"I could say the same of you," a voice growled from behind him.

Thane spun.

Ricker the War Ender stepped from a thick cloud of black smoke—and slammed a sword through Thane's chest, the blade coming out the other side.

WAIT.

Freaking wait! Elin thought.

Truth began to seep past the veil of hurt. Thane wasn't a cheater. He wasn't dishonest. And he loved her. He loved her, and Elin loved him. She trusted him. Trusted him *despite* what her eyes had seen.

He always did everything within his power to protect her. He would never purposely chain a woman in his bed—especially a bed he'd planned to share with Elin—while she was nearby, able to stumble upon the scene at any moment...without a good reason.

There was an explanation for what had happened, just like he'd tried to tell her.

Relief was a beautiful deluge, and she stopped running. She'd made it all the way to the front porch, she realized. The sun had gone down, and the moon had taken its place, high and full and silvery. She closed her eyes and breathed, her heartbeat gradually calming.

I'm sorry for doubting you, she projected to Thane. Or tried to project. There was some kind of wall in her mind, trapping the words inside. *Thane? Can you hear me?*

Silence greeted her.

Had he…blocked her?

"No," a deep, raspy voice proclaimed from…everywhere…nowhere. "I blocked you."

Her gaze darted left, right. Behind. No one was with her. Then something caught her eye in the distance. A shape. That of a male with long, pale hair. He was tall. Wide. The tallest, widest man she'd ever seen. Not fat, but muscled. Though he had no wings, he hovered in the sky, floating toward her.

His features came into view, and she could only gape. He was magnificent. Like a beam of radiant light, shining down with pure, undiluted beauty.

And yet, cold fingers of dread walked down her spine.

Fight? Or flight?

A friend of Thane's, or a foe?

Couldn't be a friend. Why block her from Thane? *Run!*

No. No way. Never again. She stood firm.

As he settled a few yards away from her, she gawked. *Handsome* didn't even begin to describe him. He was gorgeous. No, that didn't fit, either. He was exquisite. Nope. Even that word failed to do him justice.

"Who are you?" she demanded.

"I am Darkness, Destruction and Doom. I am Death. Yours, at least."

Her throat went dry. Her skin tingled. And not the good kind of tingles Thane caused, but some kind of get-out-of-Dodge-because-it's-about-to-blow tingles.

"Why are you here?" Her stomach twisted as a terrible suspicion hit her. "Never mind. Just leave. Now."

His grin was slow—and pure evil. "Oh, I have no plans to stay…not for long, anyway. But like you, your precious Thane will be dead before I go."

The prince. This was the prince Thane, Bjorn and Xerxes had talked about.

She couldn't let him get to the Sent Ones. But what could she do? She was weaponless.

Actually, no. She wasn't. She swiped up one of the boulders beside the porch stairs. "You want Thane? You'll have to get through me first."

His grin widened. "I was hoping you'd say that."

"Because you're a fool!" She launched the missile, and he didn't even try to dodge, as if he found her effort amusing. But when the rock smacked him in the chest, he blinked. Shock filled his eyes.

"You are strong," he said.

"And ticked!" She swiped up another boulder.

Bjorn raced past her, catching her by surprise, and acting as her shield. He withdrew two short swords. "Go back inside, Elin," he commanded. "Now."

Not even if you pay me.

"But I'd like her to stay," the newcomer intoned.

Suddenly, her feet felt as if they weighed a thousand pounds. She tried to lift one, failed, and tried to lift the other. Another fail. Her shoes had somehow adhered to the pavement.

"I've summoned my entire army," Bjorn announced. "You may be a prince, Malice, but you cannot beat us all."

The male shook his head, his hair so long it danced over the flowers on the ground. "I can. I will. I'll just have to work quickly." His voice was a whisper on the wind, and yet, it was now laced with screams of anguish.

Elin cringed, certain her ears were bleeding.

For seemingly no reason, Bjorn's legs collapsed, the bones in his calves snapping and pushing through his skin. As he bellowed with pain, he threw one of his swords at the prince.

Rather than take the blow, as he'd done with the boulder, Malice easily glided out of range…

…and both of Bjorn's arms broke.

Another bellow sounded. Elin crouched and reached for him, thinking to grab Bjorn and yank him behind her. *She* would be *his* shield.

Malice laughed, and though the screams were thankfully absent, the gleeful cadence of his voice scraped at her nerves. "I didn't expect to have this much fun."

"Stop," she shouted. "Enough."

He smirked. "Is it?"

Crack.

Bjorn's neck twisted to an unbearable angle. His chest stilled, no longer rising and falling.

"No!" she screamed. He was…he was…

Dead?

Unlike the Phoenix, he wouldn't regenerate. But a Sent One couldn't be killed so easily, could he?

Acid replaced blood, rushing through her veins. "Free my feet and fight me. Or are you too much of a coward?"

His gaze raked over her, and he tsked. "So brave… with so little reason to be. Let's see what we can do about that."

The next thing Elin knew, she was being lifted from the ground, floating closer and closer to the prince. Instinct demanded she flail and try to stop the motion. But she didn't. She balled her fists, ready to throw the first punch when she got to him.

Of course, he stopped her just out of reach.

"Is the big, bad warrior afraid of a girl?" she taunted.

He pursed his lips. "You're beginning to bore me, my sweet."

"I'm devastated. Really."

"Not yet. But you will be." He glided forward, and just when he was within reach, he managed to immobilize her arms without even touching her. "I'm going to do Thane both a favor and a disservice. I will make you fully Phoenix, giving you an eternity with him… but he'll have to watch me kill you over and over again."

Fully Phoenix equaled fully immortal. It was what Thane desired for her more than anything. Once, she might have worried that he would freak out over the Phoenix aspect. Now, she knew him better. He loved her, no matter her race.

"Do it," she gritted. "Make me stronger. See what happens when I unleash my wrath against you."

He chuckled as he held out his empty hand. A syringe appeared in the center of his palm, crimson liquid swirling in the belly. "I had to trade a few favors for this. I know the Sent One has come to accept your heritage…but I doubt he'll be so forgiving of Kendra's ability to enslave. Unlike the princess, you won't be able to turn it off at will."

What! "No!" she shouted, twisting and turning, contorting her body to avoid the needle. *Not the poison. Anything but the poison.* Because he was right. Thane could get over anything—except that.

Grinning, the prince held her steady and jabbed the needle into her neck. In a blink, fire spread through her entire body. Screams reverberated inside her skull.

"Blood from the strongest of the Phoenix, as well as Kendra, with a little something extra from me to help speed the process along." He brushed a fingertip along her jawline, making the pain ten thousand times worse. "You will come find me when you revive."

"No."

"Ah, well, you'll soon discover otherwise. When next you wake, you'll be bonded to me. You'll do everything I tell you."

He was too smug to be lying. She longed to respond—every fiber of her being was screaming, "Never!"—but she didn't have the strength.

He held out his hand, empty now, and Bjorn's sword flew into his grip. Her eyes widened. What did he—

He stabbed her in the stomach, once, twice, a third time. Agony. Such agony. Blood burned a path up her throat and gurgled from her mouth. The moment he pulled the metal out, she tumbled to the ground, unable to hold herself up.

"See you soon, my sweet." He stepped over her.

From the corner of her eye, she watched, horrified, as he stabbed Bjorn in the heart. If the warrior had managed to survive the severed spine, he was a goner now.

No, no, no. He was a Sent One. Stronger than most. He could survive even this.

Please.

The sword clattered to the ground. Whistling, the prince entered the castle.

Bastard. As she writhed in burning agony, her mind locked on a single fact. If he wasn't stopped, he would hurt and kill everyone she loved. *Can't let him.*

She reached for the sword, but the action caused her heart rate to increase, and her blood to pour out faster. She stilled. *I'm dying, my last minutes ticking away.*

It was okay, she reminded herself. She would come back. Malice had seen to that.

In Thane's eyes, she would be a monster.

A whimper budded in the back of her throat.

Can't worry about that right now.

To face the prince, she *had* to be stronger. And she would have to face him, not just because he'd compelled her—she could feel the desire to find him already stirring in her chest—but to help Thane.

Elin wiggled, and kept wiggling, hastening the flow of blood. The darkness waiting on the periphery spilled into her mind, closing in…growing thicker…

What if the prince lied, and you aren't really immortal?

The thought hit her, and she stilled. It was a possibility.

No. No, it wasn't. *I'm coming back, even if I'm not fully Phoenix.* No matter what, she was fully determined. Nothing could pry her spirit's kung-fu grip from her body. Nothing.

…cold slithering through her limbs. Destination: her heart.

It was coming. Death was coming. There was no stopping it.

…pooling in her chest…

"Thane," Elin said with the last of her breath.

THANE FOUGHT TO remain conscious. Ricker had freed Kendra, and the two had chained him to the bed. Kendra had wanted to kill him, and Ricker, who was clearly in the throes of her poison, had wanted to please her, but besides binding him and stabbing him a second time, neither had made a move to end him.

"What has made you like this, Kendra?" Thane asked her.

"So amazing?" she replied, flipping her hair over her shoulder.

"So…twisted."

A flash of vulnerability in her eyes, gone so swiftly he wanted to convince himself he'd imagined it—he couldn't.

"Do you really want to hear the sob story of the poor little princess ignored by her entire clan, so desperate for affection she gave herself to a rival king at the age of fourteen, and he passed her around to his troops? Well, I'm not that little girl anymore. I've learned to take what I want. The clan. Men. It doesn't matter."

He should have seen. Should have realized. She had a past more terrible than his own, and he'd only added to her problems. "I'm sorry," he said, and this, too, he meant.

"You're sorry? You're sorry!" By the end, her voice was a screech. "He's going to hurt you so bad, and I'm going to love every minute of it."

"Who is *he?*"

Her lips twisted cruelly. "Your worst nightmare."

"Is that what I am?" said a voice Thane recognized. "I always considered myself a forbidden fantasy."

Thane tensed.

The prince.

Malice glided into the room. A white robe draped his body. Pretending to be a Sent One? It was a known fact: fallen angels were insanely jealous of Sent Ones.

Thane fought his bonds. *Bjorn. Xerxes.* Since being stabbed, he'd tried to call them at least ten times, but neither had responded. He'd tried to call Zacharel, too. *The prince is here. Take the women and leave. Now.* Again, there was no response.

Dread cut through him, sharper than the blade. They would never block him and never purposely ignore him. Which meant they had to be…incapacitated. Yes. Incapacitated, not dead.

And if they were incapacitated, the women…

No. No!

"Look what we did," Kendra said, grinning as she motioned to Thane. "Just like you told us."

"It's not too late," Thane told her. "You can help me, and I can help you."

"I don't need help." But the beginnings of indecision stirred in her eyes.

"You did well," the prince said to the princess. "You have a problem, however. I no longer have any use for you." He placed a hand on both Kendra's and Ricker's brows. Striations of black appeared on their cheeks… down their necks… Their eyes rolled back, revealing the whites. Their bodies began to shake and shake… and when the shaking stopped, their skin was…stone? The black had spread, covering the pair from head to toe, creating a high-gloss sheen.

Thane had never seen anything like it.

The prince opened his hands, and the pair fell to the ground, nothing more than a pile of dust.

The evil power such an act required...more than Thane had ever witnessed. And completely unnecessary. With a little time, he could have reached her. Now, it was too late.

Malice grinned. "Your greatest enemies will never regenerate. You're welcome."

"That is the difference between us. I no longer had any desire for vengeance."

The prince narrowed his eyes. "You lie."

"And you are so afraid to face me, you had to stoop to this."

Amused again, rather than insulted, the prince said, "You mock, and yet my battle strategy far surpassed yours." He shrugged. "Did you try to summon your two favorite boy toys the way you Sent Ones like to do? Well, I'm sad to say they won't be responding. Both are currently dead."

His worst suspicion...confirmed.

Though the prince hadn't touched him, he felt as if his heart had just turned to stone inside his chest. Cracks formed, before the petrified organ burst into countless shards, cutting him. "You are the liar." Demons enjoyed twisting the truth. He couldn't forget.

"Hardly. You taste the truth of my words, I'm sure. I ran into Bjorn outside, and Xerxes in the hallway. Both had very weak bone structure...and when I left them, both had holes in their chests."

"No!" The word roared from Thane, a denial that sprang from deep, deep inside, where survival met the core of his being. The thought of losing his friends... No.

"Oh, yes."

"I taste no lie—you're right about that. You left them with broken bones and holes in their chests. But that doesn't mean they're dead. They've recovered from worse."

Irritated, Malice snapped, "Time will tell." Then he calmed and added, "They distracted you from our game...as did your female."

Thane renewed his struggles, his flesh biting into the metal cuffs. What little strength he had left rapidly drained. "Don't touch her. Don't you dare touch her."

The prince patted his cheek, and the contact blistered more than an acid bath. "Oh, I touched her. And more. I can hardly wait to show you the end result of my actions."

The relish in his tone was frightening, but his words were downright terrifying. "What did you do?" Thane croaked. "What did you do!"

"Don't worry, Sent One. She'll live."

Again, he tasted no lie. He sagged against the mattress. He could deal with anything except her death.

Malice stalked around the bed, once, twice. "Your army is on its way. Did you know that? Did you call them? Your friends did. But my minions will hold the warriors off until I'm finished here."

So cocky. "You underestimate our strength."

A tinkling laugh. "Surely you see the irony of your statement."

He did. But he didn't care.

He'd spent his life bucking against the authority of a leader—any leader. That was how he'd ended up with Zacharel, the coldest of the cold, part of an army the rest of their world considered one step above useless and best forgotten.

Those soldiers would fight for him and those he loved with the same fervency as Bjorn and Xerxes. Like Elin, they had become his family.

"You don't stand a chance," Thane said confidently.

Malice waved the words away. "I'll be long gone before your friends are even able to enter the castle." His ear twitched, and he nodded with satisfaction. "Excellent. I think your Elin is on her way."

Elin!

"Run," Thane shouted. "Elin, run!"

"She can't," the prince said with a smile straight from the depths of his worst nightmares.

She dashed around the corner and entered the room wearing Bjorn's robe. Thane experienced a wealth of emotion. Joy that she lived. Anger that she had been placed in this situation. Desperation to whisk her away to safety. Fear for Bjorn.

Her gaze met his, only to skid away quickly.

Still upset about what she'd seen?

Or upset about what had happened to his friend?

"Run," he commanded. "Please."

"Uh, uh, uh," Malice tsked. "Stay."

She stayed. Head bowed. Shoulders stooped. A pose of submission.

Something inside Thane's chest clenched. Her hair appeared lighter, he realized—because it was threaded with flames. And her once smoked-glass eyes now blazed and crackled with orange fire.

She was a Phoenix.

And she still wouldn't meet his gaze.

Did she think he would reject her?

How could he? She was a beautiful, fearsome sight. And she was still his kulta. Now and always.

"I love you, Elin. With all that I am. No matter what."

Tears streaked down her cheeks. "Let him go," she demanded of the prince, the hem of the robe swaying on the floor as she shifted from one foot to the other. "Please."

"I don't think I will, but I do thank you for the suggestion." Malice rubbed his hands together, and with his gaze locked on Thane, he said, "I wonder if your love will turn to hate when you learn your woman is now blessed with the same ability your Kendra possessed."

Thane merely blinked. *Kulta. I don't care. Do you hear me?*

She was alive. Nothing else mattered.

His lack of reaction angered the prince.

Malice whirled on Elin, who'd stood utterly still during his speech. "Did your clothes burn away, little one? Did you steal a robe from a dead man, not wanting me to see the body I will soon rip asunder? How novel." He tore the material off her, leaving her naked.

Thane tried to reach for her, desperate to shield her. And for a moment, he was transported back to the demon dungeon, Bjorn dangling over him, Xerxes raped across from him. Thane, seemingly forgotten, while all too present in that hell.

"Don't you dare hurt her. Hurt me. Hurt me however you desire. Just let her go."

"Hurt you?" Malice winked at him. "From what I hear, you'd like it."

"Thane," Elin said before he could reply, her tone trembling. "Don't worry about me, all right? I'll be okay. And…I'm sorry. I'm so sorry about what happened earlier. I trust you. I do. And I love you. I love you so much."

Words he'd longed to hear—words that eased something inside him, even as they razed the worst of his protective instincts. *Don't be sorry,* he tried to project to her. *Survive.*

"How adorable." The prince held out his hand. A sword appeared. "You love her. She loves you. Now, you can watch her die."

"No," Thane shouted, trying again to reach for her.

A shudder moved through Elin's body. "It's okay. I'll be okay. You just— "

Malice stabbed her in the heart, silencing her with an agonized gasp.

Snarling, Thane yanked so hard at his chains, the entire bed shook. Elin fell, crashing into the floor. She didn't move.

Knowing she was now fully Phoenix did nothing to temper his reaction. His woman was a boneless heap, blood pooling around her, and it destroyed him. Fury was a storm, uncontrollable and wild, flooding him with adrenaline and, finally, the necessary strength. As Elin caught fire and burned to ash in mere seconds—the fastest regeneration he'd ever seen—he split the head- and footboard with the force of his struggles. The links gave way at last, freeing him.

He jolted upright, watching as the fire expanded. In the center of the flames, Elin appeared in a burst of light. He was relieved. He was angry. How she must have suffered. *Must be* suffering.

The fire died, and she once again crashed into the floor. Gasping for breath, she fought her way to her hands and knees, then to an unsteady crouch.

"Ready for…round two?" she panted, taunting the prince.

A knot clogged Thane's throat. He made to grab her and jerk her behind him, even though his forearms and wrists were broken and set at odd angles.

"None of that," Malice said—and used the sword to hack off both Thane's hands.

Elin screamed with fury. She lumbered to her feet and launched herself at the prince, but he caught her midair, able to levitate her with his mind and lock her in place. Then…he stabbed her in the stomach.

"Oh, my," the prince said as she crumbled to the floor. "I do hope she wasn't carrying your babe."

Thane barely had time to choke on a howl of rage, for when she reformed, the male quickly decapitated her. This time, she reformed almost instantly, motionless in a pool of blood and fire one second, crouched and surrounded by smoke the next. Thane almost couldn't process the depths of his fury and helplessness.

"Please," he croaked. He would beg. Pride was nothing when it came to his woman's safety and well-being.

"Here's how this is going to work," the prince continued. "I'm going to give a command, and you, Thane, are going to obey it. If you fail, I will kill your female in a new and creative way."

"Whatever you want, I'll do." Thane stood, swayed. He didn't care about the loss of his hands, or the holes in his chest. "This is between you and me."

"Exactly."

"She's suffered enough."

"Has she?"

He watched, unable to do anything as Elin floated closer and closer to the prince…stopping just in front of him. She looked at Thane and offered him a soft, sweet smile that proved to be his undoing.

He stumbled forward, intent on stepping in front of his woman and taking whatever blow was meant for her. He couldn't watch her die again. He just couldn't.

An almost imperceptible shake of her head stopped him.

He frowned.

"Thank you," she said to Malice.

The male arched a brow. "For what, my sweet?" He gently brushed the hair from her forehead.

"For orchestrating your own downfall. You see, the second time you killed me, you severed our bond. Every time after that, I grew stronger. Now, I'm powerful enough to control the abilities that would have overwhelmed me otherwise." As the last word left her, wings burst from her back. Wings of red, yellow and black. Not made of feathers, but of flames. Thick smoke curled from their edges.

Before the prince could process what was happening, she spun, swiping those wings across his throat.

She dropped to the floor, crouched, watching, waiting, the wings lifted and spread behind her.

Blood dripped from Malice's wound several seconds before his head slipped off his body. But he caught the head midair and put it back in place.

The skin, and everything else, wove back together.

"That wasn't very nice," the prince gritted.

Horror chilled Thane. But he forced himself to look past it. Past all of his emotions and focus on instinct. All demons, no matter their rank, were susceptible to one thing.

"No," Elin whispered. "Impossible."

"Again, Elin," Thane managed.

She heard him and reacted instantly, swinging her wings at the prince a second time before he thought to strike at her.

Once again, she removed his head.

"Water," Thane rushed out next. "Robe. Pour."

She knew what he wanted, and grabbed the robe she'd taken from Bjorn, the one the prince had torn away from her, digging inside and removing the vial of Water.

The prince's head had fallen and again he'd caught it. But before he could anchor it back into place, Elin used her wings to propel herself into his chest and knock him down.

The head rolled away, out of reach.

Still the prince swung at her, though it was clear he couldn't see her, because he missed by a mile. It bought her the second she needed. She dumped what little Water the vial contained over the neck wound.

Tissue sizzled. Sulfur-scented steam rose.

The body jerked.

The head screamed.

The sizzling intensified, and spread…spread…until all of his flesh…and muscle…and bone…were bubbling like cheese in an oven.

Elin coughed, the steam so thick it saturated the air. Thane didn't have the strength to react.

Then the steam cleared—there one moment, gone the next—and there was no sign of the prince.

He was gone.

Thane had read about this. He knew the prince had just lost his body, and his spirit had been sucked into hell, where it was now bound.

Which meant…

It was over. It was really over.

Thane's knees buckled, and he collapsed, overjoyed, relieved. And still dying. Ricker's sword had punctured his heart and a lung, and now, his life's blood poured from the ends of his arms.

He'd never hated pain more. Because it meant he would be taken from Elin.

"Kulta," he gasped out.

Her wings vanished, and she rushed to his side, saying, "Bjorn and Xerxes are alive. I gave them each a few drops of the Water. And then the prince... I should have saved some for you... What was I thinking? I'm so sorry, baby."

"You did everything right." His gaze met the sweet beauty of hers. The time he'd had with her...worth anything. Everything. "Stay with...them. They'll take care...of you."

Tears caught in her lashes before cascading down her cheeks. "Don't you dare talk like that. You're going to be okay. You're immortal. You'll recover."

If he drank the Water in the next few minutes, yes. Maybe. If not...no. These injuries were far too severe. Vital organs had been punctured and they couldn't regenerate fast enough. He'd lost too much blood. But he didn't want to tell her that. She'd start to feel guilty again.

His friends rushed into the room—and they were not alone. Bellorie and the girls, plus all of Zacharel's army. Everyone had survived the attack. And thank the Most High, the minions must have sensed the prince's death and scurried off like the cowards they were, afraid to act now that they were without a leader to protect them.

While Xerxes blocked everyone's view of Elin, Bjorn

grabbed a robe from the closet and tugged the material over her head, covering her nakedness.

Zacharel surveyed the scene, and when his gaze landed on Thane, the layer of ice he wore like a second skin cracked. "You are almost past the point of aid, my friend."

"Tell me something…I don't know."

"Does anyone have the special Water?" Elin practically shrieked. "If so, you better give it to me. Give it to me now. I killed a prince, and I won't stop there."

Malcolm, who had resisted all of Thane's demands and pleas before, reached inside an air pocket without hesitation.

My little tyrant. She'd really come into her own.

He began to wheeze. His chest tightened. The world dimmed as Elin uncorked the vial and turned to him. Then he lost sight of her completely. Lost the sound of her voice, and the comfort of her scent. Lost…everything.

ELIN POURED EVERY BIT of the water into Thane's mouth. But he was unconscious and didn't swallow. Most of it dribbled from him as his head lolled to the side.

"Come on, Thane." Desperately she worked his throat with her fingers.

The black-haired warrior with bright green eyes barked, "Does anyone else have a vial? He needs it *now*."

Heads shook, and eyes gleamed with dismay. Bjorn and Xerxes looked ready to bust apart at the seams, as if they couldn't control the dark tide of emotion rampaging through them.

Without the Water, Thane would die. If he wasn't already—

No.

This couldn't be the end.

"Bjorn, Xerxes." She wasn't giving up and knew they wouldn't, either. "We're taking him to the source. Now."

"We can't force the crowd to let us pass," Xerxes said, clearly dealing with shock. "That's the only rule."

She had no idea what he was talking about. But it didn't matter—she would do anything. "We'll find a way."

The male gently gathered Thane in his arms. Blood dripped from Thane's wings, painting the feathers crimson. "You're right. We must try."

Features tight with worry, Bjorn tugged her to his chest, something that couldn't be pleasant for him. But their minds were in accord. Do whatever was necessary to save Thane's life.

Together, their little foursome flew to some kind of temple. During the twenty-minute flight—the longest twenty minutes of her life—Thane never opened his eyes, never said a word.

To her horror, there was a huge line of people waiting at a towering iron gate, and Xerxes's words began to make sense. All of these people…and she was just supposed to *wait*?

"We are next," Xerxes stated baldly. "Please."

"No way," said the petulant male at the front of the line. "I've waited too long for my turn."

"Then another few minutes won't hurt you, but I will," Elin snapped, flames bursting from her hair.

She hissed, her face breaking out into a mass of blisters, and Bjorn dropped her.

As she straightened, the male at the front of the line backed away from her.

"We can't use force," Xerxes reminded her. "Whatever method we use will be visited upon us for the rest of eternity."

Which wouldn't help Thane. She wanted to scream!

A mental command caused her wings to dissipate—her control continued to shock and awe her. "Thane of the Three is dying," she announced, lifting her chin. "He is a good man, and he is loved. Help us help him. Please."

Annnd…no response. Everyone looked away. All the moment lacked was crickets singing in the background.

Her hands fisted. "Imagine yourself standing here, in my place. Imagine your spouse or your friend or your father or brother struggling to survive. Imagine there is a way to save him…but someone is standing in your way. How would you feel? What would you do?"

Again, there was no response. Until…

"Let them pass," someone down the way shouted.

"Yeah," another called. "Have a heart. He's one of ours."

"It's not like you'll be adding more than five minutes to your wait."

"Fine," the next in line grumbled. "You're next."

Her relief was tempered by concern as she took in Thane's pale skin and blue-tinged lips. The first battle was won, but not the war.

Come on, come on, come the freak on. Finally, the iron gate opened, and as a female Sent One skipped out, smiling, Xerxes stalked past her, Thane still quiet and motionless in his arms. Bjorn and Elin followed closely behind.

This had to work. Failure wasn't an option.

Xerxes didn't stop at the River's shore, but waded in deep. Bjorn and Elin, too. At the moment of contact, however, terrible pain consumed her and she jumped out. What was that about?

Bjorn looked back at her, understanding lighting his face. "I heard what the prince said to you. He infected you with Kendra's poison and his own darkness."

"Yes."

"And now you hurt."

"Yes," she repeated, her gaze straying to Thane. He was still unconscious. *Keep it together.*

Bjorn tilted his head to the side, as if he was listening to a voice she couldn't hear. "The Water is a cleansing agent," he said. "The Most High has just informed me your defeat of the prince has earned a reward. Enter the River and be cleansed of the fallen angel's darkness, as well as Kendra's poison."

Thank you. Thank you, thank you, thank you. "What about my immortality?" She had to keep it. For Thane. Because he *would* survive this. Nothing else was acceptable.

Again Bjorn's head tilted to the side. "You will lose only the evil that came with it."

Have the good, discard the bad? *Thank you* wasn't good enough. Steeling herself against what was to come, she dived in and swallowed a mouthful. The pain was immediate and intense, and she broke the surface screaming, but within a few minutes, a sweet sense of peace took its place.

The moment she was able to, she swam to Xerxes

and Thane. The water was the perfect temperature. Not too warm, not too cold, and it sparkled against her skin, pleasant now. Shaking, she scooped the liquid into Thane's mouth, handful after handful, forcing him to swallow.

Still, there was no change.

She fed him even more liquid, desperation trying to choke her. She pressed her fingers into his neck, searching for a pulse. Nothing. Near-crippling anguish joined the desperation, and she gasped for breath.

"He helped me," she cried out, hoping the Most High could hear her. "He helped me defeat the prince. I couldn't have done it without him. Reward him. Please."

Again, there was no change.

"Thane," she rasped. "Please. Don't do this. You made me love you. You gave me a purpose. Now…give me a future. Please."

Bjorn and Xerxes exchanged a look teeming with grief.

She continued. "This isn't a debate. I told you heal, and so you'll heal. Do you hear me?"

Finally—finally!—he coughed, blood gurgling from the corners of his mouth.

She froze. Bjorn and Xerxes froze.

"Did that just happen?" she demanded.

"More. Give him more," Xerxes rushed out, and she began scooping more and more water into Thane's mouth, practically drowning him.

Another cough rang out, and there was a starburst of joy inside her.

"It's working!"

"Elin?"

Steady. Don't attack him. Not yet. But she could

hardly contain herself, was jumping up and down, water sloshing around her. "I'm here, baby. I'm here."

Thane raised his arms to wipe his face—his hands had completely regenerated, she noted. He looked around, saw that he was cradled in Xerxes's arms like a baby, and frowned. "Where am I?"

Steady. "The River of Life."

Xerxes released him. "Elin decided you needed a bath." Guttural emotion thickened his voice.

"And she was right," Bjorn said, his voice just as thick.

Steady— Oh, screw it. She threw herself against Thane. "I love you. I love you so much, and I've been cleansed of Kendra's poison. You don't have to worry—"

"I wasn't worried. You were alive, and that was all that mattered to me." His arms tightened around her. "I want you however I can have you."

"I love you." She peppered his face with kisses. "I'm so sorry I doubted you when I saw you with the girl. I—"

"Kendra," he said, cupping her cheeks. "That was Kendra, pretending to be you. But I recognized the differences, and wanted only to talk to her before you walked in. But Ricker came in and incapacitated me. Then the prince showed up and killed both Kendra and Ricker, and they did not regenerate."

"Good. That means the only enemy you have left is Ardeo."

"No." He buried his face in the hollow of her neck and breathed her in. "What he did, he did out of sorrow. Losing you…I understand, and I forgive. I'm done with that war. My weeds are gone."

Elin peppered him with more kisses, then looked,

misty-eyed, at Bjorn and Xerxes. "Don't just stand there, guys. Get in on this. It's group-hug time!"

To her delight, they obeyed.

They are my family. Now and always.

These men were a gift. Thane had told her she was the light to his dark, but that wasn't true. These men weren't dark. Okay, so they were kind of darkish. But. For once, she loved the word. And they were healing. With a little help from her, they'd go all the way.

Step one, helping Bjorn with his much-needed divorce.

Step two, finding a date for Xerxes.

"What are you thinking, kulta?" Thane asked.

"Just that I love you," she replied. "And I'm going to make you and our two little boys happy. I know it."

Bjorn and Xerxes snorted.

"Hey, Zerk," she said. "Did I ever tell you about the girl I met at one of my dodge-boulder games? She—"

"No." He shook his head. "Never. You aren't playing matchmaker."

"He already has a woman." Bjorn wiggled his brows. "Her name is Cario, and she—"

"Isn't mine," Xerxes said, cutting him off.

Elin clapped. "Ohhh, I'm intrigued. Tell me more."

Xerxes dragged Bjorn away, the two men arguing.

"I'll find out, and give her a call," she bellowed after them. "Maybe we can double-date. Yes? Great. I'm taking your silence as a yes."

Thane grinned down at her slowly, sweetly. "A double date will be interesting, that's for sure."

"Why?"

"Because Xerxes would like to kill Cario."

"Oh. Well, not every relationship can be as healthy as ours."

"True. We'll just have to be an example to others for the rest of eternity."

She rubbed her nose against his. "Slight problem, Mr. Three. I'm not sure that's going to be long enough."

EPILOGUE

"TAKE THAT, BIATCHES," Elin shouted as she flipped the bird.

She'd just come in from the edge of the court and knocked out the Erections' second-to-last player. Yes. The Erections. That was their team name. And their motto? We Play Hard So You Can Suck It!

"Elin the Side Swiper rocks and socks it," someone in the crowd shouted.

Thane had given her the new moniker—he claimed she'd sneaked up on him and stolen his heart—and it had stuck.

Maybe because Multiple Scorgasms had made it all the way to the finals. And this, this was the championship match, and all their players were still in the game. No one had been knocked out.

Because they were fierce. They were determined.

This was for Chanel.

Thane, Bjorn and Xerxes watched from the stands, cheering just like everyone else. Well, except for those stupid enough to be fans of the Erections. Okay, that hadn't come out the way she'd meant. Anyway. Those people were booing.

They must not have heard what Thane, Bjorn and Xerxes did to the last crowd to boo her. In essence, the stakes had seen another round of play. Short play, of course—they hadn't wanted to upset Zacharel—but enough to get their point across.

Gotta love my man.

On the Erections' team were Kaia, her sisters Bianka and Gwen, and Anya. They were quick on the speed trigger—ha-ha—but not quick enough. They were strong, but not strong enough.

Maybe because they were a bit distracted. Even though a couple of Sent Ones were helping to track them down, two of their people were still missing. Torin and Cameo.

Maybe there's something I can do. I'm kind of extra amazing now.

When Bellorie tossed a boulder with all of her might, the remaining player, Kaia, caught it—*crap, spoke too soon!*—knocking Bellorie out, and bringing in another player from the Erections. Kaia then darted in the air, the tiny wings on her back allowing her to hover as she selected her target. Elin. Of course.

She was without a boulder.

Kaia tossed the one she held. It was angled too low to catch…unless she dived headfirst, risking serious injury. But if she failed to dive, she would be tapped out. The game would be over, and her team would lose.

Whatever. I'll heal.

Elin dived.

The crowd went quiet with anticipation. The boulder slammed into her—into her face. *Crack.* Blood filled her mouth, but she was grinning as she stood with the boulder clutched in her hands and tossed it at Anya, nailing her in the ankle.

"Out!" she screamed with glee. She stuck her tongue out at both women. "You're both out."

And that meant…drumroll, please…the Scorgasms had done it. They'd won!

Her girls dog-piled her.

"Bonka Donk in the house!"

"We're the champs, and everyone else is a loser!"

"We're unstoppable!"

"Unbeatable!"

"And a little hideous," Bellorie said, no longer jumping up and down, but eyeing Elin with concern. "I hate to say it, but your face has been taken over by an alien life force."

"Thane will kiss me and make me better." Elin pulled from the pack and raced toward the crowd.

Her man had already pushed his way through the masses. He met her in the middle of the court and gathered her close.

"So proud of you, kulta," he said.

"Even though I had to cream your friends last week to get here?"

"Especially because you creamed my friends." He tenderly cupped her face. "Let's get you some Water."

"Nope." They had filled their vials while they swam in the River, but Bjorn needed every drop they had. His queen was summoning him more frequently now. They were looking for ways to break the bond between the two, but so far, they'd found nothing. "It may take a few days, but I'll heal on my own." It was one of the benefits of being fully immortal.

They were still trying to learn all she could do. Her strengths…her weaknesses. But Thane took everything in stride, helping her every step of the way.

He smiled at her. "There's a problem with your plan.

I need your mouth for other things. Namely, my next tongue-lashing."

"Nothing could stop me," she promised, and she meant it. "Nothing."

* * * * *

*Don't miss one of the most highly anticipated stories
in the* LORDS OF THE UNDERWORLD *saga—
featuring Torin, keeper of Disease.*
THE DARKEST TOUCH,
coming soon from
Gena Showalter and Harlequin HQN!

A no-nonsense female cop reluctantly teams up with the one man who makes her lose control in a deliciously sensual new novel from *New York Times* bestselling author

LORI FOSTER

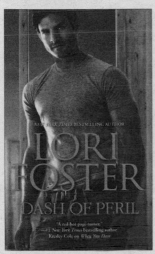

To bring down a sleazy abduction ring, Lieutenant Margaret "Margo" Peterson has set herself up as bait. But recruiting Dashiel Riske as her unofficial partner is a whole other kind of danger. Dash is 6'4" of laid-back masculine charm, a man who loves life—and women—to the limit. Until Margo is threatened, and he reveals a dark side that may just match her own....

Beneath Margo's tough facade is a slow-burning sexiness that drives Dash crazy. The only way to finish this case is to work together side by side...skin to skin. And as their mission takes a lethal turn, he'll have to prove he's all the man she needs—in all the ways that matter....

Be sure to connect with us at:

Harlequin.com/Newsletters
Facebook.com/HarlequinBooks
Twitter.com/HarlequinBooks

HARLEQUIN® HQN™
www.Harlequin.com

PHLF857

GENA SHOWALTER

77775	THE DARKEST CRAVING	__ $7.99 U.S.	__ $8.99 CAN.
77743	BEAUTY AWAKENED	__ $7.99 U.S.	__ $9.99 CAN.
77698	WICKED NIGHTS	__ $7.99 U.S.	__ $9.99 CAN.
77622	THE PLEASURE SLAVE	__ $7.99 U.S.	__ $9.99 CAN.
77621	THE STONE PRINCE	__ $7.99 U.S.	__ $9.99 CAN.
77581	THE DARKEST SURRENDER	__ $7.99 U.S.	__ $9.99 CAN.
77568	CATCH A MATE	__ $7.99 U.S.	__ $9.99 CAN.
77549	THE DARKEST SECRET	__ $7.99 U.S.	__ $9.99 CAN.
77535	THE NYMPH KING	__ $7.99 U.S.	__ $9.99 CAN.
77525	HEART OF THE DRAGON	__ $7.99 U.S.	__ $9.99 CAN.
77524	THE DARKEST PLEASURE	__ $7.99 U.S.	__ $9.99 CAN.
77523	THE DARKEST KISS	__ $7.99 U.S.	__ $9.99 CAN.
77522	THE DARKEST NIGHT	__ $7.99 U.S.	__ $9.99 CAN.
77461	THE DARKEST LIE	__ $7.99 U.S.	__ $9.99 CAN.
77451	INTO THE DARK	__ $7.99 U.S.	__ $9.99 CAN.
77437	TWICE AS HOT	__ $7.99 U.S.	__ $9.99 CAN.

(limited quantities available)

TOTAL AMOUNT	$ _____
POSTAGE & HANDLING	$ _____
($1.00 FOR 1 BOOK, 50¢ for each additional)	
APPLICABLE TAXES*	$ _____
TOTAL PAYABLE	$ _____

(check or money order—please do not send cash)

To order, complete this form and send it, along with a check or money order for the total above, payable to Harlequin HQN, to: **In the U.S.:** 3010 Walden Avenue, P.O. Box 9077, Buffalo, NY 14269-9077; **In Canada:** P.O. Box 636, Fort Erie, Ontario, L2A 5X3.

Name: _____

Address: _____ City: _____

State/Prov.: _____ Zip/Postal Code: _____

Account Number (if applicable): _____

075 CSAS

*New York residents remit applicable sales taxes.
*Canadian residents remit applicable GST and provincial taxes.

HARLEQUIN®HQN™
™ www.Harlequin.com

PHGS0514BL